Dissatisfied Me:

West Coast Larry

Bruce D. Gordon

Renaissance

Diverse Canadian Voices

First edition 2025

Cover art by Nathan Fréchette.
Cover design by Nathan Fréchette.
Interior design by Molly Desson.
Edited by Shawn Brixi, Aleksandar Cimeša, and Lorenzo Carrara.

Legal deposit, Library and Archives Canada, September 2025.

Paperback ISBN: 9781990086847 (978-1-990086-84-7)
Ebook ISBN: 9781990086878 (978-1-990086-87-8)

Renaissance Press - pressesrenaissancepress.ca

Renaissance acknowledges that it is hosted on the traditional, unceded land of the Anishinabek, the Kanien'kehá:ka, and the Omàmìwininìwag. We acknowledge the privileges and comforts that colonialism has granted us and vow to use this privilege to disrupt colonialism by lifting up the voices of marginalized humans who continue to suffer the effects of ongoing colonialism.

Printed in Gatineau at
Imprimerie Gauvin
Depuis 1892
gauvin.ca

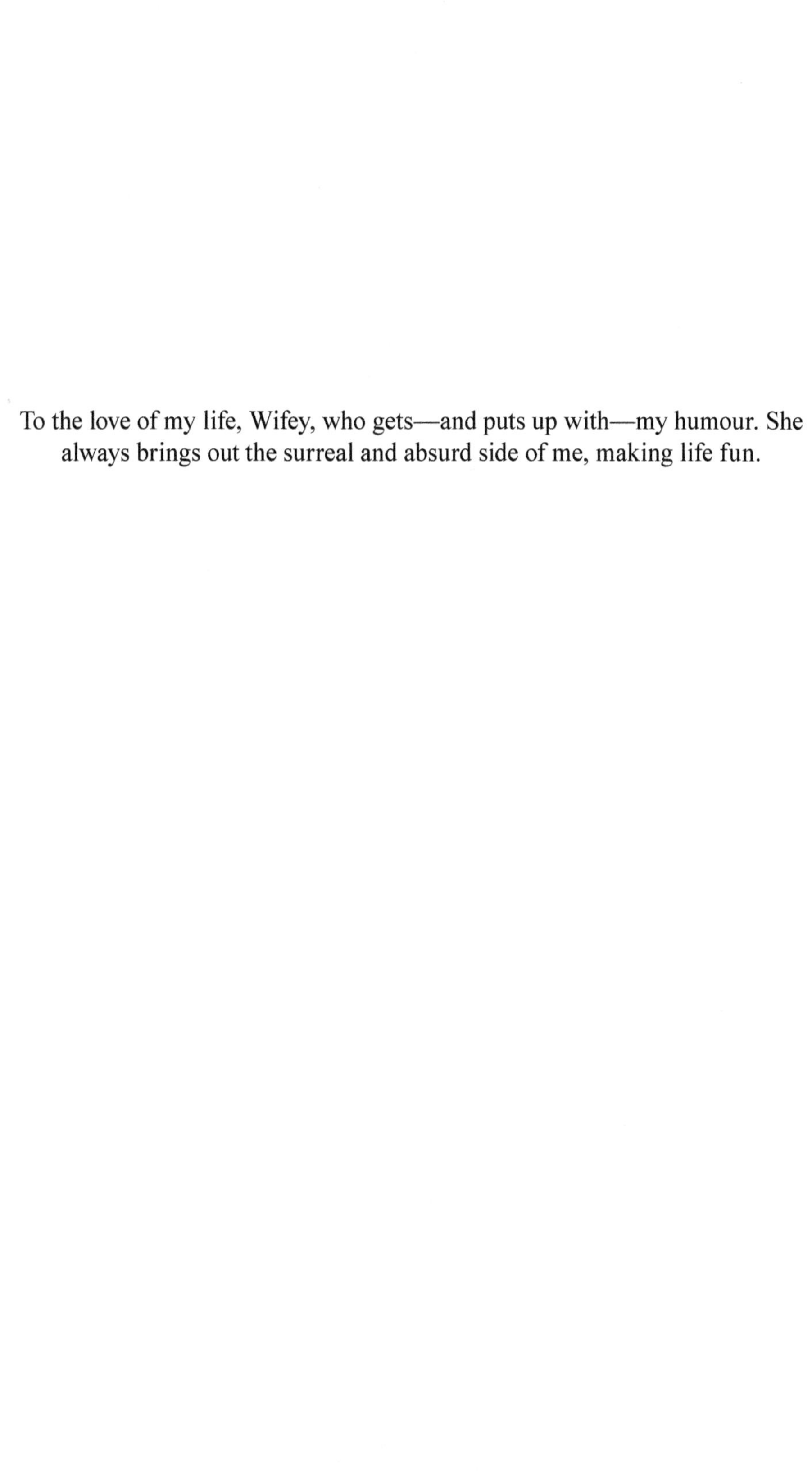

To the love of my life, Wifey, who gets—and puts up with—my humour. She always brings out the surreal and absurd side of me, making life fun.

Content Warning

Be advised that this book contains content related to death of a pet, death of person, infertility, bullying, mild drug use and implied selling of harder drugs, homelessness, implied family abuse, partner neglect, and sexual content.

DISSATISFIED ME:

West Coast Larry

by Bruce D. Gordon

Foreword

by Rick Duncan

can't believe this is happening. A book about Larry Johnstone?! Who in this freakin' world actually wants to read about that clueless tool?

Some loser who had the brain fart of writing his story called me a few years ago and requested I draft an introduction to this memoir. I asked him why the hell I'd do that? I despise the douche, and I've only seen him a couple of times over the past thirty-five years. But he thought it'd be funny, that I, Rick Duncan of all people, would endorse this wretch's life story. The caller added that Larry was an unexpected star of my book, *Dissatisfied Me: A Love Story,* and fans wanted more of him. Everyone "loved to hate him and hated to love him." That set me off. To me, he's frustrating AF. I abruptly hung up.

I was haunted by the call over the following days. If anyone has read *Dissatisfied Me: A Love Story,* they'd know what a disruptive force Larry was in my life. Not to mention the life of rock star Cheryl Smith (who most of you will know as the Red Angel). Larry wouldn't be "famous" if it weren't for us.

I mean, this guy's full of himself. He's a liar, he's conniving, and lives in his own world. Were we friends? *He* would've thought so. In high school, he'd irritate the hell out of me, phoning me every day to blather on about the latest girl who dumped him. Honestly, I could never tell if he made up those sob stories.

It's such a Larry thing to do, drawing attention to himself.

Like, I wore a kilt to my grad, so he wore one, too, claiming *my* family tartan looks better on him. When I sang in church—and no, I don't go to church, attending was his idea—he had to belt out his atonal harmonies on top of mine. Even when someone threw me a surprise birthday party, he made a huge production of proposing marriage to my bitchy cousin on *my* day. Then the clincher… he stole my identity… don't even get me started on that.

Now, once again, Copycat Larry steals my thunder with his own book.

Over the following months, his publisher kept hounding me to draft this foreword. After the hundredth time they called, maybe eighteen months ago, my wife convinced me it might not be a bad idea to write something and plug my own story. Besides, with my history with Larry, it would be prudent to have a sneak peek at his manuscript. Our lives do intersect, and he is a liar…

So, I agreed to do it and was promised a copy of the book a week later. Never received it…and yesterday, I got this call from his publisher saying that they're going to typesetting *tomorrow!* They need me to finish my foreword today! I told them, "How can I do this? I haven't even seen the book yet!"

But they said, "That's okay. Do your best. You know him well. We'll show you the final copy before it goes to print."

Did I mention they're going to print next week?

I finally received the document this morning. And like his over-inflated ego, his life story is a freakin' tome. No way I'll finish today—I don't even want to read it. This is typical Larry. He's always been bone idle and a huge procrastinator, so why should his work habits change now? You can imagine how nervous I am about all this, given my past with this layabout.

I've only had time to scan the introduction to his story. It reads so like him—from *his* perspective and through *his* eyes. No mention of me. Good. I don't want to be in his book. I'm a bit stressed, though, that the memoir might include Cheryl and me, and that he'll spread more lies about us. Maybe he'll just focus on his self-centred self. If not, Cheryl's got tons of lawyers to sue his ass.

Anyway, here's my endorsement: I doubt his book will sell. Buy mine, *Dissatisfied Me: A Love Story*, instead.

Okay, let's open the first page of this pulp and dive into this crap. So, without any further ado, brace yourself, and let me introduce you to…Larry Johnstone.

Prologue

May 2017

"OOOOOAAAAAAAH!"

Amazing! Best of the month! Ha!

The dimly lit room in the fertility clinic didn't create much ambience. Nor did the medical charts hanging on the white wall over the sink in the corner. Not that I needed anything atmospheric. When it came to ejaculating into a cup, no one did it better.

C'mon! There's barely any stuff in there! Something that euphoric should've been at least double. Sigh. *They say it's quality, not quantity.*

You know…that little squirt would've pocketed me at least fifty bucks in the States. Here in Vancouver? Nothing. After coming here for the past twenty years, that money would've come in handy. I never made much working at that men's shelter. *Oh well, volunteering my talent is the least I can do.*

I shifted position but couldn't move in the old chair—the grooves in the cushions now fitted too snug to my body. At least it's comfy and helped me to relax while I focused on my task.

Hmm… Better try to squeeze out another round. The clinic might want more.

I closed my eyes, sat back, and restarted, but a sharp knock at the door interrupted.

"Larry, finish up," yelled Margo, the apathetic nurse. "It's almost time to leave."

"But…I'm almost there," I replied. "Gimme another five minutes."

"Rules are rules, Larry, get moving."

Why on earth did this hospital ever change to a "fifteen-minute only" policy? Don't they know I'm an artist?

C'mon Larry, down to business…only a few more strokes.

Knock-knock-knock.

Damn, it's not happening!

"Larry. Now!"

"Oh, all right."

I dropped what I was doing, stood, and admired the butt grooves that remained entrenched in the chair. *BA-HA-HA, for an average-sized guy, my fifty-two-year-old ass still looks perfect!*

Yeah, the Golden Oak Hospital in western Vancouver adopted a "fifteen-minute policy" a while back. Before then, I'd park myself for hours in that comfy chair, recline way back, and peruse a huge pile of magazines they'd provide. Taking my time, I delivered gallons of baby gravy.

After each visit, the staff laughed at me. They're jealous, of course. My man sauce had always been of higher quality than the average Joe—in the top one percent, so the labs say.

My donations were always in high demand. I never understood why the hospital insisted on a once every three-day schedule. I'd be willing to come daily, and I took the forced rest as an affront. I could've easily given them three bottles each visit with no need to "recharge my batteries."

Now with imposed time restrictions—and no magazines—I worked five times faster to meet my quota. I couldn't disappoint, even if it's harder to deliver. Despite these challenges, I still rose to the occasion and left the hospital content that I contributed to the betterment of humanity. After all, I made people happy by giving them the hope of bearing my children, fulfilling my lifelong mission to father a nation. These every-third-morning visits had been an essential part of my routine.

A bell rang, warning someone was about to open the door.

I pulled up my pants—a bit tight today. *Probably shrank in the wash.* I left the room.

A round-faced, older woman sat behind her desk, sipping a large bottle of cola. Her finger twirled her short curly hair. I had to admit, her new butterfly-filled scrubs were cheerier than her usual navy blue.

"Margo, why on earth are you drinking that poison so early in the morning? Don't you know they clean hubcaps with that stuff?" She didn't seem amused. "Hey, didn't I say you should smile more?"

She'd always been cantankerous. When I first started making donations, I suggested that smiling was the first step in liberating her burdened soul. It didn't help Margo much, and she needed constant reminding.

The dour nurse peered above her aviator glasses at the janitor across the hall and sneered. "Do you see what I have to deal with day in, day out, Enrique?" She typed a few notes into her computer, and turned to face me, cocking her head. "Have you lost more hair since your last visit?"

I placed the small bottle on her counter. "I'll have you know, I've had this mullet since my teens. And...my adoring fans recognize me because of it." *Well, it's been ten years since I became a social media phenom.* I adjusted my John Lennon glasses, another trademark from my youth.

"Well, I've got two words for you. Tou-pée." She reached over and grabbed my bottle. "Okay, what do you have for us today?"

Margo was testier than usual. I had that effect on people. They were so insecure in my presence that they tried to elevate their stature with cheap put

-downs. Sometimes I wished I had lightning bolts, like the Ancient Greek gods, to put them in their place. *But I don't need to—I'm better than them.*

Margo raised her eyebrows at my below average output. "I expected more. Enrique over there was mopping to the beat of your fap—he finished his work five minutes faster."

Good, at least now she's smiling.

Enrique sat in the corner, exhausted.

"You should eat more fresh fruit, Enrique—" I said.

"And you should get more sun," Margo retorted.

My pale skin is like royalty!

Ignoring her, I finished my thought. "It might make you less sluggish, Enrique. Don't worry Margo. I'll perform better next time. I'm a little stressed. Have a lot on my plate today."

Margo laughed. "You? What's the big stressor? Deciding on drinking an espresso over a latte?"

How'd she know?

"By the way," I said, "I've said a million times this whole fifteen-minute policy you guys have is for the birds. You should make an exception for me. Oh, and another thing. You really gotta bring back those magazines."

"Hospital cutbacks, dear. Have you not heard of the internet?" Margo replied. "Most donors use their cell phones to find stimulus."

"Hey, may I remind you that I *volunteer* my time for this? I shouldn't have to use my cell data. The hospital should offer free Wi-Fi. It would improve overall output."

"I'll make the request just for you Larry. I'm sure the board of directors would be happy to pay for Wi-Fi to satisfy your porn needs."

About time someone did something about that. "Thank you, Margo." My smartwatch chimed. *Burned 600 calories this morning! Guess I can have extra cream in my morning coffee.* "Gotta run. See you Thursday. Same time. And I expect to see the Wi-Fi installed."

"Hopefully someone else will be here. I'm due for a change from this fertility clinic to do something more invigorating—like bedpan rotation." She dropped my sample into a large yellow bin labelled "Larry Johnstone's Donations."

Margo could be so silly. She loved my regular visits. I clicked my heels, did an about face, and left for Jumpin' Java to enjoy my free daily coffee.

Aboard a packed bus, part of me still dreamt for the "traditional" way of rearing a family. That was my intent when I flew over to the West Coast from Ottawa to marry my Schnookums—wife, white picket fence, tons of kids, dog, cat.... not quite the way it worked out.

Hard to believe it's near thirty years since I landed here. Drowsy, I closed my eyes reliving the day Schnookums invited me to move to the West Coast.

Part One:
Honeymooning Larry

(1989 — 1990)

Chapter One

Aftermath

April 1989

The console aboard the small spacecraft blipped and bleeped while I navigated the asteroid belt with ease.

A soft moan from behind aroused my attention.

"Larry," said the sensual voice, "space travel is sooo boring. Why don't we mate the way the ancients did back home?"

The woman with long strawberry-blonde hair lay on her side. Her mane camouflaged with the ship's interior—an orange-brown, shag carpet, covering the floor, walls, and ceiling.

The fur blanket wrapped around her suggested she had nothing else on. She held a martini glass filled with a clear liquid and took a sip. "Why don't you have one of these, Larry? It'll get you in the mood."

In a firm voice, she ordered, "Fly, autopilot." The computer took over the controls.

"You know," I said in my cool Larry voice, "I can drink anyone in the galaxy under the table. That includes you."

"The drink is strong, Larry, dear. Be careful. Why risk the pleasures you'll receive by getting intoxicated?"

"Hogwash."

I grabbed the half-filled Martini glass next to her; and with one big gulp, I downed the drink while soaking in my co-traveller's beauty.

She deserves a night of unforgettable ecstasy with me.

The room blurred, and my head erupted in pain. The smooth-flying vessel suddenly bounced up and down, forcing me to fall on top of my companion. Since I landed on her anyway, I closed my eyes, puckered up, and—

My eyes fluttered open and beheld my best friend's freckled face. Brad

Lepage was sitting next to me, shaking my shoulders.

"Aaaaaah," I yelled, placing my hands by my temples. "Stop it! The pain! The pain!" My head exploded. Sunlight beamed through the far window creating a halo around Brad's ginger hair.

"Haah…Uugh…Aaah…" I groaned and rolled over onto my side, facing the wall. I pulled the blanket over my head to escape the bright rays.

What the…?

I lowered the blanket again. My eyes bulged open as I caught a glimpse of a pair of bare legs facing me.

A life-size Barbarella *poster?*

While Brad's room was a bit like a pop-culture museum, boasting a huge collection of action figures, models of spacecraft, fantasy boardgames, and a wall filled top to bottom with books, his choice of "art" featuring posters of scantily clad sex-symbols from the sixties hanging over his bed was so…

Huh, and Brad tells me he "reads" science fiction "alone" here.

Brad shook me again.

"Leave me alone!" I curled myself into a tight ball.

I slept here last night? Couldn't remember. *Wait…is he waking me to go to church?*

"Okay, okay, I'll get up."

I attempted to sit, but the pain was so overwhelming I crashed back on the pillow and rolled on my side. I couldn't for the life of me figure out why my head thumped at the speed of light.

"Happy twenty-fourth birthday, Larry," he said unenthusiastically.

Why the sullen puss? You should be singing me a birthday song. Wait a sec. My birthday is in a couple of weeks…I think.

"Brad, did I sleep in?" I turned on my back. "I can't be late. My church's youth group needs their leader!" I massaged my face attempting to shake the cobwebs from my brain. "Ugh… Wait. You do remember my birthday is in May, right? I think we're still in April."

"Really? Shit, Larry!" Brad, agitated, stood. "You asked me to plan an early surprise party for you after church today."

"I did?"

"Don't you remember anything?" he said, waving his arms in the air in frustration.

"Uh…"

"You didn't want to celebrate your birthday so close to your wedding in a couple of weeks."

"Yes, yes, of course. Brilliant idea. Well, you know I have a lot of dates on my mind with all that marriage prep stuff."

"Yeah…don't I know it." Brad placed both hands behind his neck and moaned. "I've had way too much to do as best man for your wedding…running around coordinating stuff for you and your fiancée, Heather. Why I asked some guy who said he knew you from church to plan your surprise birthday party."

"Good stuff. Well, you might as well join me for mass and my birthday. I can pretend to act surprised. How's this?" I sat up, opened my mouth wide, and raised my eyebrows. Brad didn't budge. "Anyway, it's been months since you last attended church, Brad. You need religion for your soul."

"I don't think so. It's 3 p.m."

"What?"

"Your party, if it happened, ended two hours ago. Besides, you don't look like you're in any shape to go anywhere. Your face looks like it's been pressed by a waffle maker."

I couldn't understand what Brad was on about. My face always is stunningly handsome…and for sure the gang would wait for the birthday boy to show up! Or would they be worried? I never missed church.

"How the hell did I sleep in so late?"

Brad's eyebrows furrowed. "You mean, you don't remember what happened last night?"

"Sure I do. We had a *soirée* to celebrate me! I taught the gang about all my trials and tribulations in love! It was great! Did you guys learn a thing or two about scoring with chicks? Ba-ha-ha."

"Uh, Larry, what's the last thing you remember?"

"Some guy had this flipchart, filled with a great timeline listing the hundreds of girls I dated. It was fun recounting my love story for each one."

Brad bit his lower lip.

"Okay… Tell you what. Get yourself out of bed and wash up. Maybe you'll remember better after you have some coffee. There's a fresh pot brewing." He walked towards the door and stopped before leaving the room. "Oh, and when you're fully awake, call Father Barry. He phoned earlier. Says it's important."

"He always calls me when there's an emergency, like when he needs me to replace him at church."

Brad scoffed. "You need to finish university to be a priest."

"Details. Details. I *am* a recognized youth leader at that church, after all."

Brad stormed out and went downstairs.

Who pissed in his cereal today? Cereal? Breakfast? Wait a second. Did Brad say it's three o'clock? Crap! I missed my marriage prep meeting.

My fiancée, Heather, and I were getting married in a couple of weeks and were supposed to finalize the plans for our service with the priest. These meetings were brutal to coordinate. Schnookums—I also nicknamed her Honey-Bunny—was a busy professional living in Vancouver. She wanted to make all the wedding decisions. I didn't care about things like choice of flowers or the reception, but when it came to the church service, that was *my* domain. I fought her tooth and nail to earn the right to make the calls for our ceremony. *And I missed the key meeting where we were going to review the hymns and liturgy.*

I began to panic.

Heather wanted a non-traditional ceremony and couldn't understand that Anglican smells-and-bells were the only way to go. She argued for hours about wanting to walk down the aisle to "Another One Bites the Dust," but we had it removed. I feared with my being absent she'd reintroduce that wretched song back in the service.

Anyway, the service isn't the most important thing. The marriage is.

Through our regular prep meetings with Father Barry over the past months, we'll be ready for the "big time." Reminds me. Haven't started reading the four books he gave us in January that outline the steps to successful marriage, including one on human relations. I never understood why Father Barry wanted me to read them…Heather had taught me all I needed to know about "human relations" that one time. I closed my eyes, recalling every detail of that intimate interaction with my fiancée, when a door slammed downstairs, interrupting my pleasant memory. Sigh. Guess I'd better start my day.

I went for a leak in the bathroom. *Oops, there's a bit of pee on the floor. That's okay. Brad'll get that.* Washing my hands, I peeked up at my reflection in the mirror above the sink, and I let out a huge shriek.

What the hell?

"BRAD!" I yelled, "Where did I get that black eye?"

He didn't reply. I tried calling again. No response.

What's up with him?

The strong, fresh coffee smell lured me downstairs to the kitchen after I changed.

Didn't pour me a cup. Jerk.

Brad busied himself outside in the garden, occasionally coming in and out of view of the kitchen window.

A wrapped present and an envelope with my name awaited me on the table. A yellow note taped to it read, "Call Father Barry, eat your meal, and please leave—Brad."

Huh?

I opened the envelope. A card with a knight in white-plate armour holding a lance read "Happy Birthday Larry—Brad." Curious, I ripped off the wrapping around my gift.

Wow! How thoughtful! An amazing porcelain figurine of a wizard. Brad and I had spent many an hour at his dining room table, playing role-playing games and conjuring complex fantasy worlds.

Tossing it on the table, I phoned my priest.

"Father Barry speaking, praise God!" His booming voice echoed over the line.

Owwww. Is he using a microphone?

"Larry! So glad to hear from you! Are you doing okay? The gang from the party last night is worried about you."

Father Barry was there? Where was that again?

"My head hurts, Father. I never felt such pain. I must be paying for my sins. I'm sure it'll soon pass."

"My son, since you mention sin, let me come straight to the point. You certainly *were* dancing along the edge of the Lake of Fire last night. After all our teachings on sexual purity to our youth of late, you of all people were bragging about having pre-marital sex to our young friends."

"What? No! I'm saving my virginity for my Schnookums on our wedding night. You know that. It's just like it said in the books you told me to read." I tried hard to remember what I could've possibly said to the gang. I mean… Heather and I used a condom that one time, and we both agreed that it wasn't "really" having sex…even if she became pregnant, which she did. I took a second to imagine what "real" would be like on my honeymoon. "That big day's coming soon, you know. Anyway, why are we talking about this? Aren't you calling me to lead evening vespers or something? I really can't today."

"What? No. Listen," replied the priest. "You also announced that Heather was in a 'maternal' condition." — *I did?* — "When I preached on planting a passion last fall, it never occurred to me you'd take it in this direction."

"No, no, no! I'd never talk about sex openly in front of a group of people. I'm pure, I tell you."

"Well, you did. The boys from the youth group were all shocked you had lost your innocence."

"Father Barry, I led those kids for years. They love me. I'm their spiritual mentor. Why would I lie to them about my sex life at my birthday party?"

"It was your stag, Larry, and you were trashed."

"That's what I meant. *Stag.*"

All these dates. It came back to me. Bachelor party last night that Brad organized. "Surprise" birthday today. Wedding in a couple of weeks.

"Trashed? How's that possible? I've never been drunk."

"You were plastered, and I have some sobering news for you. I cannot officiate at your wedding. You really need to do some reflection. You blabbed more than you probably intended. I was particularly flabbergasted at that story you shared…you know, the one where you stole your friend's identity? What was his name? Dick Wank? And for what? To date girls because you had such a horrible reputation that you couldn't even use your own name?"

"Not true," I said, "everyone loves the name Larry Johnstone."

"And you were arrested for being a voyeur? That poor girl Trisha sounded traumatized!"

I spoke about Trisha? That can't be good. I promised the police and my counsellors I'd never mention her. That was all a huge misunderstanding. I only hung around her apartment building a lot—not really being a voyeur.

"Your story about that young woman set that boy off. What was his name?

You know…one of your ushers?

"Rick Duncan?"

"That's the one! I'd never seen anyone that angry in years. Why would he be so furious?"

"That's because Rick Duncan *is* Dick Wank. He fronts this rock band called Scottish Rot using that stage name. He also wears a paper bag over his head when he performs so no one will recognize him." It's how I got away with using his stage name. Trisha only knew me as Dick.

"Well, Rick clobbered you, and you were out cold. He left in a storm. I prayed for your recovery, and I'm glad at least you're up and about, praise God."

I rubbed near my bruised eye. *My best friend after Brad hit me? He couldn't have been that upset I pretended to be Dick Wank?*

"My friend," Father Barry said, "I'm all about forgiveness, so I can turn a blind eye to your shenanigans for the sake of a couple willing to commit themselves to each other in the eyes of God and man. But I can't marry you. I might reconsider if both you and your fiancée undergo some heavy counselling. Obviously, we would also have to wait until your baby is born."

I couldn't respond. *Did I really blab out my deepest secrets?*

Pfft, who needs counselling? I have all the marital advice one can get from the Bible and all the soap operas I watch.

"Thanks, Father Barry, for your concern. I'll discuss this with Heather."

"Sorry for the bad news, Larry. If you need to talk to someone, I'm here for you, praise God." Father Barry hung up.

I couldn't believe this "birthday." I reread Brad's note and glanced out the kitchen window. Brad was raking the pristine yard with agressive strokes, his grip tight on the handle, as if trying to force his frustrations out into the grass. Poor guy must've been upset that Rick ruined my bachelor party. I shook my head in sympathy and served myself some food.

Hungry, I demolished a box of Frootie-ooties—my favourite cereal. The clock read 5 p.m., so I drank the remainder of the milk from my bowl and phoned Heather.

I made all my long-distance calls from Brad's house. He never complained, maybe because he didn't notice. It did help because I needed to chat with my fiancée often.

I dialed her number in Vancouver.

"Hi, Schnookums," I sang in a kid-like tone, "it's your Honey-Bear. I love you."

"Come," the voice on the line said abruptly, then hung up.

Chapter Two
The Ecstasy of Flight
April 1989

Heather was the best thing that came out of my relationship with Prick Rick. She was his first cousin and had flown in before the jerk's twenty-first birthday party last September—that I organized. Overwhelmed by her beauty, I fell in love with the blonde bombshell at first sight. Within two weeks of meeting, we were engaged.

Heather remained in Vancouver while Brad and I ran around Ottawa doing all the preparations. She told us what she wanted, and we'd act on it. She had to have her say in everything, and we spared no expense—we had no choice but to honour all of Heather's wishes.

Schnookums had a high-paying job as an advertising executive, but never helped with the bills and insisted my family pay. My parents were poor as dirt, but my dad did co-sign a loan with me for her engagement ring, which I defaulted on. I had to convince Heather's mom, Mary Mackenzie, to give me her credit card number to help clear my debts. Thankfully, she did, and I continued to use it for other wedding expenses.

Now Schnookums is calling me to join her on the West Coast.

I rifled through Brad's kitchen drawers and found a phone book. Excited about the prospect of taking my first flight, I dialed Air Western. A ticketing agent answered.

"Hi, I'm Larry Johnstone. I need to fly to Vancouver tonight."

"Let's see, sir. You're in luck. You have the choice between two flights. They're costly. Most people book their tickets a few weeks in advance to avoid paying a premium."

"I don't care, I have to urgently return to my fiancée."

"Okay. You could take a direct flight to Vancouver, but at such short notice it will cost \$1,350. It leaves at 7:00 p.m. and the flight will take about five hours.

You should arrive by 9 p.m. The other option is cheaper; however, you'll be flying to Vancouver via Toronto, Winnipeg, Regina, Calgary, and Edmonton. You don't have to change planes, though, and it only costs $900. Better leave quick to catch it. The flight departs in an hour and a half. You'll arrive in Vancouver after midnight."

"I'll take that," I said.

"Very good, sir. Would you like economy or first class?"

Without missing a beat, I answered, "First class." *They'd better not serve meatloaf!*

"Excellent. That'll be $1,700."

Mary's credit card paid the bill, and the agent instructed me to pick up the ticket at the airport. I called Heather, and she promised to meet me.

Hmm, only got five bucks. Not enough for a cab.

"Hey Brad," I yelled through the kitchen window. "You asked me to leave. Can you drive me to the airport?"

Brad stared at me, hesitated, then nodded.

I'll have my personal belongings sent to me later. I don't have much and can't tarry. Heather beckons.

Brad drove me to the airport. He surprised me by not saying good-bye. Didn't matter. I was too psyched for my first flight and to be reunited with my Honey-Bunny on the West Coast.

My head still hurt from my bender the night before, and the airport swarming with people in frantic excitement didn't help. I stood in the entrance, unsure where to go. I couldn't believe all the slow-moving queues, and I only had forty-five minutes to catch my plane.

I must've appeared lost. An elderly woman walked by. "You poor, poor, man," she said. "Here, let me help you with your taxi fare." She gave me twenty dollars! I'd never refuse free cash, but why on earth would she do that?

Within another minute, someone else gave me ten.

I should hang out at the airport more often!

"Excuse me," I asked a porter. "Which is the line for picking up my ticket?"

He pointed to a sign marked "Tickets." Five people were waiting to be served.

A middle-aged woman greeted me from behind the counter. I figured I'd make some light conversation. "Hey baby, how'd a hot chick like you get stuck at a job like this?"

"NAME," she replied.

"Uh, hi, I'm Larry Johnstone," I said.

She checked the register. "You're supposed to be in first class. Go to the first-class line."

The queue had about ten people. "I'm in a hurry. Can't you just give me the ticket here?"

"Sorry. Economy fare only."

The nerve.

I walked over towards the other line. A young couple with their backs to me were chatting after having checked their bags. They might've been talking about playing squash, or washing a car, for all I could care; but based on their snobbish accents, I guessed they must've come straight from a prep school. At least they had good taste in clothing—dressed like me in similar golf shirts, jeans, and topsiders.

I tapped the man's shoulder. "Hi, I'm Larry. I gotta get to Vancouver desperately."

"Sorry, chum. Why the urgency?"

"Can't go into details. My fiancée needs me."

The woman chimed in, "Topher, help the poor man out. He probably got mugged… Isn't it romantic? He wants to visit his Cutie Patootie." She beamed at her boyfriend.

"You're so right, Muffy," He pulled out his wallet. "Sorry for your troubles. This should help, and hope they find the guy who did this to you." He produced a generous wad of cash. "This can be put towards a cheaper *economy* ticket."

The woman gushed. "Topher! You're so noble!" She gave him a long, wet kiss. The two gathered up their belongings and went towards the gates while I joined the lineup for first class passengers.

Who needs to work when you have airports?

I made more cash in fifteen minutes than my last semester in university.

The young woman behind the first-class counter opened her mouth in shock. Her big blue eyes widened. "My word, what on earth happened to you?"

"What do you mean? I'm flying to Vancouver tonight."

"Your black eye…and your clothes."

It occurred to me I had slept in the clothes I wore at my stag and smelled of rancid BO and alcohol.

Might as well take advantage of the situation.

"I got beat up by this horrible man named Rick Duncan. He sucker-punched me and left me lying in the gutter all night. Then my fiancée called from Vancouver in a panic. She needs me badly. I booked a ticket, so here I am."

"That's horrible! Let's see." She clicked at her keyboard. "Name?"

"Larry Johnstone."

"Here you are, right near the front of the aircraft." She surveyed me closely. "Are you sure you want to take this flight? You'll be in a small plane for almost ten hours."

"Ten hours? I was told I would arrive in Vancouver at around midnight, not four in the morning."

"Yes, but there's a time difference of three hours. The direct flight will get you there at around 9 p.m. and leaves a half hour later. Since you paid first-class, I can get you on it. At least you can grab a drink and unwind beforehand in the first-class lounge."

Excellent! I might earn more money in the meantime.

"Okay, sounds good."

"Your boarding pass." She handed me the ticket.

Score! A window seat.

"Follow those signs to the first-class lounge," she said. "They'll announce boarding in about a half hour."

Did she say free beverages? Makes first class worth it!

I stopped off at a bookstore *en route* to the lounge. Someone else gave me a fiver.

Perfect, that should cover the cost of my reading material.

I loved mythology, and it had been a while since I indulged in the Greeks. I purchased a copy of Homer's *Iliad and the Odyssey*—a nice light read for the flight.

I checked into the first-class lounge and downed a couple of vodka oranges.

Funny. They helped my headache.

"Flight 729, destination Vancouver, now accepting first- and business-class passengers. Please proceed to Gate 17."

Grabbing my book, I went to the bathroom and ran to catch my inaugural flight. I dashed ahead of an elderly couple moving slowly towards the front of the queue.

I win! Gonna be first to board the plane!

The old man tapped my shoulder, "Excuse me," his cracking voice said, "we were here before you."

"Uh-uh. No way! I ran all the way from the lounge and beat you both to the head of the line."

Before the old fart could reply, a woman in a navy-blue flight attendant's uniform asked, "Boarding pass?"

"Here. First class!"

She tore it, and I jogged down the jetway and boarded the airplane.

A striking man in similar uniform, perhaps a few years older, greeted me. "Good day sir, may I see your boarding pass?"

Odd. They already asked. But who am I to argue in the presence of this handsome thing?

I soaked in all his features: dark haired, broad shouldered, and chiselled. A moment passed, but it could've been an eternity.

I snapped out of my trance when he broke out his charismatic smile. "Sir?"

"Huh?"

"Can I see your boarding pass?" he said.

"Huh? Oh, yeah, that." I held it out for him and dropped it.

Butterfingers.

"Let me get that for you." He bent over as my eyes traced his graceful movement. An image of Schnookums looking at me disapprovingly broke my daydream.

He checked the ticket. "Nice to meet you, Mr. Johnstone. You are in seat 4F by the window on the far left."

"Please, call me Larry," I said.

"Very well, Larry." He gave me a subtle wink. "I'm David. I'll be serving drinks shortly. What will you have?"

"Vodka orange," I replied.

"Excellent. Make yourself comfortable."

I should've been a flight attendant. Must be a cinchy job, and I'd be dashing in David's uniform.

Being in the last row of first class gave me an excellent vantage point to observe my fellow travelers boarding the aircraft. When the first-class cabin filled, the "lower-class" passengers filed in.

Peasants. I stretched my legs out over the empty seat next to mine and stared at the voyagers hauling their bags.

David served me a pre-flight drink.

"Why did you become a flight attendant?" I asked. "With your looks, you could've easily landed a Hollywood gig."

He smiled shyly. "I tried auditioning for Broadway. After a couple of years of not landing anything and waiting on too many tables, I figured this would make a better career. I've travelled all over the globe and love serving fine people like yourself!"

He didn't give me a chance to reply and went on to serve other first-classers. I sipped my drink while the few remaining passengers trickled on.

A large, bald, Black man with a goatee boarded. *He must be six-foot-six, and I'm guessing...what...275-pounds?* Anyway, his muscular frame hulked over David as he presented his ticket. David pointed in my direction, and the man nodded. His bulging biceps rippled lifting his baggage.

No. Don't sit here, these are my seats.

He placed his suitcase in the overhead compartment. "Excuse me," he said in a booming voice and plopped himself in the seat next to mine. He barely fit, pushing up against my left side, forcing me to scrunch into my window.

David came back with a soda for him.

The man grabbed his beverage with his right hand and caught me staring at David. He chuckled. I wanted to give him the stink eye, but his intense glare and size intimidated me. He put his drink down and reached his hand across my seat. "Vaughn Brown."

I shook it. "Hi, I'm Larry Johnstone. Nice to meet you, Vaughn." His warm handshake and friendly tone put me at ease.

The aircraft door closed, and pinging sounds filled the cabin.

"Looks like we'll be getting ready to leave soon." Vaughn downed his drink in one gulp.

I did the same.

"Sorry for taking up so much space, can't be helped," he said with a smile. "This is why I go first class. Seats in economy are half the size."

"I go for the service," I replied, staring at David.

Vaughn nodded in acknowledgement. Reaching into his carry-on, he pulled out a small teddy bear—about six inches tall, wearing a number thirty-two basketball shirt. He also pulled out a pill bottle and popped one. Shaking it to alert my attention, he said, "Doc gave me these, 'cause I'm a nervous traveller. Might need a few of these babies to get me to Vancouver—don't want me having a panic attack."

No, I don't. You'd squash me.

He continued. "These do me wonders." Vaughn placed them in the seat pocket in front of him. Shaking his bear, he said, "You know who this is?"

I shook my head.

"He's Magic, my travel buddy. He helps me relax. Growing up, I watched all the basketball games I could on TV and had team posters all over my room. Mama bought him for me when I turned fifteen. She thought it kinda funny. I treasured it. He goes wherever I go."

Tempted to make fun of this huge man who played with teddy bears, I bit my tongue. "Do you play basketball?"

David brought me another vodka orange.

Didn't even have to ask! He knew I wanted one.

Vaughn laughed, "Nah, not my thing. I'm a professional football player." He showed me a tattoo of his team's logo on the inside of his left forearm.

"Wait a second. You're *the* Vaughn Brown?"

"One and the same."

I rarely took interest in other people, but I was sitting next to a star in Canadian football! "How come a talent such as yourself is playing in Canada, and not in the States?"

Vaughn looked glum.

"A bit of a story. I got a scholarship at a small university in Iowa. Not much to do there except study, play football, and watch the corn grow.

"I'd hopes of going pro in my senior year. Scouts scouted me, and they all said I looked promising, but I broke my leg badly. They didn't think I'd fully recover, so no team picked me in the draft.

"I kept faith, though, and Dallas signed me as a free agent. But before I could pack my bags, they cut me. Didn't even hit training camp. Ended up landing a contract in Vancouver. I've done well here, and I'm sure my success in Canada will pave my way back to the States one day."

Man, this guy can talk. I haven't had a chance to say anything about me, yet!

"It's gonna be hard to leave Canada, though. I've grown to love British Columbia. I met and married my gorgeous wife, Jacquie, there." He showed me a dragon tattoo on his right shoulder with his wife's name under it, surrounded by hearts.

With my horrible dating history, I knew implying your partner was a dragon was a virtual death sentence.

"Ba-ha-ha, it looks like you named the dragon tattoo, Jacquie," I said.

He laughed. "Get that all the time. I had this dragon when I lived in Iowa, before meeting my wife. I didn't want to give it up, nor have another tattoo on my other shoulder." He snickered. "Jacquie can be a dragon when enraged, but she's also the sweetest woman I've ever met."

While Vaughn blathered on about his college football career, I daydreamed about dragons, which transitioned to reflections of my childhood.

"I, too, am an athlete," I interrupted. He gave me a curious look. "I was in the top five for the 50-yard dash in the Ontario provincial games." *When I was eleven, and there were ten kids competing, all from my school. And I won a participation pin.*

"Really? Did you try for the Olympics?" he asked.

"Nah, I had a more pressing mission. I spent my teenage years searching for a girl to be my wife and have my kids. I finally found her. I'm going to Vancouver to get married."

"Good for you! And congratulations!"

The aircraft moved backwards. I reached for my new book while Vaughn popped a pill.

"Into Greek mythology?" he asked.

"Love it," I responded, surprised. Not many people shared my interest. "I've been reading this stuff since I was a kid. You into it?"

"Not really." My expression must have shown a bit of disappointment, because he added, "but I studied how to read Ancient Greek in Iowa. I did an undergraduate degree in—" and a woman's voice broke over the intercom interrupting him. She welcomed us to the flight and gave some basic safety instructions. David came by to pick up our cups, and he smiled at me again.

The airplane taxied to the runway and paused. The engines kicked in a heavy blast, and we rocketed forward. I never experienced such speed and noise, and I clutched nervously to the armrests for dear life while my co-traveller clung to his bear. The nose lifted, and we were airborne, land escaping beneath me as we burst through a cloud.

The announcer mentioned the flight would take about five hours.

It won't be long, Schnookums.

Several minutes after takeoff, the captain extinguished the Fasten Seat Belts sign. Vaughn appeared relaxed, no longer strangling his teddy bear. We had a few hours to kill, so I figured I'd return the favour and tell him about my life. No doubt my hundreds of lessons about women would help improve his marriage.

David came by and gave me yet another drink.

"You must be so happy to be married," I said to Vaughn.

Vaughn slurred, likely from his medication. "Yeah, she's the best."

"Yeah, so is my Heather. I love her to pieces. As I was saying, I wanted to be married, have kids, the dog, the cat, and the house with the white picket fence ever since I was a teen. I received a calling to be a director of a choir camp, and became a professional chorister…"

I went on to talk about all the girls I had dated, and how they all had dumped me within a couple of weeks. I painted a picture of how these women had victimized me for one reason or another. After all, I wanted to be the perfect boyfriend, wishing only to be married.

Vaughn soaked in my words. He even closed his eyes to reflect on everything I said. He had a slightly pensive expression on his face, with his mouth slightly open. *Is that drool?*

After talking for two hours, an annoying pinging interrupted me, and the Fasten Seat Belts sign illuminated. The plane shook violently, so much so I feared the fuselage would break apart.

Vaughn's eyes popped open. "This is why I hate flying so much." Hand trembling, he reached to the pouch in the seat ahead and popped another pill. Poor Magic underwent "the squeeze" again.

The turbulence didn't last long, and the moment the passengers were permitted, Vaughn undid his seatbelt and dashed to the washroom.

I trembled terribly after the plane bounced and jolted around, and I needed another drink. I waved my empty glass in David's general direction, who returned with a fresh vodka orange.

Curious, I grabbed the pill bottle in Vaughn's seat and read the label.

Bah, never heard of this stuff, but if it can calm Vaughn, maybe it'll calm me.

I opened the bottle and swallowed four capsules with the help of my beverage.

Instead of relaxing, I grew anxious and trembled. A scary thought entered my mind. *Did I board the correct plane?* My brain fogged. I yelled. "We're not going to" — *What did Vaughn say? Iowa? A place with corn? No, he said —*

"Dallas! I want to see my Honey-Bunny in Vancouver, not some cowboys!"

I stood and screamed like a little girl. David rushed over and placed his hands on my shoulders. It made me feel warm and fuzzy, but I couldn't shake the notion we weren't going to Vancouver. He guided me to a vacant bathroom and left me alone to splash cold water on my face. It didn't calm my jitters.

What would Heather say if I don't show up? Would she dump me? I can't risk losing "the one."

Still convinced we were on route to Texas, I rushed to the cockpit and banged the door several times. "As a first-class customer, I demand you turn the plane westbound. Now!"

After a couple of attempts with no response, my throat grew dry, and I was overwhelmed by a debilitating fatigue. I pirouetted towards my fellow travellers, but my vision blurred, and I couldn't make out any of their faces. My eyes grew heavy. Needing some sleep—and without thinking—I instinctively removed my jeans and shirt to prepare myself for bed.

A handsome flight attendant entered the back from economy. Even in my hazy state, I could make out his uniform, dark hair, and athletic frame. *David?*

I took two steps forward to greet him, but my legs could no longer contain the weight of my body. I turned and did a face plant in the two vacant seats in the front of the cabin and fell asleep to the sound of applause.

A shake woke me out of my deep slumber.

David, is that you?

"Larry," David's soothing voice said, "you need to wake up, please."

"Not now darling, maybe later." I grabbed the blanket and leaned against the bulkhead. *Wait...this isn't my seat. Where's Vaughn? And I'm clothed...and sitting upright.* I opened my eyes and faced David. *Did you dress me? And got me the blanket? So thoughtful of you!*

"Larry, can you hear me? We're approaching Vancouver airport. I need you to fasten your seat belt. Do you need my help?"

It took a few moments to regain my senses. *Glad the pilots changed course.*

"Another vodka orange?" I asked.

"No, Larry. I don't mean help with that. I meant your seat belt. We're landing."

Not that I needed his assistance, but I nodded to David who reached around my waist and buckled me snug as a bug in a rug. He returned to his duties while the plane descended to make its final approach.

Welcome to Schnookums-ville!

Forgetting to tell Heather about my change of flights, I had four hours to kill at the airport.

Maybe I could score more cash?

After looking pathetic for an hour, no one gave me a penny. Bored, I figured it might be a good idea to call home to tell my folks I had left Ottawa. I found a phone booth.

"Operator speaking."

"I would like to make a collect call."

"To whom."

"Johnny Johnstone."

"From whom."

"Larry Johnstone."

"One moment please." I heard a phone ringing.

A harsh-sounding woman answered, "Yes?"

"Collect call from Larry Johnstone to Johnny Johnstone. Do you accept the charges?"

"What?" A crash flooded my ear.

She hung up!

I phoned again, and the woman didn't give the operator a chance to speak.

The third time, I screamed over the operator. "Mama, accept the frigging call!"

She did.

"Don't you realize it's past bedtime?" she said. "And why now? You haven't called your mama in weeks, and we practically live in the same city! This better be important. Speak fast. I don't want to waste money talking to you on the phone when you can come over for a visit."

"I'm in Vancouver. Heather insisted I come. Something happened last—"

"WHAT? Larry, how many times have I told you to keep your pecker in your trousers. I made it very clear. NO FORNICATING before the wedding. Now you're taking your hard-earned cash to seek carnal delight before you officially wifed your trollop? You know I think she's perfect for you, but this is inexcusable."

"Mama, we're not getting married because—"

"You're going to live together in sin? Even worse! Wait until your father finds out… Johnny," she yelled in the background, "your son has gone to Vancouver and is shacking up with that hussy, Heather. Marriage's off. I thought you raised him to be decent—not this whoring hooligan…" She shrieked into the phone, "Don't you come home until you're ready to repent, and I don't expect to hear from you again until you do."

Mama hung up.

She didn't even give me a chance to talk about last night, and how Rat Rick betrayed me. It was his fault my wedding plans got cancelled.

A man in his forties walked by, took out his wallet, and gave me ten dollars. "You poor man. Maybe you can buy yourself something to eat."

Good idea. I had slept when the meal was served on the airplane. Just as well. They had served meatloaf.

A tall, pregnant blonde entered the terminal wearing a red dress. Glaring sternly, she altered her course towards me. She moved with incredible alacrity for someone in her condition.

She wrapped her arms around my shoulders and kissed me. I felt her tongue navigate its way into my mouth, and I savoured the moment. The passionate kiss lasted an eternity.

Heather grabbed my hand and ordered, "Come."

Without saying another word, she led me down an empty hallway in the terminal and found a door to a supply room. She opened it and she guided me in. Within a minute, I executed her command.

Despite the small hiccup with Rancid Rick, I couldn't have imagined a better way to close off my weekend:

My best friend organized a kick-ass stag; I taught a bunch of young lads how to score with women; I experienced getting tanked for the first time (and promised it'll never happen again); I ventured out of Ottawa and fulfilled a dream of flying; I made a ton of cash; I saw what could've been the dishiest man ever, after myself; and I befriended a professional athlete, who happened to be one of the biggest names in Canadian football. But most importantly, I was about to embark on a new life chapter with my Schnookums.

The black of evening made the cab ride to Heather's place uneventful. The majestic beauty of the Rockies, or any landmark, were invisible along the way. I didn't have any sense of direction, save for the bright lights of the city as we drove toward it.

Schnookums told me she lived in the Kitsilano area, near the waterfront. The taxi rolled into the driveway of an older red-brick building—my new home— and she paid the fare.

Though hard to make out, most of the buildings in the area seemed to be no taller than a couple of stories. Heather's apartment happened to be on the top floor. She unlocked the door, and I stood stunned in the entranceway. *The living room has a giant screen TV?*

"Is that colour?" I asked.

"Of course," replied Heather. She walked to the far end of the room and slid a glass door open. "Have a look."

The fully covered balcony contained a lavish table, Bar-B-Q, and a small fridge. "Va-va-voom," I said, leaning against the rail.

"There's an amazing view here on a clear morning. Would you like a drink?"

"Thanks! I'm dying of thirst."

Heather pointed to the fridge. "Help yourself to a cider. Oh, get me a lemonade while you're at it."

I opened two bottles and downed most of mine in one swig. It tasted a bit like fizzy fruit juice.

"Careful," said Heather, "that's a strong drink."

"Bah!" I helped myself to a second one while Heather returned indoors.

I followed Schnookums, walking on the dark oak floors past the living room and into the hallway. We stopped off in the bathroom. It reeked of affluence, with two sinks and porcelain bath—but the beautiful walk-in rainfall shower stole my breath. My mind drifted thinking of the wild erotic adventures we'd experience each morning.

"That's nothing," said Heather, watching me stand in awe. "Check this out." She led me to the most ornate kitchen I had ever seen. I placed my bottle on a granite-topped island, and with a dramatic swish of her hands, Heather gestured gracefully to the gas stove embedded in the countertop. "You'll make good use of it."

"Yes, I will." *After I figure it out.*

"I'm so glad you are here," she said, rubbing her belly. "We do need you. What do you think of our home?"

Beautiful balcony. Giant screen TV. Erotic showers. "Yes. Yes. I think this place will be satisfactory."

Heather smirked. "Good! Come."

Funsies? Again?

She smiled and opened the door to the master bedroom. It was huge, and the design endeared my romantic heart. The blue wall combined with the white king-sized bed created an illusion of a giant cloud, floating in the sky. I could just daydream my days away here while Heather does her work at the office, then cuddle her all night.

I made a move into our room, but Heather denied me access. "Not so fast, Honey-Bear. We're not married, yet…this way."

A little confused, I followed her down the hall. She opened a door to a smaller guest room, with a cot and dresser.

"This is yours," she said. "Remember…your mother doesn't want us to fool around before our marriage, so no entry in our room. Have to keep up appearances!" She winked and blew me a kiss.

I laughed and blew her a kiss back. "Good night, my Schnookums."

She returned to her room without saying a word.

Chapter Three

Hello City

April 1989

I slept *au naturel* last night, glad to discard my two-day worn clothes on the floor and feel my nakedness against fresh sheets. I awoke refreshed and looked forward to the beautiful view Heather had mentioned, but the sky's darkness and rain hid it when I peered out my window. I expected the city of Vancouver would've ordered sunshine on my first day, not this dismal weather.

Heather's melancholy decor for this room was also depressing. The dark grey walls reflected the gloomy skies outside, and the black and white photos hanging in their plastic frames didn't brighten things up. Most of them were of a buff blond man, posed in different positions. The most intriguing one was an aerial view of him, naked, sitting on the floor with both hands entwined behind his neck, and his head placed on his lifted knees. From a distance, the gaps between his head and elbows resembled a skull with an elongated chin.

If this is gonna be my baby's room, it will need some Noah's Ark decals, and cute pairs of furry animals all over the place. I would've loved that as a child. Instead, I had clowns painted over my walls. Mama adored them, but for me, clowns didn't belong in comedy, they belonged in horror.

I recalled many a night screaming out in fear, so Mama took me to a circus to show how funny they could be. She was right. Clowns could be hysterical, but inanimate pictures gave them a different character—very creepy. *There has to be something cheery about this room.*

I walked back to the window to look outside again. People scurried around the street below with umbrellas during the morning rush hour. Heather's right. Even without sunshine, there was a majestic charm to the waterfront view. *Maybe I will be able to see the mountains from here when the skies clear.* The rain still pattered against the building, and it blended with a sizzling sound from the kitchen.

The smell of bacon made me salivate.

Breakfast!

I spun around with intention to check out what's cooking and jumped out of my skin. Heather's sneering face greeted me from the doorway.

"Why are you naked?" she said sternly. She stood akimbo, wearing a red and white business suit. I forgot it was a Monday, and she had to work. Instinctively, I put my hands over my crotch.

"Do you have any sausages?"

"There might be some in the freezer." Heather laughed. "You know, this is the first time I've ever seen you fully naked. You really need to gain some weight." She looked me up and down. "You didn't pack a change of clothes? Wait a sec…I do have some spare clothes for you."

She left the room and came back with a pair of jeans, socks, underwear, and a royal blue t-shirt. "Try these on. When you're ready, come to the kitchen."

The clothes floated on me, and I dreaded tripping over the much-too-long pant legs. A giant Swedish flag adorned the front of the shirt. I had no choice but to wear them, given the reeking state of my own.

Schnookums could've done a better job estimating my size when she bought these for me. And Sweden? Must be a Vancouver thing.

I entered the kitchen, holding my pants up. Schnookums sat at the table, head shaking and hand tapping to the loud music pounding from a boombox on the counter behind her. She was humming along with the singer, whose voice blasted low, growly tones over the ludicrously fast, distorted, and heavy beat. Heather stopped her movements on spotting me in the doorway, coughed, and frowned.

"Horrible, uh, I mean they are a little big for you," she commented on my outfit. She had to project her voice over the aggressive guitars emanating from the stereo. I took a seat opposite her.

"What's that noise?" I yelled, covering my ears.

"Nothing like some Napalm Death to kickstart my week," Heather hollered back, somehow sweetening her tone. She reached over and lowered the volume of the music. "My friend made me that cassette. I love it. I listen to it every morning. These songs are my new favourites."

"Can you turn it off? It's hurting my brain."

"It's almost over." True to her word, "Electric Youth" by Debbie Gibson began playing within thirty seconds. "See?" she said. "My friend introduced me to these wonderful cheerful tunes."

I don't follow pop music, but that song had polluted the radio airwaves the last few months. The peppy positive energy was a violent contrast to Napalm Death.

"Listen to the rest and let me know what you think." She resumed eating her breakfast. "That eye of yours is in rough shape," she said between bites. "You better've clobbered the guy who gave you that ugly shiner."

"I did, Schnookums. He'll regret the day he insulted you for being pregnant. He'll think twice about defiling your name."

"How'd he find out?" she said angrily. "I didn't want your friends to know yet."

After a brief pause, Heather sighed and forced a smile. She went for her purse and gave me $200 cash. "Here. A small welcome gift. Buy some clothes to get you through the next few days. Can someone pack and send your stuff here from Ottawa?"

"Yes. Father George can."

My former parish priest, Father George McKinley, took in boys from out of town who attended school in the city. Since I had moved to a rural area outside Ottawa, my parents thought it best I live closer to my school. The decision was probably driven by Mama and me fighting all the time. I'd been living with Father George in peace since around Grade 6.

"Right," she said. "We'll talk more when I get home from work. My mother got a call from that priest, Father Barry, yesterday…We'll have to make alternate wedding plans."

"But I have no money."

"Pshhh. Not a worry. Must leave for the office. You can grab a bus downtown and get to know the city. I'll be home around six. I expect dinner to be ready by then and you in new clothes. Okay?"

"Okay," I said happily.

"Electric Youth" ended, followed by a similar dark-toned song to Napalm Death.

"Ah, Carcass," said Heather. "This song moves my soul."

"Sounds riveting," I said sarcastically. "I can't make out the words."

"That's because there aren't any. It's called 'Genital Grinder.' Do you still want your sausage?"

Thankfully the song didn't last too long and was replaced by Tiffany's "I Think We're Alone Now." Heather giggled.

"I'll pass," I said, figuring she was laughing at the dramatic changes of musical styles. "Can you make me waffles? They'll go good with bacon."

"In the freezer…" she barked, then chuckled again. "That Tiffany song is my friend's favourite on the tape. He's so cute when he tries to sing it…" She paused in reflection. "You know what we should eat tonight? Chicken Kiev. Can you make it, Honey-Bear? I'll give you a nice reward," she stood and kissed my head. "Gotta run, but before I go, I need you to sign for the house key."

She produced a thick document from her briefcase, stapled neatly in the corner. She turned to the last page and pointed to a signature block bearing my name. "Just sign here, Honey-Bear."

Seemed like a lot of bureaucratic nonsense for a key, but I had heard condos could have ridiculous rules.

I signed, she flipped me a key, and grabbed the last piece of bacon. Heather left, waving goodbye, while the boombox played another heavy song with guttural vocals.

Big city folks, always in a hurry. Can't remember what she said. Did she say chicken Cordon-Bleu? I must find the recipe—I want my "reward." Had to admit, I always liked what Heather called it—funsies.

I was happy to cook for her but didn't feel like making myself waffles. I opened the fridge and helped myself to some juice. Maybe she had some Frootie-ooties; she knew I loved the stuff. I looked in the cupboard—Bowel Buster Bran.

Who seriously eats this?

I called Father George who agreed to pack my personal belongings and send them via courier. Putting down the phone, I caught a whiff of my underarms. No wonder Heather hurried out the door, but before hitting the shower, I turned off the annoying music.

God gave me sunshine when I hit the streets!

I strolled east towards the bus stop, enjoying the beach view. The downtown cityscape had an unobstructed backdrop of the Rockies. I had never taken in such beauty.

"Hi, I'm Larry Johnstone," I said to the driver. "I'm new in town. My fiancée said this bus takes me downtown. Can I find a good coffee shop there?"

The driver, an older man, stared at me with odd eyes. "Have you not heard of Earl of Latteigh? That coffee chain is breeding like rabbits. Might be fun for you to check out the first one in Canada. Just have to grab the sky train for a stop at the end of my run."

What a nice chatty man. Bus drivers back home would threaten to throw me off the bus for asking questions.

"Thanks. Sounds great. How long will it take?"

"About a half hour."

I took a seat near the front. Awestruck like a child, I explored my new city through the window. Some of the buildings were architecturally inspiring.

"The Hotel Vancouver reminds me of the Chateau Laurier in Ottawa," I said.

The driver laughed. "They're a chain across Canada. It was the tallest building in the city up until twenty years ago. If buildings are your thing, the Marine Building near your stop used to be the largest in the British Empire, before the Hotel Vancouver. They're relatively small now, though, but still a point of interest."

I thanked the driver as I disembarked. I found the train, and in hindsight, should've walked—the ride only lasted a minute.

It didn't take long to find the Earl of Latteigh—a line spilled out of the shop. A variety of people wearing suits to shorts queued up. I witnessed this phenomenon with coffee shops in Ottawa. People would go and wait fifteen minutes to buy a cup of coffee and leave not talking to anyone. I never understood the fascination. Coffee was important, but I'd rather be sitting and served in a proper ceramic mug as opposed to being herded like cattle and forced to drink from cardboard cups.

I couldn't read the menu from where I stood. When I neared the front of the line, a gentleman in a nice suit ordered. "I'll have a quadruple *mòr* soy no foam latte with a peppermint shot."

The young woman at the register smiled. "That'll be $7.45, William."

Who pays $7.45 for a coffee?

"Triple, *meadhanach*, half sweet, non-fat, caramel macchiato," the person ahead of me ordered.

"$6.50, ma'am."

How do these people afford this? And what on earth are they saying?

"May I help you, sir?" the cashier asked.

"Uh, I've never been here before, and I've no idea what's going on."

"It's simple. We have three sizes based on Scottish Gaelic for small, medium and large: *beag, meadhanach,* and *mòr.* You can choose an espresso, latte, dark, decaf…"

She lost me at *beag.* "I'll have what the woman ahead of me ordered."

"Was it the triple, *meadhanach,* half sweet, non-fat, caramel macchiato?"

Spam, spam, spam.

I had no idea what it meant, but a *mòr* sounded like a gigantic size. "Yes, but I'll have a *mòr,* and make it a quadruple."

"Sounds good. That'll be $8.75. Can I get your name for the bar?"

Eight dollars and seventy-five cents? Didn't she notice my black eye? Good customer service should dictate giving me the drink, free.

I shelled out the cash. "Larry, and what is the bar?"

"When you pay, you can go to the bar on the far side where the barista will prepare your drink."

Barista. Sounds fancy. I might like this place!

"What is a quadruple?"

"You're asking for four expresso shots in the drink—about double the usual."

I'm liking coffee talk!

"How do you master this lingo?"

"Just keep coming back. After a few weeks you'll get the hang of it."

I couldn't afford this but went to the bar after the woman gave me my change.

The barista called out my name and placed my white cup, the size of a can of pop, in a brown sleeve—*that's a mòr? Eight-dollar coffee better...*

I took a sip and nearly fainted.

Soooo goooood!

I'll be back!

The shop had no place to sit, so I hit the streets with my cup in hand. Most other pedestrians carried coffee with them, too, making me feel a part of the culture.

I walked eastbound on West Cordova Street, noticing the harbour between the buildings. I ventured down Water Street into a district called Gastown. I loved the cobblestone streets laced with small souvenir shops and restaurants set in Victorian architecture. Water Street ended at a statue of John "Gassy Jack" Deighton, founder of the first tavern in the area in 1867.

Hmm. One man builds a pub, and the whole area is named after him. Interesting.

I continued eastbound on Powell. The red-bricked roads of Gastown ended, so I ventured north on Main Street. Feeling peckish, I grabbed a bag of chips from a pharmacy and continued west on Hastings munching away at them.

I couldn't believe how streets in such proximity could be so different. Many unfortunate souls lived in this district. I don't recall ever seeing so many homeless people before packed in one area. Ottawa had its share, but the magnitude here was overwhelming.

Could something be done to help them? They didn't bother me, but I never felt so unsettled in my life.

A couple of blocks further, several people stood around a huge man sitting in a deck chair, listening to him play "This Land is My Land" on his guitar. His beard crawled over top of his instrument, occasionally getting in the way of his strum. He wore a tie-dyed dashiki and bell-bottom jeans, and a huge peace symbol necklace displayed prominently on his chest. His greasy grey hair was held in place with a leather headband, filled with small white flowers. This '60s relic must've been in his fifties.

I wanted to join in the singing, but he finished the song as I approached. He placed his guitar down beside him.

"Thanks brothers and sisters," he said. "Peace and love to you all."

Many of the people surrounding him dispersed. Curious, I approached. A young couple slipped the hippie some money. He reached into a duffle bag and retrieved something for them.

Suddenly, a skunk-like aroma overwhelmed me, emanating from the young couple. They had lit up some funny-smelling cigarettes.

"Thanks brother and sister, only the best from me, man." He pointed to a blanket beside him, containing a variety of beaded jewelry. "Would you like some friendship bracelets to help spread the love?" He had a soft-spoken drawl.

The couple shook their heads and went on their way; however, the odour didn't dissipate. *Did this guy roll around in a field or something?*

"Stuck up yuppy bastards." He muttered under his breath. Returning his focus to me, he adjusted his coke bottle glasses and smiled. "Hey brother, I don't think I've seen you here before! Can I interest you in this far-out jewelry?"

"Hi, I'm Larry Johnstone. I like what you're playing."

"Groovy, Larry. The song speaks so many truths. I'm Peter Van Wagner. I hate to say it, brother, but you look like shit."

You smell like...

"Can I sell you something to pick you up?" he asked, "Hey, how about this?" He lifted a bracelet. "Will definitely impress your ol' lady." I shook my head.

"Or perhaps…" He opened a duffle bag from under his chair and pulled out a funny cigarette, similar to what that couple were smoking. "These little babies might ease some of your pain, if you're still sore from your mugging."

"I don't think so. Mama told me smoking is bad."

"No way, man. These ain't bad, brother. Like my jewelry, man, 'Mary Warner' is all about love!"

"Mary Warner?"

"Pot, man. Do you mean to tell me you never tried weed before?" Peter cackled. "You're obviously not from here." He stared at my shirt. "Sweden? I thought they were a progressive and liberated culture."

"Nah. Ottawa."

"Ottawa?" Peter reached back in his bag, removed a second joint, and inserted the two in a baggie and waved them at me. "You're gonna need more than one, man, if you're from that uptight bureaucratic town."

"Well, I live in this real cool place now. You know…the Kits?" I thought it hip to use the local vernacular for Kitsilano.

"The Kits? Yeah, I know the Kits, man. Was my first home when I landed here from California—back in the day when I dodged the draft for 'Nam. Bloody yuppies took over and gentrified the area. Can't complain. I live off the land. I'm free of rules imposed by the man. Free of materialism. Free to make love where I want. Free to spread love with my music and my pot. You'll see. One day we'll leave behind all of this capitalistic garbage and share the wealth like we did back in the day."

"Well, I love the Kits. I have marble countertops in my kitchen, and a rain shower in my bathroom. How could you possibly leave that?"

"You're kidding, right?" Peter peered over my shoulder and waved. "Did you not hear what I said? I don't live like that. Maybe you *should* try these out." He waved the baggie. "When I first smoked pot in the day, it opened my mind to a whole new reality. Try first, then we'll talk."

A few businessmen were approaching, a half a block down behind me. They grinned from ear to ear and waved in unison back at Peter.

"Look, see those suits," he said. "A few months ago, they didn't even smile. Smiling is the first step in liberating your soul, brother. Guarantee you, those yuppies never did before sampling my magic herb."

They approached Peter who retrieved more baggies from beneath his chair, and they had a cheerful exchange. Peter pocketed their money and even hugged one! Before they left, he bounded back to his blanket and retrieved a couple of bracelets for them.

"On the house," he said. "Peace, brothers, and share the love, man."

More people approached and stood around waiting.

"Larry, man, I have to help these folk." He acknowledged the newcomers. "Listen, you must smoke these if you want to call yourself a real Vancouverite and unlock a higher level of consciousness. I'll even throw in a book of matches free, since it's your first time."

He seemed pleasant, and I felt a sudden urge to help the poor and homeless. I also was intrigued by spreading love and improving my overall intellectual capacity.

"How much?"

"Three dollars each, or two reefers for five, man."

"Okay. I'll give it a try." I dropped him a fiver.

Peter handed me two in a plastic bag. He didn't seem like a gangster you'd see on the news pushing drugs on a street corner. Peter came across carefree and full of love. I wanted to explore more.

I took a "reefer" out and struck a match. I inhaled and coughed. It reeked like something I recalled from the one rock concert I attended, featuring Rabid Rick and his band Scottish Rot.

"Easy, brother," Peter called after me. "You'll get used to it. Be discreet where you smoke it. That stuff's still illegal, though you'll never get busted for it. Anyhow, enjoy, and I'll expect to see you again tomorrow, man. Peace." He smiled and greeted his next customer.

I took the cue and left down the road, puffing my joint.

Was I supposed to feel anything after a few drags? I thought this stuff made you mellow and want munchies.

My heart weighed heavier with each stride walking among the homeless. I felt overwhelmed by the bleakness of this part of the city. In hindsight, my dispirit could've been augmented by the drug I smoked.

My mood shifted dramatically walking back on West Pender. I saw another world in this remarkable city. Ottawa had a Chinatown which spanned a whole block. Vancouver's, in comparison, stretched what seemed like miles. I laughed uncontrollably as the artwork containing dragons felt more vibrant, alive, and spat colours at me. *Is this what being stoned is like?* I needed to regroup. I still had supper to make and felt hungry.

A sign for a library pointed to a prominent building, and I figured it might be a good idea to research my dinner project. Walking in, it took me a moment to regain my senses. It had been a while since I last visited a library, and in my enlightened state, it was difficult for me to remain quiet.

The librarian had the clichéd look—older, stern expression, pointed rim glasses, and hair done up in a bun. It might've been the pot, but her face seemed dehydrated and shrivelled. I screamed out in laughter, "BA-HA-HA, hey raisin lady, give me a pen, I need to make supper."

Pleased at myself, I broke out into "I Heard it Through the Grape Vine" and started a jig.

"Sir," she replied, "one more outburst like that, and you'll have to leave." She turned away to continue her work, and I resumed my singing in a hushed tone.

With no pen or paper to write on, I had to use the small pencils and paper scraps by the drawers containing all the library reference cards. I leafed through a few.

"How the hell do you find books here?" I screamed.

Several librarians shushed me.

"Bloody useless," I retorted slamming the drawer shut.

It took me a few hours to figure out the Dewey decimal system, but I found a suitable recipe and went through eight pencils copying it down.

Armed with the meal plan for tonight's dinner, I had one more stop before returning to the Kits. I needed some basic clothes to tide me over. I left the library and quickly found a store where I purchased a pair of jeans and a Queen concert t-shirt.

I modelled my new clothes strolling down the street, carrying my borrowed ones in a plastic bag like an accessory. This morning's bus driver was right. Earl of Latteigh coffee shops were everywhere. I craved another caramel latte, so I grabbed one for my ride home.

Larry, you masterful gourmet, you!

Six o'clock. The kitchen smelled of fresh zucchini, asparagus, and onion. The rice simmered in a pot, and the chicken baked in the oven. I had set the table with a checkered tablecloth and candles. I uncorked a fresh bottle of white wine just as the front door rattled, signaling the return of my Schnookums from the office.

"Something smells off," Heather roared. She smiled when she saw me holding the bottle of wine. "Aw, did you make this for me?"

"My queen, your supper awaits!" I poured a glass for her.

Something struck her, and she furrowed her eyebrows. "You know I can't drink in my condition!" Her anger turned to sweetness in a flash. "Never mind. Please pour me some tonic water and grape juice instead."

The fridge, thankfully, had plenty.

"I don't smell garlic, only onions," Heather said.

"The recipe doesn't call for garlic, Schnookums."

"I'm sure it does. It's been a long day, and I'm famished."

She sat at the table. The smell of Chicken Cordon Bleu exploded from the oven, and I placed her dinner on the table.

I took a bite. What a taste explosion! The ham, melted Swiss cheese, and chicken blended perfectly together.

"Bleh! I knew I smelt something wrong." Heather spat up a half-chewed piece of chicken on the side of her plate. "Chicken Kiev doesn't have ham in it. It's supposed to be full of garlic! I hate ham! It makes me sick. Ugh. For that, I might not buff your banana tonight!"

I didn't know she hated ham. She ate bacon this morning!

"But Honey-Bunny, you asked for Chicken *Cordon Bleu*."

"Don't be silly, I'd never ask for something with ham in it." She ate a forkful of vegetables. "These are acceptable." She batted her eyes at me. "Could you make up something without ham?"

"I have some extra pieces of uncooked breaded chicken. I can fry it up for you. Shouldn't take more than a couple of minutes."

Heather broke a grin. "That's why my friend says you'd make a great house-husband. The baby is going to so love being with you." Her eyes brightened as she looked up to me. "I think someone's gonna get their rub and tug time tonight!"

I couldn't help but smile.

I talked cheerfully about my adventures of the day while preparing Schnookum's second dinner. Heather read a document from her briefcase and placed it back when I set her meal down.

She chewed on a piece of meat. "This'll have to do," she grunted. "I am feeding two, after all. Next time, please be sure to have plenty of garlic. I'd do anything for melted butter and garlic."

"Noted, sorry."

"We have a problem," said Heather reading in the living room after supper. "Mom's extremely upset. I can't have her calling me at work! She's phoning me hourly!"

"How's it possible we have a problem, Schnookums? I love you so much!

I'm willing to do anything for you. Look at the meal we just ate. It was a huge effort."

"Yes, yes, and you'll be good at keeping this house neat, but she's still upset at that call she got from that dreadful priest you liked."

Phew, not about her credit card bill.

"Father Barry?"

"He won't marry us."

"Why won't he?" I said, knowing full well the truth. "We're the perfect couple!"

"I know! He has some rod up his butt about my expecting a child. He says we need marriage counselling. I mean, I understand why he'd suggest *you* needing it, but me? And Mom is insisting we marry before the child is born." Heather looked down and rubbed her belly. "Says the kid needs a father figure in his life." She stopped and looked me in the eye. "I suppose you'll have to do. I don't get it. I never had a father…and I turned out fine."

I sat next to Schnookums on the couch, reached over, and placed my hand on her shoulder. "What do I have to do, Honey-Bunny, to get our marriage plans back on track? I so want to get married in my home church by my pastor."

"Mom made other plans. I can't believe this Barry cares so much about our sex lives. It's none of his damn business!" Her voice changed to a cheerful lilt. "My mom said we should get married in city hall, fast!" She brushed her hair over her right shoulder. "She's made the arrangement. Auntie Maggie" — Repugnant Rick's mum — "will send me the dress from Ottawa."

"But I wanted a church wedding with all my friends."

"Not enough time. We have no choice. You'll need to pay for the ceremony. It only costs $100. We get married in three weeks. Baby will have a male presence like my mom and friend want. You can pay for your friends to come if you like. We're in luck, though. My friend will be our witness and can act as your best man."

My face must've shown my disappointment. Heather reached over and placed her hand on mine. Seeing her beautiful eyes, and her pregnant belly, I saw past our wedding ceremony and envisioned our future as man and wife. I'd do anything for love.

Rolling into the first week of May, my clothes arrived, I bought myself a Bible, and settled into a routine.

The days were simple. I woke at six, made my Schnookums her breakfast, and packed her lunch. When she left for work, I'd go to my special Earl of Latteigh and read my Bible for a couple of hours. The barista was right. I mastered the lingo for ordering coffee.

I loved the Kits. Though it rained a lot, the picturesque city appealed to my soul. On the days when the sun shone, I made my way to the waterfront and sat outside to read my scriptures.

Peter Van Wagner sold his wares at the same intersection each morning. We hit it off, and, wanting to do my part to spread the love, I bought joints daily from him. Fully relaxed by noon, I'd grab some groceries, clean house while watching my soaps, and make supper.

Schnookums loved my cooking. I could tell because she'd often say nothing during meals, and sometimes ate everything. After dinner, I'd prepare her favourite drink, asparagus water. She'd enjoy it while reading in the living room on her own while I washed the dishes and put away any leftovers.

Every evening, at 7 p.m. sharp, the phone rang. Heather'd pounce the moment it sounded. She didn't want me to hang around during her calls, so I washed the dishes while she chatted in the living room.

Heather would be transformed into a sweet pussycat when she hung up. In fact, the calls made my Schnookums so happy, she'd immediately dive into "funsie" mode. Funny. The phone ring now triggers a weird Pavlovian effect, so I, too, looked forward to seven o'clock.

During the weekends, Heather attended company retreats in some Okanagan Valley resort. She claimed the world of advertising needed creative settings in the country. I didn't like being left on my own but understood. She was an important executive, requiring frequent meetings with distinguished clients.

I had spent my last dollar on a peppermint mocha with almond milk one Friday in May. With my wallet now drained, I needed an income fast. I couldn't imagine a day in this city without a latte injection.

Peter, at his usual spot, waved. "Hey, peace brother, what can I get you today?"

"Hi Peter," I answered, "I'm hard up on cash. Think you can give me a 'reefer' and open a tab for me?"

"I'm all about love, man, but can't give this stuff away free. Tell you what. Business has been so hot—I need help. A prep like you can sell a ton of this crap."

I was a little confused about how "love" related to "business." But wanting to support Peter in his desire to spread peace and goodwill, I nodded.

Peter gave me a duffle bag. "I got about $1,000 worth of stuff here. There's a college west of the Kits near you. Man, those kids on University Hill will go wild for my shit. Sell it all, and I'll give you $250!"

"Cool!" I never did sales before, but my charismatic self should find it a snap.

Peter's cheery expression turned stone cold. "Don't fuck with me, man. I expect either $1,000 bucks in my hand tomorrow, or the leftover stash with the correct balance. Anything less, I'm gonna mess you up. I know moves you'd never heard of! Got it?"

I couldn't tell if Peter was being serious, but I'd never screw over a friend and wanted to support his mission.

"No worries."

He was right. I blended well with the university crowd. My natural charm did all the work. I didn't need a juicy pitch—this stuff sold itself. Word spread like wildfire on campus, and my stock depleted quickly. I'd make a fortune coming back here every day spreading the love.

Peter was thrilled with my success. He gave me the promised $250, though he refused to let me sell at the university daily—he didn't have enough stock for the demand. He also wanted to be discreet when dealing with those kids— their parents didn't buy into his "love" philosophy. Angry parents call cops, which could cause him headaches. He gave me a free joint and promised me more work.

Yup, I think I'm gonna love this city.

Chapter Four
Today is the Day
May 1989

My month-a-versary in Vancouver started with a bang. My soon-to-be mother-in-law dropped off the wedding dress on Monday.

"Heather, what am I going to do with you?" she yelled. "My credit card statement came in and it's over $12,000! And for what? Him?" She pointed emphatically at me.

I smiled and waved. She ignored me. *Odd. I put most women at ease.*

"Don't worry, Mom" — Heather spoke in a condescending tone — "You know I'll cover it after the ceremony."

"Oh, you will," she said. "He'd better be worth it." She continued to point at me. That happens sometimes with mothers. Never figured out why. "Do you know what you're in for?" she asked me.

"He does," said Heather, "Besides, he's kept my place sparkling clean. Come." For a moment, I felt aroused, but she led her mother to the kitchen. "Try this *Ärtsoppa*." She gave her mom some leftover yellow pea soup I'd prepared. Heather acquired a taste for Swedish cuisine while traveling on business in Gothenburg last year. She had insisted I learn some popular recipes.

Mary softened. "Mmmmmm. That is good. Maybe he is worth keeping around." She kissed Heather's cheek. "Gotta run. You're going to need to get the dress altered."

I waved as she walked by me. She was too focused on leaving to reciprocate.

I gave my Honey-Bunny's mother credit; city hall marriages were cheap and fast, unlike the high costs and months of preparation we put into our Ottawa wedding. We were both angry it was cancelled after all our hard work. I really did, though, want something more traditional.

At least we were getting it done. Maybe we could do a vow renewal ceremony in a church a few years from now, and our kids could bask in my Anglican traditions!

Would it've been too much to ask Schnookums to organize a bachelor party on the eve of our wedding? I'd only met a few new people since arriving in this wonderful city—Peter and some baristas.

Heather refused Peter entry to our home, or inviting him to the wedding, on grounds he contributed to my new habit. Heather hated my marijuana smoking, and I had made the mistake of insinuating that she should try it. Honestly, I thought it'd mellow her out. The suggestion cost me two nights of "knob polishing."

My Schnookums didn't want a honeymoon, either. Her rationale made sense. The baby was due, so why go away to some exotic place only to give birth?

Like clockwork, the phone rang at 7 p.m. on our wedding eve, and Heather pounced on it on the first ring. I took my usual spot in the kitchen, cleaning dishes. After fifteen minutes, she skipped to me with youthful energy and kissed me.

"No funsies, 'cause we're not supposed to see each other tonight! I'm off to bed early. You should do the same. Oh, and your best man is arriving just in time for our wedding. He should be here early in the morning." She gave me a big smile and hugged me so tight, I thought I'd lose circulation to my extremities. "Good night, Honey-Bear," she said and went to her bedroom and closed the door.

"Good night, Honey-Bunny," I whispered after her.

I crawled into bed but was too excited to fall asleep.

I had weird dreams all night. At 2:30 a.m., I could have sworn I heard the front door opening, and a glass crashing to the floor. A prolonged squeal filled the air followed by a galloping sound down the hallway. After a pause, another fast trot, and a door slammed. Then silence. I dismissed it all as part of my dreams and closed my eyes and returned to sleep.

I awoke at 5:30 a.m. The soft sheets against my naked body could make a ten-minute nap feel like a full eight hours, and even after a night of broken sleep, I felt energized.

Jumping out of bed, I began my morning exercise ritual, including toe touches, knee bends, and quadricep stretches. Sleeping and exercising naked were new habits since arriving in Vancouver. There was something mystical about the combination of the sheets, the damp city air, and my nudity.

No pain. Nice way to start my wedding day. I walked down the hall for my morning OJ. *Curious. I don't recall leaving the kitchen light on last night, and Schnookums never wakes before me.*

Turning into the kitchen, I jumped out of my skin. A strange man with dark blond hair sat at the table, reading a book. He wore a familiar looking t-shirt with a Swedish flag and boxer shorts. His ice-blue eyes sparkled, and he broke a dazzling smile. *Damn, he's handsomer than that flight attendant David. Might even be a bit younger than me.* He stood and extended his hand.

Still naked, I instinctively cupped my left hand over my ding-a-ling and reached to grab his hand with my right. My head tilted up, looking at the taller man straight in the eye.

"Hee-hee," he said. "I'm Sfeem. Yuoo moost be-a zee huoose-a-hoosbund. Vhy zee heek ere-a yuoo neked? Bork bork bork!" He sounded identical to that guy from *The Muppet Show.*

"Huh? Sorry, are you speaking Swedish?"

He smiled a smug grin and broke out in laughter. "Eee HEE-HEE hee hee!"

I couldn't understand him. "Maybe speak slower?"

"Nah, it's okay. Just pulling your leg. I speak perfect English. I sometimes pull the old 'Swedish Chef' routine to freak people out. I hate that foam fucker." He sat back in the chair at the table. "So, you're Larry, the househusband, right? I'm your best man, Sven Lindgaard. Come, join me at the table." He settled into a chair, but I remained standing.

This striking man would up the quality of our wedding photos...now if only we could find a comelier replacement for Heather's mother.

"Ah, yes, I'm Larry," I said. "So, you must be Heather's friend. She didn't mention you'd be Swedish."

"Well, I am!" he grinned. "I'm looking forward to the wedding." Sven stretched his arms in the air and placed his hands behind his head. The flag on his shirt stretched tight across his chest and his biceps bulged. "It will be important to have someone look after the baby when it's born. It helps. Heather and I have tons of business to do."

"Business?" *And of course I'll take care of the baby! Why should you care?*

"Yes." Sven lowered his elbows on the table, keeping his hands clasped. "She represents a critical partnership of my life. She is, you know, a very important lady."

"Uh, yes, agreed." She was, after all, an advertising executive who made tons of cash. "You're up early." I looked around awkwardly, wanting to leave the room to change.

"Arrived here a few hours ago. Couldn't sleep." He rubbed his hands through his thick hair and placed them back behind his head. "Bloody jet lag makes my body think it's past lunch. I noticed you had some *lax* in your fridge. Mind if I eat it? I'm starving."

"Knock yourself out. I don't feel like eating fish today, anyway."

"Hey, you staying in the back room? What you think of the pictures of me?" Sven winked, and without moving his arms, flexed his left bicep, then the right.

He's the guy in those creepy photos?

Sven stood to help himself to some food, but before he opened the fridge, Heather walked in. I never saw her in a bathrobe with her hair in such a dishevelled mess before. She always left her room perfectly coiffed.

"Morning Honey-Bear, why are you naked?" she asked. "And hellllllllo Sven." She went over to our best man, wrapped her arms around him, and gave the Swede a big kiss on the lips!

"What the hell?" I said raising my arms in protest, then quickly covered myself again.

"It's okay Larry," said Heather, releasing her grip. "That's how Sven greets everyone. It's a European thing."

Really?

"Come, Larry," said Sven. "You seem like a pretty open-minded guy, given how you flaunt your little bird. I'll give you a European greeting, too." He advanced a few steps towards me.

"No, thank you." I raised my right hand. "I'm spoken for. I only want to be kissed by my Schnookums."

I left the kitchen, wanting desperately to dress, but strained to listen to them talk from my bedroom. Heather giggled.

"I'm surprised he didn't want to be kissed by a guy like me," said Sven. "No matter. He *seems* to like you. I mean, why wouldn't he? You're the hottest babe I've ever met!"

"I know. Did I mention it only took him about ten seconds to…" Heather's voice faded.

"No way! You did it?"

"Not really, Svenny, you know I have a…"

I struggled to make out Heather's whispers. I gathered Heather was explaining to Sven we had used a condom that one time we had intercourse—why neither of us never called that encounter "real" sex.

"Eee-HEE-HEE-hee-hee. Good. Hard to find someone who lasts thirty minutes, eh? Missed me?"

"Oh, yes!" roared Heather.

What? Schnookums never laughs like that!

After changing, I stared at myself in the mirror. It'd been a while since Repugnant Rick slugged me. My black eye should've healed by now. *Dammit.* I wanted my wedding photos to be perfect.

I dressed and stared at the creepy pictures on the wall. *Impossible to tell they are Sven.*

Heather still laughed in the background. Probably be a good idea that I join them and get acquainted with my "best man." At least Sven gets along with Heather. *It helps.* I stood in the entrance of the kitchen, dropping in on the middle of a conversation.

She had her arm wrapped around Sven's shoulders and was laughing so hard tears welled in her eyes.

"Eee HEE-HEE hee hee, didn't we love the midsummer festival last year?"

"I ate so much herring," said Heather. With eyes closed she leaned forward, chuckling, holding her pregnant tummy. "I burped fish for three months. I mean, for breakfast they served it smoked. Snacks, fermented. Dinner, with dill and oil. I couldn't stomach fish anymore."

"It made our annual frog dance difficult," said Sven. He stood and squatted up and down. "Hard to hop around with sick stomachs. *Sötnos*—my darling—you made such a great frog, hopping around the maypole singing the *Små grodorna*." He sat back in the chair.

Heather giggled and slapped his arm.

The two were in their own world.

"I can out-hop real frogs," I said, leaning against the entranceway, "and with my professional voice, I could sing the *Smug Road Dorna* better than any of you. What is this festival?"

"The Midsummer Maypole Festival?" said Sven. "We call it the *Midsommarstången*. It's an annual festival that has a huge pole with two large loops at the top. Sort of looks like a giant cock, which makes sense, given the festival is based on an ancient fertility rite.

"Why we imitate frogs jumping around the pole?" Sven shrugged his shoulders. "I don't know. The *Små grodorna* is a song telling their story. It's all part of the ritual. I have no idea why we do it each year, but after drinking and singing 'hup-de-la-la-lah-lay,' one can do anything."

Heather's eyes widened, and she clapped her hands together radiating a bright smile. "I can't wait to go back."

"I guarantee I'd win the prize for best frog," I interrupted. "When is it? I'd love to go, too."

Maybe we could honeymoon in Sweden?

They both looked over to me. Sven raised an eyebrow.

"I'm going to be the master of ceremonies this year," said Sven. "It's part of our business, being in promotion and advertising." Sven stroked Heather's back, then stared back at me. "Too bad you'll be too busy taking care of the *bebis*."

"What? Maybe Heather's mom can take him in," I answered. "She'd love to take care of her new grandchild for a few weeks."

"Not a good idea. *Bebis* need lots of attention with people they're comfortable within the early months."

"Yes," Heather said abruptly. "Taking care of the baby will be your core responsibility."

"When is the midsummer thing?" I asked again.

"In June," Sven answered. "If you please excuse me, I'm exhausted from my flight. Mind if I go crash for a few hours?"

"Poor Svenny," Heather cooed putting her hand through his hair. "Larry, you should be happy. Sven flew in from Sweden just for us."

"Yes," he said waving his finger at me. "You should be grateful. I'm literally in and out of here for the wedding. Besides attending the festival, I must fine-tune some details of my invention, so it's ready to market. It'll be a hit in Canada, thanks to Heather." He patted her back again.

"It's going to blow this country away," she said with excitement. "Svenny and I have been developing the marketing plans for it this past year. He calls his invention the *Lax Och Köttbulle Bärbar Ugn*. We wanted to keep the Swedish name—it just rolls off your tongue. Calling it the Salmon Meatball Portable Oven simply doesn't have the same *panache* in English."

"Yeah, it's small," said Sven smiling. "The size of a large bread box." Sven illustrated its dimensions with his hands. "Canadian department stores have already pre-ordered 10,000 units, mostly thanks to my honey!" He leaned over and kissed Heather on the head, much to my consternation. "It can do amazing things, like cook your meatballs or fish." He changed topic and looked over at Heather. "Househusband, do you really want to get married to this fine woman?"

"Please don't call me househusband, but yes, I'm so in love with my Honey-Bunny, and marriage has been my lifelong dream."

"Good. I'd personally hate to get married, and it's important for the kid to have some family stability. *Sötnos?*"

Heather seemed nonplused. "Yes. Agreed. Another perk, Larry, of being a family means we get a tax credit!"

Sounded good to me. I heard some family allowances can be extremely generous. Kid might pay for itself.

"Okay, it's sleepy times!" Sven stood, shook my hand, and walked down the hall. He turned into Heather's bedroom and closed the door.

"Why is he going into your room?" I asked.

"Oh, Honey-Bear, that's not my room, it's his. He owns this place."

"Ohhhhh."

Wait a minute, her room is Sven's room?

"I'm going back to bed for a while. We have a big day ahead of us." She got up, kissed my head, and returned to her room.

What the...

A sunny day in the Kits. I figured I'd spend the remaining few hours of bachelorhood roaming the streets, grabbing a coffee, and reflecting on my new life being a husband. I had been richly blessed to have Heather in my life—something I didn't want to take for granted.

I'd dated so many girls, and they all left me for a variety of reasons. Mostly, I found they simply did not want to participate in my life journey. The mere mention of having children on our first date risked sending them running. I offered so much love to them, only to be spurned and rejected. Heather happened to be the first woman to fully give herself to me from the get-go. I loved her for it, and I wanted to ensure she remained happy and content. I'd hate to make a mistake that would ruin our future together.

Sitting in a new Earl of Latteigh, I sipped a regular espresso. Sven coming in from Sweden meant a lot to Schnookums. He travelled far to witness our marriage, but I found it shocking he owned the condominium. Also, Schnookums had no problem with him crashing in her room. I guess it wouldn't be fair to boot him out, given he owned the place, but it felt wrong and annoyed me.

Pondering my conundrum, I consulted the Good Book. Normally, I seek divine inspiration by reading random verses, then reflecting on how they might apply in my situation. It sometimes took a few tries before something made sense.

Today's readings were particularly validating, and my resolve to love Heather became stronger than ever. They stated that my embitterment could cause serious issues in our marriage, so I needed to suppress my jealousy; I fathered a child, with which came great responsibility; and I am biblically commanded to stay at home from work or military service for one year to ensure happiness for my wife. The last would be a breeze to fulfil.

I chugged back the remainder of my drink and checked the time. Just after lunch. Better rush for the ceremony. I had to be at city hall for 2 p.m.

Barging through the door of our condo, I yelled, "Hi, I'm home! We have to hurry." No answer. "Hi?"

I walked in the kitchen. A note was taped to the fridge. *Awww, my Honey-*

Bunny and Sven went to mother-in-law Mary's to prepare for the ceremony, and they left me some money for a cab to drive me to city hall.

Opening my closet door, my prized possession hung neatly on a hanger—my kilt, bought for me by my dad for the wedding. The last time I wore a kilt was for my high school prom. I thought it unique, but Replicating Rick stole *my* thunder by wearing one himself.

Time flew. I only had twenty minutes to get to city hall. I called a taxi, and luckily, one came within five. We zoomed off to the ceremony.

I tracked down the room where Honey-Bunny, Sven, Mary, and the Justice of the Peace were waiting. I was late.

"We were starting to worry you got cold feet," Sven chuckled.

"Wish he had," said Mary.

"No worries," I chirped happily. "Lots of traffic. I'm here, so let's doooooo this!"

I took my place beside Heather. What a radiant bride in her $2,500 wedding dress! A photographer snapped some shots while Heather and I posed in front of the judge. Odd. Heather never smiled.

The judge read from a script. "A wedding is such a wonderful occasion filled with hopes, dreams, and excitement. We're here today to celebrate the love that—" he pointed to Heather.

"Heather."

"And—" he pointed to me.

"Larry."

"Have for each other, and to recognize and witness their decision to journey forward in their lives as married partners."

Heather interrupted him. "Can we cut to the chase?"

The judge was a bit taken aback. "Okay. Heather and Larry, by the power invested in me, I now pronounce you husband and wife. You may now kiss. That'll be $100."

The judge cued a soundman in the corner who cranked "Heaven Knows I'm Miserable Now" full blast on the stereo.

"Who chose this song?" I hollered.

"I did," said Sven. "I love the Smiths and thought it a nice touch."

"Awwww, is poor Svenny having a hard time?" cooed my wife.

Why are you asking? Sven's not fazed at all.

"Screw the song," I said.

I puckered up to kiss my Honey-Bear, and she turned her cheek as my lips landed.

"Don't want to spoil the make-up," she said.

The photographer gathered us for a group picture concluding the one-minute-long wedding ceremony—a tad shorter than I had expected, and cost over $18,000, thanks to Reprobate Rick who ruined our original plans. We signed the register and received our license, making our marriage official. Sven kissed the judge on the cheek and paid a clerk for the ceremony.

A limo awaited us outside the building. Heather had made reservations at the Purple Pigeons. They had an awesome reputation for making the meanest chicken burgers on the West Coast. Sadly, Heather did not permit us to have champagne in the car, so we settled for tonic water instead.

Mary said nothing.

"To many years of a fine partnership," said Sven raising his glass. "A toast to my Heather and her househusband."

Heather shifted in her seat and groaned. "I think I have wetness in my perineum."

"What, sweetie?" said Sven.

"What, Honey-Bunny?" I said.

"Crap, my water broke."

Lying on the floor of the limo, a puddle formed at the base of Heather's seat.

"Driver! We need to go to the hospital! NOW!" Sven cried.

"I want my chicken burger," Heather moaned.

Chapter Five
Hello, Little Larry!
May 1989

Heather didn't want anyone to join her in the delivery room. From her perspective, she was undergoing a "medical" procedure. We respected her wishes, but my curiosity was killing me. *Which of my features will the baby have?*

She gave birth to a 7.6 pound, 19-inch boy. When we finally had a chance to see him, I noted he inherited my good looks. His eyes were blue. Not quite the same blue as his mother, but greyer—maybe it was my brown eyes' influence. His hair: dark like mine. Nose: sort of resembled mine or my mother's. Size: average. I ached to find out which of my features would become more dominant as he grew older.

Heather and the baby stayed in the hospital a couple of days. We were all excited to bring them home, though my Schnookums looked beat. She placed the newborn in his special seat in the car, and she and Sven joined him in the back while Heather's mother, Mary, drove.

Sven seemed proud. "Look, he has his father's nose."

Like I thought!

Mary turned her head.

"Keep your eyes on the road!" barked my wife.

"And he has his father's hair," I said, turning in my seat.

"Honey-Bear," said Heather. "His hair and eye colour may change over time."

I cocked my head, confused.

"I love this child," Sven said, staring down at the baby. "We should call him Lars. Always liked that name."

I didn't care for his suggestion and wanted to pass my own name to my son. "We need to name him after me, Lawrence, and maybe add my middle name,

Johnathan, which happens to be my father's name, too. Lawrence Johnathan Johnstone. Love it!"

"Lawrence and Johnathan are such weak names. Lars is stronger," said Heather, admiring her baby. After a moment of reflection, she added, "I have always loved Rupert the Bear. This little bear will be my Rupie. Rupert Lars Mackenzie."

"Lars?" I said. "C'mon, you can't be serious. I'm going to nickname him Little Larry."

His last name will be Mackenzie? I had assumed she'd take my family name when we'd be married. Not the time to discuss it, though. Honey-Bunny is exhausted.

Schnookums bestowed me a great honour and responsibility—to care for our child while continuing my cooking and house cleaning duties. I had no problem with it as I had committed to keeping myself free of employment for a year, as the Bible ordained, to care for both child and wife.

I longed to sleep in the wedding bed with Schnookums, but when we returned to the apartment with the baby, Heather insisted I continue to stay in the backroom of the condominium. Heather mentioned she didn't want me around at night in case her "post-natal depression" flared. I'd never heard of it, but she claimed she had an acute case. She also alleged that Sven had the experience and the "magic touch" to heal her, so it was necessary he remain in her bedroom. I worried for Schnookums. Sven would return to Sweden soon, and even though he stayed longer than I'd expected, I had no clue how to help her through this difficult time. No matter, we'd have eternity to figure it out.

My early days sharing the baby's room were awesome. He screamed a lot in the crib Sven had assembled, but I had the knack of keeping the child calm. I loved soothing him with my beautiful singing voice. Heather occasionally joined us to give the baby a cuddle, but the moment he dropped his guts, she'd give him back to me and leave.

Poor thing. She must've suffered severely from the postpartum depression. In fact, she and Sven rarely ventured out of the master bedroom for nearly a week. I didn't mind. After all, Sven travelled from Sweden for us, paid for all our living expenses, and cleared our wedding debts, including Mary's. We were blessed because of Sven's generosity, and being an old friend of Heather's, I figured they had a lot of catching up to do. It gave me the opportunity for some quality father-son time.

My dreams of consummating my marriage with my wife intensified during the first days of Little Larry's life. In my mind, all the hype around the wedding night revolved around "the two becoming one." It didn't happen as scripted because our wedding night was spent in the hospital. I confronted Heather at breakfast about "doing it" while Sven took a shower. It was hard to get a word in edgewise, Heather had her favourite mixtape cranked on the stereo. Competing with "Carcass" in the background was near impossible.

"Honey-Bunny, it's been a while since we had funsies. We're now married, so funsies should now be super-funsies! Can we make love like husband and wife tonight?"

"Are you mad?" Heather answered angrily. "Don't you realize I just blew a watermelon through a garden hose?"

I never thought about it in that context. But still, does it matter?

"But we're married!"

"Yes, legally, but even if I wanted sex with you, the doctor told me not for at least six weeks." She poured herself an orange juice. It must've been sour. Her eyes squinted.

"Can I at least join you in our matrimonial bed?" I asked.

"This orange juice is not fresh," she said.

"Well, can I?"

She set the glass on the table. "Hmm…you want to leave the baby alone in his room in the crib?" Her eyes narrowed. "What would Sven do?"

I thought about it. "We can move the crib so baby could be with us."

"No." She lifted the glass and debated having another sip but placed it down. "No. The baby needs to learn he isn't permitted in Sven's room. He needs to learn independence by staying in his own."

"You mean, my room?"

"Technically, it's Lars'. You share it with him."

"Like technically your room is Sven's, because he owns this place?"

"That's right. I know, Honey-Bunny, this is all complicated. But we don't have enough space for all of us living together. Would you prefer Lars to share a room with you, or Sven?"

Better for the child to be with the father.

I nodded.

"Sven returns to Sweden soon. We'll discuss the living arrangements when he leaves." Heather kissed my cheek and left to have a shower.

A few more weeks passed. Sven was still living with us. I was still in the baby's room.

Little Larry stared at a mobile above his crib the morning of his month-a-versary while I climbed out of bed. Sven and Schnookums usually got up an hour later, giving me plenty of time to put together a special meal for the occasion including cake, kippers, eggs, and bacon.

Like clockwork, Sven came in dressed only in boxers, and Honey-Bunny in her bathrobe. I served them, and Little Larry started to cry from the back room.

I brought the baby to the kitchen. The whole family was together to celebrate the "birthday."

"Aw, our baby Lars is so cute," Sven fussed. "Let me hold him."

I passed him the baby.

"Larry," said Sven, "would you mind getting my camera from the bag in the hallway? I'd like to capture this moment for my friends and family back home."

Heather and Sven were sitting shoulder-to-shoulder feeding the baby on my return.

"Take a picture of the three of us," Sven requested.

"Oh, Sven, I'm not even made up!" Heather said. She began primping her hair.

"No worries, you're always gorgeous, dear," Sven answered.

I had the couple face the camera, and they smiled while I snapped the photo of them with the baby. I had to admit, Heather and Sven would've made a striking couple.

Too bad Sven, I snagged her.

Sven smiled. "Larry, you're doing so well with Lars that I asked Heather to return with me for the Swedish midsummer festival next week."

I couldn't believe my ears! "But I want to do the frog dance and drink beer!"

"Honey-Bear," said Heather with a sweet tone, "you know I love Swedish culture, and this is a dream opportunity for us to promote Sven's invention. You'll need to stay and care for baby Lars. It's way too early for him to go on a plane. The doctor has cleared me to travel this week. We'll call every day at seven to check in on Rupie-Bear."

"We'll be gone only a month," said Sven. "I'll leave you $1,000 for your household duties. I'll even give you a special coffee allowance!"

Free coffee didn't sound too bad, but I had hoped Sven's departure would finally give me some special alone time with my wife!

I recalled my scriptures commanding me not to be embittered with my spouse. I lost so many potential wives because of my pettiness and jealousy. I couldn't refuse Heather.

"No problem, Schnookums, I'll take care of Little Larry."

Heather squealed and gave Sven a big hug. Sven passed Little Larry back to me and patted my shoulder.

The condo's silence after Sven and Heather left for Sweden was unbearable. Little Larry broke the stillness every now and again with a wail for food or diaper change.

I hadn't sung since arriving in Vancouver and being alone gave me the opportunity to keep my strong vocal chops going. I couldn't understand why every time I practiced Gregorian chant, Little Larry cried. It soothed my soul, and I thought it created an atmosphere of reflective calm, but my baby didn't agree.

For sure he should have the same musical passions inherited from my super genes.

My dad always sang '50s rock to me. I dug deep in my musical memory bank, and my baby, like me, loved those oldies! Little Larry would "dance" while I sang Elvis Presley—wiggling the most to "Jailhouse Rock." *Didn't know I had a knack for singing old time rock 'n' roll!*

My neighbours vetted my newfound talent. They loved it! They'd bang the ceiling floor and walls to show their appreciation. Glad they did. I wouldn't have heard them clapping from their apartments. I'd respect their ovations and would sing louder, and they'd accompany me by increasing their volume, too! When I stopped, there'd be a sudden peace in my home.

I kept to my routine. Baby loved our visits to Earl of Latteigh. He napped to the cool jazz played in there. Peter loved him too, and though he happily sold me my morning joints, he refused to permit me to peddle them with baby in tow. I didn't mind. I had more than enough cash, courtesy of Sven, to keep me going.

Heather didn't call the first day they left. I figured they had problems with travel. I became concerned when I didn't hear from them after a couple of days.

The phone rang shortly after I woke Saturday morning.

"Hello," I said wearily.

"Morning, Honey-Bear!"

A cheerful Heather always makes my day!

"Hi, Schnookums!"

"Hi. Hard to find phones here for long distance calls." Her tone changed. "Put my little Rupie-Bear on, now."

I hate it when she calls our baby Rupie.

"You mean, Little Larry?"

"No, Rupie-Bear."

I put Little Larry on the phone, who sat motionless while his mother talked to him.

"Thanks, I'll call you the next chance I get," said Heather.

"When will that be—"

The line cut. *It happens to me so often!* Heather even forgot to leave her phone number!

I went to take a shower and sang "Blueberry Hill," and Little Larry began to cry.

So much for the '50s music soothing baby's spirits.

Chapter Six
The Prophecy
June 1989

Being alone with a baby made me yearn for adult time. Desperate for intellectual conversation like the Bible studies led by Father Barry back home, I needed to find a church, fast. Armed with a Mocha-Dough-Espresso, I dropped Little Larry off for his Sunday morning visit with grandma, then explored the Kits. My father would love this city—in fact, he'd love to visit *any* city.

When I was a child, living at home, Dad ached to travel. He wanted to return to his homeland, England, but Mama had zero desire to leave the house. She also refused to let him go alone, saying something about it would lead to "promiscuous" behaviour, and "fornication" would soon follow. I didn't know what fornication meant, being so young, but I figured it had something to do with happiness for my melancholy father.

I didn't enjoy vacation time like typical children. Hearing the wonderful stories of classmates going on trips to their cottages, or to the beach, I often begged Mama and Dad to take me somewhere. Dad loved the idea, but Mama insisted we'd have more fun at home.

One Sunday in mid-June after my eighth birthday, Mama changed her tune.

"I heard of this wonderful place in church this morning," she said to us. "It's an ecumenical facility called the Mount Bethel Family Renewal Centre and Resort. It's a place for families to connect." She pulled out a flyer, and I had to admit, even though religious, it looked promising.

There were cabins, a lake, canoes, pools, and outdoor fire pits. I bounced all over our home—a trailer—while my dad called the resort owners to book a two week stay in early July.

The grounds were located 150 kilometers west of Ottawa, and the site was a carbon copy of the brochure. Kids were playing in the pool, adults were cooking over an open fire, and groups of people were congregating doing activities ranging from volleyball to praying. We checked in and received our cabin assignment.

The second we parked the car, I dashed into our little cottage, threw my bag on a cot, grabbed a towel, and bolted out to the lake where other children were playing on the beach.

Unlike my school, the kids welcomed me with open arms—literally. They hugged me and patted my back and seemed genuinely enthused when I joined. A couple of girls my age asked me to help them in a sandcastle building contest. They entrusted me with gathering the decorative elements, like small rocks and twigs.

The girls were kind. One dug a moat around a huge pile of sand to form the base of the castle, while the other talked about when she accepted Jesus. They complimented me on my fine sticks and stones collecting skills and requested I fill some pails with water. I walked off to do their bidding, but a stern English accent screaming from the distance broke the tempo of our building.

"Laaaaaarrry!" my dad yelled. "Come here. Now!"

I had to obey. I returned the buckets to the girls and ran to my father who approached the beach.

"You'll have to leave your game. We must go home immediately."

"But why?" I asked. "I'm having the best time in my life. I'm making such close friends." I looked back at my girls.

He didn't answer.

Mama waited for us in her seat in our car. I recalled driving away from that wonderful place and staring out the back window longing to be with the other children.

The ride home was deadly silent. I didn't understand why we had left. Mama did complain later that the cabins didn't have TV and smelled of mildew; and didn't like the idea of venturing to a "common" shared bathroom. Hints of the truth leaked out over the following weeks.

"I didn't know that place was run by 'those' *Pent-y-costals*," she'd say. "I thought it'd be for us Anglicans only. They're so loud, singing their 'modern' hymns everywhere! Don't they know that we Anglicans only do that in church? And they used the swimming pool for baptizing people? And the fuss they make, dancing and singing in gibberish under the open sun? Imagine if they continued at night? We'd never get any sleep!"

She slagged off the Pentecostals all summer. It amazed me how much she picked up of their culture in a little over an hour's stay. All I could think of was how nice they were, how warmly they welcomed me on the beach, and the fun I had building sandcastles with my first girlfriends.

Outside an elementary school, a sign promoted an upcoming event for the pending 1989 Summer Solstice. Past the parking lot, a huge banner hanging over the building's entranceway caught my eye. "City of Heavenly Praise Church. Worship this morning. All Welcome!" I had always loved the pomp and circumstances of my traditional church roots, but my memory of those few hours at that Pentecostal resort changed my perspective. I'd be willing to try a different Christian denomination in my new city.

But church in a school? Can I walk in with a coffee in hand?

Signs guided me to the gymnasium entrance where a middle-aged couple wearing large "Welcome" badges on their shirts stood smiling. They introduced themselves as Penny and Harry Lee.

"Hi, I'm Larry Johnstone."

"Welcome to the City of Heavenly Praise Church, Larry." The woman stuck out her hand to shake mine, so did her husband.

"I've never seen you before, is this your first time here?" Penny asked.

"Yes. I'm a professional chorister. I miss my traditional Anglican church and need to stretch out my vocal pipes. Your sign outside intrigued me. I've never been to church in a school before. I mean, where'd you put the pipe organ?"

"Oh, we don't play organ here. We sing by spirit," said Harry.

What the hell does that mean?

Penny opened the door revealing a gymnasium packed with people. They were making a cacophony of noise. "Why don't you see for yourself? Sorry, it's standing room only."

"No problem. My voice will carry over this ruckus no matter where I am in the building."

The heat and smell of body odor overwhelmed me, and the floor was saturated with perspiration. I found a space along the back wall.

These people are singing whatever they feel like! How do I harmonize to this?

The man standing to my right had his eyes closed and repeated the words "la la la" while swaying back and forth. The older lady in front of me screeched like a seagull and waved her arms, occasionally hitting the people next to her. I was certain I heard a man hold an extended "woo" like a siren in a high-pitched falsetto.

A leader in a short-sleeved shirt and tie stood at the front, head bowed, with a microphone. His voice dominated the noise in the gym. He held his left hand in the air, and sang the words, "We praise you, we praise you," using different melodies, tempos and timings. Some people responded with resounding "amens" and "praise Hims."

"If you worshiped as an animal," said the leader, "what would it be?"

Someone let off an "ack-ack-ack-ackawoooo-ack-ack-ack" sound, distracting me from the man at the front.

Sort of sounds like a wounded bird. Animals were never part of Anglican liturgy!

I had no clue why they did this, but figured, if you can't beat them, join them. I screamed, "Eek eek eek oo oo oo. Eek eek eek oo oo oo." I couldn't contain myself and broke down in laughter. I dropped my empty coffee cup and bent over to pick it up.

Seagull woman in front of me turned and placed her hand on my shoulder and stretched her other straight up. "Praise Him, the one who gifted me with an interpretation for this man's prophecy."

Ew, her hand is hot on my shoulder.

Nearby congregants encircled me. The atonal voices faded in the background.

Seagull woman said, "The brother, through his prophetic tongue, proclaims: 'He will be with you if ye humble yourselves before him. Reach out and touch him. For I am with thee. Touch him. Touch him. Touch him.'"

In a blink of an eye, a dozen moist hands were touching my back and arms.

She continued, with people echoing grunts around her: "Be humble and true, and ye shall be married to the voice of this generation. Honour her. Love her. Cherish her. Protect her. Never seek glory for yourself and edify the Lord. Also, like Abraham, you'll be blessed with many children. Go forth and multiply."

She got all that from Eek eek eek oo oo oo? Glad I didn't throw in a "moo!"

A drum beat broke through the din, and the leader in the front picked up an electric guitar and strummed chords. An overhead projector lit a screen above him with lyrics. *At last, a coherent song!*

The congregation sang, finally, in unison, despite the guitar being out of tune. Even though the melody was easy to pick up, I remained silent, thinking about what just happened. I had never heard of prophecies being mentioned in my Anglican services. Was it something directed specifically at me, intended for everyone, or was it a metaphor?

I began singing, loud enough to be heard above the rabble. The crowd around me gave me a ten-foot birth in respect of my powerful voice, and as I hit a high harmony, I spotted a cute family towards the front. The parents were middle-aged and both blond. Beside them were five children, also blond.

Heather and I have one child. If we had one a year for the next ten years, we'd be double the size of that family. Of course, there would be the technicality of consummating our marriage, and Heather would have to stop working... but it is possible.

I longed for the leader to play traditional music, but after one song, he stopped and led the congregation in prayer.

"We are gathered together, here, as a family of God…"

If we are all "family," why did this prophecy feel so directed at me? If Schnookums and I get down to it, we might be able to crank out twenty children before she'd have to stop. Maybe Heather would see the importance of the prophecy and permit additional wives so I could father a nation? I dismissed the thought, knowing full well she wouldn't allow it. Though the thought amused me, I didn't have the heart to spread my love beyond one woman. *But how many children constitutes "fathering a nation?" Do my descendants count?*

"Lord, bless now the words of Pastor Vaughn…"

Vaughn?

The hulking frame of my airplane buddy Vaughn Brown took the microphone from the leader.

A professional athlete is the rector here? No wonder the place is packed!

He gave a simple, yet inspirational, message about how he gave up a life of dating beautiful women and wild parties in Iowa—a gorgeous young Black lady standing near him scowled and crossed her arms—so he could follow religious pursuits and lead Bible studies. He continued about his own marriage, how blessed and complete he was to have a wife like his Jacquie—the woman unfolded her arms and looked at him adoringly—and offered words of encouragement for those who remained single.

I, too, am blessed to have Heather. She's an advertising executive…not a celebrity like you, Vaughn. Your voice can inspire millions. How on earth could Heather's be the voice of a generation?

I checked my watch when Vaughn concluded his homily. *He spoke for an hour?* I never had sat through a sermon longer than ten minutes.

The service concluded with a song that reminded me of a commercial jingle you'd hear on TV for laundry detergent. Throughout the hymn, I was still scratching my head about all this prophecy business.

I wanted to get Vaughn's take on all of this and meet his wife, but everyone made a beeline for him after the service. I couldn't stay long, anyway—I had to pick up my baby from Grumpy Grandma's. I exited the gymnasium and was intercepted by Penny, and we chatted about the service, specifically about the prophecy.

"Miracles happen all the time here," she said. "Generally, they are for the edification of our community—"

But Seagull woman said she had the "gift" to interpret THIS MAN'S prophecy. She didn't say the church's. It must've been something directed only at me.

"—Sometimes they are dramatic and immediate, like in a healing. Others can take a lifetime to unpack.'"

A huge hand walloped my left shoulder, making my knees buckle.

"God will provide an answer," a familiar booming voice echoed with confidence. "You must always be seeking clues throughout your life to understand exactly what He means. Do so, and you *will* receive his blessings."

I turned to face him, and Vaughn smiled.

"Hey, aren't you the athlete I met flying over here?" he said. "Yes, I remember. You're going to get married."

"Vaughn? It's so great to see you! And yes, I just got married. Is she going to be the voice of a generation?"

Vaughn laughed. "Like I said…who knows what God's mysterious plan is for us. That said, I'm so happy for you and so glad you could join us. Hey, since you are new here, would you like to come over to my place for a small group session? We meet weekly, and we can introduce you to some cool folk and learn about faith…maybe study about Biblical prophecies. Might help unpack yours."

"Well, I certainly can teach you all a thing or two about Christianity, and it would be great to meet new people."

Vaughn laughed. "Great…and you should bring your bride. We'd love to meet her, too." He quickly checked his watch. "Gotta run. Hope to see you there."

I nodded and Penny wrote Vaughn's address on a church flyer. I looked forward to sharing my superior Bible knowledge with a gang of theological pathfinders. They also didn't mind my bringing the baby along, and there'd be a potluck dinner.

The service and church were weird for my Anglican sensibilities, but there was something uplifting about it. Something stirred in my soul, and I left feeling ready to take on the challenges of life.

My marriage.

And the prophecy…it did say I'd have many children, like Father Abraham, and my Honey-Bunny will be the voice of a generation!

Vaughn and Jacquie lived in the Kits, too, a bit to the west of me in a similar styled home, though much more modest. The beautiful woman from church greeted me at the door.

"Hi, I'm Larry Johnstone." I extended my hand.

"Hi… Jacquie Brown. Welcome to our group. Wow, what an adorable little baby. May I hold him?"

"By all means. I think Little Larry likes you." The baby didn't budge while she cuddled him. I peeked over her shoulder. Her apartment was spotless. "Do you have any children? Maybe we can organize some play dates."

"No, not yet." A tear welled in her eye. "Vaughn and I have been trying for a couple of years. So far it hasn't been meant to be."

"Sorry to hear that. Would you believe when we conceived ours, I used a condom?"

Funny, she didn't respond.

"Come in," she said. "There's food out on the table in the dining room. Serve yourself, then come join the rest of us." She let me in and carried the baby to the large living room.

There were some interesting dishes. One intrigued me. Rice rolled around something orangey. I grabbed a bit of that, helped myself to some bread, and piled a couple spoonfuls of a fishy smelling pasta dish. I plopped in an empty chair to join the gang.

"Hi, all," said Jacquie, hushing the group. "I'd like to warmly welcome Larry Johnstone tonight, along with his adorable child, Little Larry. He recently moved here from Ottawa."

I took a huge bite out of the rice patty stuff. A fishy taste exploded in my mouth, promoting a gag reflux. I had to spit it out in front of everyone.

"Pt-ah, what the *hell* is that?"

"Larry, you will not use profanity in my house," Jacquie said.

A sophisticated man, with a round balding head and thin moustache spoke in a British accent. "That, my friend, is sushi. Quite popular here."

Pompous git.

"Ugh, no way. We don't eat such crap in Ottawa."

"Larry! Second warning," said Jacquie.

"I'm sure you'll come to like it," said the British man. "Take smaller bites until you're used to the flavour."

I took a nibble.

"I'm Reginald Windsor-Perkins."

"Nice to meet you, Reggie."

"That's *Reginald*. And that's Windsor like the Royals. We might be related…" Reginald paused. Not sure if he wanted me to be impressed. I wasn't really. "I'll have you know I sung as a child in the Westminster Cathedral choir."

"Really, well *I'm* a professional chorister."

Reginald stroked his moustache. "You don't say, old boy. Well, I won a scholarship to attend a church school, for my voice."

I took a second small bite of the sushi. *He's right. This isn't so bad. And he's a singer. Maybe he's not so bad.*

He drawled on. "I landed in Canada, because of that scholarship, you know. We were on a summer mission with the school. One of our stops was here, in Vancouver, helping at the Hospice of Good Hope. It's a homeless shelter. Have you heard of it?"

Why are you telling me your life story?

"No." I said, squinting while taking another bite of fishy pasta. "Hospice is a funny word for a homeless shelter. I thought hospice was another name for hospital."

"We think it an appropriate name. After that summer, I decided to complete my degree and volunteered there." He pulled on the lapels of his blazer. "After a few years, I became managing *director*.

"We take in many homeless people from the downtown core of the city and rehabilitate them into society. In a sense, we are a hospital. We nurture souls, by ministering to their various needs—"

Why hasn't he stopped talking?

"—Another way you could look at it…the word 'hospice' also comes from the days when cathedrals opened their doors to be a lodging for travelers. We open our doors as lodging for those travelling the streets and seeking a permanent home destination. There's a multitude of reasons why people wander the streets, with a variety of needs. I'm blessed to be working with them and seeing so many lives transformed."

I took a few more nibbles of sushi. I loved it!

"You should join us, some time." Reginald concluded. I nodded. Might be interesting to find out if this fellow chorister has decent vocal chops.

The rest took turns introducing themselves around the room.

"Hey Jacquie," said Vaughn, "this is the guy from the airplane I told you about. The *athlete* who taught me so much about women. How's your running going?" Vaughn winked. "Where's the wife you flew across Canada to be with? I'd expect you would've brought her along, too."

"Well, she had to go to Sweden with a friend. But that's okay, I get more time to develop a father-son bond with Little Larry."

"That's good," said Vaughn. "Enjoy your time with him, but personally, I think he's too young to be without his mother. These are cherished moments for a family. Anyway, I would've loved to meet this woman you rushed out here for."

I gazed proudly at my little baby. I'm going to be such a positive influence on him.

A strong looking middle-aged woman with angular features put her plate on her lap. "He's such an adorable child. I love his eyes. His mother's?" The tone of her voice soothed me.

"Yes, with a hint of mine. And he has my nose."

After we ate, Vaughn opened our session in prayer. I never prayed aloud in a gang outside of church before. When Vaughn said "amen," all the members took out their Bibles. They also opened accompanying booklets.

Jacquie came over to me. "We usually do Bible studies here." She gave me a Bible, and a copy of the booklet. She flashed a radiant smile. "The booklet is a guide we use to help us understand the Holy Word better."

She faced the group. "Please turn to page fifteen. Today we'll be discussing how Jesus fed the 5,000."

The thin guide was entitled, "The Simplified Book of John for Small Groups." I leafed through the table of contents and judged the group was about halfway through. I had hoped they'd be discussing prophecies, but figured they might chat about it at another time.

A woman volunteered to read the study lesson. When she finished, Vaughn asked the first question from the guide. "Jesus fed how many people?"

Really?

Harry Lee raised his hand. "Five thousand."

"Very good, Harry," Jacquie encouraged. Everyone nodded their approval at the correct response.

Jacquie asked, "In verse one, what sea did Jesus cross?"

I reviewed the list of questions. If one could read the chapter, one should be able to easily answer them. *What a boring discussion.* My academically superior brain wouldn't last long here if we continued like this.

I had to do something. "Why do we have slightly different accounts of this story in the four Gospels? Let's read them…"

The gang responded to my taking over, and we spent our time exploring the spiritual significance of the miracle, the fact there were leftovers from the five loaves and two fish, and how the lesson applied to our lives.

I recanted my academic knowledge of the Greek interlinear, discussing the various translations throughout history, impressing everyone. Vaughn broke out his university texts, giving a scholarly approach to the study.

After a lively couple of hours, Vaughn opened a notepad and asked people to share personal concerns to offer as prayers.

Reginald requested intercessions for his hospice. Harry needed a job. Vaughn and Jacquie asked for continued support in their quest to have children. Vaughn also asked for God to fulfill a personal dream to play professional football in the States. I asked for the safe return of my Honey-Bunny, who I missed so much, and a deeper understanding of the prophecy bestowed on me.

The evening concluded, and as I left, Vaughn offered me a two-handed handshake, and Jacquie gave me a warm hug. They were an amazing couple, and for the first time since arriving in British Columbia, I felt like I had friends.

I promised to return the following week.

Schnookums didn't call daily. She insisted European phones forced her to pay in advance with coins, which she never carried. When I challenged her by asking why not call collect, Heather said they didn't permit collect calls in Sweden—something to do with the economy. She did finally give me an emergency contact number, where I could leave messages at the hotel's front desk.

Our chats were brief. On connection, she'd ask to hear Little Larry's voice. Of course, he didn't say anything, then she'd blame me for his silence. But when he began to coo, she took the credit for it.

Our calls were cut off abruptly because time would expire. In one brief conversation, she mentioned enjoying the Garden Society of Gothenburg, a nineteenth-century green spot in the city. It sounded exotic and beautiful. The blossoms she described appealed to my botanic sensitivities, and I longed to gather some samples for my pressed flower collection.

The two-minute interactions offered a thrilling highlight to my routine. Caring for the baby was a big deal, and I couldn't fathom why she found Sweden more important than our son. Each night, I stared at the phone anticipating its ring. Most nights it stood silent. *She's missing so much. Little Larry's hair is turning lighter!*

Earl of Latteigh, Peter, church, and small group sustained me while she gallivanted around Scandinavia with Sven.

I loved the Browns. Jacquie invited me over most days for dinners. She mastered making a "spread," bringing out fine dinnerware and placing candles lit near a nice centre piece. Vaughn was seldom home. It was football season, so he often travelled with his team across Canada. I think Vaughn might've joined us twice.

Little Larry loved Jacquie. It didn't surprise me. With her motherly charms, she'd put any young child at ease. Little Larry often slept with a content grin on his face while she rocked him in her arms close to her chest.

I trusted Little Larry with Jacquie. I was grateful when she volunteered to babysit for me for two reasons. One: I needed to smoke up, which helped keep the edge off. It was a habit I knew she'd disapprove of, especially with a baby, so I needed to hide it.

Two: I missed earning some cash selling Peter's dope. He never seemed at ease when I brought my son around, saying things like "I don't like kids that age, man, they're basically just lumps that shit."

Along with the company of the small group, the Browns, and especially Jacquie babysitting, my life resumed some normalcy…sort of.

Chapter Seven
Chicken Kiev—Take 2
July 1989

S chnookums is coming home today! Joy!
I harnessed all the lessons about meal presentation from Jacquie by buying some nice paper plates, a tablecloth, and some candles. The garlic smell from the Chicken Kiev baking in the oven filled the condo. *Schnookums will love it.*

The phone rang at 5 p.m.

"Honey-Bear, it's me," said Heather. Her tone could've melted butter.

"Hi, Honey-Bunny."

"Sven and I never left Europe. We must stay in Sweden for another six weeks."

"What? But I've a special dinner for you. It'll be ready in a couple of hours!"

"More for you, then!" said my wife harshly. "We're having problems. We've been having numerous conference calls with our North American reps. Sven's trying to convince them that *Lax Och Köttbulle Bärbar Ugn* will be a good name for marketing his invention in Canada.

"They want to anglicize it to something cheesy like 'Amazing Portable Oven.' Garbage. The Swedish name has more uniqueness, though I'm trying to convince Sven and our reps it would be better to simplify the name to only *Bärbar Ugn.* Say it…now!"

"Huh?"

"Repeat after me…baaah"

"Baaaah." *I feel like a fed-up sheep.*

"rrrrrrr."

Easy.

"Beau – roon."

"Baaah-rrrrr-bo-roon?"

"See? Mastered in one try." Heather seemed pleased. "Anyway, both Sven and the reps are resisting. Svennie is protesting that without the *Lax Och Köttbulle* prefix, how will anyone know the oven is for meatballs and salmon? Our American reps don't like the Swedish.

"It's a nightmare! We've already begun manufacturing them using the longer name. It'll cost us a mint to rebrand now and might take time to sort out, but I'm sure everyone will see the brilliance of my suggestion."

Honey-Bunny will be gone until the fall?

"You're missing your child's earliest moments," I said, "and you aren't supposed to be working on maternity leave."

"Don't be silly. This is a vacation for me. Take lots of pictures of Rupie-Bear. Sven and I will be back soon and will care for him then."

"You're not making any" — the phone disconnected — "sense."

Damn, why does that keep happening?

Angry!

The huge effort to make Heather's return home special, ruined. She would've orgasmed at the buttery taste of my Chicken Kiev. Pity. *No one to share my mad cooking skills with. Or is there?* I picked up the phone and dialed.

"Hello?" answered Jacquie.

"Jacquie, dear," I said, "how are you?"

"Oh, Larry!" said Jacquie. "So wonderful to hear from you."

"Hey, Jacquie, I made my world-famous Chicken Kiev. I realize it's last minute, but would you and Vaughn like to partake? Say, 7 p.m.?"

"Sounds yummy! See you then!"

She always is happy to hear from me!

My dinner will one-up the Browns'—a challenging task. Jacquie was a killer cook and belonged to a family of hardcore chefs. It's a pity she had a demanding job with irregular hours—she never had time to prepare anything from scratch for me. Despite Jacquie's elegant table settings, her meals were usually straightforward fare—comprising reheated frozen foods and ice cream. Didn't bother me. I went over to their place more for the company.

Tonight, they'll receive the full Larry experience.

It occurred to me I hadn't bought any alcohol since my first day on the West Coast—over two months. A proper meal begged for cocktails, wine, and aperitifs.

Feeling the urge to go on a bender, I called Heather's mother, Mary. I seldom contacted her, though she'd swing by to visit Little Larry on Sundays. Her visits were annoying. She'd gallop into the condo without saying "hello," demand a cup of tea, and played with her grandson until she left. The rude buzzard rarely uttered a single word to me.

After a thirty second telephone conversation, Mary agreed to take Little Larry overnight. *Finally, doing grandma's duty!*

I dropped him off with Grandma Crabby-Pants and ventured into town to buy all the necessary alcohols to make the evening memorable: wine, whiskey, and some crème de menthe should cover it. Fully armed with booze, I returned home to reheat the Chicken Kiev.

I forgot the dessert! The Fates smiled upon me! Our fridge had enough ingredients for a Blueberry Fool. *Perfect.* Makes for a nice complement to the dinner. Expecting the Browns in a half hour, I whipped everything together.

The doorbell rang at 7:00 p.m. sharp. Jacquie stood outside, waiting alone, wearing a navy-blue flirty skirt with white polka-dots. Her white tank top complemented her dress which clung to her curvaceous figure.

Jacquie's straight, shoulder-length hair with coppery highlights had a perfect part on the left side. She produced two carnations in her hand—one pink and one white. Her face radiated a bright smile as she held them out.

"For you." She gave me the flowers followed by a hug.

"How thoughtful! How'd you guess carnations are my favourite?" I placed them beneath my nose and took a deep whiff.

"Just a hunch. They happen to be mine, too. Thank you for having 'us' over."

"Us?" I said coyly, doing a little circle on the floor with my foot. "But where's Vaughn? I made enough food for four."

"Oh!" Jacquie placed her hand over her chest, feigning surprise. "Didn't I mention? He sends his regrets. He's playing in Montreal this week." Jacquie winked. We both followed football and Vaughn's schedule. Playing the flirtatious "where's Vaughn" game became an in-joke. "They're playing now. Can we watch on TV? You know I don't like missing them."

"I'll turn it on!" I loved sports but stopped following due to the time-zone shift from the East Coast. Most games ended by the time I finished dinner.

I escorted her into the living room, and we began watching TV. The match was in the fourth quarter.

"Wow, this place is beautiful," she said when the action cut to a commercial. She closed her eyes and inhaled deeply. "And man, whatever is cooking sure smells delish."

"Dinner is almost ready," I said, but I noticed Jacquie focussing her attention back to the TV, "but we can wait until the game is over."

"Look!" she pointed at the screen excitedly. "There's my Vaughn! He's number 91 on the field."

Vaughn steamrolled over a blocker and annihilated the opponent's quarterback. The poor man didn't know what hit him. Vaughn gyrated his hips and twirled an imaginary lasso while trainers placed the QB on a stretcher. Jacquie's husband transitioned to a running man dance while watching his victim carted off the field.

Jacquie clapped her hands. "Ha-ha, that's my man!"

"He's quite the football player!" I raised my hand in a drinkie-drinkie motion. "Would you like a cocktail before dinner?"

"Larry, you know I don't drink too often."

"Honestly, I haven't had a drop since arriving in Vancouver, so I wanted to have some with our meal. It makes dinner a little more special."

"Okay, what do you have?"

"Not too much, but I wouldn't mind mixing a special cocktail for us. Feel adventurous?"

"Well...why not! But are you okay with drinking around Little Larry?" Jacquie scanned the entire room. "Hey...where's my little man?"

"He's spending quality time with Grandma tonight."

"Oh, okay." Jacquie sounded disappointed.

Aww...she's pretending to sulk.

I mixed some ginger-ale and whiskey in a couple of glass tumblers and placed one next to Jacquie on the couch.

She took a sip. "Yikes! That's strong, but sooooo good." She paused, tilted the glass to look at the bottom, then gulped the remainder of her drink in one large swallow.

Impressive, but she won't out drink me!

"I find the mix quite flavourful," I said. "Would you like another?"

"Yeth."

Poor thing can't hold her liquor.

I prepared us a second drink. I downed mine, and Jacquie nursed hers for the remainder of the game. When the match neared the end, Jacquie took a last sip, smacked her lips, and placed her glass on the coffee table in front of her. She rubbed the plush texture of the fabric on my expensive couch with both hands.

"Oooh, so velvety...Larry, how on earth can you afford to live in this place? My Vaughn and I can barely make ends meet on his salary and my job."

"I don't concern myself with finances. My Schnookums is an executive at an advertising firm."

"Where is she?" Jacquie swiveled her head looking for my wife.

"Still in Sweden with Sven..."

Jacquie appeared concerned and before she could comment or question, I changed the topic. "Would you like a pre-dinner glass of wine?"

She nodded, and I went back to the kitchen and opened a bottle of white. I didn't expect Jacquie to follow, and when I reached for the bottle opener, I felt the warmth of her hand covering the top of mine. She gave an affectionate squeeze, then released her grip. Electricity filled my body with her touch.

"You poor soul," she said.

"Oh, it's not so bad." I popped the cork, set the two glasses on the kitchen table, and partially filled both. Jacquie seemed impressed with my beautiful table setting, and her eyes bulged at the colourful array when I began serving the food. "It's their business that enables us to live in such a fine place. And I get to spend quality time with my son."

"I find it remarkable you have a son so soon in your marriage." She took a sip of the wine, nodded, and motioned for me to top up her glass.

"What's wild for me," I said, pouring the wine, "is that we only had sex once, and like I had mentioned, with a condom. But I guess I'm special."

The one statement about my sex life with Heather opened the flood gate of conversation about my dating experiences with women, and how my Heather promised to be the fulfilment of my lifelong mission. I expressed my sorrow for my many failed relationships, and my concern for not consummating our marriage.

I talked for an hour while we ate dinner, ensuring our glasses were always full. Tipsy Jacquie expressed sympathy through her beautiful eyes.

"Women treating you so horribly…that's a topic we'll get to another day," she said while enjoying dessert. "But let me get this straight. You had sex once with a condom…how can you produce such a fine child?"

Her question opened the door to my retelling the story of how I met Heather at Rancorous Rick's house, the details of our relationship, and how we had "intercourse" shortly after meeting.

I poured some *crème de menthe* after we finished our desserts. Couldn't really tell how much we were drinking, though Jacquie sipped where I gulped.

Jacquie slurred, "We talked much about your prophecy. I don't know how it will be fulfilled with you and Heather, let's say, not living like husband and wife. I mean, it's clear you both can produce children. I imagine it's just a matter of time where you'll have more."

"Nothing can hold back my super sperm." I downed my drink and poured myself another.

"I envy you both. Vaughn and I've been trying to have a baby for years now. And nothing. Nada." Her tone turned to bitterness. "We got into an argument the other night, and Vaughn said…can you believe it…he said that it might be my fault because of some 'unconfessed sin.' I understand he's into his faith, but how dare he pull that out of his behind! How could it be my fault? I betcha he was no angel before we met!" Her voice choked and without saying anything further, her eyes told me she longed for Vaughn to produce sperm like mine.

After a brief pause, I asked, "How's that possible? You have the perfect body for child rearing?"

Jacquie blushed. "He claims that because I had another man before meeting him, God is punishing me."

I slammed my glass down on the table.

"What? That's ridiculous. God has blessed me with a child, and he was produced with the aid of latex and outside the bounds of matrimony."

Jacquie slugged back her drink. "Yes, Larry. I get that. But do you understand the guilt he put on me? I must be paying for my sins. Don't get me wrong. I'm so happy you've been blessed with such a wonderful prophecy to have many more kids to follow." A tear welled in her eye. "I only wish I could have *one*.

"That Vaughn is never around. It's always football, football, football. If he's not practicing with the team, he's flying down to the States to chase his American dream. When he's in town, it's all about the church. Heather's got it so good having a kind man like you around. She should be here, with you, taking care of Little Larry." Jacquie reached out and placed her hand on top of mine. Once again, a tingling sensation traversed my arm down through my chest within a nano-second.

"She knows I'm the best thing for her. She'll be home soon."

Jacquie pulled back her hand, nodded, then sniffed.

"Would you like some more *crème de menthe*? Hey, we still have some more wine. Prefer that?"

She nodded. I wobbled over to the counter and struggled to pour out a fresh glass for her—some spilled on the table. Jacquie didn't even flinch.

"Can you show me around your condo? I'm curious to see how folks live in the east side of the Kits."

Raised as a gentleman, I offered Jacquie my hand. She took it and carried her wine glass in the other. I led her down the hall to my bedroom, bringing the bottle of wine with me.

"Rich folk live like this?" she said sarcastically. "This room barely fits a bed and the crib."

I slugged back a good quarter of the bottle. Tasting wine between my lips felt good. *She must be close to blotto by now. Yet, she walks straighter than me!*

"Let me show you the master bedroom. It's much larger." Heather had forbidden me to enter Sven's room—a rule I respected even while Heather flew around Sweden. It might've been the alcohol, but I didn't care that night.

We walked arm in arm down the hallway, leaning into each other. I opened the door to Heather's room, and...

Squish.

We molded into each other cramming through the door at the same time. After remaining stuck for a moment, we inhaled deeply and stumbled on through, laughing.

Jacquie placed her hand on my back while our giggles subsided. In a moment of still and silence, she slowly moved her hand up and down, sending chills through my spine.

I turned my head to face her beautiful eyes, and we held each other's gaze for what seemed like an eternity. Her lips parted, breath hinting of wine, and the tip of her tongue touched the edge of her lower lip.

Does she know how alluring she is? I leaned my head closer towards hers...

It broke the spell. Jacquie dropped her arm and took a few steps deeper into the room.

"This room feels like we are riding clouds in a sky," Jacquie said observing the blue walls and white decor. She sat at the foot at the bed, kicked off her shoes, and slowly rubbed the duvet beside her.

I took a sip of wine.

"What's in the closet?" she asked. "Rich homes always have beautiful walk-ins."

Heather had many clothes, but I'd never experienced the depth of her wardrobe. I opened the doors and flicked a light switch. To my right were shelves with dozens of pumps, flats, and other shoes. A little beyond, the red dress Heather wore to greet me at the airport hung first on a rail filled with clothes that extended deep into the closet.

On my left were tons of loafers, boat shoes, and sneakers. Beyond them, three-piece suits, ties, and fancy casual wear. *Sven's? He did own the place, but how often does he stay? This should be my closet! In my room, I live out of a suitcase. What else does Sven have that I don't?*

Heather.

Jacquie read the shock on my face.

"Laaaaarrry," she said patting the bed beside her. I took a big swig from the bottle, placed it on a wardrobe, and sat. I put my head on Jacquie's shoulder but didn't cry. I couldn't trust my negative thoughts of my Schnookums, especially after an evening of heavy drinking.

Jacquie stroked my hair, and I closed my eyes comforted in her embrace.

The phone screamed the next morning. My head hurt like the devil. It reminded me of the pain I had experienced when Brad had woken me after my bachelor party. The curtains were drawn, and I felt disoriented. Accustomed to a soft, fluffy bed, Heather's brick-hard mattress risked throwing me in a chiropractic clinic for a year. My back and shoulder ached almost as bad as my head. The sheets were soft against my naked body, though.

Wait! Where are my clothes?

The phone kept ringing!

Can't you see I'm dying here?

Wait! I'm in Schnookum's room. Was this Sven and Sweden thing a dream? How'd I end up in my wife's bed? The only logical conclusion hit me.

Heather and I had officially consummated our marriage!

The phone's irritating chime persisted. Annoyed, I bolted out of bed to the kitchen and answered. It hung up the moment I said hello.

You let the phone ring a trillion times, and you couldn't let it go once more?

Pots and pans filled the sink, dinner plates were left on the table, and bottles of alcohol were strewn all over the place.

Smells like Chicken Kiev. One of Heather's favourites.

But where's Heather?

I stood naked, alone in the apartment, and the accursed phone buzzed again.

Oh crap, it's true. She's in Sweden. Maybe it's her on the line.

"Hello, Honey-Bunny?"

"No, it's Honey-Bunny's mom. It's 1 p.m. You were supposed to pick up Lars over an hour ago. I must meet some friends soon. I expect you here in fifteen minutes."

Click.

That freaking dial tone again.

What is that bat talking about?

I figured I'd better oblige and try to put together the missing pieces like I did the last time I blacked out.

Chapter Eight
The Return of the Queen
September 1989

Schnookums announced her return to Vancouver in mid-September. After spending our first months of marriage apart, we'd finally be able to resume where we left off after our wedding ceremony. The following morning, while sloshing back a mocha at my local Earl of Latteigh, I formulated a plan to kickstart our new beginning when Schnookums returns next week.

I'll buy her something to symbolize my affection and our future life together. But what?

I consulted the Bible. Today's study featured a genealogy, and I imagined myself walking through a graveyard reading names on the tombstones found in the verses. Daydreaming, my mind drifted to scenes of Ancient Greece.

"Hey Herc," a high-pitched voice echoed through my brain. A pointy-eared, orange-haired centaur entered my reverie with a cartoon-like backdrop of Mount Olympus. Lightning flashed all over the place.

Great Zeus! Something clicked. I should buy something with a Hercules Knot! Heather would love it. The symbolic emblem denoting my commitment and undying love for my Honey-Bunny would bowl her over. An added bonus and little-known fact: Hercules was a legendary fertility God, which promised many children to come. *Perfect!*

Stoked, I downed my drink and rushed downtown in quest of a Hercules Knot trinket. It shouldn't be difficult to find. It's simply a knot comprising two entwined ropes.

My brain flooded with ideas. Maybe we could take our long overdue honeymoon. Maybe I could incorporate a Hercules Knot in my bride's "protective" girdle. Maybe I could ceremoniously untie it on our belated wedding night! *Woof!* This is the perfect way to officially "tie the knot."

After speaking with a wonderful travel agent, she suggested I whisk Schnookums away to a honeymoon suite at a luxury hotel in Whistler for a weekend getaway. The brochures promised a swanky and potentially sexually satisfying experience.

Needing a break from all the strenuous planning, I tracked Peter down on his usual street corner and bought my daily joint.

A couple of weeks later, Peter asked me to sample a "newish" product. Wasn't sure I quite liked it, so had to try a few to confirm. When the effects of the joints died down, a sudden realization hit me like a ton of bricks falling on my head…*Heather returns today! Crap! I haven't even set foot in a store to find my Hercules Knot!*

With the Hercules Knot idea flushed down the toilet, I stumbled into a local department store that afternoon to find something else. The nicest jewelry was way too expensive! My eyes gravitated to a huge heart-shaped locket. *Only ten dollars? That could work!* The two-inch silver-plated pendant sparkled on the long chain. *Heather'll love it!*

My Bible contained all my dearest photos cemented between its covers. I removed a nice one of the two of us around the time we were engaged. *Too bad she frowns in every picture.* I also retrieved a favourite shot of Little Larry being held by Jacquie. It was so cute. He had just started smiling last week, and only when in her arms!

The clerk offered me scissors, and I cut the photos to fit neatly on each side of the hollow shell within the locket. I paid the man after he gift-wrapped it, and I left the store proud as a peacock.

It took a half hour to flag down a taxi. We still had time before Heather's plane landed, but within a few minutes of pulling away from the curb, my nose erupted from something foul.

"Hey, did someone die back here?" I asked the driver.

He pulled the car over. "Dude, your baby dropped a bomb. Go change him in that burger joint. I can wait."

"We can't stop! I'm in a hurry! I'm meeting my wife at the airport. It's an important occasion! I have to be there on time."

"And time is money." The cabbie tapped his meter.

I went on to tell the cab driver an abbreviated version about my marriage and Sven.

"Meter's running," reminded my driver.

I carried on talking about my dating, lifelong desire to father children, and have a happy marriage.

"Still running," he said. I could tell he was listening attentively while he leafed through some receipts.

I went on discussing my church history concluding with the prophecy.

"Buddy," the driver said, tossing his papers on his passenger's seat. "My taxi is stinking. I'm going to give you two options. You either go out and change your baby's diaper now, or you stay and talk to me more. I don't mind. At this rate, I'll be able to pay my mortgage this month."

The taxi meter read thirty-one dollars.

We barely drove three blocks! I checked the time. *What? I blabbed for over an hour?*

In a huff, I grabbed Little Larry and reached for the door handle.

"Hey buddy," the driver said. "Pay me now. How do I know you won't make a dash for it?"

"Weren't you listening? I'm going to pick up my Schnookums?" The meter increased to $33, and the driver's stone-cold expression didn't flinch. "Oh, all right." I tossed him two twenties and left. "Wait here."

Little Larry cried in discomfort as we walked into the empty washroom. I'd become an expert in changing him in difficult areas, and the men's bathroom in the burger joint was a challenge—with just a pedestal sink.

I needed paper towels. *Crap, they only have hand dryers. What to do?*

I rushed into the only stall. Three rolls of toilet paper were available, plus a half a one in the dispenser. I grabbed them all, bypassing a man who entered to use a urinal. I laid out the toilet paper on the floor to define a nice, clean, dry space to change my son.

The man left—without washing his hands—and an older teen entered. He stepped on the corner of my toilet paper bed.

"Hey, walk around!" I yelled.

The boy crept along the edge of the wall and into the stall, closing the door.

I placed Little Larry down on the ground and changed him. *Can't pick up after myself and waste more time getting to the airport. The staff is paid for these menial clean-up tasks, anyway.*

The youth yelled from his stall, "What the fuck? Where's the toilet paper?"

Little Larry and I slipped out the door.

It might've been my toking that day, but the amazing smell of French fries overwhelmed me. *Must have meat and spuds!* I joined the queue to satisfy my craving, and the line advanced at a snail's pace. My stomach, though, felt sated when I finally indulged in my meal.

One more pit stop to the washroom, and we returned outside. The cab was nowhere to be found!

Jerk! It's 5:10 p.m.
Schnookums has landed!

Heather glared in the distance with her arms crossed, tapping her gold pump, with two large suitcases parked beside her. Every few seconds, she turned her wrist to check the time. She stood out in the hustling and bustling crowd in a red dress, radiating under the Air Western sign at the baggage claim.

"Schnookums!" I waved at her and weaved slowly through the horde, pushing Little Larry's stroller.

She turned her head, eyes locking into me like a missile acquiring its target. Within ten yards of her, her expression softened, making me fall in love with her all over again.

"Look how big my little Rupie-Bear is growing." Heather reached out for the baby and lifted him. Little Larry cooed and fussed, cuddling into her like two close friends reuniting after a long time apart.

"Wow! Amazing he knows who you are after all this time!" I might've been a bit sarcastic.

Heather scowled. "Of course he does. Why wouldn't he?" She looked down at the baby, smiled, and said some gibberish which Little Larry responded to. "Why were you an hour late?" she growled.

I didn't want to tell her I was taste toking for Peter.

"Wait." She paused. "Sven told me to be nice." She drew a few deep breaths. "I'm sorry," she sang. "I forget that the Vancouver traffic can be brutal. How are you doing my Honey-Bear?" She placed her hand on my shoulder, making me feel all warm and fuzzy, and kissed my cheek. "Maybe we'll have funsies later?"

I never heard her apologize before. *And funsies? Yay!*

Seizing her cheerfulness as an opportunity, I put down my knapsack, bent to one knee, and offered my wife her present.

"Stop making a scene," she barked. After a brief pause, her stern expression turned into a radiant smile. The shift of mood reminded me of how the sun bursts through dark clouds.

"Sven insisted I be kinder, because we need you," she said softly.

Smart man.

She maintained her fixed grin as she spoke. "Is that a present for me?" Her voice took on a girlish timber.

I nodded while she placed the baby in his stroller.

She unwrapped the gift and stared at the blue felt jewelry box. "What the hell?" The cloud returned, and her face became stern again. Within a blink of an eye, she smiled. "Oh Sven—I mean Larry—why?" She stared adoringly at my gift. "Oh Honey-Bear, how thoughtful!" She opened the box and lifted the chain which dangled the large heart-shaped pendant.

Her eyes flared in anger. "What an ug" — and the smile returned — "beautiful gift. I'll cherish it always."

She giggled!

"Let me put it on you." I reached forward.

She tapped my hand. "No, the weight of that pendant will put a permanent chain mark in my neck." *That freaking cloud is back.* After a second, her voice softened. "No, wait. I'd prefer to put this lovely necklace on myself. My neck is stiff from those seats on that long flight."

That made sense. When she attached the chain, the heart-shaped pendant rested in her cleavage.

"Today is a special day," I said.

Heather looked confused.

"It's the anniversary of our meeting? Don't you remember?"

"No."

A little put off, I dismissed her answer as a joke. "Anyhow, this gift is a token of my continued commitment to you and our love. It will symbolize our togetherness for all eternity."

Heather began to laugh!

"This freaking thing? It looks like something out of a cereal box." She paused and regrouped herself. "No, right. I need to be more respectful. Is it really our anniversary?"

"Darn tootin' it is. I have something special to show you." I reached out for the dangling pendant.

Heather slapped my hand hard. "Not. Here," she repeated. The cloud passed again. "I told you. You *might* get funsies later."

"Huh?" I replied, "Oh, that would be nice, but I simply wanted to open the locket."

Heather permitted me to hold the pendant, and I showed her the two pictures. "Why would I want *that* picture of Rupie-Bear?" She smiled again. "What a lovely memory. Wish I was there for it." She kissed my head. "I missed my little Rupie-Bear so much." She inspected the image. "Larry! What—"

"—a beautiful picture. Yes, I know."

"No. I was going to say…whose hands are those?"

Heather pointed out some beautifully manicured fingers.

Jacquie's!

"Er, they belong to a friend."

The cloud shifted. "What? You know how I feel about the sanctity of marriage." And it passed. "Wait, no. I really should try to trust you. It would make Sven happy."

Who cares about Sven?

She looked over to our baby in the stroller. "I like his hair. It's turning blonder."

Should've been here to see all the wonderful changes.

We strolled outside and flagged a taxi.

Heather wanted to return straight home. I was a little disappointed. I'd hoped she would want to eat out at Purple Pigeons, like we were supposed to after our wedding ceremony. She was too tired after her long flight.

"If you need some rest, we can leave Little Larry with Jacquie for the weekend and take our belated honeymoon in Whistler. They have hot tubs and a spa! I've booked everything!"

"Who's Jacquie?" Heather hissed.

Why the attitude?

"Jacquie? You remember… I mentioned her before you left for Gothenburg. She's the pastor's wife of my church."

"What? I leave you for two seconds and you shack up with other women?" She relaxed, recomposed herself, and laughed. "No, wait. Sven told me you wouldn't be the type to cheat on me. Do you trust her to care for my son?"

Little Larry cuddled into Heather.

"For sure. She's helped me care for him on occasion. You know I wouldn't want to disrespect our marriage Honey-Bunny. I missed you so much. So did Little Larry."

"Little Larry, Little Larry…" she looked down to her child. "That's not my Rupie-Bear's name."

"Everyone calls him Little Larry. Besides, I think he only started responding to Larry over the past couple weeks." I smiled.

"We'll have to recondition him. Larry is a horrible name for this child."

"What do you mean? There's nothing wrong with it."

"Of course there is, it's not even close to his real name," Heather said. The cloud shifted again. "That's why I call you my Honey-Bear." She placed her hand on my lap. Combined with her sweet tone, I swooned.

"Well, like I said, Schnookums, would you like to go to Whistler this weekend and finally have a honeymoon? We can unwind in their mud baths, and I've always wanted a seaweed facial!"

Heather looked mortified. "No."

We sat silent while the cab drove into the Kits.

"I won't be around much," she continued, "so I want to spend the time with Rupie-Bear. Besides, Sven returns on Sunday from Sweden.

"What? Sven is returning?"

She told me of their ambitious plan to travel across Canada to work on promoting Sven's oven. She insisted they required me to care for the kid because Sven "needed" her, and by extension, me. I protested her galivanting across the country with the Swedish interloper.

Heather attempted to reassure me by rubbing my leg. "Don't worry, we'll be back every now and again over the next several months to check in on our little bear."

Next several months?

Heather explained they were going to film "infomercials." She figured Sven, who happened to be a Swedish celebrity—both playing pro hockey in his late teens, then anchoring a national TV sports program—would blow Canada away with his charm and sell millions of *Bärbar Ugns*.

"It's exciting. We're going to film infomercial spots in all the cities we visit. Gives our *Bärbar Ugn* ads a more local flare. You'll see, Sven will become a household name here. It's been a lifelong dream of mine to be affiliated with such a celebrity. You should be thrilled!"

"Overwhelmed."

"Aw, don't be like that. I'll make it up to you." She slowly rubbed my thigh.

We pulled into our building. Heather paid the driver and began unpacking in her bedroom when we settled in our condo. Not permitted into "Sven's" room, I stood by the door and watched.

"Oh, I have a present for you," she said, reaching into her suitcase.

"For me?" My mood lifted. "I thought you forgot our anniversary?"

"I did. But you'll find my gift fun, and practical."

Must be some serious kinky Swedish thing.

"Here." She handed me a bag adorned with Swedish flags. "Enjoy." She resumed her unpacking.

"What are these?" I said opening it. "Wooden butter knives?"

"That's right! Everyone uses them in Sweden. We should try them with our dinner rolls tonight."

"I don't have any dinner rolls. Remember? I was planning on us going out."

"Oh, and while you pick up the dinner rolls at the store, get me some fresh asparagus. I'm dying for some asparagus water. I haven't had any in months."

I sighed. "I'll go shopping now." I left Little Larry with his mother and went to put on my raincoat.

"By the way, I got you a second gift." Heather followed me out into the hallway and handed me a flyer. "You should give it a spin when it arrives. It's one of the first to come off the factory line."

I read the *Bärbar Ugn* brochure. It reminded me of a plastic toy oven I owned as a child.

They made great cakes, but meatballs?

Chapter Nine
The Viking and the Maiden
September - October 1989

Heather and I spent a great week with Little Larry—like a family. I skipped church that Sunday morning, and we went downtown to grab a coffee at an Earl of Latteigh. Little Larry stared intently with his ice blue eyes at the baristas serving customers. I, as usual, read my Bible. Amazing story today about how children were a reward from God.

Little Larry. My first child of many in fulfilment of my prophecy. I couldn't love Heather more than I did at that moment. She radiated as a maternal beauty, sitting in silence while holding our baby. She had been extra sweet since her return.

"I want another one," I said, staring at our son. I placed my empty cup on the table.

Heather stopped eating her yogurt. Little Larry shifted his focus to her dangling pendant. "Why? This coffee is overpriced and fetid."

"C'mon, Heather, you know what I mean." I was positive she understood I meant having a second child. "Anyway, this is the best coffee in town. You have to try it."

"I can smell its quality in the air, and it reminds me of a dirty ashtray. This isn't the European coffee I like."

"Give it a chance," I insisted. "Let me buy you something that'll rock your world."

I requested a quadruple caramel latte for Heather—one of my favourites. The steam hissed out of the machine, and the barista handed me the mouthwatering drink.

Heather stared at the cup in my hand like a spider had crawled from under a rock. After a long pause, she grabbed it and took a sip. Her eyes lit up like a baby tasting chocolate pudding for the first time.

"It's okay." She suppressed a smile.

Okay my arse. Her smile reminded me of how she used to tease when we first met.

"So, do you have an answer to my question about a second child?" I pressed. "You're too gorgeous not to have more children."

"I know."

"We are destined for greatness. With your infomercials, for sure you'll be a voice for this generation." *And fulfil my prophecy.*

Heather stared at me blankly. "What on earth are you babbling about? Sven's the star."

Okay, but there's the father of a nation part...

"Let's have another baby," I persisted.

Heather sighed. "I'd have to talk to Sven first. He wasn't too keen on having this little cub."

"Sven? What does Sven have to do with anything? It's our family. Our decision."

Little Larry's ice blue eyes reacted to the arrays of sounds in the shop— people ordering long-named coffees, the noise of the espresso machines, different tones of chatter surrounding us.

Heather noticed our child's curiosity. "My Rupie-Bear is so cute!" She rocked him. "It's Sven's house, remember? He's part of the family, so he needs to be part of the plan."

"That makes no sense."

"Of course it does. Where will you put the second child?"

I thought about it. "The baby could share the room with his brother."

"And what if the baby is a girl? Can't expect them to share space. And where will you sleep?"

Why is this even a question?

"I was thinking that I could move into your bedroom."

"It's *Sven's* bedroom. Where'd he go?"

"Listen, I should sleep with my wife. Sven could sleep with the bratwurst, or whatever the Swedish word for baby is."

"So should Sven."

"So should Sven what?"

"Sleep with his wife."

"That makes no sense, I've never met Sven's wife. I didn't even know he was married."

"You've met his wife...sort of."

"Huh?"

"You met me."

"What does that have to do with anything?"

"It's complicated." Heather placed the baby in the stroller next to the table and took another swig of coffee. "Yes," she said, staring at the cup. "That's acceptable." She placed it on the table. "Sven bought the condo around the time we became business partners, and we both had dreams of success. We had a wonderful arrangement…you have to agree, the Kits is a remarkable place to live."

True.

"Sven threatened to leave me," continued Heather, "when he found out I was pregnant. That was unacceptable. I didn't want to give up the life I was building with him—or lose out on my dreams of life with a celebrity—so he agreed you and I should be married."

"He *agreed* we should be married?" My voice escalated.

"Of course he allowed it. I mean, he doesn't want anything to do with raising a baby. In fact, he loves you raising the child and caring for the home. It frees him up to pursue his passion to become one of the highest earning businessmen in the world. Besides, he has a playboy image to maintain in Sweden."

Little Larry fussed. Heather bent over and tickled under his chin.

"You know, my mother didn't want me to be unmarried with a child, too. So you see our marriage, Honey-Bear, became *über* important. It benefits us all. Rupie-Bear has a father-like presence in his life; Mom has her wishes fulfilled that I be married with a child; Sven stays with me comforted that he isn't bearing the responsibility of raising the baby; I get to launch his success and ride the fame of a celebrity. And you? You get your dream—wife, child, and family. It all works out!" She took a moment to stare at her half-empty cup. "But there's something missing in it for me."

Little Larry began to cry.

"What's wrong with him?" asked Heather.

A mother should know.

"He needs a diaper change." I shouldered a packsack and took Little Larry to the washroom. On my return, a young couple stood, chatting to my wife. They waved and departed when I took my seat.

"Who were they?"

"Some business associates. There's a lot of people here from my office."

Heather reached out for our son, and I passed him back to her. She made a googly face at Little Larry, and they both laughed.

"See," she said, "you have all that you wanted. I didn't. Why? Because Sven never wanted a committed relationship—with me or anyone. He often joked about being 'off the hook' now that we have you as 'househusband.' When we arrived in Sweden, he completely forgot our anniversary."

You forgot ours!

"You can imagine how angry that made me. But he made up for it. He proposed, and we married!"

"What?" I shook my head. "You can't be married to two men. It's against the law."

"We found a way. See, Sven's and my marriage isn't bound by the laws of this world. Our marriage is bound on an ethereal plane laid for us by the ancient Vikings of old. It wouldn't be recognized in any country, but it has much more profound roots than any conventional marriage."

"Huh?" I downed the remainder of my drink, and my head buzzed from the caffeine rush.

"Sven had struggled with the notion of marriage. To him, modern marriage is an insignificant ritual with little meaning. He broached the topic of committing our lives together after we arrived in Gothenburg. My frustration of my dreams not being fulfilled—and my threatening to leave him and abandoning our multi-million-dollar business—might've had something to do with it.

"He surprised me. A day later he presented me with a *kransen*. It's a headband to symbolize my virginity" — Heather giggled — "and he placed it around my head. Sven mentioned his mother had worn a *kransen* before she got married, so I took it as a step in the right direction.

"You know, Nordic tradition dictates the *kransen* be passed down from women of previous generations. But because he didn't have his mother's, Sven gave me the sweatband he wears while playing squash." Heather squealed at the memory. "I proudly wore it the whole time up until our ceremony. I look forward to passing it on to my daughter one day!"

I was shocked. "Marriage is my whole purpose in life."

"Yes, but it's not for everyone. Over half the people in the world are divorced within the first two years of marriage. Sven didn't want to cheapen our relationship with something that could end so easily. But after spending all that time with me, he told me he couldn't be with any other." Heather sparkled at the memory.

"During the midsummer festival, we were hopping around like frogs, and Sven expressed his undying love for me. He suggested we perform the 'Viking Rites,' an ancient tradition that's eternally binding, but has no legal commitment whatsoever." Heather beamed. "I finally got him to want me! I couldn't say no, and the ceremony was like it was out of a fairy-tale.

"Larry, I mentioned I dreamt of building the career of a celebrity, but I had another dream—a dream of becoming famous through my spouse. Not only am I in love with Sven" — Heather blushed — "but he promised to make me famous, too! He'll complete my life ambitions. It didn't take long for me to say yes. I stopped my hop and kissed him under the maypole."

I stared at Heather in disbelief, but she ignored me.

"Sven led me away from the festival deep into the woods. We needed a cemetery for the first part of the ritual—something he called a sword ceremony. The ancient Vikings practiced it to rid themselves of bachelorhood and destroy the vestiges of their unmarried self. To achieve this, Sven had to break into a grave and retrieve a sword of one of his ancestors.

"Of course, he didn't really break into a grave, nor did he have a real sword. He simply walked out of my sight into the woods, symbolizing his entering a tomb, and he retrieved a stick, pretending it was an ancestral sword.

"Through this action, he entered death as a boy and emerged into a life as a man reborn. Larry" — she reached across the table and grabbed my hand — "I swear, he changed." She released it. "Oh, he didn't have a traditional Viking costume like he was supposed to, but he had bought a plastic helmet with horns from a tourist shop to surprise me." Heather lowered her voice. "When he returned to me from the forest carrying his stick and wearing his horns, I wanted to do him then and there."

She took a sip of coffee.

"Mmmm…you know, this isn't bad. Anyway, I had to perform my part of the ceremony next. It was supposed to happen in an ancient bathhouse, but there wasn't one available; so, we used the bathtub in our hotel room instead. I stripped naked, dressed only in my *kransen,* and took a hot bath. Before I realized it, he opened the door wearing nothing but his plastic helmet, and he helped me wash away my maidenhood—all in that pink tub.

"We stood and embraced. Our skin touching and caressing each other in the steaming hot bathroom. We cemented and consummated our eternal commitment right there and then.

"When we finished our love making, he removed my *kransen* and replaced it with a diamond tiara. Of course it was costume jewelry, bought at the same place he found the helmet, but the meaning had a profound effect on me." Heather put down the cup and fanned her eyes. "We're now united forever, under the stars of the ancient Vikings—even if they were blocked by the ceiling of our hotel bathroom."

"Hogwash," I said.

"It's true. It's real. Sven wouldn't lie about such things. He gave me this."

Heather pulled out an old book from her bag. She turned the yellowing pages to hand-drawn pictures of ancient marital ceremonies. I reached over and grabbed it, flipping to the front cover. I couldn't understand the script—it might've been Scandinavian.

I couldn't believe what I heard. "What about *our* marriage? Aren't you happy with me?"

"Of course. Sven and I are okay with our arrangement." She returned the book back to her bag. "It's very convenient for him having you around as a *househusband* to mind his property and care for Rupie-Bear, so, no need for you to fret, Honey-Bear. You're married, fulfilling your dream; I have Sven still in my life; and Sven has me to grow his business. Besides, Sven likes you, and you're doing him a huge favour. We'd hate to lose you on a technicality. But as you see, you and I are still legally married, and should behave as such."

Technicality? So, I'm the husband to the house, not to Heather.

"What do I get out of this?"

"I told you. A family. Oh, and you get to live in the Kits. That's pretty luxurious living, no?"

I do like the condo's rain shower...

With no idea what to do or how to answer, I went back to the Bible. There must be some solution there. The random verse said something about an assassin boring his sword deep into the belly of a king, and his guts spilled everywhere.

Not quite the inspiration I longed for. But the image of death did speak to me. My marriage wasn't quite what I had expected. And she didn't answer the question about having a second child.

How could a prophecy be wrong?

Heather finished her drink and took Little Larry to meet Sven at the airport, leaving me alone to ponder this bizarre arrangement.

The rain poured around while I walked away from the Earl of Latteigh. Consumed by anger and disappointment, Heather had dashed all my dreams of a traditional "white picket fence" life over a single latte. My frustration clouded the thoughts racing through my brain.

All my life, I had one ambition: to be married and have children. In that quest, I had dated non-stop and was continuously dumped. Until Heather. She was the first woman who wanted me—and to be married. Sure, like me, she had life ambitions. But to be driven to the point where she'd want a lifelong commitment with someone else? Didn't make sense.

Sven's ceremony was an obvious farce—but not to my Schnookums. *Will she find out one day that she, too, is being played?* My mind raced, practicing a dialogue of a huge confrontation with Sven and Heather. I held a trump card. They both needed me for their success. *But does it make sense to risk irreversible damage and ruin everything by blowing up at them?*

Can I lead this life supporting my wife's dreams for her sake? And what about my dreams? How will the prophecy play out? Is Heather supposed to be a part of it? Marriage is forever, in my books. My parents' marriage endured many bumpy roads; they persevered, and time heals—but is this grounds for divorce? I wasn't sure.

Peter sat at his usual corner under a golf umbrella. He wasn't playing guitar today, thanks to the rain. He simply shared the love with a bright smile and waved to anyone who walked by.

"Peter, hit me," I said.

"No problem, man!" He grabbed two joints. "You look pissed, brother. This'll take the edge off."

I paid for them and continued strolling towards the downtown core, smoking.

Sven must be a passing fancy. She can't possibly believe his little "mating ritual" is binding...I'm sure Sven will leave her if it conveniences him. And I will be there waiting...proving my love is a rock, and that I'm the better man. I'm sure it won't be long for her to see the light.

I turned down a road lined with many shops. I'd been walking around a while, and the munchies kicked in. I walked into a Buck-o-rama for a bag of chips.

I need a plan B. I've been dumped too often. Maybe, since she's having a fling, I better have one, too—it would be smart to have someone waiting in the wings in case Heather doesn't see the light...maybe someone like Jacquie.

A book rack featured some cheesy romance novels, the kind I read by the bucketload in high school. Jacquie did, too, in her youth—a fact we'd often joke about. She sometimes lent me some of her "prized" ones. We'd laugh at their campiness, and comment about the "love lessons" found in each. This shop had its share of over-the-top titles.

One cover, featuring a topless man, caught my eye. *Great chesticles!* Chiseled like a bodybuilder, he held a gorgeous woman with deep brown skin by a campfire. Both had black hair, blowing in the wind. Both looked longingly into each other's eyes preparing for a deep embrace, with the man's brim of his cowboy hat separating them. The guy on the cover sort of looked like me.

Loving the title, *You Move My Steers—Book Two of the Chuckwagon of Desire Series*, I grabbed a copy. *Jacquie'll love this!*

Oh, look what they have...

I left the store with a toy gun in a holster and wearing a cowboy hat. I picked a good day to wear plaid. She'll get a kick out of my get up when I give her the book.

The rest of the afternoon didn't go too well. The moment I opened the door to my condo in the Kits, I was greeted by Sven's annoying "EEE HEE HEE HEE!" from the kitchen. He advanced into the hall and opened his arms to give me a "European greeting," but I instinctively drew my pistol at the interloper.

"Whert der ferk?" he said, ironically imitating the Swedish Chef.

I pulled the trigger, and the toy gun made a shooting sound.

"EEE HEE HEE HEE! You're a terrible shot."

"Svenny..." said Heather gently from her room, "what's all that racket? Where's my drink?"

"Coming right up, *Sötnos!*" he sang back. "Househusband...fetch us some asparagus water...and knock before entering." He swiftly returned to the master bedroom.

"You fetch it!" I yelled. Fed up with all of this, I grabbed my *Bärbar Ugn*—since I was supposed to make the dinner at the Browns'—and decided to head over early for small group.

I was expecting Jacquie to open the door, but Vaughn did instead. He was never around for my Jacquie visits.

"What are *you* doing here?" I asked.

"I should be asking you the same thing," answered Vaughn.

"What do you mean? I come over most afternoons!"

Vaughn furrowed his eyebrows. "You do know that our special small group meeting doesn't start until dinner time."

I peered over his shoulder. He had guests.

Noticing my curiosity, he opened the door wide. The living room full of strangers were all dressed in suits. "Hey, gang!" said Vaughn, "Check this out. Billy the Kid is paying us a visit." Everyone snickered when I walked in.

Jacquie was sitting in the far corner of the room, looking rather sad.

"Hey, you guys shouldn't laugh." I handed Vaughn my portable oven and reached into the bag and pulled out the book with the beautiful Black woman on the cover. I waved it so everyone could see it. "Hey Jacquie, have you seen this? I'm sure we'll learn a lot from it!"

"What?" said Vaughn, noticing the cover. His eyes bulged while his eyebrows joined again. "How dare you!" He looked back at his wife. "What have you two been up to?"

Jacquie rolled her eyes, stood from her chair, and walked past her husband to join me in the hallway. She waved him off and beckoned me to follow her to a room they used as an office.

"Larry" — she snickered — "that is very thoughtful, and I love your get up. But you should've called. You've interrupted an important meeting. Maybe read the book until it's time for small group to start."

She gave me a much-needed hug and left to join her guests, closing the door behind her.

I leafed through *Book Two of the Chuckwagon of Desire Series,* but I couldn't get into it. I had too many visions of what Heather and Sven were up to in their bedroom back in our condo. Also, I tried hard to eavesdrop on the conversation going on in the Browns' living room, but I couldn't make out any details. Eventually, the familiar chatter from my church-mates filled the air, so I ventured out into the living room. The usual small-group gang was there, and they were bantering with the strangers. They all erupted in laughter when they saw me.

Crap! I'm still wearing my cowboy hat!

Jacquie smiled and enveloped me in a warm embrace. "Howdy, partner. Don't let them tease you, my big cowboy."

"Larry, brother," Vaughn said with harsh tone. He stood out of his chair and advanced forward.

There's that look Vaughn gave me earlier.

Jacquie glared at her husband.

He sighed. "Okay, look. I snuck in a quick chat with Jacquie before everyone arrived." He lowered his voice so only the three of us could hear. "She explained things…"

"And…" filled in Jacquie.

"I'm sorry for getting mad earlier," Vaughn grumbled. He lifted his eyes to my oven. "Hey what's that thing you brought?"

"Oh, this thing is called the *Bärbar Ugn*. It's supposed to make meatballs. Jacquie, did you pick up the ingredients I asked for?"

"I'm sorry, Larry," said Jacquie. "There's been a change of plans for dinner."

"Yeah, we're feasting!" said Vaughn "We called this special meeting because we've got a huge announcement!"

After Vaughn's bad attitude—and pissed after lugging the *Bärbar Ugn* over to their home for no reason—I didn't feel like listening to anything he wanted to say.

I sulked in a corner chair, thinking about my quagmire of a love life. I refused to help myself to the food set on the table by my Jacquie.

"Awwww," she said bringing a plateful after everyone served themselves. She sat next to me and wrapped her arm around my shoulder. "Does Larry have the sulkies? You must try this out." She handed me the plate. "It's my mama's recipe."

I removed my cowboy hat and took the meal from her. "Well, I really wanted to speak to you about Schnook—"

"Everyone," Vaughn said cutting me off. "We won't be studying the Word tonight. Because we have so much to be thankful for, I figured we'd celebrate." Vaughn left for the kitchen and returned with two large bottles of champagne.

"We have some really big news! Guess what? Tampa Bay wants me to play football for them! I'm going to the States! All our dreams and prayers have been answered!" Vaughn jumped from his chair making the room shake when his feet crashed to the floor. He introduced the strangers as his agents.

Everyone but me applauded, and Jacquie didn't show much enthusiasm. Her arm around my shoulder went limp.

Vaughn continued when the clapping settled. "This will have an impact on where we live. So, we now solicit your prayers for our future decisions. Jacquie's family lives here. Though they are a huge blessing to us, she doesn't want to leave them, even though this is our opportunity of a lifetime."

Jacquie glanced over to me. Her sad eyes projected she didn't want to move. I didn't want her to, either.

Vaughn continued. "You won't be seeing me much in the coming weeks 'cause I'll be joining my new team in November. If I impress them with my play, I might be offered that multi-million-dollar contract we've always dreamed about. God is good."

God never granted me money for being my school's chess champion. I could've beaten anybody.

"I have some additional news, equally exciting," Vaughn added with a lilt in his booming voice. Everyone perked to attention. "Jacquie and I are expecting a baby! We've been so richly blessed. Football *and* a baby! What more could a man ask for?"

A faithful wife?

A tear formed in my eye, but I put my emotions aside and turned to hug Jacquie in her chair. I couldn't be happier for her knowing that her dream came true. She smiled, but not with the usual radiance. I expected her to bounce off the ceiling with such fantastic news.

"The baby is due in March," Jacquie said to the group. Her voice lacked the vigour of her husband's. She paused and a tear rolled down her cheek. "He'll be born here before we leave."

"I can't wait to be a father," said Vaughn. "I plan to spend every minute possible with my boy and teach him football!"

We all drank in celebration, though the drink had a bittersweet taste.

This group was more than a social circle. It was my extended family. They were an odd and eclectic lot, but they revered my superior intellect, and I loved my Jacquie. And the leaders will be leaving.

Funny. Jacquie and I were both left alone while our spouses sought their lifelong dreams and desires.

The days leading up to Sven and Heather's departure in October were brutal. Most nights, I'd lay awake in bed, staring at the ceiling, trying to listen to Little Larry oohing at his mobile. It was impossible. All I heard in the condo was the perpetual racket of Sven going "EEEeEEEeEEeEEEeEEEeEEE...Uggggh" accompanied by Heather moaning and egging him on. It made me wonder if that was what marital sex was really like, but their racket made me crave peace from their wild antics. I finally got it.

Sven and Heather hit the road that fall. They had planned to visit many cities during a long and busy trip across Canada—all to develop the promotional campaign for their little oven. They had to coordinate studio times, attend huge events, and set up booths for people to sample the *Bärbar Ugn's* meatballs. Camera crews traveled with them capturing everything, including interviews with everyone they met.

I hoped Sven would get punched by someone he greets with a "European kiss" along the way. Maybe they could knock his block back to Copenhagen,

or wherever he's from.
   Didn't happen.
   And the Viking and the Maiden left me alone, again.

Chapter Ten
Ping-pong Hero
October - December 1989

My friend, Reginald Windsor-Perkins, came to Canada from London in the mid-sixties. He loved the country so much, he stayed and completed his university degree in Vancouver, then found permanent work at the Hospice of Good Hope. Every small group session, he'd mention "his" great achievements at the shelter and pestered me to volunteer. I sort of connected with his pompous ways, and we spoke often about singing and church history. Reginald would've made a fine Anglican, and it didn't surprise me that he was raised one.

Impressed by the idea of the *Bärbar Ugn*, he wanted me to show his staff at the men's shelter how it could be used to prepare dinner. Not having anything better to do with my time, I agreed to visit.

"Super-duper!" he said. "Let me know what you need, and we'll see you Friday."

The hospice was situated near the harbour beyond Gastown. The street was laced with older buildings, which, by comparison to the city core, looked dated. The Friday night gang hung around the shelter's front door. Many were smoking and chatting; a few younger ones were kicking around a bean bag. They were performing some impressive tricks, all while keeping the ball-sack from hitting the ground. *I could do better.*

The smallest lad spotted me staring. "Hey old man, how's your freestyle?"

Old? I'm in my mid-twenties! I'll show him!

With *Bärbar Ugn* in hand, I raised my leg in the air without problem. The bean bag landed square on my foot. I flicked my ankle upward, but the sack must've been of inferior quality—it dribbled off my toes and hit the ground.

"Looks like you need some practice, old man."

Before I could blast an insult at the brat, Reginald emerged from the building dressed in his usual tie and blazer.

"Ah, there you are. Don't mind this cheeky monkey. Everyone's 'old man' to him. Is that the *Bärbar Ugn*? What a clever looking device. Come, follow me."

Reginald led me through the building's doors. The foyer reminded me of one of those schools that hadn't seen a drop of paint since the early 1950s. The yucky green stucco walls gave a woodsy feel, and the dark hardwood floors creaked with each step as we walked down the hall.

We entered a cafeteria not much newer than the entrance. The white linoleum floors reflected the bright florescent lighting, and long tables were set up with chairs on either side. A buffet backed on to a kitchen where I left my little oven before continuing our tour.

We strolled through the cafeteria to a recreation room. A few people were sitting on worn-out furniture, watching a small TV in the corner. Two men were playing ping-pong on the opposite side. I ached to join them—and Reginald noticed.

"One of my wealthier acquaintances donated this ace table a couple of weeks ago. Been used non-stop," he said. "Your timing is good. We're having a cracking tournament tonight!"

"Woah-ho! No one will beat me!"

"We'll see. Some of these lads are pretty good."

A stairwell behind the table led to the top floor and living quarters. The huge room fitted about fifty cots, neatly arranged in rows. It smelled musky and reminded me of a gym locker.

"What a hovel!" I said. "You should see my condo! I have granite counter-tops!"

"This place was in even worse shape before I arrived," Reginald whispered, beckoning me to lower my voice. He pointed to a man asleep in the distance. "This is home for many. You might've guessed by how run down the facility is that we don't have much money. We manage with what we have."

Reginald explained the hospice's fascinating program which "he" implemented. His program took around six weeks to help homeless men find employment and housing. According to Reginald, the shelter had transformed many lives.

Even though some men fell back on hard times, it didn't matter. The hospice would accept them back unconditionally and would repeat the process again. There were residents who'd been in and out of the system for years.

I checked out some single rooms used by permanent staff before returning to the kitchen via another stairwell. A team of cooks huddled around my tiny oven. One was reading the instructions while another prepared the ingredients.

"This will be your station," said Reginald. He motioned to one of the kitchen staff, who fitted me with an apron. "You will stand here and serve your meatballs. In the meantime, go to the back and help the others."

How does this place pass health inspections?

The kitchen looked like a bomb hit it. A cheap metallic island consumed most of the floor space in the small rectangular room. Appliances fit underneath it, and a counter with sinks spanned the width of the far wall. Two men were busy chopping vegetables, placing them in a large aluminum serving tray. I heard a toilet flush, and a third joined us from the bathroom on the far side. *Did he wash his hands?*

"You're the new guy?" he asked. Before I could answer, he flung me a hair net. "Must wear these in the food prep area. For health reasons."

I resented the idea of putting up my mullet in that hideous headwear, but I didn't argue. The man showed me how to chop lettuce and left me to it.

I was bored, going through the same motions repeatedly. Reginald had explained they were a tiny operation, maybe serving fifty people per meal on a busy day. They didn't feed everyone, only those who registered seeking a life off the streets. Still, couldn't imagine chopping lettuce all the time like these folks do.

Is that a cockroach crawling on the floor?

A couple of volunteers manned the *Bärbar Ugn*. They oohed and aaahed while the magic machine rolled the meat after mixing everything together. By the time I finished lettuce duty, the little oven crapped out over 150 meatballs.

One of the cooks placed them in a chaffing dish, and I followed him to the dining area, hauling the salad. We both dropped the food in the buffet.

"Ah, excellent, Larry," said Reginald. He was talking to a staff member. He clapped his hands. "Stations everyone!" He gave me a ladle to serve the meatballs.

Our diners formed a queue at the far side of the bar. I served everyone while singing a rousing chorus of "Roll out the Barrel." My energy and song kept the line moving. They were an eclectic lot. Some were social and wanted to chat. Others didn't seem to have a clue where they were.

A peace symbol flashed in front of my face while I scooped out a serving. A familiar man with coke-bottle glasses and long grey beard stood in front of me.

"Peter?"

"Those look yummy!" he answered while I served him a fresh spoonful of meatballs. "This place has great grub!"

Peter found a seat in the dining area opposite another man who had been playing ping-pong. "This is the best meal I've eaten in days, man. Sure beats those brutal tuna casserole Tuesdays!" A couple of hear-hear's echoed in agreement.

I scooped my ladle into the serving tray and sampled a meatball for myself. It tasted okay. *Are Swedish meatballs supposed to be crunchy?* I opened the little oven's drawer.

"What's all this stuff mixed in with the meat?" A golden powder piled high in the tray.

My "sous-chef" wearing a white apron responded. "That? I thought it needed a bit of zip. I added a dash of salt."

"You call that mountain a dash? It's not salt. It's orange." I licked my finger, dipped it in the powder, and sampled it. "Tastes sweet to me."

"Did I add a corn flake cereal instead of salt? Oh well. Old habit. It's my mom's recipe. Gives it texture."

I practically threw up. "Don't do that again." I served the next person but made a mental note to tell Sven to include some Frootie-ooties in his recipe.

When all the gang settled with their dinners, I grabbed a plateful of food and joined Peter. Peter's friend left for the recreation room and started a ping-pong game.

"You know, this place is a great deal, man," Peter said eating away. "I earn some cash peddling my crafts in the streets, then come here for six weeks. They find me a home and a job. I try the job, I hate the job, go back on the streets for a few days, then come back here."

Wait, you have a ton of cash from your business, "spreading the love."

"You don't have to," I protested.

"True. But I live off the land, man. My credo." Peter wiped his mouth with a napkin. "Brother, these balls are amazing! What's the secret?"

"Can't say for sure, it's Sven's recipe."

"Sven? Who's that, man?"

Never having an opportunity to share my life with Peter while working the street, I went on to tell him about my disappointing wedding, and how my spouse and the interloper left me alone for months.

"Well, she still wants me around, and I do love her," I concluded, batting a meatball with a fork.

"You really need to get out of this sham of a marriage, brother." He scooped the remnants of his meal off his plate. "In my commune, back in the day in San Francisco, if we felt like making love, we made love. If you wanted to live with someone, you just did, man."

"You might be right." I stared at my now empty plate. "I'm sort of dating someone now. My new girlfriend is beyond hot. She, not Heather, might end up being the one for me anyway." *Well, maybe Jacquie and I are not quite dating...*

"Brother, I'm with you. Go and get down with this chick. Sounds like a new era is in front of you. Open the door and see the light on the other side. Time to move on."

"Look," ping-pong man bellowed from the other room. "This meat turd actually does bounce!" A meatball flew from the other room into the caf, smooshing into the ground.

"Stephen…don't ever do that again! Last warning!" yelled Reginald in the distance.

"Oh," I said to Peter, "not that easy to move on. See, my new girlfriend is married, and she's expecting her first baby. Anyway, I do have some morals."

I continued sharing my life story with him. Peter appeared captivated, so much so he had to leave to get more food, saying he needed to stock up on energy to focus on my every word. He grunted in frustration when he noticed all the meatballs were gone and helped himself to some bread and veggies. Before he returned to the table, Reginald stood in front of the cafeteria to address the group.

"The ping-pong tournament will start in fifteen minutes. Please sign your name on the sheet on the wall if you want to join the fun."

The second Reginald stopped talking, I bolted and placed my name on the list. *First of course!* I rushed in the recreation room and commenced some pre-ping-pong tournament warmups—finger stretches, wrist curls, and windmills.

"First game of the night," Reginald announced, "Larry against Stephen. Good luck gentlemen."

The meatball-mushing man will taste my wrath for defiling my cooking!

I finished my stretching. *Why isn't anyone coming to watch us play?* The few men in the recreation room didn't budge and remained huddled around the TV. Others were finishing their dinners and sipping coffee in the cafeteria. Reginald was the only onlooker. I wasn't discouraged. *The crowds will come once I start doing my fancy spin shots and smashes!* My opponent took his place at the other end of the table.

"I'm gonna kick your ass for forcing those shitballs on us!" Stephen said.

I served first. Stephen wound up and took a huge swing at the ball, and missed, whiffing his paddle through air.

"Fuck this game." He threw his racket on the table with a bang and bolted out of the room.

"I win!" I screamed. "Who dares face the 'ping-pong-inater' next?" I waved my paddle over my head in victory.

"Looks like you and Stephen were the only ones to sign up tonight," said Reginald. "Everyone, let's congratulate the Hospice of Good Hope's new ping-pong champion, Larry Johnstone." Reginald led the applause, though I only heard him clapping.

I sang a rousing chorus of "He's a Jolly Good Fellow" with my powerful voice. The men watching TV turned around, and looked like they might want to join in the singing, but they stared at me with furrowed eyebrows and blank expressions on their faces. I was surprised they didn't join in. Maybe next time.

I was also shocked no one awarded me a trophy.

"That was excellent Larry, and so was the meal," said Reginald when I was leaving. "If you ever felt the call to serve us here at the hospice, you'll always be welcome."

I felt badly for these guys. The least I could do is pick up their morale by feeding and singing to them. I returned to the cafeteria with Reginald. Many people were still hanging around.

"I'd love to come back, but Reginald, I can't do lettuce duty. Could I just serve the food and play ping-pong?"

Reginald nodded, while I glanced around the room.

"Reginald, you see that hippie-like man?" I asked.

Peter was laughing loudly, chatting to a few fellows.

"You mean Peter?

"You know him?"

"I do," replied Reginald, "he's been in and out of our residence for years."

"Then you know he's taking advantage of the system," I said.

"Yes, Larry. Peter is a bit of a dodgy character. But remember. We're like a hospital, dealing with lots of types of people. For every Peter, there's a hundred who need legitimate help. Everyone, including the Peters, have various needs. We don't know what Peter's motivations are for doing what he does…but we don't judge here. We welcome all with open arms."

I could nurture and care for people here! Offering my invaluable and irreplaceable service to the hospice became part of my new routine in Vancouver.

"EEEeEEEeEEeEEEeEEEeEEE. Ugh." Silence.

Only forty-five minutes this time.

Sven and Heather were home in early November and resumed their nightly carnal routine. My blood boiled over. They'd been back two nights and had intercourse seven times. Thank goodness the in-house porn ends tomorrow. Their flight out east leaves early in the morning.

Their racket woke me from my slumber again at 5:30 a.m. I wished they'd set scheduled times for getting romantic so I could plan my sleep better. It never happened at the same time twice. In fact, they had mated right after my splendid Beef Wellington "welcome home" dinner. Sven didn't care much for it—but despite his complaining, he had mentioned the bacon made him horny. My Honey-Bunny had paid me a rare compliment saying my meal was "tolerable" before joining Sven in his bedroom.

This is unreal. Heather married me, a shagging dynamo, and we haven't even slept in the same bed since we wed. I wish I had married someone like Jacquie. We'd be so happy together.

Remembering how the Browns were expecting their first baby, I recalled my desire to produce a second child with Heather. *I am the man. I am the husband. Enough of this nonsense.*

Before I could get out of bed, a light flooded my room. Heather entered, wearing a bright red floor-length nightie. Little Larry began to cry from his crib. He calmed as soon as Heather held him.

"Morning," I said coolly.

No response. Heather rocked her baby back and forth. After a minute, she said, "I should've been here more for him. I missed a special bonding moment with my Rupie-Bear."

She regrets leaving our child behind during her trips! Maybe there's hope for our marriage!

I jumped out of bed and walked behind her. I placed my hands on her shoulders and stared at Little Larry. He rested contently cradled in his mother's arms. I had dreamt of moments like this since I received my spiritual call to have a wife and children.

Here's to a fresh start!

Heather looked up at me, bleary-eyed.

I reciprocated, using every fibre of my being to push aside her recent transgressions from my mind.

"We're going to have a second child!" she said.

I couldn't believe my ears. *I knew she'd come around and want one with me!* I brushed up closer to her, wrapping my arms around her waist.

Heather gasped and stepped away.

"We can start now," I said. "I guarantee, Schnookums, you'll be carrying a baby right after we do it for the first time as man and wife."

"No," she said.

"What do you mean, no?" My suppressed temper thermometer began to rise. "You said we're going to have a second child. So, why wait? You'll be leaving again soon."

The sobering reality hit me like a semi-truck, and my wife validated it.

"No, Honey-Bunny. You don't understand. I think I'm pregnant. I'm late," she stared at our baby. "I guess our family is growing."

I paused stunned. "With Sven's baby?" This wasn't supposed to be this way. *I'm supposed to be the father here!*

Before I could erupt, Sven walked in, half-naked. My eyes zoned into his perfectly sculpted midriff. He raised his muscular arms and locked his fingers behind his neck, then shook his hips while manipulating his abs like some belly-dancers I'd seen on TV.

"You like what you see, househusband?" he mocked.

You cheeky interloping bastard!

I curled my hand in a fist and wound up far back, then let my punch go with all my might. He stepped back, and my momentum swooshed by him throwing me to the ground with a resounding thud.

"Woah, woah, woah. What's going on here?" said Sven. He picked me up and held me in a bear hug. My arms were trapped.

"I just told Larry I'm pregnant," said Heather.

"You're what?" Sven's tone changed from levity to stern. "Two? We can barely manage one with our schedule. Does he know it's mi..."

Heather shook her head. Her eyes were so wide open, I thought they'd pop right out.

I struggled a bit under Sven's grip but couldn't budge.

"Please don't be angry," said Heather to Sven. "I need you."

"Why would you think I'm angry, *Sötnos*? You know I need you, too. I just don't need that." He pointed to Heather's tummy. "I'm just surprised you told Larry first."

"I was having a moment with my son, and it slipped out. Larry makes a great father, doesn't he?"

Sven let me go. His ice blue eyes shot into mine like a laser. There was a strength, then surprisingly, a vulnerability expressed through them. He placed his hands on my shoulders.

"Larry, Larry, Larry, this is amazing news. A new child will enter this world."

"Your child, dickwad."

"Tut, tut. Mind your tone." Sven didn't seem affected by my anger. "Larry, I have the highest respect for you. You know that? And you strike me as an ambitious and enterprising person, yes?"

I thought about my achievements since arriving in Vancouver. I cared for a child. I taught a church group in-depth knowledge of their faith. I helped expand Peter's love business. And I'm a ping-pong champ at the shelter.

I nodded.

"I can also tell you are passionate about family, Larry. Doesn't surprise me you are destined to father children. Your care for Lars is proof, no? Heather's right. You've done such a great job with him."

The baby laughed in Heather's arms.

"Larry, you're clearly someone of high intelligence. You can see, here, that this little hiccup has a great opportunity for you."

"What are you smoking?" I said. "Opportunity? For me? In this? Heather's my wife!"

"Well, you can be the father to more than one child."

One of many for Larry Nation?

Thinking of the prophecy cooled me down a bit. I said, "I can father many children. But there is a difference between fathering a child and being a father to one."

Sven raised his right hand behind his head and flexed his bicep.

"Larry, anyone can make a woman pregnant. Sperm is just that. Sperm. Whether it's mine, yours, the man who lives down the street. It doesn't matter. I mean, hell, I just did it without really trying."

You've been trying hard this week...

Sven walked the width of the narrow room, like he was on a stage giving a lecture. "No Larry." He pointed to me. "It takes a real man to be a father. I humbly admit" — he placed both hands flat on his chest — "I don't have that in me. Nor did my father." He began pacing again. "Besides, I have too many ventures planned to be bogged down with kids. You see, we need you more than ever. And I'm sure if you look deep down into your soul, you'll see it, too."

I needed more time to mull this over. *Could I be a father to someone else's child?*

"This condo is a pretty nice place too, no?"

He had me there… "The shower. I love the shower."

He slapped my arm, and I winced from the pain.

"He-he. So do I. Then it's settled."

Heather gave me a hug, though I didn't reciprocate.

"Svenny says that with a bit of training, I might be on TV with him! That is even better than anything I could've dreamed for. We will both be household names across Canada!"

Is this how Heather becomes the voice of a generation? Is this how I father a nation—through Sven? No, certainly this wasn't what the prophecy meant.

Or was it?

"*Sötnos*, we must rush, or we'll miss our flight. Larry, I'll give you some more money for free coffee. Like that?"

I didn't respond.

The enterprising couple left, and I crashed on the couch and turned on the big screen TV. Of late, there was nothing but infomercials on, which pissed me off. I turned it off and strolled out on the balcony to take in the view. A taxi pulled onto the street driving my Schnookums and Sven away on their escapade.

Little Larry began to cry. I went back into the condo, and I sang some Elvis while feeding him. My routine resumed like nothing had happened.

I heard nothing from Sven and Schnookums until Christmas Eve, over a month later. They dropped in to celebrate a "family" dinner. We sat silent around the table eating turkey. Of course, I had prepared an excellent meal, but frankly, I didn't know why I had bothered. Maybe I did it for my son. He loved the Christmas spirit with my singing carols and trimming the tree. He'd stare in awe at the coloured lights for hours leading up to my Schnookums' return.

Sven gave me a stuffed beaver he picked up in Toronto for Christmas. I hadn't bought either of them a gift.

"Larry," said Sven, "we're only here for the evening. We're off to Winnipeg tomorrow to celebrate the holidays with my family."

I didn't budge and took a few more bites of my dinner.

"That's nice," I said, "I didn't know you had any family."

"Well, they're really business associates. Close to me, like family, in a professional sort of way. Anyway, we'd like to take Lars along for the ride."

"Isn't this great, Honey-Bear?" said Heather. "Svenny wants to take the baby."

"Does he, now." I refused to make eye contact with the couple. *Sven will hate caring for the baby. Maybe he will dump Heather, and this will all end.*

"You can stay in the condo if you like," Sven continued. "My associates are key distributors for the oven and have television contacts. They are important for realizing our dreams and have deep rooted family values. Seeing such a cute child would only help our cause."

"Besides, Larry," said Heather, "these people are just part of our business strategy. This is only for a little trip. We still need you here to fulfill your responsibilities."

My blood began to boil. Heather placed her hand on my forearm. I read her eyes. They pleaded with me to let her take the baby. I couldn't say no to my Schnookums, especially knowing this Sven chapter should soon be over.

"Anyway," said Sven, "I'm sure you need a break from caring for the child and have some special 'Larry time.'"

Not doing this for you, jerk.

The next morning, they left me again. I didn't bother asking how "baby number two" was coming along. I didn't care. The more I thought of being "father" to another man's child, the more I wanted out of this.

Something had to change. Within a week of their departure, the condo took a new life, or should I say, lack thereof. The quiet drove me loopy. I needed friends more than ever, and the hospice offered me a fresh community.

Sven's and Heather's "short" trip lasted a few months. They did send me pictures of their various stopovers, mostly with people I didn't know. I had to admit, there were some cool photos with my baby being held by some TV celebrities and even a famous politician. I did feel sort of proud at that.

As for me? I dreamt of a perfect marriage—with someone like my Jacquie. Despite that, for whatever silly reason, I couldn't let go of my Schnookums. She was my first and only woman who had considered a life with me. I clung on to our love, our vows, and the hope that Sven would leave the picture, and my marriage would return to normal.

And even after a few months of my new routine with the shelter and no baby,

I still owned the ping-pong champ crown at the Hospice of Good Hope.

Chapter Eleven
A New Life

Rain. *Rain. Rain.* The novelty of the Rockies had worn off during the cold, damp winter. Only one more month to April, signaling the end of my first year in Vancouver. I knew in advance my anniversary gift—more precipitation.

I'd been spending my free time at the hospice. In fact, it became my home away from home. It completed my new normal: most mornings with Jacquie; selling for Peter, which some days included a nice train ride to a university east of the city; and then helping serve meals and singing at the shelter.

Jacquie and I grew closer, having many "heart to heart" conversations. She's such a wonderful woman. I had loved watching her change while the baby grew inside her—a process I missed and longed to have shared with Heather. Through Jacquie, I witnessed the evolution of maternal beauty with each passing month. Now in the final days of her pregnancy, her excitement—along with desire to "offload" the baby—peaked.

Vaughn had signed his dream pro football contract, and the two planned their move to Florida during the following summer. It must've been a tough decision for them, given how Jacquie didn't want to leave Vancouver. She even mentioned once during small group that she didn't want to abandon me—her "dearest friend." It prompted a curious expression from Vaughn.

I never mentioned my pot habit to Jacquie, though I suspected she knew. We spent too much time together for her not to be aware of my *eau de marie-jo* odour. Anyway, she never asked.

Jacquie was, though, curious about Peter. I talked often of my friend, skipping some details, like the pot selling. I kept spinning that we sold touristy trinkets to "spread the love." It's a partial truth, but Peter's jewels were hardly the hit of his catalogue.

She insisted I invite Peter over for tea one afternoon, the second week of March. I couldn't imagine Peter being the "tea drinking" type, but I extended the invitation to him.

"Thank your woman for me, brother. I never get asked over to people's homes."

We planned to visit the Browns' at 3 p.m. the next day, a few hours before small group. Loving any excuse to spend bonus time with Jacquie, I arrived early to tell her more about Peter and explained how I'm "witnessing" to him. Arriving a little late, Peter rang the bell, and Jacquie greeted him at the door. Vaughn wasn't around, doing some business with a real-estate agent.

"Wow, man, you're far out," Peter glowed when he set eyes on Jacquie. "What a breathtaking beauty. If I were fifteen years younger, I'd seduce you!"

I had no idea how Jacquie kept from erupting. Ever gracious, she looked at me from the corner of her eye and took a deep breath. "Oooookay, thanks. Come in."

"What a beautiful pad, man. You guys live like royalty." Peter walked in, dropping his bag on the floor in the middle of the living room. He turned his head around soaking in the environment. "Mind if I brew the tea? I have a special recipe which I'm sure you'll love. May I ask, how long you've been expecting?"

"I'm thirty-seven weeks pregnant."

"Cool," said Peter. "Too bad we didn't meet several months ago, man. My tea guarantees a cure for morning sickness and other health issues. Just need butter, man. You got?"

"Of course I have butter," said Jacquie coolly. She gave me the side eye again. "What do you need it for?"

Peter ignored the question. "Larry, would you mind boilin' about five cups of water?"

He entered the kitchen with a plastic bag containing a ground herb, and carefully measured some, spooned some butter, and mixed them in the pot of water. A familiar smell filled the air, and I had a Pavlovian urge to eat potato chips.

Jacquie noticed, too, and exploded. "What on earth are you doing to my house? Are you boiling drugs?"

"Best tea in the world, man. With the butter, it tastes like a latte."

"No drugs in my house or around my baby!" she yelled wrapping her arms around her stomach. "You should know better!"

"Hey, relax, man. I promise this'll be the best thing you've had to drink in months. It'll take the edge off you, too."

I recalled Vaughn telling me about his dragon tattoo on the plane with his wife's name written under it. I had never seen Jacquie angry before, but Vaughn's dragon woke in a fury, and she breathed fire.

"What makes you think you can walk your nasty self into my Christian home, and pollute it with your rancid tea? And you, Larry…" She waved her finger at me.

"But doesn't Peter's tea smell great?" I said, anxious to have a cup.

"No, smells just like him," snarled Jacquie. "You, Larry, you should know better than to bring such people here when I'm expecting a child!" She faced Peter. "I'm giving you thirty seconds to get out of my house!" She pointed to her door. "Starting now!"

Peter didn't move. "But it's so nice here. I never get to visit people's homes." He poured himself a cup of tea, returned to the living room, and slumped on the couch.

Jacquie continued to berate Peter. He listened while calmly sipping his drink. I poured myself a cup of his concoction and sampled it. *Tasty.* Peter's right. Just like a latte.

A knock on the door rapped the "shave and a haircut" beat, and Vaughn walked into the apartment. He sensed his wife's anger. "Jacquie, love, what's going on? And why does it smell like weed?"

"This man is one of Larry's friends. You know what he did? He walked into our house and talked of seducing me! I gave this burned out, drop-out, drugged up, tree-loving hippie thirty seconds to leave, and you know what he did? He crashed on your couch and stunk up our home. If he doesn't exit fast, I'm gonna—"

Vaughn read his wife and yelled at full volume. "If you don't leave now, my brother, my foot is gonna have a deep conversation with your upper intestine."

Jacquie's words would've caused most men to panic. The huge Vaughn's made the room tremble. Peter moved with an alacrity I didn't think possible for him.

"All right, all right, man, I'll go." Peter stood, grabbing his bag from the floor. Before leaving, he turned, faced us, and placed both his hands together. "Namaste," he said, bowed, and left. Vaughn slammed the door behind him and hugged his wife.

"Guys," I said, "I understand Peter is eccentric, but you must have a sip of his tea. It ain't half bad!" I held out my cup for Jacquie.

"Larry," Vaughn said angrily, "you of all people should know I can't go any-where near drugs now that I signed my new football contract. Even having the smell of the stuff on me could cause me trouble. It's gotta be thrown out. And NOW! And not in MY house! LEAVE!" Vaughn stormed off to the washroom.

I turned to Jacquie. "You sure you don't want to try it? I get why Vaughn won't, but you complained about cramps. Maybe this could help."

Jacquie rolled her eyes. "Larry, I can't believe you would even say that. Do what my man says. Leave. NOW!"

I don't understand why she'd be mad at me. Besides…Peter only wanted to help.

But I left.

I couldn't imagine Jacquie staying angry at me about Peter for long, so I showed up for small group at the Browns', as usual, a few hours later and rang their bell.

Odd. No answer.

I rang it several more times.

Still no answer.

Two days later, Heather called in the morning to announce she'd be back home with Little Larry later that night…without Sven. My heart leapt with excitement. *Did she see the truth about Sven and dump the bastard?* It started my day on the right foot. I left my building and enjoyed the breezy air.

I had to leave the condo door unlocked because I had lost my housekeys at some point that week. But with such a good start to my morning, I didn't fret. I rarely locked the door, anyway, so security was never an issue.

After a delicious cup of coffee, I enjoyed some fresh herbs from Peter; sold dope to university brats; and rushed over to the hospice to prepare to win another ping-pong tournament.

When I arrived at the shelter later that afternoon, I kept checking the time, anxious to return to the Kits to see my wife and my child. They were not due to return for several hours, so I tried to focus on the task at hand and began my stretching routine for the upcoming tournament. Reginald walked into the recreation room, catching me in a middle of a knee bend.

"Ah there you are, I haven't seen you in days. Getting ready for another match? It's still a little early for the tournament…do you think there will be any takers tonight?"

"Oh, there will be. Hey, what happened to small group this week? No one was at the Browns'. Where was everyone?" I hadn't seen Jacquie, or Vaughn for that matter, since the "Peter incident." I even popped over a few times, like I usually did, and no one answered the door!

"How peculiar. I wondered what happened to you," answered Reginald. "We were all at the Purple Pigeons for dinner. One of the ladies in the group secretly organized a surprise baby shower for Jacquie. It all came together quick this week. Vaughn was in on it. I thought he was going to tell you."

Did Vaughn forget? I for sure would have remembered Jacquie's shower. I would've loved to have seen her open presents filled with some cute one-piece clothing and baby booties for the soon-to-be newborn. Miffed at missing out on the fun, I assumed my station at the buffet to serve the now traditional Friday night meatballs.

The Browns couldn't possibly be mad at me for what Peter did?

Peter, as usual, showed up for the meatballs and went to his seat. I joined him after everyone received their meals.

"Larry, brother, I felt terribly for upsetting your girl, man."

"I should've warned you. She gets mad fast but cools quick." I chuckled, though I couldn't be certain what I said was true. I had never seen Jacquie angry before. "No harm done."

"Well, I still felt awful, so I went back to their place first thing the next morning to apologize. The big man opened the door—you know the one, man—the guy who booted me out? Anyway, I left an apology for him to pass to your girlfriend. I forgot her name. He's a scary dude. Is that her brother?"

"No, Peter, that's her *husband*. Don't you remember? I told you. She's married."

"No."

"Yes, I'm sure I did." Worried, I propped my elbows on the table and leaned my head into my hands.

"No, I'm sure you didn't," he responded back.

"Damn it!" I slammed my hands on the table. *How could he forget?* "What did you tell him?"

Peter didn't flinch. "Oh, I only told him to say I think Larry's girlfriend lives there, and that I'm sorry for upsetting her. I also mentioned that I wanted to assure her I'd never bring drugs in the house again if ever invited back."

Oh...no! Is this why the Browns didn't want to see me?

Reginald entered the cafeteria. "Looks like Larry's the only one who signed up for the ping-pong tournament again! Smashing, Larry! Your unbeaten streak survives another week!"

I couldn't revel in my victory. My mind was elsewhere...the uncertainty about the Browns combined with Schnookums coming home later without Sven! *Did I leave the house in spic and span condition?* I wanted her in the best mood possible! I set to leaving.

Reginald stopped me in the hallway while I put my coat on. "By the way, I just received a call from Vaughn."

"What?"

"Can you believe it? They rushed Jacquie to the hospital this morning—"

My heart accelerated in excitement. *Ah...maybe that's why they didn't answer when I knocked! They weren't home!*

"—I anticipate the baby'll be born soon, if not already. It's earlier than expected! Vaughn was soliciting our prayers."

He's soliciting my prayers? Maybe he is not mad at me!

Schnookums is coming home, and my best friends are having a baby? What a wonderful day!

The evening bus arrived forty-five minutes late. There'd be a bit of a hope I'd get back to the condo before Heather arrived. The place was presentable, but my Schnookums expected her home to be "hospital clean." She sometimes wore a white glove to do inspections when I first arrived in town.

The bus dropped me off, and I ran all the way home from the stop. *Why are the lights on in the living room window? For sure I turned them off.* I fumbled for my keys. *Where are they?* I dug deeper in my pockets. *Damn! I forgot. I lost them.* I tried the door, but it was locked and had no other choice but ring the doorbell. Heather opened it, holding Little Larry in her arms.

He's grown! And his hair is blonder!

"Hi Honey-Bunny." I opened my arms to embrace her.

"Someone's here to see you," Heather said, voice extra cold. She turned away curtly and walked into the hallway.

Before I could set foot in the apartment, a large man blocked my path.

"I trusted you, you son of a bitch," Vaughn said.

I opened my mouth to reply, only to eat a huge fist knocking me down to the floor. I lost time. When I regained consciousness, I rolled my tongue along my gumline, tasting blood, and noticed a large gap between my upper teeth. *My looks! My smile! What will women think of me?*

I groaned and rolled on my side. My knocked-out teeth stared at me from the floor. I stayed still. *How long have I been out?* I tried to stand, but my head spun out of control, and I could only rise to my knees. I wiped tons of blood from my mouth with the sleeve of my shirt.

Heather approached me from a chair in the living room. "Get out you filthy beast! I knew you being alone here was a bad idea, but how dare you betray our arrangement by committing adultery with that woman!"

Me committing adultery?

I sat there, quietly, on my knees. My head cleared, and Heather stood blocking my access to the apartment. She placed two books on the floor in front of me—my Bible, and the *Iliad and the Odyssey*—the only two things in my possession when I first landed in Vancouver.

"Take, and leave."

I picked up my stuff.

"Oh wait," said Heather.

I turned. *Has she changed her mood again?*

"Don't forget your smut." She threw my romance novel with the cowboy and the Black woman.

I turned around and left. Anger could hardly describe my emotion. *How dare she say I dishonoured our marriage? She's pregnant with another man's baby and wants to be married to him. And she calls me unfaithful?*

With nowhere else to go, I crashed at the Hospice of Good Hope.

Heather stormed into our Earl of Latteigh the next morning, pushing Little Larry in his stroller. She was wearing a similar form-fitting red dress she had on the day she greeted me when I arrived in Vancouver. She must've been four months pregnant by now, and yet, no sign of a potbelly. She parked herself in a chair and pulled the stroller up to the table.

"I spoke to Sven. We're getting a separation."

Did my Schnookums come to her senses and pick me over Sven?

I smiled, forgetting my upper top teeth were knocked out.

"Why are you smiling?" she asked. "You think this is good news?"

Can I forgive you for having another man's child? We still have Little Larry as ours. Maybe the new baby can live with his father.

"Frankly, yes. Sven sort of puts a damper on you and me being married." Heather's perfect form reminded me to ask about her pregnancy. "Why aren't you showing? Did something happen to the baby? Did Sven have something to do with it? Is that why you are leaving him?" I was raising my voice. People in the busy shop stopped their chatter and stared.

"No, genius. I never did get pregnant. I just missed my period." Her voice calmed. "Believe it or not, I'm an old-fashioned girl, and Sven and I cannot have you disrespecting our arrangement. Besides, Sven is taking a stronger liking to Lars. He wants to try being his father now. I don't trust it, so I still want you available, in case he changes his mind and we need a househusband again."

I erupted. I rarely exploded in front of Heather, but after the burden of last night, the months of solitude, and disrespect to our marriage, I couldn't contain myself.

"You marry me; sleep with another man; you commit to him in some hokey-pokey bathtub ceremony; you tried to have his baby; and you accuse *me* of adultery? All I give you is love! All I want is to be with you and our child! I've waited patiently for you, in a conjugal way, since I arrived in this city, and know what? I've had it! I don't want 'separation.' I want out. I'm going to take you and Sven to the cleaners with a divorce. You won't have a dime. And…I'm not the househusband. I'm *the* husband."

Proud of myself, I crossed my arms and glared at my wife. "I guarantee… you'll soon realize you'll never have anyone better than me. Love to see how long Sven changes diapers!"

Silence filled the café. You could hear a pin drop. No one ordered mochaccinos or lattes. The baristas stopped steaming milk and preparing espressos.

I am a star.

"That is not acceptable," said Heather. "I need someone around in case Sven changes his mind about Rupie-Bear. There might come a time where the novelty of having a small child will wear off. So, no. We won't divorce."

"No way." I said. My patience was exhausted. "I want that condo and some cash for all my hard work."

Heather reached into her purse.

"These are your house keys," she hissed placing the key ring around her finger. "You left them at that woman's house. That man returned them last night."

Did I leave them at Jacquie's?

"That man," she continued, "said he heard from your hippie friend that you were calling his wife your girlfriend." She twirled the keyring around her finger. "And he said you left these there to proposition her?" She caught the twirling keys and place them back in her purse. She then retrieved a thick manilla envelope and placed it on the table. She shuddered in disgust, pulling out a wad of paper from the envelope. "Remember this?"

I looked down at the thick stack and leafed through it. *Bah, just a bunch of legal mumbo jumbo.*

"This," said Heather, "is the document you signed to obtain the keys from Sven. You should remember." I shook my head. I didn't. "Well, you signed it the first day you arrived in Vancouver. I suggest you refresh your memory and read it, as well as any document you sign in the future.

"You'll see, when you're done reading, that you've no right to any of my property, or Sven's. So drop the bravado. You don't want to divorce me. Besides, like I said, we still might need a househusband." She stood up, leaving the papers and the envelope on the table. "Think about it."

I looked down at the paper and at her. "I thought about it. I will never be the househusband!"

"We'll see!"

She exited the cafe in a dramatic huff.

Business resumed in the Earl of Latteigh. I lifted the document—clearly a photocopy. It read, "Prenuptial Agreement between Larry Johnstone and Heather Mackenzie." I skimmed through the pages.

I scratched my head. *What does this mean? I didn't sign for the keys to the condo?*

She did say that Sven might leave her and needs me...there might still be hope.

I stared down at the pile of paper. *I loved you when we met. You were my "first" in so many ways. I flew over here to marry you and care for our child. I established my roots here. I've bonded with Little Larry. We've had our moments, even though they were few and far between.*

In my heart, I know Sven is a fling. I still haven't stopped loving you, my Schnookums. One day you will realize this.

"See you soon," I whispered aloud alone at my table.

I had much to be thankful for that Christmas Eve.

Reginald had taken pity on me and had offered me a permanent home and job at the Hospice of Good Hope. He assigned me the charge of program coordinator, and I continued to serve dinners to the inhabitants.

Reginald knew I'd bring positive energy to the residence. I met many people coming in and out of the doors of the shelter, and everyone loved me and the community-based programs I developed. Last month, I encouraged the Board of Directors to institute chess night. As expected, I beat everyone who played the game.

I had no idea why Vaughn had knocked me out. Was it Peter's comment about Jacquie being my girlfriend? Though I continued to attend church, the small group had fizzled after the birth of the Browns' baby. Jacquie and Vaughn moved away shortly thereafter.

And what about my Schnookums and Sven? I had no notion what got into her brain last spring about my infidelity. I never took our marriage for granted. Unlike her, I had worshiped my wife and child. Even though it had been over nine months since Schnookums left my life, I had no burning desire to build a relationship with another woman.

I needed a fresh start. Working for Peter supplemented my meagre income from the hospice, but my Earl of Latteigh habit became too expensive—especially since I had to save money to buy a denture bridge to fill the gap left in my mouth by Vaughn. I couldn't believe the con artist dentist wanted to charge me near $1,500 for an appliance! The nerve! If they knew how important I'd become, they would've given me not only the bridge-work free, but veneers too!

I struggled to ditch my caffeine addiction. It had been a too important aspect of my life. I needed a cheaper way to obtain my daily fix.

Caleb Schwarz, a Jewish man from Montreal, owned the Jumpin' Java coffee shop. The kind man had a bald head with dark hair above his ear, and when he smiled, I could never tell if he had any front teeth because his thick mustache covered his mouth. He often visited the shelter, delivering a large bag of day-old baked goods. They were mostly bagels, and even though they weren't fresh, they were the best I'd ever eaten.

"If you like those," he said with an endearing German-Yiddish accent, "you should try my pastries. My shop is only a few blocks down the street."

I loved the name, "Jumpin' Java," so I decided it was worth a visit.

Caleb ran a popular business, and the queue extended out the door. I waited in line, and by the time I arrived at the front, the store was emptier. A kind gentleman bought me a coffee, and I was blown away by the quality of the roast. I parked myself at a table and read my Bible.

I couldn't stop thinking about the intimacy of the small shop and craved a second visit. I returned the following day, and, like the first, someone else bought me a coffee.

It happened again on the third. Then the fourth. After a week, I became a fixture in the shop. I made it a point to arrive first thing in the morning, a few minutes before the crowds, to ensure I'd grab the same table, making it my "home base." Someone always bought me a drink.

I needed the caffeine because I didn't sleep much. I'd hang out late at night in the recreation room to watch TV alone. It depressed me. Great syndicated shows like the *Brady Bunch* weren't on TV anymore. Now, infomercials ruled the air.

They bemused me, at first. I mean, who on earth would seriously buy spray paint to cover male pattern baldness? Maybe some loser. But yeah, infomercials became boring fast—always the same ones on at the same time.

Reginald shook me awake Christmas morning. I had fallen asleep in front of the TV again.

"Larry, you overslept and are missing the food deliveries, hurry up. They left the stock outside."

Caleb, the kind soul that he was, purchased a special delivery this morning for our annual Christmas dinner. I had finished bringing the last of the turkeys to the kitchen, when Reginald came down to the cafeteria waving an envelope in his hand.

"I forgot to show you this. A Christmas card from Vaughn arrived yesterday. It has a nice shot of his family."

I had not heard from Jacquie or Vaughn since Schnookums gave me the boot. Reginald handed me the card—one of those studio family portraits. It was a lovely shot of Vaughn and Jacquie. Sitting on my Jacquie's lap was their baby, who I noticed had much lighter skin than his parents and shoots of copper hair. They were all wearing Santa hats.

The kitchen bustled preparing the holiday meal. Though I started a new life here at the hospice, I so wished to spend time with family again.

Part Two: Daddy Larry

1995 — 2005

Chapter Twelve
Beach Day
May 1995

1 a.m.
Another sleepless night. I slapped on the old TV at the hospice and a familiar infomercial flashed on screen. It had aired every night over the past few years and featured dancing bikini-clad women—so it still got my attention. They kicked off the show chanting a horrible rap, all out of key:

You too, can *Bärbar Ugn,*
Make some meatballs,
Eat them too
You too, can *Bärbar Ugn,*
Sweden's finest,
Here for you

They repeated it non-stop. Every time they mentioned the oven, *Bärbar Ugn* flashed on the screen, making me dizzy.

The crew had filmed footage from trains, planes, and boats while travelling across Canada. They captured people in the street sampling meatballs, testifying how the *Bärbar Ugn* transformed their lives and how they now desired to explore Swedish culture. The infomercial had predictable structure, each night featuring a different Canadian city. Tonight's was Halifax.

The dancers paved the way for Sven who took the stage. The audience went wild for him. I had to admit, it was hard not to avert my eyes from the charismatic Swedish celebrity.

He demonstrated how the meatballs were made and served the women samples on toothpicks from a tray. They seductively licked them, acting ecstatic with each nibble. He then encouraged members in the live audience to try them, receiving hugs and kisses in the process.

Like all versions of this infomercial, this nonsense was followed by a city segment; voyage clips; more bikini models; studio segments; and at precisely eight, thirteen, and twenty-eight minutes into the show, messages explained how to purchase the *Bärbar Ugn*. I never felt the urge to pick up my phone to order one.

Sven dominated the late-night airwaves—this night was no exception. I changed the channel. *Bärbar Ugn*. I changed it again. *Bärbar Ugn*. A third time. *Bärbar Ugn*. Even the American channels had them. What I'd give to watch Tony Robbins' or Tony Little's face appear on screen for infomercial variety.

The remaining seconds of Sven's show aired. At least there'd be a different infomercial in a couple minutes.

1:30 a.m.

An announcer blared over the speakers. "You wild Canadians, get ready for a huge life transformation!"

Finally, something new in late night TV hell.

"Brace yourself."

I sat tight.

"Get ready."

I moved to the edge of my seat.

"For the new, and improved, *Bärbar Ugn II*."

The hell?

I ran my hand through my hair. On the cusp of turning thirty, it didn't have the volume it once had—though still ran down to the tip of my shoulders.

The screen flashed to the new crop of dancing women wearing tight white t-shirts labelled *Bärbar Ugn II*. Clearly taken with a hand-held video camera, the image bopped up and down with their motion. After a minute, Sven emerged between them carrying a microphone.

"You thought meatballs were scrumptious with the *Bärbar Ugn*? You love the taste of Sweden? Well, now you can enjoy salmon with the amazing *Bärbar Ugn II*. It dices, it slices, and debones your fish while broiling it to perfection. Everyone loves it!"

It's the same freakin' oven...

"Ever buy fish with a fishy-fish smell? Worry no more! Press this button, and *voila*! The *Bärbar Ugn II* injects the special spice formula—sold separately—to disguise any undesired tastes." Sven gave each of his dancers a piece of fish on a toothpick, who, like the first infomercial, let out silent moans with each bite.

"I can't take this anymore!" I slammed the remote on the couch, walked over to the TV, and turned it off "old school." *What I'd give for an* Another World *rerun right now.*

Maybe a movie can settle my mind so I could sleep. I browsed through our collection of five VHS videos. I chose *Sister Act 2* and popped the tape in the machine. Only watched it three million times—*why don't we have the original?* In fact, all the movies the hospice owned were terrible sequels. I'd watched them all, including *Troll 2*. I fell asleep to a kids' choir singing "Oh Happy Day." My "happy day" ended with dreams of Sven and his dancers eating fish.

The next morning, the common shower pissed out lukewarm water like an elderly man with severe prostate issues. How I longed for the luxury jets of that Kits' whirlpool!

I missed my former life and wife. I'd been waiting over five years for Sven to drop Heather. It hadn't happened yet. I was convinced she and Little Larry would eventually come back to me—the better man, her steadfast rock.

Since she left, I'd spend most mornings sitting in a discrete spot across the road from my old condo in the Kits, dreaming of a life with Heather and Little Larry with Sven out of the picture. I hoped to catch a glimpse of Schnookums and my son entering or leaving the building, but they were never around. Didn't surprise me with their busy schedule. In fact, she was so busy, she never contacted me. I'd heard she spent most of her time now with Sven in Toronto.

Bored and feeling bluer than usual, I quit my daydreaming and returned to Jumpin' Java. Entering my thirtieth year of life and still married, I hadn't dated anyone since Heather booted me out. I had struggled. Part of me clung to a fantasy of being with her, another wanted to move on. Regardless, I had no clue how my prophecy would be fulfilled without a woman in my life.

Despite my not seeing anyone, most people still considered me a playboy, playing the field. At least, that's what I tell my friends. It was important to maintain my stud image, for they had depended on me for dating advice.

Crap. There's Jumpin' Java's new waitress, Dana, waving at me from behind the counter again. She's proof women still found me irresistible. I averted her gaze, picked up a newspaper, and pretended to read at my table.

Dana was hired a few weeks ago. She ogled me all the time like a starving dog staring at a piece of steak. At six foot tall, I'd hardly call her a bombshell, but she did have expressive brown eyes. She had gangly limbs, a largish nose, and long brown hair with burnt ends. She flirted with me all the time, but my head and heart were elsewhere. She'd never take a hint.

Dana skipped over.

"Hi Larry, rare I see you twice in the same morning!" she said cheerfully, placing a coffee in front of me.

"Yes." I looked down at my drink, then my watch. "Ten minutes. Bit slow, don't you think?" I returned to my paper.

"Going to be a sunny week, for a change," she said, ignoring me. "Would be nice to go to the beach." Dana clasped her hands in front of her waist and swayed her arms from side to side.

"Yes. It would."

Awkward pause.

"Well, have a nice day," she said.

"Thank you, I will."

Sigh.

I had some spare time to visit Peter. I planned to drop by the university to unload some weed on the local campus dipsticks and needed some fresh stock. Glad Peter kept his business alive. He'd just park himself in the same spot each day and did his thing—and never had problems with the law. In fact, he had several people working for him now.

"Hey, man, you look so sad," said Peter. He reached into a baggie, handed me a joint, and smiled.

"You giving me a freebie?" It would've been the first time in five years.

"Well, not completely free, brother. I need your help in exchange."

"Sure, but you know I'm off to the university, right?" I took a deep drag from my reefer. It tasted a bit different today.

"Yeah, man, far-out. You see, brother, my business is booming, and my homegrown supply has maxed out! I needed to find a new supplier, and I think I've found one. Cheaper stock and more profit!"

"Profit? What about spreading the love?" I said taking another puff. I pulled out the joint and stared at it. "This tastes a bit off."

"The more weed I sell, the more love, man!" Peter waved and smiled at a police officer walking by. I was always amazed how no one ever arrested him. "Still need your help, man."

"How?"

"I have to visit the supplier Saturday. You've worked long enough with me, so I think I can trust you with some business secrets. Besides, your pathetic yuppie look is just what I need."

I brushed back my mullet.

"Glad you recognize my beauty."

"No, not really, man," Peter said. "You have a suit?"

I nodded.

"By the way, that joint you have? It's a new spin on the product from that new supplier we'll see. Yeah, it tastes a bit different, but let me know what you think when you're done. Be careful. It's more potent."

Last time he changed things up, it took a few tries before getting used to it.

But he was right. The new sample made me giddier than usual, and I took a long route back to the hospice to enjoy the sunny day.

The warm spring air encouraged most of the hospice's regulars to stay out on the streets, so fewer people visited for meals. Supper took more a "self-serve" approach, and we'd have plenty of food left over. Not having to serve freed my time to enjoy the hockey playoffs. I crashed in the recreation room to mellow out and enjoy a match.

Despite the boring "trap" game one of the teams played, I found it a welcome relief to the non-stop *Bärbar Ugn* infomercials. Reginald interrupted, tapping my shoulder.

"Telephone." He pointed to the hall leading to the office.

"Who is it?"

"President Bill Clinton, he wants your advice on the Bosnian crisis."

Not surprised. He must've heard about my brilliant chess strategies the other night.

I took the phone. "Hey Bill, it's Larry."

"Bill? No, it's me, Honey-Bear!" a woman chirped.

"Schnookums?" Dating memories flooded my brain at the tone of her cheerful voice.

"I'll be in town and need you to take care of Rupie-Bear on Friday. I'm going to drop him off with you. Can you meet me at our old Earl of Latteigh for 9 a.m.? Is that okay?"

She's asking permission? What's wrong with her? Stoked to spend time with my son, I debated what to do with him.

Dana mentioned beach. Great idea! I'm going to take my son fishing, make sandcastles, and go out in a boat! Basically, he's going to enjoy everything I didn't as a kid. He'll never want to go back to life on the road after spending a day with his super Dad!

I agreed, hung up, and performed a jig.

I couldn't fall asleep—too excited to see my Little Larry. It had been way too long, so I went downstairs and flipped on the TV.

I hadn't watched more than two minutes of that new *Bärbar Ugn II* infomercial, figuring it'd be more of the same dull diatribe with Sven's face contaminating the screen. I was wrong. Sven wasn't the only star!

Heather now co-hosted with him! I knew she'd film well, having the looks of a model, but I never thought she could be so animated and emotive—perfect for sales on TV. Heather's enthusiasm infected everyone she interviewed in the streets, and people were so excited to eat the fish she offered.

The show concluded with her announcing how to buy the *Bärbar Ugn II*, adding that the original *Bärbar Ugn* could be purchased at half price if both were bought together. They also promised to throw in some wooden knives, imported directly from Sweden, at no additional cost if buyers acted on the offer within the next half hour.

She still could be the voice of a generation, through these silly infomercials. My prophecy could still be fulfilled.

If it wasn't for Sven.

Dana greeted me at Jumpin' Java Friday morning.

"Good morning, Larry!" she chirped, "Another sunny day on the 'Wet' Coast. Got big plans for today?"

Her smile creeped me out. She poured my usual free coffee while I read the paper. *Has she been buying me coffee since she started working here?* I avoided talking to her, but she tried making conversation. *I'd better answer her.*

"Going to take my son, Little Larry, to Kits Beach this afternoon. Looking forward to seeing him. First time in years."

"You have a son? That's so sweet. I'm sure you're a great dad. You should have a blast. Weather is perfect." Dana beamed an awkward smile.

I never understood why people chatted about the climate when they want to talk, and there's nothing to say. It's such a waste of breath.

"You haven't been working here too long," I said.

"No. Summer job to help pay for university."

"I remember university. Not a good fit for me."

"Too bad. You seem an intelligent man."

Maybe I should give her a bit more of my time. She's insightful.

"I'm an academic. I study theology and Greek mythology in my spare time."

"Oh my gosh! You have to be so smart for that type of stuff! Why'd you give up on school?"

"I had a higher calling. Something that'd fulfill my life purpose."

"Love to find out more but have to serve others."

"No problem. I've got to run soon anyway."

I returned to my paper and pretended to read.

I arrived at the Earl of Latteigh a half hour early, wanting to ensure I found a seat in the busy shop.

It'd been years since I last been here. I drooled at the smell of a young man's quadruple peppermint latte, but only had enough money for a boring, plain coffee.

My wife walked in with her head wrapped in a kerchief, wearing sunglasses. A little man about three and half feet tall walked behind her in tow. My Little Larry might've grown, but I'd recognize those ice blue eyes anywhere. I didn't care for what he wore, though. Shorts with suspenders just didn't work.

I stood and opened my arms for a hug. Heather might've come in for one, but I'll never know for sure. Someone intercepted her for an autograph.

I held out my hand to my son. "Hi Little Larry, you remember me, your Dada?"

"I'm Lars." Little Larry looked up at his mother. "Who's that?"

"Him?" said my Schnookums sweetly. "That, my little Rupie-Bear, is the one who cleaned our home and looked after you when you were my sweet baby cub. But you haven't seen him in a long time because he was very naughty. But I think he's sorry" — Heather's eyes pleaded with me, so I nodded for the sake of the child — "and he'll take good care of you today. Call him, Larry."

Larry? You mean Dad, no?

"If you behave," she added, "we'll go out for some ice cream later tonight."

The boy clapped his hands. "I love ice cream!"

"Honey-Bear," Heather said gently to me, "I'll pick him up around seven." She kissed my cheek and abruptly left. For a second, I felt like the couple we were when we first met.

"Hi Little Larry," I said to my little boy again.

"Call me Lars. You're Larry."

"Yes, I know, but Larry is such an amazing name! Don't you want to be cool like me?"

"No. You're not cool. My Papa is cool. He's on TV. You're not."

There's something so wrong with a blond boy in suspenders saying what's cool and what's not.

Silence.

"How old are you, Lars?" Calling him Lars felt weird.

"I'm five, Larry!" His eyes wandered towards an elderly lady carrying a huge tray full of donuts to her friends.

"Well, I'm thirty, and don't call me Larry," I answered.

"But Mama said that's your name."

"You can call me Dad."

"No."

I sighed. Explaining the truth to him probably wasn't appropriate.

"You sure you don't remember me?"

The lad shook his head.

I kept some cherished photos in my Bible, which I pulled from my bag.

"See this picture? That's you when you were just a little over a week old. You recognize your Mama there, don't you?"

He nodded but seemed more interested in the big book.

"And that's me, and that's you!" I said.

"That's not me! I'm no baby!"

"You don't believe me?" I returned the photos to the middle of my scriptures and placed my hand on the book. "I swear it's the truth!"

"What do you mean, swear it's the truth?"

"This is the world's most important book." I waved it in front of his face. "It's called the Bible."

"What's the Bible?" he interrupted.

"It tells God's story from the beginning of time. I prefer reading the Greek interlinear, but this version is a decent translation. It starts in Genesis…"

"What's God?" He cocked his head and scratched it.

The heathen Sven never introduced God to my son? This is going to be a long day.

"Uh, it seems I have a lot to teach you. Anyway, this book has some amazing stories in it, like how a little man like yourself kills an evil ferocious giant. Maybe I can read you one from this amazing book sometime?"

He nodded. "I love stories."

I pulled out the Pocket Fisher Pro from my sack. Little Larry stared curiously at it. They were all the rage in the '70s. I had it since my first year at choir camp, and fishing helped me cope with a difficult time. I spent many hours by the lake with it, but never caught anything. It didn't bother me. I just loved sitting in peace waiting for a nibble.

"Ever go fishing?"

"No. What is that?" He pointed to my Pocket Fisher Pro.

"A special fishing rod. See, we take this," I said, snapping it open from the handle case, "and we cast this line in the water, and the fish eat this hook." I pointed to the metal object at the end of the line. "We then reel them in, and if the fish is any good, we could eat it for lunch! Wanna try it with me?"

Little Larry nodded enthusiastically.

I put the rod back in my bag and took him to the bus stop. I'd figure we'd go to the beach and try to catch some big ones from the pier.

Little Larry loved the bus. He said nothing and sat motionless, staring out the window.

It reminded me of my first bus ride with my mother when I hit the tender age of six. I'll never forget the well dressed, middle-aged man who boarded and sat in the front. He started clapping in rhythm and broke out into an old gospel song. His majestic voice sang "I'm Going Home, On That Morning Train," which still haunts me to this day. Everyone applauded him when he finished.

He rose then walked around the bus with hat in hand asking people for money and exited at the next stop.

I turned to Mama, "That's what I want to do when I grow up."

Mama said, "Why wait? You can learn to sing, but only choral music."

From then, I dedicated my life to song.

One should never dismiss the effects of public transportation. The life impacts could be humungous. Today, Little Larry is guaranteed to have some.

"Little Larry—"

"Lars."

"Sorry, Lars. Do you like singing?" I asked.

He shrugged his shoulders.

I began. "When you're happy and you know it, clap your hands!"

A few teens sitting opposite clapped. "You get it," I said, pointing to them.

The ride passed quickly singing the song with Little Larry and a bunch of passengers joining in. Everyone seemed to be in good spirits as we stepped off the bus at our stop.

He'll remember this bus trip with his dad forever.

We walked hand-in-hand out on to the pier. Like his father, Little Larry enjoyed casting and reeling the line in and out of the water. He repeated the action non-stop.

"When will I catch something?"

"You need to be patient. Maybe leave the line in the water longer."

The next time Little Larry cast the line, he waited a few minutes before reeling it in. It produced zilch. He grunted in frustration and tried again.

He's starting to bore! I need something to happen soon!

An old man with a long pole walked by. He stared at us and noticed Little Larry sighing in disappointment.

"What are you guys using for bait?" he asked.

"Bait? What do you mean?" I said.

The man laughed. "You need to put something on your hook, like a worm, or you won't catch anything."

The stranger motioned to Little Larry to reel in his line. He opened his duffle bag, withdrew a small container, and lowered it for Little Larry to see. It was full of earth.

"See here?" The man dug his finger in the dirt. "Those pink and red squiggly things? Those are worms. You need them to catch fish." He deftly removed one and placed it on the hook of the Pocket Fisher Pro. "Now you're ready for action. If you catch one and need more, don't be shy. I'll be further down the pier."

Little Larry looked at me. "Why didn't you know that? Haven't you ever caught a fish?"

I thought fast on my feet. "The Pocket Fisher Pro's hook has a special fish magnet. Maybe it doesn't work in the salt water of the ocean. I only used it in freshwater lakes."

Worms. Might've been the reason why I've never caught a single thing in my life.

Little Larry cast the line into the ocean. Within a couple minutes, the line jerked. I stood behind him and helped reel in his catch. My child gasped in excitement at the site of the little fish emerging from the water. We lowered it to the ground. *Hmm...a bit bigger than the palm of my hand.*

"What did I catch?" Little Larry asked.

I had no idea. I only knew a few fish species—the ones I ordered in restaurants. "Congratulations! You caught a sockeye salmon!"

"Wow! Papa loves *lax.*"

My son knows Swedish? Must be Sven's slimy influence. *The bastard.*

"Hey, it's getting near lunch time. Wanna see if we can cook this puppy?"

"It's not a puppy, it's a fish!"

"Uh, okay. Fish, right."

I'd no idea what to do with the tiny fish lying on the dock. I had bought a Polaroid camera a while back which I seldom used, but now wanted to capture the moment. I posed Little Larry holding my Pocket Fisher Pro in one hand, and the fish still attached to the hook in the other. It was a tiny creature, but he seemed proud of his achievement. He burst in excitement when he saw the camera shoot out the photo and demanded I take another. I placed the two pictures in my Bible and promised I'd give him one at the end of the day.

I attempted to remove the hook from the poor fish's mouth, and almost cussed when I cut my finger in the process. I threw the slimy scaly thing in my bag, along with my Pocket Fisher Pro. *Have to figure out how to cook it. Do I just throw the thing in a pot and boil it?*

I shouldered my bag and grabbed my kid's hand, then a big fat idea hit me. We hopped on an east-bound bus to a local pub I had frequented. A foul smell permeated the air as we took our seats, and my child plugged his nose.

The lunch time crowd filed into our restaurant, and the host ushered us to a window table near the front. When the waiter took our orders for drinks, I asked him for a pen and paper.

"This restaurant specializes in preparing fish caught in the ocean," I said to my son. "They'll take our catch and make it the way we like. Do you like fish sticks?"

Little Larry nodded enthusiastically.

"Great, so do I. We can also get some fries, too."

I quickly wrote on a piece of paper: "Take our order and ignore anything I say to you, but simply agree and play along. Take the fish I give you and throw it out, and bring us one breaded haddock and chip dinner, with two plates."

"What are you writing, Larry?" Little Larry enquired.

"Stop calling me Larry. It's Dad!" I forgot I was speaking to a five-year-old who'd been living a lie with another man as his father. I placed my head between my hands over the table.

"Why do you want to be called Dad all the time? Are you sad you don't have kids of your own?"

Sigh. *I'm going to be a father of a nation.* "You remind me of my son."

"Can I take your order?" interrupted a waiter.

I straightened myself up and slipped him the note. "Here are some special instructions how we want our meal prepared."

He acknowledged.

"You see," I said, "we just went fishing and caught this HUGE salmon. Would you mind asking the chef to serve it with French fries?"

"No problem, sir!"

I opened my bag. The ensuing explosive smell made my eyes water, soliciting a gag reflux. The waiter recoiled and turned away. Pinching my nose, I fished around the sack, pulled out our dinner by its tail, and passed it to the waiter. He wasn't impressed and walked away from our table carrying it while all the other patrons plugged their noses as he passed.

Waving his hand in front of his face, Little Larry said, "I don't think I can eat that stinky fish."

"Yeah, it's gross, but this place works wonders with freshly caught seafood. You'll see."

The waiter returned in about fifteen minutes with an empty plate and a huge, battered piece of haddock, about the length of my forearm. A second waiter brought the fries and a bottle of ketchup and malt vinegar.

"Wow," Little Larry replied, "my little salmon made all that meal?"

"You bet!" I said grabbing a knife and fork. "Enough for four!"

"But my fish was so puny."

"Well, they expand when they're fried." I served some haddock and fries on Little Larry's plate. "Would you like some ketchup?" Little Larry nodded.

He took a bite out of his haddock and let out a big, "Mmmmmmm. I never tasted salmon like this before!"

"Glad you like it. They prepare the fish really well here."

"I love fishing. I never get to do this with my papa, Uncle Larry."

I'll take being called uncle.

The waiter came back with the bill. My heart stopped! *They charged me twenty bucks for disposing our catch on top of the cost of the meal?*

I stood and grabbed Little Larry's hand.

"Ever hear of dine-and-dash? It's a lot of fun. Like a race. First one to make it out of the restaurant, and to the end of the block, wins. We start when I count to three. Ready? One. Two. Three!"

I won the race, of course, but after eating a huge meal, my tummy cramped. We sauntered our way to the beach to check out what was going on.

I showed my son how to build sandcastles, making huge piles decorated with pebbles. We dug a moat around it to allow the ocean tide to fill it. Little Larry took all the credit for the architectural feat—the apple does not fall far from the tree. I took more photos to capture the moment.

A group of young children maybe a few years older than Little Larry were playing soccer about a hundred yards from us. We joined in. I knew Little Larry couldn't contribute much to the game, but one team would have a huge advantage thanks to my advanced skills.

My boy walked around staring at shells and dug in the sand while we played. I, on the other hand, couldn't resist the lure of competition. I made an initial contact with the ball and dashed from one end of the pitch to the other, weaving around my nine-year-old opponents. I heard cries for my teammates to pass, but there wasn't a need. I had full control of the situation. I wound up my leg far and released a cannon of a shot past the goalkeeper. She barely had a chance to leave her feet and could only watch the ball sail past her fifty yards down the beach.

"Gooooooooooooooooooooooal!" I yelled running to my teammates giving them high fives. Little Larry dropped some seaweed, ran over, and slapped my hand.

"This is boring!" he said. "I want ice cream, NOW!"

"Aw, c'mon Lars. This is an awesome game! Give it a chance."

The other team kicked off. Leaving Little Larry, I pounced on the ball. No one could stop me! This time, I deked out the goalie and snuck the ball in for a goal! I did ten celebratory jumping jacks while my opponents moaned in defeat. Everyone stared at me in awe.

My teammates didn't cheer me when I scored for the third, fourth, or tenth time. It didn't matter. I'm sure they were learning my technique so they could apply it for their next match.

Parents began signalling their kids to leave, concluding the game. *Quitters!* I checked the time. Yup, ten goals in twenty minutes. A personal best by seven!

Crap! Where'd Little Larry go? He's supposed to be playing soccer with us!

Panic set in. *How can someone just vanish into thin air?*

He's nowhere around!

I'd hoped to prove that I'm a great dad and grace myself back into Heather's life. Losing our child would slam the door on that possibility forever. *Where could he be?*

No one on the beach had seen him. There were so many children, I didn't know how on earth I'd find him.

Retracing my steps to the sandcastle led to nothing. A familiar voice called my name from behind. I turned and about twenty meters in my wake advanced a tall thin brunette with a big nose. She waved while smiling.

Dana appeared different in a bikini top and shorts—a little less frumpy. With her hair in a neat ponytail, and less awkward smile, she looked kind of cute. In her hand, a little boy in suspenders followed, eating an ice cream cone.

"Oh Lars, where on earth did you go?" I asked.

"I got iced cream! It's good!" he replied.

"He walked to the road from the beach," said Dana. "I saw you playing soccer with the other children and figured he belonged to your group. Better keep an eye on this one. He likes the ladies and loves his ice cream."

"Yeah! I love iced cream!" Little Larry took a big lick of his cone.

"Thank you, thank you, thank you."

"No problem," Dana answered.

She looks kinda hot. Maybe I should take a picture with her. She'd love it!
I was right.

Dana squealed and clapped her hands and flagged down a passerby to take a photo of us. She permitted me to wrap my arm around her waist while we posed. I requested more pictures, including one with Little Larry on my shoulders and Dana by my side, and some with just Little Larry and myself.

"She's nice," my son said, pointing to Dana from my shoulders. "Hey, maybe, she can be your wife, and you can have kids."

"That's a great idea!" Dana giggled.

"Uh, oh. Okay," I said. "Maybe we should start with a date?" *Did I just say that?*

Dana clapped her hands cheerfully. "Yay! Well, I don't work again until next Thursday cause I'm going out of town for the next few days. Can we plan something then when you come in for coffee?"

Maybe she'll forget by then.

"Okay."

"Ever hear of colonic hydrotherapy? Maybe we can go for one. It's the rage! You'll love it!"

Never heard of it.

"Sounds refreshing," I said.

She laughed and slapped my arm. "Oh, I'd better rejoin my friends. Take care Larrys."

"Lars," Little Larry corrected.

Little Larry waved to her from a top of my shoulders, and I trotted across the road to the bus stop to catch our ride back to the hospice.

I wanted to teach Little Larry how to play ping-pong before dinner. His head barely cleared the edge of the table, but it didn't deter him from trying to swing at the ball. He had decent hand-eye coordination and managed to return a few. After a few good rallies, I concluded my son might offer competition for me in about fifteen years—if he practiced.

We hung out in the recreation room after supper, and I introduced him to a few regulars who were playing board games. Reginald entered, informing me I had a phone call.

"Hello."

"Bring Rupie-Bear to the front of the building at 7:30 p.m., sharp," Heather said.

Before I could respond, I was interrupted by a dial tone. *Damn, that happens to me all the time.*

I returned to the lounge area. "Would you like to hear some nice Bible stories that I told you about?" I asked my son.

He nodded enthusiastically.

I checked the time. 7:20. *How'd get so late?*

"Maybe some other time. We have to take you back to Mama."

"Awwww," Little Larry protested.

I took him by the hand and waited outside the building. A metallic blue sports car screeched to a halt in front of us. The passenger window lowered, and loud heavy metal exploded over the woofers.

Heather greeted me warmly. "Good. He's still clean. Time to leave Honey-Bear to his filth and come home!" I noticed she wore a red strapless dress.

"Mama, I had such a wonderful day with Uncle Larry."

"Uncle Larry?" Heather gave an approving look.

"Yeah! We went fishing, and I caught this huge fish. Oh, and we built sand-castles and played ping-pong."

"You did all that?" Heather's eyes had a genuine hint of affection.

"I don't want to go back on that plane tomorrow."

Atta boy.

"Aw, but you have to, dear. Papa has been very naughty, and we need to make sure we fix him."

Fix Sven? Like snip-snip?

"He is expecting us in Toronto tomorrow. You know he has important meetings and needs us there."

She stepped out of the car and opened the backdoor for her son.

"Mama, can Uncle Larry come home to read me a bedtime story?"

Heather whispered in my ear, "Sven never reads to him." She placed Little

Larry in the back seat. "Well, since *Uncle Larry's* been good, you can bring him home." She stroked my back gently with her hand. "Come?"

A flashback of funsies at Vancouver airport overwhelmed me.

Yes! Little Larry will be the key to bringing us back together!

I could've sworn I saw a brown-haired pony-tailed girl duck around the corner of a distant building while I jumped into the passenger seat.

"Snazzy car," I said, "the *Bärbar Ugn* must be doing well."

"Let's not talk now. Listen." She reached and cranked the radio.

"What is this noise," I yelled.

"Shhh. It's Rammstein. I find them soothing."

Little Larry attempted to mimic the German singer's deep voice from the back. His gibberish aped the melody well. Heather placed her hand on my lap, occasionally gripping my thigh during intense parts of the music. *Like old times.*

We pulled up to the old condo in the Kits, and we followed Heather into the apartment. *Place hasn't changed at all.*

"Go. Read to my son," Heather said.

I helped little Larry prepare for bed in the back room where we spent his initial days of life together. He cuddled into my arm while I read him the story of David and Goliath. He enjoyed it and wanted me to read another. But before I could choose a second story, Heather walked in holding a glass of wine, wearing a black negligée.

"Lights out, my little Rupie-Bear," she said in a cool slur. "Say good-night to *Uncle Larry.*"

Little Larry turned to me. His eyes told me he recognized me to be his one true father.

"Papa never reads me stories."

"Well, maybe you should ask him to read you some more from the Bible," I said. *Bloody heathen.*

"Papa doesn't do many papa things, does he?" said Heather. "Except, perhaps, for making little bears." Her voice sounded melancholy as she bent over and kissed her son's head.

Huh?

"Thanks for the wonderful day, Uncle Larry. I love you." Little Larry turned on his side, and I pulled the covers over him.

"I love you too, Lars." I choked up. "Oh wait, didn't want to forget these." I gave him some photos taken during the day, and he reached out to give me a big hug.

This'll guarantee me getting back Heather's good graces.

I opened my bag and retrieved the Pocket Fisher Pro. "May I leave him this?"

Heather's eyes expressed an emotion I hadn't seen in years from her—maybe it was the night we produced this fine child. She downed the contents of her glass.

"Yes. Come." She reached her hand out.

I took it, and Heather led me down the hall and took a pitstop in the kitchen. She refilled and downed her glass of wine, twice. She retook my hand and led me to the master bedroom.

"Wait," I said, remembering. "We can't go into Sven's room."

"Of course, we can. That *Swede's* not around," slurred Heather. "And besides, don't you remember? He did say many years ago, 'I should be nice to you.'"

Why would she say that now?

We entered the room. Heather wrapped her arms around my shoulder and looked into my eye.

"You were good to my boy." She gently placed her hand around the back of my head and drew me in so our lips connected. Her breath tasted of alcohol, and I wanted to drink her all up.

She broke apart and looked me in the eyes.

"Do you remember our first date?"

I nodded enthusiastically. Heather let go of me and walked over to her dresser along the wall. She opened the drawer and produced a box labelled "Cock Socks," and withdrew two square packages.

I sat motionless, reliving that one encounter we had many years ago.

Heather staggered towards me and pressed both condom packages firmly in my hand.

"For tonight," she whispered.

I sat on the edge of the bed, and we necked for a while. Before I knew it, funsies led to super-funsies. But something felt different. The condom packages remained unopened.

Twenty seconds later, Heather smiled. "Good…and thank you. Please leave when you've had a chance to catch your breath—and not a word of this to anyone." She left the room.

Sigh, just like the first time. I stood, buckled my pants, and left.

Good night Schnookums.

Chapter Thirteen

Seattle

May 1995

Peter entered the hospice the following Saturday dressed in a high-end Italian suit and hair slicked back in a ponytail. If it wasn't for his long beard and thick glasses, he could've passed for an executive.

"I don't know how you guys eat this, man," he said to me, struggling with some oatmeal. "Glad you're up early, brother. Remember the favour I asked you earlier this week?"

"No."

"Don't jive me, man. I need you to go with me to meet my 'friend.' Go get your suit on."

I reluctantly returned to my room to don my kilt and collared shirt—pretty much what I wore at my wedding. Still fit.

He laughed at me!

"Brother, I'd hoped you'd look a little more officious. Don't you have any other nice clothes to wear?"

I shook my head.

Peter should talk. He looked like a cross between a gangster and St. Nick. I didn't have anything else formal to wear, so I went upstairs, kept the dress shirt, and put on my newest pair of jeans. It had to do. At least I looked neat and pressed.

We walked outside a few blocks, and Peter unlocked the door of a luxurious SUV.

"Wow," I said, "where'd you get this? Love the leather seats." I parked myself inside and wiggled my bum around.

"I live off the land, brother," Peter said, "but this cat had an amazing deal I couldn't pass up."

How could he afford this?

He turned on the ignition and cranked the sound system with flower-child era music. Transported in time, we hit the road.

"We're off to Seattle," said Peter, driving. "It'll take us a few hours. You've been working with me the longest—reason why I wanted you to tag along."

"Everyone wants my company," I said.

We crossed over a bridge and continued towards the highway. Peter didn't say anything until we hit the open roads. He appeared deep in thought.

"You know, man," he said, "it just hit me. I'm fifty, have no kids, and don't know who to pass my legacy to."

"Well, I have a kid, and a prophecy promising me a nation of children."

"Yes, you've told me numerous times. But what's your legacy, man? What will you pass on when you die?"

He stumped me. I didn't have many possessions and never thought of death before.

"Part of the prophecy says my wife will be the voice of a generation."

"Your wife's influence is not what *you* have to pass on."

He had me again. Being thirty, I never thought about life "beyond Larry."

"I dig you, brother," he said solemnly, "and I'm thinking, if you continue with me and work hard, maybe you'll carry my torch when my days are done—continuing to spread the love. But enough bleak talk, man. That day is far away."

I never looked to Peter as a father-like figure. In fact, I knew nothing about the man outside our working relationship. Peddling weed for him took way too much effort to earn a fast buck. My future plans were simple: live off my wife when she comes back to me.

After an awkward silence, Peter said, "Brother, I also dig your spiritual connection. Gives life purpose. Like it does me."

Before I could respond, saying I've no idea what he's talking about, he cranked the volume of the stereo.

"Hope you like psychedelic music."

"I don't get its appeal."

Peter tapped his finger against the steering wheel and hummed a few bars of the song.

"Man," he said when it finished, "the sixties were the best, brother. I blacked out most of it." Peter chuckled and slapped my thigh. He noticed my blank face. "C'mon man, don't you know anything about the sixties? Sit back and let the tunes move your soul."

"In-A-Gadda-Da-Vida" blared. It made little sense—surreal, lyrics all over the map, long, repeated lines with similar tone.

I listened to the song for a half hour. We reached the border when it finally ended.

Peter declared to the border agent that we were travelling on business, attending a medical conference. She raised an eyebrow but let us through uncontested.

"Still don't get it?" he asked.

"Get what?"

"The music."

"No," I said, "I really don't. How can anyone call this music?"

He lowered the volume.

"I feel badly for you, man," said Peter. "The sixties were a huge time of change."

"Like what? My birth?" I slouched back in my chair.

"Man, it's more than just you. There was a movement to break away from the stranglehold of our parents' generation. I don't know what your papa was like, but man, my dad was drab."

"My dad's great," I said. "He's British."

"Well brother, my pop was American, and he was typical 1950s. Pure square. Colourless. Heavy into materialism. He woke up each morning and drove his boat-sized car to toil away at his nine-to-five job. Then he'd drive home, eat supper, and read. He had no soul. No spirit. No purpose."

The way Peter described his father sounded pretty good to me. House with picket fence. Secure job. Siblings. A car. A dad who encouraged him to go to college. I would have loved that.

"My father represented a society that had a dull, soulless existence, and was void of any humanity. I wanted to open my mind to a wider reality, man."

A dull ache came from my belly. *Maybe downing that giant sixty-four-ounce soft drink at the border wasn't a great idea.*

Peter blathered on about '60s society and meeting some guy named Artie Greenburg in university. It seemed he did everything with Artie—frequenting coffee shops, smoking weed, and listening to counter-culture poets. He even saw Dylan, which influenced Peter to pick up the guitar and write his own music. I tuned him out at that point, as he began recanting the history of the beatnik movement. The increasing cramping in my stomach was a distraction, and I twitched my leg in attempt to relieve the discomfort. By the time he started talking about the Vietnam war, my bladder was at DEFCON1.

"Peter, I need you to pull over, NOW!"

I ran out of the car into a wooded area by the edge of the highway and relieved myself on the trunk of a red cedar. It must've taken a whole five minutes. When I returned to the car, Peter was hunched over the steering wheel, sobbing.

"Are you okay?" Concerned for Peter, I reached in my pocket for a tissue. It was used, so Peter waved his hand at me dismissively.

"My best friend Artie was a year older than me, man," said Peter, choked up. "I told him not to enlist in his dad's war, but he caved in to his father's pressure to perform his 'patriotic duty.' Like that old bastard of a father ever did!"

"I'm sure your friend Artie came out okay in the end," I said, trying to be positive.

Peter's eyes widened. "Don't you get it? I lost my best friend to that fuckin' war!" Peter took a few deep breaths to gather his thoughts and drove back on the highway. "A week before Artie's departure for Nam, we got word of a literary event that promised to blow people's minds sky high. Artie dragged me to this building. Many school buses were parked outside, man, all painted in dayglow bright colours. The poetry was mind blowing, and the loud music was different. It was the first time Artie and I experimented with acid…

"I remember sweating, then seeing bright lights like I'd never seen before. The music had increased depth and meaning, man. I swayed to and fro with the beats of the songs. I was in my own world, until a woman standing next to me placed her hand on my forearm, making me tingle like pins on a cushion. My mind had been exposed to a new art. A new reality.

"I remember snapping out of it, maybe several hours later. I was sitting in one of them school buses, surrounded by people having these out of mind experiences. I had no idea how I landed there, but recalled the first thing I saw was a road sign saying we were deep into Pennsylvania…but I had no clue where Artie went.

"So, this pretty girl, my age, was sitting next to me. She said that I was on a new journey now—not one of simply reading poetry and smoking up, man, but that I have embarked on another movement—to spread the love and share the wealth of our materialistic land. I unwittingly that evening joined a crew travelling to California. We were seeking out the maker of the music we had heard that night in the school. A band called the Grateful Dead. I found my calling with my new family."

"But Peter, what happened to Artie. Why wasn't he with you on the bus?"

Peter broke down in tears. He became so consumed with emotion that he nearly veered the SUV off the road. I instinctively grabbed the wheel and straightened the car out.

"Sorry, man. My head went into a cloud. I sometimes relive the grief that I never saw my friend Artie again. I don't know why he didn't board that bus to California. He should've dodged the draft with me. If only I didn't lose sight of him while I was on that trip at the school."

I never experienced the death of a beloved friend before, and seeing Peter so distraught invoked a confused feeling of empathy. How could you grieve someone so many years after the fact? I patted the back of my friend while he drove up into the city. We exited the highway and travelled down a few side streets.

"See that hospital sign?" said Peter. "That's where we're heading."

We drove by a statue of Jimi Hendrix, and Peter cranked "Purple Haze," as he said, "in tribute" both to the guitar god and Artie, lost in Vietnam.

If I thought Vancouver was a hotbed for coffee, Seattle took it to a higher level. Everyone in the hospital carried the familiar Earl of Latteigh cups with cardboard holders. I felt conspicuous not having one in hand. I asked Peter if we could fix this.

"Might not be a bad idea, we can grab one at the hospital diner and meet my contact. It's near his office."

Ordering an espresso peppermint mocha, I noted a sign for a fertility clinic. It made me chuckle, especially watching a man leave with a sheepish expression on his face.

"Twelve dollars, please," a voice behind the cashier said cheerfully.

"What?" I said.

Peter laughed and paid for my drink. "Should've told you. Coffee is expensive here, and it's in American dollars. Oh look, there's my man." He waved at a tall and handsome doctor walking towards us. Peter introduced me to his associate, and they left together, leaving me to my latte.

People milled in and out of the fertility clinic, often taking a pitstop for a coffee. A woman, in nurse's gear, exited rapidly with a worried expression. She asked a nearby orderly a question, and he pointed in my direction. Relieved, she approached me.

"Mr. Spencer?" she said.

She's cute!

"Sorry? Have we met?"

I surely would've remembered this American beauty.

"No. You were supposed see the cashier before leaving. You forgot to receive your payment for your donation."

"My donation?"

"Yes, your sperm donation. Just need you to sign here." She handed me a clipboard.

"You're giving me money for spanking my salami?"

She appeared surprised. The form had too much fine print. I scanned it and found the signature block. Steven Spencer. I signed accordingly and handed it back to her.

"Thank you. We'll see you next week." She passed me some money, snapped around, and returned to the clinic.

Rolling the fifty-dollar bill in my fingers, I bought myself another twelve-dollar coffee.

Nice way to pass a Saturday afternoon! Donate sperm and make money for it? Not a bad score for a few minutes' effort. I should move here. That'd be much easier than the $250 I make hauling Peter's weed across the city to a university campus.

"Larry, man," Peter's voice called in the distance. He beckoned me to join him at the far end of the hall.

He led me to a back room where his associate and a couple of orderlies were loading up five carts full of toilet paper, all packaged neatly in boxes.

"Ba-ha-ha! What a shit-load."

"Shh," said Peter winking. "We need to bring this to a hospital in Vancouver, man, got it?"

"Which one?" I asked.

The orderlies stopped loading the boxes and stared. Peter stiffened and coughed into his hand. After a moment, they resumed and finished.

"Follow me," said Peter.

We rolled the carts through the building to the car. Peter asked me to help load the boxes, but one was too many for me, so I left the task to the orderlies.

The cab was filled from floor to ceiling, with not an inch to spare. Our helpers left, and Peter handed his partner a thick envelope. The man verified the contents, nodded, and walked off.

We drove back on the highway with the boring "Astronomy Domine" playing over the car's speakers. At least I understood the word Domine from my many Gregorian chants.

"Thanks, man!" said Peter hitting the highway. "I'll need the extra body to haul all that toilet paper out."

"I don't understand it."

"You don't get what, brother?"

I shook my head. "Why would we come down to Seattle to pick up thousands of rolls of bum wad? Couldn't we have gone to the local grocery store?"

Peter shook his head in disbelief. "You've got a lot to learn, man, if you ever are going to step into my shoes."

"Huh?" I scratched my head.

"We are not bringing toilet paper across the border, it's what's *inside* the rolls that's important."

"What?"

"The toilet paper rolls are filled to the brim in hashish."

"I thought you sold marijuana."

"I did, but hash makes things easier for me. It's a more potent form of marijuana. Remember the 'new samples' you tried?"

I recalled the amazing buzz after sampling it. "Do I ever!"

"That was using my new hash. A little bit goes a longer way. I'm making a killing on the stuff."

"I thought you were about the love," I said. "You don't strike me as a businessman."

"I'm not, man. I love the freedom of living off the land, but I've always had a sense of making money—even with very little. Funny, eh, how some cats are like that. You give some guys a little cash; they make a lot. Others you give a lot, and they blow it in seconds."

"That would be me!" I said.

"Hmmm. Are you sure this work is for you?"

"Well," I said, thinking about the embarrassed faces leaving the fertility clinic, "sperm donation would be easier. Hey, did you know they make fifty bucks a pop! But, heck, I like selling for you."

"Good. Encouraging marijuana use with young people feeds that spirit I was telling you about."

I gave him a blank look.

"You know, man, about opening one's mind. Seeing purpose in life. Something deeper than this materialistic society we live in. Love is a gateway to all that stuff."

"Oh, yeah." *No clue.*

"That bus I was telling you about that took us on the Grateful Dead quest?"
Oh please, can't we listen to some Vivaldi instead?

"It landed us in San Francisco. Man…there was nothing like the Haight-Ashbury experience." At this point, I think he talked about his life as a hippie, where everyone shared in community. The love-ins in the parks perked my interest, and Peter missed them the most.

Peter stopped in deep reflection and sighed. "You talk about how you score with women, brother? You ain't scored until an experience like that. In fact, I never been with a woman since…must be near twenty-five years, man!"

Get a haircut, wear clothes like me, and shave. You might have better luck, but not likely. And maybe smoke less.

Peter chain-smoked cigarettes the entire drive back to the border. He went on and on about how the press made hippies both trendy and a scorn to society.

"Some asshole capitalists conducted tours of our loving home in San Francisco, selling us hippies as part of the excursion. Made us feel like animals at a zoo, being stared at through cages. Some bad apples stole from us, just for the sake of stealing. Some even beat on us!"

He extinguished his cigarette in the ashtray and lit another.

"Then I received news from an owner of a psychedelic shop I frequented, that he received a call from my dad—how did he track me down? I'll never know, but I blame the press. Anyway, man, good ol' Pop had reported me to the pigs, for not doing my patriotic duty. Could you believe he was forcing me to fight in *his* war?"

"The pigs?" I asked.

"Yeah, brother. Pigs. The cops. Anyway, the experience of San Francisco started to become less appealing. I tried to convince the folk from my bus to move. They wouldn't budge. I finally told them the Dead were playing Vancouver, and that did the trick. Within minutes, we were gone and set up a commune in the Kits. Been living off the land here ever since."

We arrived at the border and Peter pulled into a line of cars. My eyes were tearing from all of Peter's smoking. He had consumed most of a pack.

"Weird thing, man," said Peter. "shortly after landing in the Kits, the City of Vancouver started rebuilding the area. Bastards kicked us out…and you know the weird irony of it all, man? Most of my commune went on with life, looking for work and buying homes! Not cool! They moved on from a paradise of loving and sharing their wealth to become the bloody yuppies they hated! They turned into their parents!"

Peter advanced the car to take his place by the border agent.

"Guess they didn't want their kids to have free love, or share a joint with them—who knows, it would've made them all happier."

Peter rolled down the window, and the border agent coughed from the cigarette smell after greeting him.

"How long have you been in the States?" the agent asked, covering his mouth.

"Only the day."

"Were you there on business or pleasure?"

"Business."

"Doing what?"

"Obtaining bathroom supplies for a local hospital."

The agent looked at the cab.

"That's a lot of boxes for a day trip."

"Yes," said Peter. "There was a sale on toilet paper we had to take advantage of. We're on a tight budget. It was purchased by a hospital in Seattle on our behalf. We didn't pay for anything."

"BA-HA-HA, and this TP makes our bums happy," I said.

Peter glared at me.

"Do you have any documentation and identification?" asked the agent.

Peter opened the glove compartment and passed him some papers.

"All this is going to the Hospice of Good Hope?" she asked.

"Yes, bit of a crisis at that hospital. They go through a lot."

"It's not really a hospital," I said.

Peter glared at me. "Yes. It. Is," he said with teeth clenched.

"Oh…yeah…that place," I said. "Yeah, those guys go through tons of that stuff! Especially on meatball night!"

Peter looked back to the agent. "It's true. There is a crisis."

"I will need to inspect the contents. Please pull over."

Peter groaned and obeyed. "Keep your trap shut, man," he said to me while he left the vehicle.

Peter opened the cab and unloaded a couple of boxes. The agent removed the packaged toilet paper and casually inspected a few more boxes and was satisfied. Peter returned and breathed a sigh of relief as we drove off.

"Yee-haw!" Peter said slapping the wheel and smiling. "Those guys in Seattle did an amazing job. It's near impossible to see the tubes of hash inside each roll. The plastic wrapping's too opaque! Thank the stars, man, that agent didn't dig too deep."

A thought occurred to me. "Peter, if you dodged the draft, how can you cross the border?"

He removed a wallet from his jacket pocket and tossed it to me. There were several IDs in there, all with Peter's photo. I read the name on the first one and busted a gut.

"No way!" I broke down in laughter. "You go by the alias Mike Rochburns?"

Peter chuckled. "Well, the ID says Michael officially. No one ever noticed the joke. And if someone asks me to say my name, I make the 's' silent. They buy it all the time."

We drove down the boring road making a game of listing "joke" names until we pulled into Vancouver.

"Does Reginald know about all this toilet paper?" I asked.

"In a way. He's expecting me to deliver, but not for a couple of weeks. I have to make a pitstop first."

We parked outside a temporary storage facility away from the downtown core. While I helped Peter unload all the boxes into a large locker, he told me how his assembly team would start prepping the joints for sale. After I unloaded the last box, Peter locked things up and drove me back to the hospice.

When he dropped me off outside the hospice, he left the SUV to join me on the sidewalk. He placed his hands on my shoulders and looked me directly in the eye.

"Thanks for joining me today, man. You're a good friend. If I had kids, I would've kept my dream of spreading the love through them, but since I don't, I hope that one day, you can do all this. Want to watch my production team prepare the hash for sale tomorrow?"

That sounded like too much work.

"Not this time. I need some rest. Thanks for the trip."

"No problem, man. What do you think of it all?"

I didn't give Peter's business much thought on the way home from Seattle. In fact, I hadn't stopped thinking about how easy it was to make money donating sperm since leaving Seattle—but there was something to be said about what

Peter was saying about "legacy." Inheriting his love-spreading mission would be awesome, and he wanted to take me under his wing. It was a long day, I was exhausted, and it must've shown on my face.

Peter seemed to be disappointed from my lack of enthusiasm. "Well man, I hope you see the great opportunity for you working under me like this. Think about it."

Peter hugged me, hopped into the SUV, and drove off.

Chapter Fourteen
Whiskey and Frootie-ooties
May 1995

A week later, utensils clanged loudly while the residents ate their Saturday morning breakfast. The noise roused me from a blissful evening of erotic dreams, reliving my night of ecstasy with Schnookums. My body ached for a repeat performance. I stretched my arms, sat up in my bed, and rubbed my eyes.

Four Beanbag Babes sat on my dresser, staring back at me. The baby dolls came in hundreds of varieties and were the rage earlier in the year. Beanbag Babes were hard to come by, and they promised a huge return on investment. My hope was they'd quadruple in value in a few weeks. They'd better…I dropped the remainder of my fifty-bucks I "earned" in Seattle on them. Since I had no money and needed something to eat, I went down to the cafeteria. A pungent odour filled the air.

Le meal du matin. Blech. The hospice called it porridge. I called it sediment.

Not wanting to ingest that sludgy breakfast, I ventured out to Jumpin' Java for my usual freebees. I parked myself at my table. A new weekend waiter didn't understand the "routine." He refused me my free coffee, so I left without paying. I didn't have the money, anyway.

Pushing 10 a.m., I jogged to Peter's corner. He just opened for business and strummed some hippie song I didn't recognize on his guitar. The streets were quiet.

"Hey man," said Peter. "What gets you outta bed so early on this sunny morning?"

"Ha! You're so funny Peter. I need some cash, bad! Hey, are you going to pay for me spending the day with you last week?"

Peter's expression turned cold. "What do you mean? I take you on as an apprentice and you want payment? You barely helped moving the boxes, and you missed preparing the stock for delivery. Screw that!" Peter strummed his guitar a few times, and suddenly stopped. He raised his eyebrows as if struck by a brilliant idea. "But man, you're in luck, I do need you for a Saturday job.

"There's some wild pre-summer school party at the university tonight, man. Got time to swing out there? We should make a killing. Give you a quarter of the take, as usual. Oh, and try to push some of these, brother. I got an over-stock." He tossed me a duffle bag of the prepackaged joints and crappy jewelry.

Under the crushing weight of the bag on my shoulder, I headed out to the train station.

This backbreaking work will all be worth it when you inherit this one day, Larry.

The campus was void of life, being a Saturday. I parked myself under the shade of a big tree near the largest building. It'd been a month since I last hung out here, and none of my regulars were around. It takes only one to bring all the bees to the hive, but not a soul stopped by.

A quiet hour passed, so I meandered over to the soccer field where a crowd of students were gathering. A few skateboarders zoomed passed me and stopped near the pitch. Figuring there'd be a ninety percent likelihood they'd need my services, I approached them with my usual pitch. I'm always discreet.

"Need some joints? Check out this fresh stock!" I opened the bag, and they hovered around me like a pack of wolves about to eat their prey.

I sold a ton. I loved these rich brats—they never seemed to care about money. I closed my duffle bag and watched the soccer match. Two women's teams were playing. I scouted them out, feeling good to cruise chicks like a teen—it'd been a while. After scoring with Schnookums last week, and her leaving, I wanted to get back into the game.

Two hands slammed my shoulders from behind, making me jump out of my skin.

"Larry Johnstone!" a familiar voice said. "What on earth are you doing here?"
I instinctively spun around.

"Dana? What on earth are *you* doing here?" I placed a slightly flirtatious tone in my voice, being in my old "Larry spirit."

Dressed in soccer gear, she must've been in the match.

She blushed. "I'm on the varsity team. Didn't you say you were working at the hospice this weekend?" She grabbed the tip of her ponytail over her left shoulder with both hands.

It's what I had told her to get out of our date—the one I promised her on the beach. She had reminded me of it last Thursday at Jumpin' Java.

"I am, but I made a mistake in my schedule. I'm only working there tonight."

"Oh, but what are you doing here?"

Think fast. "I'm a philosophy student. I work and live at the hospice to pay my way through school."

"You told me, 'I remember university. Not a good fit for me.'" She laughed to herself imitating me. "I didn't know you were still in school."

"Matter of fact, I am. I'm trying to finish off what I started many years ago."

"Philosophy, eh? That's neat!" She peered over my shoulder at my duffle bag. "Hey, what's in your sack?"

"Huh?"

"I thought I saw you sell stuff to the skater boys. You took it from your bag."

I looked behind me. The skater boys had crashed under a tree, smoking and laughing. Not a care in the world.

"Do you mean smokey-smokey-stuff, or this?" I pulled out some of Peter's crappy jewelry.

Dana's eyes popped out of her head. "That looks beautiful! How much?"

If I knew you'd fulfill my prophecy, I'd give it to you free.

"I'll give it to you half-price—ten dollars. They're handmade." *I'll make a killing. Ten dollars is double.*

"Too expensive for my blood. I'll give you a toonie for one bracelet, but eight more if you throw in two joints."

I lose three on the bracelet but gain three on the joints? Break even. Okay.

"Deal." I took her cash and gave her a bag with the stuff. "I didn't know you went to college here."

"Yeah, I'm in med school. Just started. I want to become an obstetrician."

"That's like the doctors who deliver babies?"

"You bet. As a kid I dreamt of mothering hundreds of babies. When I learned about the birds and the bees, I realized it's physically impossible for one woman. So, this helps fulfill it in another way."

Interesting approach.

"Anyhow, gotta go back in the game," said Dana. "You going to the party tonight?"

"No. Like I said, I can't. I'm working."

"Right, well, we'll figure out our date for next week" Dana ran back to play soccer after throwing her purchases in a bag by the field, ponytail swishing playfully from side to side.

I couldn't explain why, but her forward nature made me uneasy. On cue, the skater boys returned with some friends to buy more joints. It didn't take long to sell out of stock.

Many of the hospice's residents were hanging outside, smoking and carrying on before supper. They cheered as I walked in. One cried, "Hail the ping-pong king." A few burst out laughing.

Glad someone recognizes royalty.

Off duty for the evening, I lined up with the few who braved our Saturday evening dinner. Tonight, they served some slop they called "stew." I opted for a quick fix peanut butter and jam sandwich to fill the void. The food had really deteriorated at this place.

I plopped myself on the couch to join a couple of men watching exhibition football on TV. I wondered how Vaughn and Jacquie were doing. Vaughn now played in San Diego. I did miss Jacquie's company and warm hugs.

A chorus of catcalls interrupted.

Dana stood in the entranceway. *What on earth is she doing here?* She looked a little different than when I left her on the soccer field. Her usual messy hair was washed and had tons of wavy volume to it, and she wore a simple one-piece summer dress that clung nicely to her figure.

"Larry! I happened to be in the neighbourhood and figured I'd pop in to see you at work. Guess what I brought?" She lifted a plastic bag. "Frootie-ooties cereal and whiskey! Your favourites!"

How the hell did she know I loved them? I began to salivate. My sandwich didn't satisfy me like I'd hoped, and the prospect of eating the stew made me puke.

"Can I come in?" she asked.

I motioned her to follow me.

"I like the place. Quite homey." *She has to be kidding.* "Do you have a room?"

"Yes."

"Show it to me," she giggled mischievously. "Bring some bowls, spoons, and glasses."

Being a staff member, I had a small room to myself—barely large enough to fit a bed, a small bureau, and a closet. It looked like a bomb had hit it, with clothes strewn all over the place and unmade bed. It didn't faze Dana. I sat on my mattress while Dana poured us some cereal and milk, filled our glasses with the alcohol, then joined me on the bed.

"You gotta do as I do, to get the full effect." She took a bite of cereal, then downed the drink. Glunk glunk glunk. "HHHHAAAUUUGH! I'll bet I'll drink you under the table." She wiped her mouth and winked.

"No way." I did the same. *Wow, the two together are amazing!*

She repeated the process. I followed. We downed a few shots before Dana started talking.

"You know, Larry, I find you hot."

Of course.

She munched some cereal. "Did I mention to you I had this lifelong dream of having babies?"

"Yes, you implied it this afternoon."

"Do you know why?"

Do I have a choice? "No."

"It happened at church."

"What?"

"The City of Heavenly Praise Church. I've been going there since I was a little girl."

Woah. That's the one I go to!

"Yeah," she said, "I loved it there. Reminded me of visits to the farm."

I laughed remembering my first visit, filled with people imitating animals.

I downed a glass of whiskey, bracing for a long blah-blah-blah moment.

"I'll never forget that life-transforming day. I might've been eleven. I joined three people, standing near me, clucking like hens. A woman, who flapped her arms like a seagull, said, 'I hear a divine interpretation of this prophecy. This child will be the mother of a nation.'"

I dropped my glass, stunned at the similarity to my experience. It shattered on the floor.

"Oh my," she said, placing her own glass on my night table. "Let me help with that."

I shook my head and left my room to fetch a broom and a fresh cup from the kitchen. When I returned, Dana refilled my drink while I swept the floor. I cleaned everything quickly, wanting to find out more about Dana's experience. *Maybe I can get some clues as to how to fulfill my own prophecy!*

"Please," I said, sitting back down on the bed, "continue."

"Okay…where was I? Oh yeah, the mother of a nation. Since then, I'd been on a quest to fulfill that prophecy. When I knew I could bear babies, I started asking every guy out to complete my mission. It's weird. You'd think I'd have it easy, but it wasn't! Sure, they would want the sex part, but they all dropped me on the spot. Why? Because I mentioned I wanted their children followed by a life commitment. I'm now at a stage of life where I'd be happier to cut to the chase and skip matrimony. But part of me does want both—it would make the church happier."

Yawn. Why is she telling me all her life story? Give me the abridged version!

She blathered forever. She recounted all her dating woes, enumerating all the men she attempted to entice to father her children. Now in med school, the desire for having her own kids increased more than ever.

I couldn't help but drift in and out while she spoke. It might've been the whiskey, or her boorish droning. Something she said snapped me awake.

"…and you want children as much as I."

Yes, but not sure I do with you.

"I don't know. I'm still young and exploring my options."

A stern expression came over her face. "You're lying, Larry Johnstone."

"No, I'm not!"

"Remember. We go to the same church."

Was she there that day I received my prophecy?

She stood and stared down at me.

"I know all about you: your hoax of a marriage, and your son. You were with them that night after we met at the beach! I heard that you talked to anyone who gave you an ear about your life mission—to have as many children as possible, with your spouse being the voice of a generation. I don't know if I'll be your voice, but I'll willingly be your vessel. Don't you get it? It would fulfill yours and my prophecy. I'm gonna make you forget about your 'Schnookums.'"

She removed her dress in a single swooping motion.

"Fill me with your babies!"

I stared open-mouthed at her. I had never seen a woman in her underwear before. Even funsies with Schnookums only involved partial nudity—all mine.

"Stand," she ordered.

I obeyed, and she gave me a hug, caressing my back.

"Dana, I can't." I squirmed out of her grip. "I'm married."

"What? You must be kidding me! We're a perfect match for each other—you with your life mission, and me with my desire to have children. And Heather? You do realize she doesn't respect you or your marriage, don't you? Where's she now? Is she even in this city? Why are you clinging on to her?"

"Of course she respects our marriage. She'll come around—you'll see. She still has a part to play in my life. Besides, you and I would need to be married to have sex…in my book."

"Damn it Larry, no we don't!" she yelled. "Our prophecies outweigh marriage…in MY book."

Exasperated, she dressed as quickly as she had undressed.

"I thought we'd be on the same page!"

I didn't care for her tone.

"I can't believe you don't see the opportunity right in front of you!" She stormed out and slammed the door.

I downed the remaining half-bottle of whiskey and passed out on my bed.

The sun rose over the horizon of my tropical paradise island. From the edge of my bamboo bivouac, I sat overlooking the beach dressed only in a damp leather thong. My loins had an uncomfortable itch. Must've rained last night.

Slugging back my morning coconut milk, I meandered towards the shore. Nets were trolling the waters to catch breakfast, bobbing up and down between the crests of the waves. I pulled in the rope.

A brunette emerged from the water holding the line. Her tall slim body slowly unveiled itself as she walked towards me on the shore. Standing in front of me, she said, "Larry, I want your babies."

Of course you do.

Before I could answer, a red head surfaced. She, too, said, "Larry, I want your babies."

Yes, yes.

A third, then a fourth, then a dozen, then maybe fifty women came out, all surrounding me. They pushed me back to the shore all chanting, "I want your babies, I want your babies."

They piled on top of me. I felt used, elated, and exhausted all in the same breath. Their collective weight suffocated me in a weird dysfunctional paradise.

I gasped for air and bolted straight out of bed.

Where am I?

My head ached. I looked around the room. *Did I black out again? What happened last night?*

An empty whiskey bottle, a carton of milk, and a box of Frootie-ooties sat on my dresser, beside my Beanbag Babes.

Score! A quarter-box of cereal remained—better than hospice porridge. I poured out the rest and some milk in the bowl and shoveled in a huge mouthful. *Ugh!* At room temperature, the milk had soured.

I gagged and vomited all over the floor. My mouth tasted like a combination of whiskey, bile, and fried strawberry-oats. *What happened again last night? Oh yeah, I was chatting with Dana. What about?*

Glad I didn't wake up next to her. My Schnookums would've not been pleased. I stared at the mess on the floor. *Someone will clean that up later.* I took off last night's shirt and draped it over the puke.

Thirty people were in line in the caf to feast on eggs and bacon. I decided to skip the greasy breakfast, grabbed a newspaper, and set myself to read in the recreation room.

Reginald came over. "Want a lift to church?"

"Sure."

"Okay, we'll leave in about twenty minutes. Oh, by the way, this came in for you." He held out a neatly gift-wrapped present with an envelope attached.

"Who dropped that off?"

"Don't know. Benny at the front gave it to me when I arrived."

I grabbed it from Reginald and stared at it like someone being confronted by a cobra about to strike. *What's the harm in a gift? Maybe it's from Schnookums!* I unwrapped it before the card. A book—*The Complete Sophocles Anthology.* I leafed through it. *It has Oedipus! Incredibly thoughtful! But who knows about my love for ancient Greek works?*

Everyone knew about my passion for religion and mythology, so the present could've come from anybody. After thinking about it, I came to one conclusion. Vaughn bought it. It's taken several years, but he must now feel guilty for punching my teeth out.

I ripped open the envelope. A hand-drawn donkey with eyes shut and a rose in its mouth adorned the card. The words, "I'm sorry, I was an ass," were written on it. *Yup, Vaughn*—but I opened the card and read:

I really am sorry.
Dana
P.S. I hope we can still be friends.

What on earth happened last night? Oh yeah, the "discussion."
Before I could dive back into reading my newspaper, Reginald told me it was time to go.

We left the building for church, and as we walked towards his car, I had an eerie sensation of being watched. I turned quickly around. There was no one. I had the same feeling when I opened Reginald's car door. I scanned the street, and still did not recognize anyone. My paranoia of being spied upon continued while we drove off to our church in the Kits.

My morning creepies were soon forgotten, thanks to an excellent worship service. I was particularly inspired by three people howling like wolves, and someone interpreting their noises as being a blessing of prosperity for all. I never had any money, so I looked forward to seeing that vision fulfilled, and took the opportunity to discuss investments with a financial expert during the coffee fellowship. Investing in the stock market sounded fascinating, almost like playing a complex game.

"Hi Larry," a voice transcended the hubbub of the crowd, interrupting my conversation. A head taller than most people, Dana was yelling at me from across the gymnasium.

I downed my coffee and gave Reginald a high sign to leave fast. We dashed out of the building, hearing in the background, "I can't wait to have babies with you Larry Johnstone!"

Peter had me venture back out to the campus the next day. I parked myself at my usual spot. Like the previous weekend, there weren't too many people around. I guessed not many students went to school on Mondays.

"Hi Larry, what are you up to today?" a familiar voice said. Dana had her hair done neatly and was wearing casual pants and a preppy shirt. She was accompanied by some friends. She whispered to her clan, and the air filled with "oohs and ahhs" when they discovered what I was selling. They practically cleaned me out of my stock.

Before she left, Dana insisted on taking me on a personalized tour of the campus after her class ended. I initially resisted, but she didn't take no for an answer. She went off to her course, and I waited for the next hour for her to return.

The tour bored me. I had seen most of the buildings before, and Dana's stories of what classes she took in them didn't really thrill me. The faculty of medicine, though, was intriguing. Located on the far edge of the campus, it was an older building. The red bricks and size made it stand out over the others.

The entrance reminded me of a typical medical facility, with waiting area, reception, and halls extending to examination rooms. Dana walked towards an elevator, wanting to show me some of the labs, but I stopped to read a Bristol board sign that caught my eye.

Subjects needed for medical research! Make money! Free meals! Enquire within.

"What's this?" I yelled over to her. She returned and grabbed my hand and pulled me to the elevators.

"That's why I brought you here. My faculty is looking for sperm donors for their research. I wanted to show you around the fertility labs and introduce you to the people running it."

We walked on the elevator together. Dana pressed a button. We were only going up one floor.

"The sign says I can make money?"

"Yeah. Seems pretty easy. You shag yourself off into a cup, and they feed you. I might even get a commission for bringing you in." She winked at me as the doors opened.

Dana showed me around the labs and introduced me to a couple of profs, including the lead researcher for the upcoming clinical trial. Like Dana had said, they were looking for sperm donors, and he appreciated my infectious enthusiasm. Dana put in a few good words for me, too. The man suggested we make an appointment to see if I could qualify.

We returned to admittance.

"I'm sure you'll be a natural at this, Larry," said Dana.

"I know I will," I said. "I'll do it."

I made the appointment for late Thursday.

Dana smiled shyly. "Tell you what. When you return for your appointment, I can take you for a burger and a movie after. There's a new Bruce's Burger Emporium near here. They have awesome shakes!"

Hmmm...free grub and cash? And a movie?

"Okay, sold!"

"Great! By the way...here's a tip. To get a head start on the other candidates, don't ejaculate for the next seventy-two hours. It should take you right to your appointment, and you will be primed and ready to go!"

"Wait? Seventy-two hours?"

I'll die!

Chapter Fifteen
My First Time
May - August 1995

I didn't look forward to the long trek to the university's fertility clinic the morning of my assessment—even if a "release" from my painful abstinence was forthcoming. The vibrations from the tracks during the train ride combined with a severe attack of the "horns" would be absolute hell. Needing to mellow from my stresses with a toke, I grabbed an umbrella and went out to see if Peter had made it out in the rainstorm.

Standing on the corner, dressed in a trench coat, soaked head to toe, Peter didn't have his stand set up and wasn't selling his crap. Instead, he was asking people directly for money.

"Morning, man! Funky day out in the city," Peter said to a woman. She dashed by him. He approached someone else. "Hey, buddy, can you spare an ex-Vietnam vet fifteen dollars for breakfast?" The man ignored him and walked hastily down the road.

"Bastard," Peter said.

"You know," I said, "words like bastard won't help. If you were nice to him, maybe he'd have given you a loonie."

"Nah, brother. All these guys are bastards. Even the ones who give money, man. I despise these yuppie pricks. They'd rather dump ten bucks down the drain drinking coffee than helping someone in need. I'll show them." He looked around at the four corners of the intersection, surveying the people waiting for the traffic signal to change. "See the man over there in the expensive raincoat?" He subtly pointed. "Hold my bag."

He limped towards the gentleman. "Hey brother, sorry to bug you, but do you have a second?" The man stopped for Peter and extended his umbrella to cover his head. "Thanks, man. I'm an executive here in Vancouver attending a technology conference."

"Oh? So am I. Which one?" replied the man.

"Ummm, the computer one… at the Vancouver Hotel," answered Peter.

"Is that the Fast-Track Business Solutions one?"

"Uh, yeah. That's it. But hey, something horrible happened. A man mugged me this morning on my way to Earl of Latteigh. This bastard pushed me to the ground and kicked my gut several times, and I twisted my ankle badly. He made off with my wallet. All my cash, credit cards, and IDs—all gone. He has everything, and I'm really stuck. I was just on my way to the police to report the incident, but thought I'd ask people for help on my way to the station."

"My word. Vancouver is normally such a safe city to walk in."

"So I heard. I need cash to buy a new airline ticket, which was in my brief-case he also took. See, my wife's sick in the hospital. Though she's being cared for by her sister, I'm sure you understand I'd want to return to her tonight. She's been so down in the dumps. Hey, can you spot me 300 bucks? It should cover my flight back to Calgary."

The man raised his hand behind his ear in thought. "I don't have that much money on me. Tell you what. I can give you what I have, and maybe someone else can make up the difference." He took out his wallet and gave Peter some cash. "Maybe you can take the bus back? It'd be cheaper—sorry you went through all this. Vancouver is a great city." With that, the man hustled off.

Peter counted the money and quickly pocketed it before returning to me.

"See? Over a hundred dollars! A day's work in five minutes! People buy what you sell, man. I sell a sob story and aim for the big bucks. Why I'm wearing the trench coat. I look wealthier, which helps. I was lucky. Doesn't always work on the first crack. Anyway, been doing that since my days in San Francisco. I've kept my skills up for those moments when I feel like 'kicking it to the man.' I love it when they cough up the cash!"

Impressive.

Part of me thought Peter's conning young businesspeople cruel and decep-tive. Another side thought it brilliant. *Does he worry about the risks? Couldn't it lead to an arrest?*

"Want to sell stuff today in the pouring rain?" Peter asked.

I nodded, and Peter gave me my usual quota of weed to bring to the univer-sity. I shouldered the soaked bag and left for the train. Along the way, a couple of homeless people asked me for some change. I had some and gave it all away. They weren't Peter. These people were in genuine need, and I worried Peter's tricks would give these poor folk a bad reputation, making it more difficult for them to make ends meet.

That creepy sensation of being watched still followed me.

The train arrived an hour early for my 1 p.m. appointment at the fertility clinic. To kill time, I stood at the centre of campus selling weed. The damp cut right through my bones, and the wet made my long hair frizzy. *One day, I will inherit Peter's business, and I won't have to schlep this heavy bag all over town in the pouring rain.*

Dana greeted me at the entrance of the medical faculty with a warm embrace. I didn't reciprocate.

"Hi Larry, you're going to so rock this fertility thing! Come in."

She sat with me in the waiting area. I couldn't tune her out while she bleated about how a few boys already dumped her this year; and whingeing over having no results maternity-wise for her efforts. *She's pushing hard to have babies! Too bad she hasn't found the one guy to settle with who can give her all the children she wanted.*

A nurse holding a clipboard escorted me into an examination room.

"Good day. We have some preliminary screening questions to ask you. Name?" asked the nurse—and she began rifling through a ton of basic questions:

Age? Thirty, but was told I should've started donation five years sooner. Job? Pharmaceuticals (sort of true). Salary—had no idea, so said 120K, figuring that sounded impressive.

I was getting fed up with all these questions. "I thought you were conducting a research experiment. Not some kind of inquisition."

I was lectured and interrogated for the following hour. They needed to create a profile to help with their studies. My background, habits, and interests could support some of their data analysis. There was an interesting promise that if I scored well with their treatments, my samples might be used for real insemination. That excited me, though a weird question popped up in the conversation—one I never considered before.

"You need to understand that you may be a biological father to many children and never see them. Are you comfortable with that?"

I'm going to be the father of many? Will this be my ticket to birthing a nation? Does it really matter if I actually see them? A quick vision flashed through my mind of all those little Larrys roaming the streets, fulfilling my prophecy. *No doubt they all would inherit my strong genes, making it clear who is their father. I'd spot one of my spawn from a mile away, and be satisfied!*

I nodded.

The nurse jotted some notes. "What would you do if one of the 'Little Larrys' actually wanted to meet their biological Dad?"

"I'd welcome them with open arms." *As long as I don't have to pay for them.*

She went on to explain the challenges I could have not being able to see all my children. The nurse also talked about the sticky issues one could have if not transparent about sperm donation with family. She suggested that I might need to consult a lawyer to draft a contract to define my parental and financial rights and obligations. I felt confident Schnookums would be okay with it and nodded solemnly.

"Noted…Okay, I've answered your questions. When can I jerk off in a cup? I haven't touched my weenie in days, and my boys are aching to explode."

She stood in a huff. "I don't need this." She left the room.

Another nurse returned to complete my interview. He had one of the deepest voices I'd ever heard. "We have a few more questions, then we must give you a full medical." He raised the clipboard left behind by the other nurse. "What are your hobbies and interests?"

Masturbating and picking wildflowers?

"I read mythology and theology." *Now to up my profile with these peasants.* "I received a bachelor's degree in business administration; I completed a master's in theology; and I am now pursuing a PhD on the effects of erosion on archaeological samples—all in my spare time. Oh, and of course, I have a passion for board games and choral singing."

He continued, "One last question. Tell me about your sexual history."

I spent the next half hour listing all the girls who dumped me, reiterating my desire to have children. I concluded with mentioning my marriage to Heather, and how I impregnated her using a condom.

"Enough," yelled the nurse. His voice boomed me to silent attention. Poor man looked drained when I finished. He was slumped in the chair, wrists resting limp on its arms dangling the clipboard. "Rare we see people getting pregnant using contraceptives," the nurse mumbled. "We're done. Stay here for your medical."

I sat on the examination room bed, swinging my legs while waiting. The doctor arrived and thoroughly checked me out—warts and all. He also confirmed I was free of venereal diseases.

"Okay, Larry, all's good. If you ever decide to be a sperm donor full time, you'll need to do these checks bi-annually."

Another nurse entered wearing yellow scrubs. After performing a blood test, she gave me some magazines. "Go to the bathroom and complete the act in there." She passed me a cup. "When you're done, drop off your sample at the registration desk. They'll schedule you for some additional pre-trial tests. We need to do a comprehensive analysis of your semen before admitting you for the full clinical trials."

"What's the pay?"

"Sorry?" said the nurse.

"I get paid for this, don't I? A man got fifty bucks for a single toss at a clinic I visited in Seattle."

The young women's eyes widened. "Oh, no. I'm sorry. We didn't receive enough funding to pay testers for the trials. The food is still free, though, but we'll insist you follow our diet…if you qualify."

WHAT?

Pissed, I snatched the magazines from her hand and stormed into my "reading" room. *They'll change their minds and pay me a fortune when they see my results. My sperm will be like gold.*

The first magazine had a French title with a woman on the cover. After leafing through some interesting articles, my eyes practically jumped out of my skin. I never expected there'd be such graphic images!

It took me less than a minute to do my business with the inspiration of the colourful photos. When I returned to the waiting area, Dana bounced out of her seat and pounced on me, giving me a long hug. She must've waited two hours!

"Larry, let's see how you did." Before I could react, she grabbed my specimen bottle. "What a great output! I knew you could do it!" She gave me another awkward hug.

Dana placed my specimen on a tray, then clapped her hands and said, "I'm so proud of you! Hey, ready for dinner?"

Crap. I had completely forgotten about our "date."

We ordered our meal at Bruce's Burger Emporium. The shakes were touted to be the best in the West, but I'd never know—Dana spilled mine all over my lap when she stretched her long arm across the table while making some emphatic point. The burgers, though, did remind me of my days in Ottawa hanging with my best friend, Brad. They tasted the same as those he made on his old barbeque.

Dana chatted away non-stop, while I daydreamed, staring at her big nose. Her awkward looks did grow on me. It gave her character. I only wished her "character" would stop blabbing. I am a good listener and would always extend an ear to my friend's "woe is me" stories. I wasted many hours listening to that pathetic nitwit…

"…Rick could've been the one." she said.

What, what, what?

"We only saw each other twice when I last visited Toronto. The first time we sat next to each other at a Blue Jays game. We talked baseball the whole time. He's such a charming guy, and I loved the fact that he played in a punk band. I'll never forget the name: Scottish Rot."

Wait, you know Rick, aka Dick Wank?

"Anyway, I bumped into him after the game at a club near the ballpark. We danced up a storm. He's so awkward and gangly." Dana laughed.

You should talk.

"I really liked him. He did tell me about how he babysat for his neighbour's daughter most of his life…what was her name again? Was it Cheryl? Anyway, he reeked of being a dad, so I thought it made sense we'd spend the night together." Dana giggled mischievously "Did you know Rick was a virgin? Poor guy was so nervous, but we still had fun. He had to take off early the next morning before I could get his mailing address."

Hmm…can I pawn Dana off to Randy Rick?

"I have it."

"What?" said Dana.

"I have his mailing address. I can give it to you." I reached into my bag, pulled out a pen, and jotted it down on a napkin. After all these years, I still remembered that jerk's home address. Dana squealed when I handed her the napkin. I could tell she was committing the information to memory.

"How do you know him?"

"I've known him since he was sixteen. Great guy." *Bullshit.* "Totally get why you like him. He's a sweetie." *Vomit.* "He still lives in Ottawa." *I think.* "He'd make a great dad for your kids!" *Assuming he's fertile…*

"That would be amazing!" She re-read the napkin. "His last name is Duncan?"

I nodded.

"Oooooh! I'm gonna follow up on this. You're so awesome!"

She leaned forward and kissed my cheek, paid the bill, and we walked back to the train.

"Thanks for the wonderful day, Larry. When do we go out again?"

Never.

"Maybe after I've completed all these medical tests?" *I said that?*

"Great! Can't wait!"

Dana was unshakeable during my six-week clinical trials to support the research. The daily commute to the university was gruelling, and the mornings she didn't work at Jumpin' Java, she'd "coincidently" bump into me leaving the hospice for the station. She'd join me on the train to the university and chitter-chatter about the importance of "her" mission, then left to attend classes, giving me a break…though never felt like they lasted long enough.

Dana often intercepted me before I returned home, and we'd take the train back together. I didn't understand why she bothered. She lived on campus. Dana would try cuddling into me by leaning against my shoulder while we commuted. It felt like needles to my skin. *Why doesn't she write Rick?*

I had little doubt I'd be selected for the trials. The chief researcher had mentioned my results put me in the top one percent of donors, making me an ideal candidate for his work.

The schedule was strict and included daily feedings, and twice a week I had to provide sperm samples. I also endured regular injections of their "experimental serum." One awkward thing—which amused me—I had to freeze my balls after breakfast. They even had special undies for that!

The things I do for my mission!

It'd been quite a juggling act going to and from the university and the hospice to balance my clinical trials with my work. Fearing the constant train rides risked bankrupting me, I played "nice" with Dana. After my first week she had agreed to support "her" mission by paying for all my transportation.

Despite the occasional kindness, like paying for my train fare, Dana became an increasing nuisance. A couple of weeks into the trials, she started skipping classes to hang out with me. Often, I'd see her in the clinic's waiting area when I finished my work and applaud my efforts like a cheerleader, then we'd go back to her dorm to watch some television.

TV silenced her chattiness. She enjoyed soap operas—we did have that in common. She set a VCR to record her shows daily and invited me to watch them with some of her friends from school. It was fun cracking jokes at the bad acting and the unbelievable plots. I'd return to the hospice shortly after the soaps ended—but never alone.

Each night, Dana dropped me off at the door of the hospice. She'd insist on a goodnight kiss, which I'd grant, but tight-lipped. She couldn't take a hint I wanted to go to sleep, and sometimes insinuated wanting to come up to my room. I forbade it saying it would be too upsetting for the residents, and besides, I had to follow the medical clinic's "rules" for sleep.

Yeah, weekdays were tiring, but the weekends were worse. I still had to go to campus, and Dana didn't have classes.

She accompanied me everywhere, not giving me any peace. Even though I told her we couldn't go out on dates because I couldn't eat at restaurants, she still wanted to spend time with me. She'd suggest going to the movies, paying for my ticket, or going for long walks between my meals. I had tried to dismiss her by saying it was my "homework" time. Didn't faze her. She'd drag me out to a park and we'd both study together on a bench. Killed me. Hard to read Ancient Greek when you're not in the mood. I'd often just stare into space for hours.

After the fourth week of my trials, a new habit started. Little notes of encouragement were left for me in the entranceway of the hospice—strategically placed so I'd notice them on my way out for coffee. Sometimes there'd be a small gift, like a book of stickers or a funny pen. My Bible reading at the Jumpin' Java would be interrupted by her asking what I had thought about the latest one. If I didn't make a comment, it'd upset her. She would exercise some restraint for the sake of the customers, but I knew if we were alone, she would've blown her stack.

She never directly said she loved me, but I felt she inferred it through her notes. They often thanked me for the day before, and how she longed for the next time we'd be together. I grew concerned when she began dropping hints about bearing my children. Some notes contained cutesy hand-drawn animals caring for little babies swaddled in linens.

During the last full week of my trials, a second note was glued beside Dana's. It simply ordered me to call an anonymous number. I phoned when I returned home late in the evening.

"Hello?" a familiar, yet husky, voice said.

"Schnookums?"

"Honey-Bear," Heather's voice chirped. Her tone changed. "It's after midnight here in Toronto."

"Oh, sorry. "

"Doesn't matter. I called to let you know I'll be in Vancouver for business on the weekend. Want to get together with Lars and me on Sunday?"

I couldn't believe my ears! Excited, I told her we'd have to go out to the university, but we could spend some time swimming at a nearby public pool. Heather agreed.

I left the hospice Sunday morning for my wife to collect me. Dana, as usual, was waiting outside on the sidewalk. She grabbed my hand to begin walking towards the train station.

"Not today, Dana," I said.

"What?" She spotted my wife's fancy blue sports car slowing down in front of the building. She released my hand, stormed across the road, crossed her arms, and stared at us like a vulture.

Heather lowered the window. "Who's that?" she barked.

Relieved Dana didn't create a scene, I whipped open the door. "I dunno. Some weirdo. Can we split?"

My wife peeled down the road cranking some ghastly song called "I'll Make Love to You."

"That was great timing," I said. "Thanks for saving me from her." Though I embellished the truth a bit for the sake of my marriage—I painted a story of Dana being a huge source of stress.

Schnookums placed her hand on my thigh and squeezed. "I wouldn't let that tramp interfere with my marriage."

We took a long and wonderful drive together before arriving at the university. The clinic surprised me with some coupons to local restaurants for all my meals that day—though I was limited to what I could eat. It was their gift to celebrate my trials nearing an end.

We found a nice family restaurant. Dining alone with my wife and child made it a special occasion and being permitted to enjoy a greasy cheeseburger for the first time in several weeks was near orgasmic.

Did I see someone staring at us through the restaurant window?

I shook it off.

My family spent the afternoon swimming, and we went for another long drive before dinner. The evening ended at Heather's hotel, where I read Lars a story about Moses.

With my son tucked away in bed, Heather whispered, "Do you still have those condoms I gave you?"

I did keep them on me, specially reserved for my next encounter with Schnookums. I fumbled in my pocket and produced a square package labelled Cock Socks.

She squealed. "You are so romantic. But I don't think we'll need them. Come."

She opened the bathroom door not to disturb our child, and led me in. We began to kiss. Given it had been a few days since my last sperm donation, it only took a few seconds for me to "be in the mood." But then remembered...

My last appointment...

I let out a prolonged moan, not out of desire, but frustration.

"What's the matter. Honey-Bear?"

"I can't do this," I said. "I have to go back to the university tomorrow. I have one more donation to make to complete my clinical trials."

"Skip it," Heather murmured in my ear and lowered her hand to grasp my buttocks.

A dilemma hit me. I had a choice: a night of ecstasy with my wife, one which I might never have again for a while; or keep true to my mission to father a nation.

Heather hasn't exactly been "ever present" in my life.

"I'm sorry Schnookums. I can't. I must finish what I started."

"No one has ever refused me before." She walked out of the bathroom and opened the room door. "Leave!"

Walking down the street, I ached in remorse. *Did I blow it with Heather?* Entering the hospice, a card of a hand-drawn snarling wolf was taped to the wall.

Dana had pushed my last button.

Dana poured me a cup of coffee, like normal, Monday morning. She returned several minutes later after serving a few more customers.

"What'd you think of the card?" she said with cutting bitterness.

I didn't answer.

"You had one more sperm donation to make today." Her voice rose. "You refused to have babies with me, and you spent the evening with *her*?"

She's been spying on me!

Not knowing what to say, I raised my cup for a refill.

Dana erupted. She poured the contents of her decanter on my lap. Thankfully, I jumped out of the way in the nick of time, minimizing the effect of the burning liquid. I wiped off the small splash of coffee that landed on my pants.

"You dickhead," she yelled. "I gave you everything. I paid for coffee, gifts, and a fortune in train fare. I even accepted that you didn't want to have your babies with me. Then you go back to that bitch wife? I never want to see you again Larry Johnstone!"

She pivoted around to face the stunned customers, walked a few steps, and turned back to me. "One more thing, jerkoff. Do you know why you were eligible for the sperm donor trials? It's because you can't cut it 'man-wise.' They might've said you were in the top one percent, all right—but they weren't looking for the highest sperm count. They were looking for the lowest! It would've been a fluke for us, or anyone, to have your children. Why I rooted for you to succeed. It would've been a miracle. But you know what, you prick? Your balls will probably rot with all the drugs they gave you!" She slammed the glass decanter down on the ground causing it to shatter and stormed out of the shop.

Pffft. One percent lowest. She doesn't have a clue what she's talking about. I, after all, already HAD a child!

I checked my watch.

I better put on my Freezie Undies—gotta protect my balls-ies for one more shows-ie.

I left the shop coffee-stained, but free.

Life returned to normal for me after the trials. Sadly, I had to eat the slop at the hospice instead of the better food at the clinic. I resumed my daily coffee routine at Jumpin' Java, free of worry from Dana. The owner, Caleb Schwarz, had fired Dana for her outburst.

I had peace for a week before Dana left an "I'm sorry note" on the door of the hospice. I read it while standing outside the building. It was odd. She wrote a message that she hoped that both our prophecies would be fulfilled one day. I looked up and thought I saw her hiding around a building in the distance.

I hoped I'd lose these illusions of her stalking me one day.

Feeling nostalgic one August day, I sweated, walking through the Kits under a blazing sun one morning. I passed by my old home, where Little Larry and I spent so many months alone together while Heather and Sven went travelling all over the place. I watched a man hammer a sign in the lawn outside the building. It read "Condo For Sale" with a photo of a striking real estate agent named Hugo Nilsson. I stared at the sign in disbelief. The handsome picture of Hugo gripped me. He could've been Sven's older brother.

I couldn't believe Sven was selling the place. We had so many memories. I missed life in the Kits and living in the lap of luxury with the beautiful views and majestic bathroom. Sven selling the condo felt like an end of an era.

It didn't take long to sell the condo—maybe a few weeks. I "celebrated" by purchasing a bottle of whiskey and crashing on the couch in front of the TV at the hospice. Though tempted, I didn't buy a box of Frootie-ooties. I couldn't stomach the memory of Dana. Dumping her and having consummated my marriage with my wife filled me with a confidence deeper than I've ever had before. I flicked on the TV.

Hmmm, Sven is becoming less and less a fixture on these horrible Bärbar Ugn commercials—and Schnookums is taking more of a lead!

She had on the same flattering red dress on the TV that she wore when I first landed in Vancouver.

Odd she'd wear maternity clothes on TV surrounded by sexy half-naked people.

Chapter Sixteen
The Lion's Den

November 1995

A short, stocky man heaved a large monitor from a box and placed it on the office desk. He wiped a bead of sweat from his bald head, stretched, and cracked his back.

"You'd think with all the technological advancements, they'd be lighter," he said.

"I've never owned a computer, Troy," Reginald exclaimed. "This one is called a *Pentium*. Sounds so science fiction."

Troy left the office.

"Yes, *Pentiums* are a type of computer," I said, using my authoritative voice. "They're a piece of cake. You type what you want it to do and poof, it's done."

"You make them sound so easy peasy, Larry," said Reginald.

Troy returned with a big box.

"That's because they are! I'm a computer master. You should've seen me on my friend's video games back in the '80s, manipulating his joystick."

Troy snickered. "They're not that easy. You know how many hours I've lost on mine at home to make it go 'poof.' Where do you want the printer, Reginald?"

"Oh, place it to the right of the monitor. That'd be super," said Reginald. "Did you bring in the software?"

Troy nodded and patted an unopened box by the door.

"This is great!" I said and jumped in the seat at the desk.

I had seen the movie *The Net* with Dana during my clinical trials last summer. I had hoped with a name like that it would've been an erotic thriller. Instead, the film featured the internet. I had never heard of it before, and this machine could open the doorway to explore this new frontier.

I pressed the power button on the monitor. Nothing happened. *Hmmm...*I applied more pressure the second time and held it longer. Still nothing. I banged the side of it. "Stupid computer, you worked all the time for me back home."

"Not likely without these." Troy lifted the wires out of the box and began hooking everything together. He plugged a power bar into the wall, flicked a switch in the back, and the computer beeped.

"Excellent! Space Invaders, here I come," I said.

I half expected an animated clip like "Mozart's Ghost" from *The Net* to kick in and be my portal to the web. Instead, some text with words I didn't understand flashed, making way for a screen that simply read "login" a few minutes later.

"Smashing, Troy, everything looks tickety-boo," said Reginald. "Larry, seeing you have experience with computers, would you like to help install the financial software?" He pointed to a box labelled "Easy Accounting."

"You bet!" I opened it and pulled out a black disk a little over three inches square. "What's this?" I read the label: "Easy Accounting—disk 1 of 42." I reached into the box and found a user guide. It must've been a thousand pages, forty of which were consumed by the table of contents! *No way I'm reading through this thing.*

I placed the manual down on the table. "I just remembered... I have a very important phone call to make. Can I come back when you have the internet all set up?"

"No problem, Larry," said Reginald. "Troy will help. I want all the staff to start using the computer for email. This is so exciting!"

I had little doubt my body would respond well to the treatments during my clinical trials. Starting in the top one percent of candidates with a sperm count of five million, by the time we finished treatment, I hit an epic proportion of sixty million! My math sucked, but I figured it was a quagillion percent increase.

The university had distributed my load to various fertility clinics around the city. It'd been a few months since the conclusion of the testing, and they'd never told me how my "little boys" were doing. I had faith Larry nation was *en route* to growing and had made a mental note a few weeks back to call the university to get the scoop.

"Hello," said the familiar voice of the office administrator at the lab.

"Hi, this is Larry Johnstone. I'm calling to find out how my samples are doing across the city."

"Larry, so nice to hear from you! You know we can't divulge that information. Besides, we have to wait for all the fertility clinics to report back their results in order for us to officially complete our research. It might take a couple of years."

"A couple of years? It can't go any faster?" I was hopeful that I'd receive confirmation Larry nation was growing. I also hadn't heard from Heather since her visit last summer. I missed my wife, and part of me wished I hadn't spurned her.

"You know, Larry, your results are decent. Have you ever thought about being a sperm donor? There is need."

This could totally work for me to father more kids. She promised to make an appointment with a nearby fertility clinic, and we arranged a time for me to drop by and pick up my file.

I hung up the phone and walked by the office. It looked like Troy was still ploughing away at installing the accounting software. Based on the piles of disks he had arranged, he'd be at it for another couple of hours.

I left the building to grab a few brews to celebrate a renewed hope to grow my kingdom and fulfill my prophecy.

Troy something-or-other, a long-time member of the staff at the hospice, and I shared a similar problem. We both struggled to find love in our thirties. He had a few strikes against him, in my opinion. Being short, bald, and near forty didn't serve him well in the looks department. He was also a quiet introvert— which didn't help either. I couldn't imagine a woman desiring his company. I mean, Troy to me was the clichéd computer nerd, whereas I maintained my "cool."

He noticed me standing in the office door when I returned from the pub. "Hey Larry, you didn't miss much—that software was pain to install. You mentioned something about the internet?"

"I'm there!" I said, pulling up a chair next to him while we waited for the computer to complete its starting sequence.

I instinctively grabbed the mouse, and the arrow on the monitor matched my hand movements. *Ooh, easy!*

"What's this?" I exclaimed.

Troy glanced over my shoulder. Before he could say anything, I clicked on the InternetServe icon. Nothing happened, I frantically tapped the mouse several times. Squeaks and whistles erupted. *What the...sounds like "The Net."* The whistles surrendered to a grinding whir, followed by some white noise, then silence. An InternetServe screen displayed topics of interest, including sports and music. *Ooh! The world is my oyster.*

"Woah, Troy! See what I did?" I pointed emphatically at the screen.

"You're amazing, Larry, a natural," said Troy.

I didn't care for his sarcasm. "Yeah, you know it. I know more about computers than all you neophytes at the hospice combined! I played *all* the video games in the '80s!"

That shut him up.

I chatted to him about how I wanted to be like that high-tech heroine in *The Net* while we waited for a "Welcome to the Internet" message to load. Troy pointed out a link to create an email account. I clicked the "register now" button, revealing a colourful page boasting a system called Torpedomail. I had little idea what email was or why I needed it, but since Reginald mentioned it earlier, I figured it might be worthwhile checking out.

I followed the steps to create an account carefully. *This is too easy!* Didn't even need Troy's help! When prompted, I typed my name, Larry. *What is it with this keyboard? The letters are not organized alphabetically.* It took me a couple of minutes to key it in and hit enter. After all that effort the computer responded the name wasn't available and suggested I use Larry97891.

Pfffft. Who dares take my first choice?

Exasperated, and tongue firmly in cheek, I typed "SuperSpermLarry." The page loaded a congratulatory message indicating I created the account "superspermlarry@torpedomail.com."

Yeah baby! I clapped and high-fived Troy. *Perfect!*

I read the user instructions on screen. I had no one to send messages to yet, so Troy, who also had an account, showed me how to do it. We practiced bouncing emails back and forth until I mastered it. *Could email open the door to reconnecting with Little Larry and Schnookums?*

He patted my back and laughed. "Congratulations Larry, I'm your first email contact! I'll be sure to write you often!"

What a kind gesture!

One of Troy's best qualities was his love for people. His care and compassion for those down on their luck inspired us all. He went out of his way seeking folk in the street to help those in need. Maybe Troy could've let that side of him shine more when he spoke with women. But he, like me, struggled with the same question: Where are all the chicks hiding in this city?

We had often talked of our dilemmas and shared the same sense of desperation. It had a strong negative impact on Troy's spirit, who wanted to marry. The whole issue of women depressed him.

"Hey," he said, "you doing anything tonight?"

"I'm weighing my options."

"If you're bored, and alone, why don't you join me at my gentlemen's club? It's great! It gives me a nice break when I feel low."

I took him up on the invitation, always being open to meet new people. I hoped they played board games, smoked cigars, and served whiskey. I could teach the members my masterful chess strategies, but Troy didn't elaborate about the club activities. I didn't care. I looked forward to visiting his hangout.

After supper, we strolled down to the harbour. We approached an establishment called the Lion's Den Gentlemen's Club. The sign outside the joint had a caricature of a smiling lion's head with a crown inviting people in. Neon lights flashed "live shows" and "free buffet." I didn't realize Troy belonged to such an exclusive establishment—and I made a note of the free food. *Might ditch the slop at the hospice if this place is any good.* The building had no windows and resembled a large concrete warehouse.

Two gentlemen dressed in tight polo shirts greeted us at the door. Their bodies spanned twice the width of the average guy.

"Five-dollar cover," one said.

Troy looked expectedly over to me. "Nuts, I left my wallet at the hospice. Larry, how much money do you have?"

I had huge stack of cash—it was payday with Peter. Begrudgingly, I gave the bouncer ten bucks. It surprised me this club needed to charge an entrance fee. I mean, every church potluck I ever attended was free.

"Two drink minimum," the man yelled from behind as we entered.

I expected a room filled with billiard tables, board games, and books. Troy's club had blue lighting that created a dark, melancholic atmosphere. We turned the corner and there, in the middle of a large room, a stage jutted with men sitting around it. It prominently featured a couple of golden poles in the middle.

Troy found an empty table in the half-full room. A young woman took our drink order. I couldn't help noticing that most of the women serving were beautiful, but scantily dressed.

"Troy," I said, "I thought you said we were going to play games tonight. I so looked forward to a round of *Parcheesi.* Had I realized there'd be bombshell babes here to meet, I would've put on my sexy kilt!"

"Don't sweat it, Larry. The women here don't care what you wear. They're pretty laid back and super friendly. See the girl in the far corner?"

"What? The one wearing the candy-cane striped bikini?"

"Yes, that's the one. Her name is, ironically, Candi. She's my favourite. I'll introduce you. She'll swing by when she notices me. Always does."

"Always does? You come here often?"

"Maybe a couple of times a week. Usually when I know Candi is around."

Candi spotted Troy in the distance, and her face lit up with a smile that screamed personality. She advanced to our table.

"Hi, Troy," she said. "I've missed you! How've you been?"

Troy laughed but quickly changed expressions to that of a sad man. "Been a tougher day. In fact, I'm a bit down in the dumps."

"That's horrible, babe. You've been having a lot of those lately. Do you want some cheering up?"

"I'd love some."

Candi grabbed Troy's hand and led him away.

"I won't be long," he said, leaving me alone.

Jerk didn't bother introducing us. Guess that's smart. He would've lost Candi to a guy like me.

A voice over a speaker boomed. "Good evening gentlemen, and welcome to the Lion's Den. Please give a warm round of applause, for your viewing pleasure, our featured entertainer, Fanny Foof."

The waitress dropped off our drinks. I lifted a flyer lying on the table. It promoted Fanny who apparently was a huge name in the adult industry. *Why would she hang out at Troy's club?* I downed my drink while the DJ cranked "I Want to Know What Love Is" by Foreigner.

A middle-aged woman moved to the dull song with a grace of a cobra swaying to a snake charmer. *Must've spent a fortune on collagen to keep her going.*

The waitress brought two more drinks, even though I didn't ask for them. I couldn't break my gaze from the stage while she placed them on the table.

Fanny's taking her clothes off!

Watching the naked woman dance embarrassed me. I didn't understand why Troy thought this place would help our loneliness. If anything, it augmented it. I really didn't like the atmosphere of the club.

Some men sitting around the stage were laughing, others catcalling. Some sat motionless, staring, soaking in every motion Fanny made. These men all wore the same blank expression—all of them alone, absorbing the dark atmosphere. The louder ones tended to be in gangs.

A group from the military were the rowdiest. They were talking to a blonde woman wearing bunny ears in a one-piece bathing suit with a cotton tail. She caught my eye in the distance, and she flashed me a sexy smile. The Larry charm even worked in a place like this!

The Foreigner song finished, and Fanny left the stage. "Ladies and gentlemen," the DJ announced, "give a warm round of applause for Fanny Foof. She'll be back in an hour."

Where on earth did Troy go?

Thankful the performance ended, I helped myself to one of Troy's drinks. Bunny-girl went back to the bar and caught my eye and smiled again. She put down her tray and approached my seat while the DJ cranked "Pour Some Sugar on Me."

"May I join you?" she asked.

"Okay, my friend disappeared."

She sat in the chair next to mine and inched it close. "You mean Troy? He'll be gone for at least a half an hour with Candi."

"How'd you know his name?"

"He comes here often enough. We all know him. Candi is his favourite." She laughed and gently touched my knee with her left hand. "What's your name?"

"Hi, I'm Larry Johnstone." I reached and shook her hand.

"Nice to meet you, Larry. I love your glasses. They make you look like John Lennon."

Yup! She has a thing for me.

"You look a little familiar, Larry," she continued. "Have we met somewhere before?"

"I don't think so. I've dated hundreds of women, and for sure, I would've remembered someone as beautiful as you."

I can play the game as well as any.

The woman blushed and placed her hand on my forearm. "Go on, Larry. A guy like you must've been with many gorgeous women."

I laughed. "Well, I am quite the stud muffin, and you'd better be careful. I'm in the top one percent of potent sperm donors. You might get pregnant by just looking at me!"

She cracked up and slapped my arm. I loved her energy.

"I don't hear that every day! I'll make sure I'm on my guard, Larry," she said with a twinkle in her eye.

"Ever play around with the internet? I even have an email address with my nickname in it! It's superspermlarry@torpedomail.com —easy to remember!"

She laughed again.

"I didn't catch your name," I said.

"Oh, it's Honey Buns."

Honey Buns? In rabbit ears?

"Funny," I said, "I sometimes call my wife Honey-Bunny. She's sorta looks like you, Honey Buns, only you're smaller."

"Wife? I hope she doesn't mind you talking to me!" She rubbed her hand slowly on my forearm.

"I don't think she'd mind. Hell, we haven't lived together in years," I said.

"I'm so sorry to hear that." She stopped stroking my forearm and held my hand in both of hers.

I choked up a bit. "She was my everything. She had beauty, intelligence, and a great personality. We had a wonderful child together."

"Larry, many would kill for what you had." Her expressive and sympathetic eyes made me tear. She placed her arm around my shoulder. "What on earth happened?"

"That snake, Sven, happened. He filled her brain with dreams of fame and business success. They've been travelling all over Canada the last several years selling those ridiculous ovens. I can't believe they're still popular."

"You mean Sven Lindgaard? The inventor of the *Bärbar Ugn*? Would you believe I passed an audition for the infomercial here in Vancouver?"

I knew she looked familiar. She's one of his dancing girls.

"He's a bit of an ass," she continued. "Instead of paying me, they gave me a *Bärbar Ugn*. It's a useless piece of shit." She cuddled a bit closer.

She digs me.

"Why'd you audition for the infomercial?" I asked.

"A couple of reasons. I love dancing and entertaining. I'd like to act one day. Who knows? It's a TV credit to my resume. I also have to pay my way through university. Did you get a degree?"

"Yes, a couple. I have a Master of Theology and a doctorate," I spewed my usual half-truths.

"Oooh. So nice to have an opportunity for intelligent conversation. I rarely have any here. You must be brilliant to have received your doctorate."

She recognizes my superior intellect!

The song ended. Troy still hadn't returned.

"Why don't we continue our discussion in the back?" Honey flashed me some bedroom eyes. "We'll have more privacy there."

I couldn't argue with her. The music and lights were distracting. She took me by the hand, I grabbed Troy's drink, and she led me out through a door marked "VIP."

We were alone in the Valentine-pink room at the back of the club. Honey directed me to sit in a velour chair. She then squatted in front of me and balanced herself with her hands on my knees.

"You've had it so hard Larry. Dating many women and losing the one you loved." Honey's alluring eyes hypnotized me.

The room filled with a wretched song with a heavy guitar lick. I never liked rock music, and AC/DC might've been the worst of the lot. The main lick of "You Shook Me All Night Long" kicked in, and on cue, Honey stood and started to swing her hips to the beat.

She turned around and bent over to touch her toes, leaving her bunny tail inches from my nose. Beyond awkward, I pushed myself deep in my chair turning away. She spun dramatically to face me and re-assumed her squat position. Honey looked down to the zipper at the top of her one-piece bathing suit, then back to me. She placed her hand on top of the zipper and slowly began to lower it.

This isn't the way to cure loneliness!

"Stop it!" I yelled before the zipper hit the top of her chest. "I didn't know you'd do that."

Honey, a bit stunned, stood and zipped up her suit quickly. "Larry dear, what did you expect in the VIP room?"

"You said we'd continue our chat in private. I have so much to tell you about my life. We could talk for hours, and I guarantee you you'll be hanging on my every word. You're right, too. I have had it hard with women—and I do pine for my Schnookums."

Honey laughed. "Schnookums? Your wife? That's so sweet! But look, Larry. I really enjoyed our time tonight, but if you're not interested in my dancing, I need to tend to other customers. I'll have to charge you for our time. Are you sure you don't want to stay? It's thirty dollars for the first dance, but fifteen for any after."

"I don't want a dance. I want a chat. I don't want to pay to talk."

"Sorry dear," said Honey Buns. "It's club policy."

"But we're getting along so well. Talk should be free!"

"You're a peach, Larry. But rules are rules. If you come back to the club, I'd love to spend more time with you."

Disappointed about club policy, I shelled out the thirty dollars. *Isn't the cover charge enough?*

"Thank you," Honey said, "it's also customary to give a tip as well. Whatever you feel is right."

Extortion! I gave her ten dollars. Clearly, I'm in the wrong line of business. We only spent about fifteen minutes together.

I left the VIP room on my own. Troy waited for me at our table. A large bald gentleman with a goatee wearing a Lion's Den polo shirt stood beside him, arms folded.

"Larry, I'm so glad to see you. I spent a little too much time with Candi. I owe the club a hundred bucks. Can you bail me out?"

Is Troy nuts? He knows the costs and the way this club works.

"And if I don't?"

"I'm in a world of hurt." Troy looked up to the bouncer.

I dished out the money.

Wallet thoroughly drained, we left the dark and depressing place.

A week passed and I didn't see a dime from Troy. He must've had money. He went back to the Lion's Den often. *Jerk!*

I couldn't stop thinking about Honey Buns. Stupid club policy. It interrupted a wonderful evening. She wanted to be in the entertainment industry. *If she becomes famous, and I married her, Honey could fulfill both elements of my prophecy!*

I couldn't imagine how one could find any job satisfaction in a place filled with lonely and desperate men like Troy. Maybe if she found the right person…

The next morning, I was shocked to receive an email from honeybuns@ lionsdengc.com. It was my first from anyone not named Troy.

Dear Larry,

Loved being with you the other night. I haven't seen you in a while and hoping you can come back.

Love,

Honey xxx

She misses me! What a sweetheart!
A second message caught my eye from info@thelionsdengc.com.

Dear Larry,

Nice to have seen you at our club!

We hope you enjoyed our featured dancer, Fanny Foof. She will be continuing her performances until the end of November. If you are interested in receiving future updates from our club, including our hot newsletter, simply click the link below.

Keep your pecker up,

Denny from the Lion's Den

Where on earth did they get my email address?
I clicked the link to subscribe to the newsletter and responded to Honey:

Dear Honey,

I loved our time together, too. Look forward to reconnecting with you soon.

You have a precious heart.

Love,

Larry xx

I didn't hear back from Honey Buns, but I received an important message from nearby Golden Oak Hospital's fertility clinic.

I jumped in the air.

Goodie! I'm going to be an official donor! Golden Oak boasted the largest fertility clinic in the province.

I walked into the west-end hospital for my appointment later that week. A round-faced nurse who might've been in her forties sat behind a counter in the admitting area, reading one of my favourite magazines, *Cosmopolitan.* A finger twirled in her short dark curly hair. Her black scrubs complemented her dour look.

"Hi, I'm Larry Johnstone. I'm here to give you my sample." I put a copy of my file from the university's fertility clinic down on the countertop. "You'll see I'll produce the highest quality sperm in the world! My tests are off the charts."

"They all say that." The woman peered up at me above the rims of her aviator glasses, nonplussed. Her badge read Margo.

I didn't care for her tone. "You know, you really should smile more. Might help lift your spirits."

She put down her magazine. "You have to be kidding me."

"It's true. It's common knowledge. Smiling is the first step in liberating your soul."

She grinned from ear to ear, then frowned. "Nope, doesn't work. What are you here for?"

I explained while she glanced through my file.

Straight-faced she said, "You're results look pretty average. Still, you might qualify."

Anyone with a half a brain would appreciate my potency.

"What do you mean, might? The university referred *me* to *you*. Don't you see my results?"

"Sure I do." She opened a desk drawer and pulled out a thick stack of paper. "Here, you'll need to complete this questionnaire. Take your time. The board will review it and determine if you're suitable."

"Great. When do I get started and how much will I get paid?"

"There is no payment, sweetie. You donate for the sheer pleasure of it. We reap the rewards." She forced a toothy grin.

I stared at the woman in disbelief. "You know, you really need to practice smiling."

"I don't have time for this nonsense," she said. "The questionnaire will take you a lot of time to complete, and we'll need a sample for our evaluation. When was your last ejaculation?"

"Last night." The effects of the club still lingered.

"As you're well aware from your file" — she lifted it — "you need to go without for seventy-two hours. You may as well come back next week with your paperwork completed. How old are you, by the way? You look a little old. Most of our donors are in their twenties."

"I'm thirty."

"Not exactly in your prime. By the way, nice mullet."

"I'll be back," I said with my deepest Arnold Schwarzenegger Terminator voice. Margo didn't react. "C'mon. That was funny. Not even a grin?"

"Like this?" Margo stretched her lips from ear to ear revealing perfect teeth.

A little over the top, but that's the idea.

There were over forty pages of questions the clinic wanted me to complete—and I had answered most during my trials at the university! They included all the details about my health, sexual history, and my physical characteristics. Per usual, I filled them out to present myself as a perfect candidate, even if it stretched the truth a bit.

No one could accuse me of lying. All the responses were based on my true personae—a man who produces children with natural good looks, and superior intellect. I made a point of memorizing my answers in case of further questioning.

I returned to the hospital seventy-two hours later. Margo maintained a fixed grin during my visit, even when she showed me the room where I squirted a sample. A few days later, they announced I qualified to be a donor.

Since then, I went twice a week—at first, to donate, but I developed a passion for my work in fulfilling my calling. The team at the hospital loved me because of my enthusiasm and the overall quality of my output.

Content with my new routine, I had kick-started my journey to father a nation.

Chapter Seventeen
Cupid Larry
March 1996 - April 1999

I never heard back from Honey Buns. Being the end of March, she could've been wrapping up her term and studying for her finals. I missed the chat we had a few months prior, and despite not really liking the club, I debated returning on my own—without Troy. He still owed me cash from our previous visit, and I didn't want to risk losing more. I knew he never went on weekends because he visited his family in Victoria, so I planned a Saturday night excursion to the Den. I vowed not to fall into the trap of "club policy" again.

Well, I did.

Troy's friend, Candi, spotted me in the crowd, and we had a nice chat. Like Honey Buns, Candi was congenial, and before I knew it, she led me back to the "VIP room" to continue our discussion, which cost me forty dollars. Candi claimed that "club policy" dictated she charge me more money than my last visit, because it was a Saturday night.

I couldn't believe I got sucked in again! It added to my frustrations of the Saturday experience in comparison to my previous mid-week visit. I had to wait in a long line to enter the building; wall-to-wall men filled the joint; I had to settle for a seat near the stage surrounded by three strangers; the customers, as a whole, were rowdier and more obnoxious; and Honey-Buns was nowhere in sight. However, there were more women at the Den that night—though Candi was the only one I recognized.

After Candi had sucked me into the VIP room, I spent the rest of the evening chatting with her friends. I loved interacting with them. Tiffany, Isabella, Ginger, and Destiny were all super nice and interested in me—though they often cut the conversation short when I mentioned I didn't want to join them in the VIP room.

After my third drink, I spotted a familiar looking woman in the distance. Her black hair draped straight down her back while she served another table. I squinted for a better look, and maybe it was the alcohol, or the dark setting of the club, but I couldn't see her face clearly. She might've been my age, but I couldn't be a hundred percent sure. *Who is she reminding me of?*

When she finished dealing with her customer, she dropped off her tray at the bar, walked to a bouncer, and whispered in his ear. *It's so hard to see her through the crowds. Wait...could that be my first love Trisha? Nah, it couldn't be.* I stood, hoping for a better view, but she was no longer in sight.

The old feelings I had for my ex-girlfriend stormed back in a flash. I never loved anyone so much before then. In the moment, I dreamed of what our life could've been like together, if not for the misunderstanding we had in university.

If you truly love her, you'll prove you learned from your mistake and give her space. My heart and head debated what to do next.

I intercepted the bouncer when he passed by.

"Sir," I said, "you know the person you just spoke to? Would her name happen to be Trisha?"

"No. Angelica," he answered.

It sure looked like Trisha. But how can I be certain?

"When does she work?" I asked.

"Only on the weekends."

I thanked him and left the club.

My email inbox flooded with messages from Candi, Tiffany, Isabella, Ginger, and Destiny, all begging me to return to the club to visit them! I couldn't say no to these lovely ladies, so I became a regular at the Den that spring to visit my fans. Odd I didn't see Honey Buns working anymore.

Dreams of Trisha haunted me ever since I first saw Angelica that Saturday night. I hadn't thought much about her since leaving Ottawa and wanted to return to the Den on the weekends to try to confirm if Angelica was in fact Trisha. Something in my spirit, though, forced me to stay away.

Trisha had called me Dick Wank—Ridiculous Rick's stage name. I went by Dick instead of mine for a while to help me date women that year. I had a bad reputation, and the mere mention of "Larry Johnstone" had all the girls running away from me. Dick Wank had served me well because no one had seen his true face under the paper bag he wore on stage. Trisha had never known me as Larry.

I ached to find out more about this woman at the Den. If it was Trisha, I wanted to apologize and show her I've changed and make amends.

How could I send a message to this woman?
Troy announced his arrival at the hospice by singing the hymn, "How Great Thou Art."
My Hermes, the Greek god of messengers, just walked in.

I had been watching TV when Troy arrived. It was getting late, and I'd been flipping through the channels grateful the *Bärbar Ugn* no longer ruled the airwaves. A new slew of infomercials flooded the networks, including some hosted by my Schnookums—and on her own. She must be well on the way to forty, and still looked great—though she had surgical alterations. And where's Sven? The two had started promoting the *Bärbar Ugn 3* on TV just before last Christmas—an oven that looks identical to the other two and made Swedish bread.

I stopped channel surfing and settled on one of Schnookums' shows. I laughed. She dressed like a 1950s housewife, cleaning ovens. *How on earth did the producers goad her into that?* Heather appeared content, smiling radiantly while scrubbing dirt and grime with a steel wool pad and some guck.

The following one also starred my wife, and it had a more local flair, set in the Rockies. I rather enjoyed it, promoting the Spuzzum Micro-brewery. It bemused me watching Heather wearing a white tank top, red cap, and shorts, trying to slug back some ale. She hated beer, and I could tell from her frown she didn't enjoy the gig.

"Wow! She's hot! I don't think I've seen this infomercial before." Troy flopped down beside me on the couch.

"Have I ever told you about the woman I moved out here to be married to?"

"Yes, only about a dozen times."

I pointed to the TV. "That's her. Looks like they're trying to entice viewers to subscribe to a beer delivery service."

"Who wouldn't like beer delivery?" asked Troy.

"True," I replied. "The price is low if you purchase the monthly six two-four tier."

Troy ignored me. He stared intently at my Schnookums on TV. She stood on a bank of a wooded river with torrent rapids rushing over rocks behind her. She held a beer can with the label facing the camera and reached to open it. The can hissed at the same time she whispered, "Spuzzum."

It made me laugh.

The screen grabbed our focus again. Heather tried her best to drink the entire can of beer in one shot. She struggled. In fact, most of the ale spilled down the side of her mouth, around her chin, and navigated down her body to her shorts.

Troy's mouth gaped wide open.

"You married *her*?" he asked.

"You don't believe me?"

"Well, no."

"You'd be surprised how many chicks want a piece of the ol' Larry action."

"I don't doubt it," Troy said sarcastically.

"Watch your tone. I could score more women in a week than you'll do in a lifetime."

"Enough of that. You know my bad luck with women," Troy grumbled.

"Of course, I do. I'm very sympathetic."

"But you had a gem" — he pointed to the TV again — "and let her get away."

He had a point. We watched the final fifteen minutes of the infomercial while I shared intimate details of my life with Heather.

"Hey Larry," he said when the show ended, "have you heard the news? Your Honey Buns stopped working at the Den."

"I missed that." My heart sank. "I'll miss Honey. What happened?"

"Who knows. They sometimes find work in another club or earn enough money to move on. Speaking of which, here's yours." Troy reached into his pocket and took out a handful of twenties. "Thanks for the loan."

"Keep it," I said pushing his hand back.

"What? You've been bugging me about it for months!"

"Yeah, I know but I decided you can pay off your debt with a favour. Game?"

"Nothing illegal, I hope."

"No, no. I want you to go on a quest. You'll likely have to use some of that cash to complete it."

"What?" Troy's face scrunched, puzzled.

"I want you to skip your trip to your family and stay in town next weekend," I said, "and go to the Lion's Den for me."

"Uh, you know where it is. Why do you need me to go?"

"Let me explain," I replied. "I've been going to the club of late, on my own, and I should forewarn you, your Candi has a crush on me."

"You ..." Troy stood in anger.

"It can't be helped," I said, shrugging my shoulders. "I promise you it's true, but don't worry, I'm not interested in her...I visited one Saturday and became enchanted by another dancer."

"So?"

"I need you to deliver something for me. No questions asked."

Troy sat back down, curious. "What am I bringing?"

"A present to a woman named Angelica. Would you believe this woman might be an old friend I haven't seen in years? All you must do is give her my gift and card. I'll buy it this afternoon. If you can, confirm her real name and find out what she does outside the club or where she lives. Report to me anything you find."

"Why would I do anything to risk my relationship with Candi?"

"I'm sure she'd be okay with it." Candi and her gang had no qualms "befriending" me, after all. "Thanks Troy." I stood and patted Troy's head and left.

"What a night!" Troy beamed as he skipped into the hospice Monday afternoon to start his shift. He smiled and danced his way into the cafeteria.

I sat in the dining room slushing back a pathetic bowl of watery leftover Brussels sprouts soup.

"Did you do as I asked, Troy?"

"Larry, you're the best friend, ever. Thank you so much."

Troy bent to hug me. He placed himself in a chair.

"I did as you asked. I got Angelica's attention and talked to her for a long while. She's so wonderful. So warm. So kind. And she led a sad and difficult life, virtually living in the streets of Toronto. She made some cash in the adult industry, and even appeared in a cheesy flick called *Saturday Night's Beaver—a Musical*. Have you heard of it?"

I'd never watch sleezy stuff like that.

"But a volunteer from a woman's shelter plucked her from that world, and they helped her finish her high school diploma. She's such a strong and bright woman."

"Did she mention anything about living in Ottawa?" I attempted to shovel another spoonful of soup in my mouth.

Troy shook his head. "No, but she mentioned a situation which forced her to quit school and moved out here for a fresh start. One reason or other, it didn't quite work the way she had hoped, and now she's at the Lion's Den. She didn't go into details, but I felt terrible for her. Angelica's been working there for a while, and I don't think she's too happy. Know what? Despite her difficulties, she still had place in her heart to be warm and kind to me last night. I thought Candi was the only one that cared for me there, but Angelica is the real deal."

"Why on earth would you say that?"

"We're going out on a date."

I dropped my spoon in the bowl with a loud clang. My blood started to boil. *Baldy scored a date with her?*

"I gave her the gift like you asked," Troy said, "and when she opened it, she burst into tears."

Interesting. Trisha owned many of these items in her home.

"She told me she'd cherish the snow globe I bought—"

Correction. "I" bought.

"—and no one had given her anything since arriving in the West Coast. Then she opened the card—"

My masterpiece.
"—and melted."
I recalled what I wrote.

Dear Angelica,

It's never too late to make things right
I have always loved you
Even though I watched you from afar
I am a lonely man, in need of love
I'd give anything if you'd be mine
With you, forever won't be too long

All my love,

You know who... xx

I knew I didn't have to sign it. I had bought Trisha a few snow globes when things were going well for us back in Ottawa. If it was Trisha, who else would've given her one?

Troy added, "She gave me a huge hug and a kiss. I don't remember the last time a woman kissed me. Maybe when I was a child? And on the cheek at that. We went for coffee together when the club closed and talked the night away."

"And her name is—"

Troy wagged his index finger at me. "I promised not to tell anyone. She wants to make her life better, and I swore I'd help her. I'm confident she'll succeed. You know what I'm going to do for her, Larry?" He paused and sat up straight in his chair. "I'm going to pay for her university tuition and residence fees so she could complete her degree without having to work at the club again."

I nearly erupted.

"You're going to do *what*? You can't afford that on your salary." *He's not supposed to go out with her!*

"Are you kidding?" said Troy. "My mother is one of the wealthiest women in British Columbia. It's why I work here. Money isn't an issue, and I want to make a difference in people's lives. My parents were excited about my career choice, working here at the shelter, and insisted on helping finance me, since it's so philanthropic. I've already spoken to Mom. She'd love to help Angelica find a different path, especially if she's unhappy with what she does."

I sat back in my chair, thinking. "Wait. Why Angelica? You've been *courting* Candi forever."

Troy nodded his head. "I've never been out with Candi, and I'm only scratching the surface with you about Angelica's tough life."

"You stop now and tell me everything you found out about her."

Troy stood to leave the room. "I can't," he said. "I promised I wouldn't talk to others about her. Anyway, Larry, I told you way too much already, but I couldn't contain myself, and you're a friend."

Yeah, really?

"Oh," said Troy pulling a wad of cash out his pocket. "Here's your hundred dollars. I can't carry this debt. I'm quitting the hospice because I decided to go back to school with her, too!"

See you on campus...

Our paths never crossed.

Yeah, Troy lucked out scoring with a dancer, but he was wrong—strip clubs weren't a place to meet women. It took me a few more years of visiting peeler bars around the city to finally realize I'd never find the voice of my generation nor the vessel of my children in one. Believe me, I was optimistic after witnessing Troy's success. In reality, I couldn't even get a single date with these exotic dancers and burned a ton of cash because of "club policies." So, I made a New Year's Resolution in 1999 to stop going to these places.

A few months later, a week after Easter, Reginald and I were working away in the hospice's office. The phone rang and Reginald picked it up.

"For you," he said. He resumed typing away on the computer.

It was a rare call from Heather. Without asking how I was doing, she demanded I buy stationary for Little Larry's schooling and mail it to her. It baffled me why she couldn't do it herself from a store near her home in Toronto, but she insisted on a particular brand from a special shop in Vancouver. I didn't have the chance to question the weird request—it seemed ridiculous she couldn't buy such a cheap item in a local pharmacy. The odd conversation lasted all of two minutes—basically to give me the instructions and her mailing address. She sounded happy to speak to me, though, but hearing her voice put me in a funk. Between striking out at strip clubs and having nothing relationship-wise with Schnookums, I was at an all-time low when I hung up the phone. I looked over towards Reginald who was too focused on his computer work to have paid any attention to my call with my wife.

"These horrid financial reports are due tomorrow. They call this software Easy Accounting. That's rubbish. It should've been named Overly Complicated Accounting. And why is this computer so slow? How can something three years old be so dead?"

"Mind if I check my email before I head out?"

"Sure, Larry. I need a break for breakfast. Take your time." He left me alone in the office.

My Torpedomail displayed a small subset of the hundreds of emails I received each day—all from women who worked at various exotic dance clubs. I did my best to follow up with them daily. Some responded to me, but they all read impersonal. In fact, most were identical to the original messages.

Another weird anomaly I had observed with email over the past couple of years was that for every one of these messages I responded to, I'd receive five new ones! All from complete strangers inviting me for special one-on-one encounters! Sadly, both Honey and Candi dropped off the face of the earth. I guessed they had lost my email address—*but c'mon, who could forget it?* Regardless, the sea of emails proved impossible to keep up with and kept piling in at a ridiculous rate. I gave up processing them all.

Scanning them compounded my emptiness. Fed up, I clicked "Home" on the web browser. The usual "link" options to subjects of interest appeared. Most days, I'd click the "Religion and Spirituality" link, but the "Search" box at the top appeared larger than normal. Wonder if I can find…

I typed "girls" in it. After a minute, a long list of options appeared. Each one read the same, saying things like "meet hot women here," "You alone? You won't be for long," or "Come in for an adventure you'll never want to abandon!"

I clicked the adventure link and waited again a few minutes for something to happen. The web browser loaded a white page. *Odd, not quite the adventure I'd expect.* After another minute, it spawned a second window. In it, a picture I'd rather soon forget. Another popped up with another dirty picture. A third opened with a link to a casino. A fourth tried to entice me to click a link to obtain the secrets of penis enlargement. *Tempting...*

The windows kept opening faster and faster and didn't stop. Each promoted something sexual, gambling, or pharmaceuticals. I couldn't close any of them. If I closed one, two more would pop up! The rate of the new windows opening slowed, but it didn't stop the computer from opening more and more. There were hundreds littering the screen.

"Stop it!" I yelled at the machine and, in an attempt to end the crisis, I clicked a link in one of the windows. *That should put an end to this.* A different message appeared. "Would you like to install the Bloated Goat toolbar?"

Of course! Anything to stop this insanity!

I clicked "Yes," and a timer turned on and stopped. Another message appeared prompting me to click to reboot the computer. *Why is this asinine machine prompting me with these silly questions! YES, it's always YES!*

The computer restarted, with a beep, and after twenty minutes of churning, the familiar login screen appeared.

"Are you finished reading your email?" Reginald stood at the door.

I jumped out of my skin. "Uh, yeah!" How long was he standing there? I got up to leave.

"Hmmm, why did the computer reboot?" he said while watching the computer roll through its opening sequence after relogging in. "Seems to be running even slower than before."

Being the ever-loyal husband, I left the office to do my task for Schnookums.

I grabbed a bus for an "artistic" section of town. Expecting a speciality stationary store, the address Schnookums gave me had a green sign reading "The Happy Apothecary" hanging over a small entrance.

I browsed the contents of the shop—mostly pill bottles and naturalist products. They didn't have any school supplies whatsoever. A young man in his twenties noticed my frustration.

"Can I help you, dude?" he said, smiling from behind the counter. He could've been a skinny, university-aged Peter.

I showed him the product number I had written. He grabbed my paper and said, "Oh, that's a special order." He went to the back and dropped a rather ordinary pad of legal-sized paper on the counter. "That'll be fifty-two dollars."

"What?"

"Two dollars for the paper, fifty for the shipping."

It sounded shifty to me, but it was what Heather asked for, and she'd pay me for it. The lad had me complete some mailing labels, and I left the shop to return to the hospice.

"I can't understand it!" Reginald yelled at the machine the next morning. It looked like he didn't get a wink of sleep. "Every time I try to go on the internet, sleezy stuff always shows up. And what is this vile Bloated Goat tool bar attached to my browser? Where on earth did that come from?" Reginald clicked and gasped. "Oh, my word, that's horrible. We can't have that here. Crumbs, I can't get it to stop, and it's running so slowly."

I looked over his shoulder. "That's disgusting. You shouldn't watch such filth. Is there anything I can do? It was working fine when I finished reading my email."

"I'll have to ring the technicians. We might have one of those viruses. I hope we don't have to replace this system." He banged his desk. "I need to submit the quarterly financials today! Now I have to deal with this?"

He didn't seem happy, and I needed to leave because I was late for my morning joint.

I should cheer him up.

"Have a nice day," I said with chipper timber then sang a verse of "Always Look on the Bright Side of Life" before he dismissed me. When I returned later, a computer technician busied himself on the keyboard. Reginald looked over his shoulder nervously.

"I can't do anything about that Bloated Goat software," said the technician. "You're gonna have to replace the computer."

"What about my reports?" asked Reginald. He looked like he was about to have a heart attack.

"We'll do our best. It'll probably be expensive."

The technician, with Reginald, performed emergency work to attempt to recover the financial data from the old computer. The process took several days, and by the end, Reginald appeared exhausted. He ended up submitting his report to the government over a week late, knowing he'd be at risk of some heavy fines. I had never seen the man so stressed.

I gave him his space the morning he submitted his reports and went to Jumpin' Java for my usual coffee. It was unusually empty. The quiet helped me concentrate on my scriptures. I closed my eyes to pray, and my thoughts went back to my Lion's Den adventure.

In my usual seat, I flipped my Bible to the back cover and took out my photos. An unopened letter I had received yesterday was bundled with them. It contained a wedding picture of Angelica and Troy. The card read:

Dear Larry,

Thanks for bringing us together. We're no longer in Vancouver. I can't tell you where we went, but you changed our lives. We're happily married now and are expecting our first child soon.

Your buddy,

You-know-who

P.S. Angelica is not her name.

No kidding, bastard! None of the strippers use their real names!
Fuming with jealousy at Troy's success in finding love, I opened a lesson from "Philippians." The verses were a directive saying not to do anything out of selfish ambition, placing others before you, and taking on a servant attitude. I put my book down and stared at the photo of Troy and Angelica.

I need to let this go. Maybe I haven't found the perfect woman for myself... but I have found one for someone else...and others. Rick's relationship with his first girlfriend, Sandy, was completely driven by me. Foolish Rick had such a crush on her all his life and didn't even realize she liked him. It was so obvious! If it wasn't for me pushing Rick to ask her on a date in high school, he'd never have gone out with anyone—never mind his dream girl. Even then, he blew it with her because of his jealousy and insecurity. Who knows...maybe my sending Dana his way might start a new romantic chapter in that jerkoff's life.

And my best friend Brad? He'd been seeing someone named Jen for a long time since high school. Brad is a complete nerd, and can't even talk to anyone human, especially a girl he liked. If it wasn't for my introducing the two, he, like Rick, would be miserable and alone.

The one thing Rick, Brad, and Troy had in common? I set them up with girls I would've given anything to date. I reflected on how much happiness I gave these guys by putting my needs last. I was bitter for losing an opportunity to date some wonderful women, but in the long run, I think it was worth it. I actually felt good helping them out.

I need to think more on that good feeling by helping others first.

Chapter Eighteen

Never Too Old

May 2005

"Hey, Larry-o," the woman said.

Well, hello there. What have we here?

I sat in a comfortable leather chair, beckoning her to enter my dimly lit den.

A six-foot tall woman with long blonde hair stood in front of me. She grabbed my attention—wearing an orangey-yellow track suit with black stripes down the sides, and standing with one hand perched on her hip, slightly tilted, in the doorway. My eyes fixated on her and the long samurai sword she held in her hand.

"You and I have some unfinished business," the blonde said.

"I always wanted more children, Schnookums," I replied. "It may be tricky for us to have another at your age."

The woman angered. "Wrong!"

She walked towards me and pointed her sword at my most vulnerable spot between my legs. I dared not move for risking losing what I prized the most.

"Watch where you point that thing!" I shrieked. "I'm still on my mission! You're supposed to be a part of it!" I instinctively moved my hands in a defensive position, but...

"You won't be needing these anymore." She pushed the blade.

I gasped. Short of breath, I woke in mid-snore with a start. The specimen cup I held in my left hand fell to the floor. My pants and underwear were off. *Did I waste some of my Larry seed?* I never fell asleep "in the moment" before.

A loud knocking at the door made me jump. "Larry, you okay? You've been in there for over an hour. Someone needs to use the room now!"

Bloody hell. I examined the cup. *Empty.*

I finished what I started in less than thirty seconds, dressed, and went to the reception.

"Here you go, Margo!" I dropped my specimen on her desk. "Another couple of million babies for you!"

"With your sperm count? You would be lucky to have two." She grinned at her joke.

"Nice to see you smiling today." It's true, she always welcomed me with a huge smile since I mentioned it to her years ago.

Margo scoffed and inspected the contents of my jar. "Light load today," she sneered. "Before you leave to take on your busy day of doing nothing, Dr. Williams needs to speak with you. He won't be long. Take a seat please."

Why on earth does the fertility administrator need to see me?

I waited twenty minutes, and Margo escorted me to the doctor's office.

Dr. Williams stood from behind his desk when I entered, smiled, and shook my hand.

"Hi Larry," he said, peering at me through his round glasses. "I realize it's still a couple of months before we do your biannual check-up." He gestured for me to sit in an empty chair opposite him.

"What's this about? Are you finally going to pay me?"

He opened a file, then took his place behind the desk. "Uh, no. Larry, but I do want to thank you for your hard work. We have a huge overstock of your donations and are grateful for your efforts. There is something important we need to discuss. We're approaching a milestone."

"Yes," I acknowledged. "Later this month, *Star Wars: Episode III—Revenge of the Sith* will open. I'm stoked for the conclusion of the trilogy."

Dr. Williams remained silent. "No, no. I mean your milestone birthday."

"You mean, my fortieth in a couple of weeks? Yes, 2005 will be a big year for me. But hell, I feel and look like a thirty-year-old."

"No doubt, you're in excellent health. No symptoms of stress or aging. However, we're facing a reality. When men hit forty, their sperm quality starts to deteriorate. Therefore, we won't be able to accept your donations beginning next month. I realize you've been helping us for many years, but rest assured, we'll find recipients for your leftover donations. It's rare we find such dedicated people like yourself." He paused and smiled. "In fact, if we had a Sperm Donor Hall of Fame, you'd find a photo of yourself hanging proudly on the wall. You must have the record for most donations in Canada—definitely in the top one percent!"

I can't believe this!

"You can't do this! I have super sperm! I'm still potent! I'll maintain a high quality, even when I'm older! Where are those freezie undies?"

The doctor stood and extended his hand. "Good luck, Larry, and thanks again."

I will defy him. I must fulfill my calling.

I bolted from the hospital without saying bye to Margo. *Why is she smiling? This is outright depressing!*

Angry! How dare they say I'm too old!

My mirror the morn of my fortieth birthday reflected a twenty-two-year-old man. Hair, still long in the back and looked cool despite having less on the top. Mullets were the rage for teens in my day. I loved it. Feeling the hair brush on the back of my neck, while not having an unruly birds nest on the top, gave me strength and sense of virility.

I'll prove the hospital wrong. I am that twenty-year-old youth in the mirror.

Maybe I need to celebrate my frustrations away. Hanging with the university crowds selling them pot keeps me young—so does smoking it. Maybe I'll start there.

Foregoing the runny eggs at the hospice, I went to Jumpin' Java. I wanted to make this day special. I never celebrated my birthday, let alone milestones, because my parents didn't throw me parties. Dad, to his credit, wanted to make a big production of them, but Mama never permitted him. She didn't like kids messing up her home.

I'll never forget my seventh birthday. Dad snuck me out of the house to do something special. He took me to the Humane Society to look at all the doggies and kitties. My dad explained to me these animals needed a nice place to live like ours. My excitement rose, thinking I might be bringing home one of these cute creatures. A dog would've been wonderful company for me, an only child, leading a lonely existence.

We walked around the kennel. All the dogs looked so sad. Their eyes pleaded with me, saying "pick me, pick me."

Many barked and jumped on their cages soliciting my attention. The shelter let a few out for me to play with. I adored them all. They all jumped on me and licked my face, showing me much love. After a few minutes, two of the three dogs began to play amongst themselves, but one continued to hang around me. The small beagle hopped and followed me around the room, and when I lifted him, he laid still in my arms savouring the warmth of being cuddled like a baby.

I nuzzled his face while holding him close to my chest. Dad smiled with pride.

"You like him, son?"

"Yes, very much! I want this one. I love him, and I'm going to name him Ulysses."

Dad laughed nervously. "Son, we're not here to get you a dog. Mama would never have one in our house. I just wanted you to have some fun with them.

You'll have to put him back and let others have the chance to play with him."

"I won't! Ulysses is mine!" I clutched him tighter. The dog yelped.

"Sorry son, but he isn't." He removed the beagle from my grasp and returned him to the attendant who placed Ulysses back in his cage. I stared at the pup as the door shut. Ulysses cocked his head and gave me sad eyes. I broke down and cried.

I wailed at the attendant, "What will happen to Ulysses if he doesn't find a home?"

The surly teenaged boy replied, "He'll be put to sleep."

That didn't sound too bad to me. I asked my dad for clarification.

"Putting to sleep means being put to death, son."

"NO!"

"Don't worry, son, I'm sure he'll find a nice home."

Dad had to pull me from the building kicking and screaming. I wanted my Ulysses!

We drove off.

"I'm sorry, son," Dad said. "I didn't mean to build your hopes up. I'll buy you a special pet for your birthday. One that Mama will permit in the house."

Dad dropped me off at home and took off on his quest. Mama served me some special birthday lime marshmallow gelatin. I slugged back the hard-topped dessert and gagged. She never could make it right. Bored, I sat alone in the living room rereading a book about Hercules.

Dad returned an hour later, carrying an aquarium.

"Here you go. Something guaranteed to be your friend well into your adult years."

He put it down on the floor and I peered in. A small turtle, the size of a silver dollar, laid motionless in the tank. I stared at it for an hour. It didn't move. I waited another. Still didn't. His head didn't even budge. I put my hand in the tank and tapped the shell. Nothing. I resumed my post for another hour. It lay still as ever.

Mum called us for dinner. My parents were pleased I was enjoying my new pet.

I returned to the aquarium after we ate, and I lost patience with this lifeless creature. Placing my hand in the tank, I lifted the turtle out and gave it a little shake. The head didn't move. I shook harder. No life came from it at all. I put its underside next to my ear. No heartbeat, though I didn't know if turtles had them or not.

I shook it like one would a bottle of pop trying to build pressure to make it explode when you opened it. Nothing.

My dad stopped reading his paper. "What on earth are you doing?"

"Trying to wake it. It's not moving."

"It's not napping, it's brumating."

"What is boo-mating?"

"Brumating. It's in a deep sleep."

"I know. I'm trying to wake it. It smells awful and needs a bath." I put the turtle on its back. No movement. My father came over and stared at the lifeless creature.

"It's dead now, son. He would be moving frantically trying to right himself if he were alive." Dad picked up the turtle. "You must've killed it with all that violent shaking." He opened the front door of the house and threw it out like someone skipping rocks by a pond. I watched my turtle bounce down the driveway and onto the main road. I bolted through the front door and stopped halfway to the roadway when an eighteen-wheel semi ran over the remnants of my pet.

Back at Jumpin' Java, I sipped my free birthday coffee and sighed. Yeah, maybe Dad didn't skip the turtle down the road, but he did flush the damn thing down the toilet. I would've much preferred a dog, anyway. *Did my poor Ulysses ever find a home? Only half of dogs in shelters ever do.*

After thinking more about that little beagle, and how much love he showed me, I picked up the paper, looking for a distraction from my funk. I leafed through the headlines but couldn't concentrate, so I placed it back down on the table. An advert on the back page for the BC Highland Games caught my eye before I started daydreaming out the window.

A man and a little girl were passing by. She was walking a grey mutt, about the size of a small cat, and when they arrived outside Jumpin' Java, she handed the man the leash, and he attached it around a lamppost. The girl looked like she had been crying as she walked into the coffee shop, and the man placed his hand on her shoulder. I watched them ordering some drinks and a couple of donuts, and they sat at an empty table next to mine. I wondered what was making the child so sad, so I listened in to their conversation. Sounded like they were planning a move to Calgary.

"Sorry, Courtney, we tried everything we could. We couldn't find your pup, Hector, a home."

Hector? Hector was the greatest warrior in Troy. It's not often you hear a name of a dog from Greek mythology, especially one so tiny!

Courtney broke down in tears. "We've only had him a month. Can't we just keep him, Daddy?"

The man nervously took a bite of the donut. "We've been through this already, our new home doesn't permit pets. I'm going to have to put Hector up for adoption."

If I didn't know any better, it sounded to me like the father was a little cold… almost like he was relieved to give the family pet away.

"Adoption? Will he find a home there?" asked Courtney.

I peered casually over to them. The girl had tears on her face.

Courtney cried harder. "He's only a puppy!" Maybe she had learned like I did as a child that if a pet does not get adopted, they would be put down.

The father placed his hand over Courtney's and tried to offer some reassurances. It didn't work. The little girl was angry at her father. She whipped her hand free and clasped hold of her cup.

"We're not putting up my dog for adoption!" she yelled.

Many patrons in the restaurant stopped what they were doing, wanting to know what was going on. I peered out the window. Hector was lying down. All I could make out is this tiny ball of grey. I didn't want to risk this cute dog being put down like my Ulysses. *Hector? Ulysses? Both characters from Greek mythology? Could this be the Fates speaking to me?*

"I can give Hector a nice home," I said, not realizing I vocalized my thought loud enough for Courtney and her dad to hear.

"Really?" said the father. He swivelled towards me in his chair. "That would be great!"

"Uh…" I had no idea how the hospice would react to a dog, but after thinking about it quickly, I didn't care. "Yes, and I promise you can visit him whenever you are in town."

The father brightened up, and though the girl remained sad, she did stop crying. We discussed his care, exchanged our phone numbers and addresses, and planned a time for the father to formerly transfer the ownership of Hector and drop off some of the dog's belongings at the hospice. After we finished our drinks, we left the coffee shop together.

The little dog stood and wagged his tail. He was mostly grey, but his chest and muzzle were white with hints of brown speckled in his wiry fur—and his small ears above his head flopped forward. I fell in love with Hector's little face. *Who could resist those dark eyes!* His overall appearance reminded me of what a dog could look like if it licked a lamp socket. I didn't care. It added to his cute.

"Hector is a Snorkie," said Courtney. "Half Miniature Schnauzer, and half Yorkie."

He began to whine and pulled on its lead, wanting to greet me. I walked closer and he balanced himself on his hind legs while I bent down to pat him.

"And look, he seems to like you," said the father, removing the leash from the lamp post and handing it to me. "See, Courtney? I think Hector will be in fine hands."

I couldn't agree more. I picked up the dog, and he loved being held like a baby—just like my Ulysses.

My two new friends turned to walk away, but suddenly, the father stopped.

"Oh, by the way," he said, "be careful with Hector. He piddles when he gets excited."

"Don't we all?" I answered, putting the dog down. Maybe they didn't understand I was joking. They both seemed confused. After a final wave goodbye to their pet, the two left me alone with my new dog.

My fortieth birthday was starting quite well. I helped a family with their problem, and I now have a new pet! I stared down at Hector. I loved how he always wagged his tiny tail!

"Hey, my little warrior. Wanna go check out the Highland games?"

Hector trotted alongside as we returned to the hospice. He occasionally would stop and sniff a lamppost or a corner of a building, but as a whole, he was well trained, walking by my side. Pedestrians looked down at him and smiled. Some said hello, including a few young women who stopped to fuss over Hector. Had I known owning a dog would've been the secret to popularity, I would've gotten one sooner! Even the small group of men hanging around the front of the hospice wanted to interact with the pup, and though Hector wanted to say hi, I went right by them and into the building.

"Welcome to your new home, Hector," I said in the recreation hall, removing his lead.

Hector ran around the room, exploring his new territory. He was social, making quick friends with those who were watching TV. Before Hector made himself too comfortable, I whisked him into my arms and took him upstairs to my room.

"And this is where we sleep, Hector."

The dog jumped onto my bed and walked around in circles. Once he found a comfy spot by my pillow, he lay down and looked up at me expectantly. I gave him a few pats.

"Good boy!"

Hector stared at me while I prepared for our outing to the Highland games.

My kilt hung inside a plastic wrap in my closet. I tried it on. Still fits. *The old body hasn't changed a bit!* Hector barked his approval. After tying my sporran around my waist, a thought occurred to me. *Whiskey will be essential for my outing.* Scots love their drink and sipping back the stuff to wailing bagpipes seemed like a match made in heaven. I had a couple of bottles stashed in my dresser.

While I opened the bottom drawer, Hector stood, hopped onto my nightstand by my bed, and jumped on top of the dresser next to my Beanbag Babes. He playfully wagged his tail and barked a couple of times while I placed the two bottles and a package of plastic cups into a knapsack.

"Nothing for you here, Hector."

Hector retreated a few steps, knocking over one of my Beanbag Babes in the process.

"Be careful, Hector! These are going to be valuable one day!"

Hector understood. He jumped back onto my nightstand and returned to a comfy spot on my bed. He let out a big yawn and lay down for a nap. I left the room to let him sleep, figuring I'd grab a lunch from the cafeteria before heading out.

I settled to a fine meal of "brittle burgers." These hamburgers were so deep fried, they were more crisp than moist. I was finishing my meal when Reginald joined me, and we exchanged a few pleasantries. When…

"Who let that dog in the kitchen?"

Reginald and I left the dining area immediately to see what was going on. The senior chef—if you can call him that—was standing with his hands on his hips, chiding a junior cook. My Hector was chewing away at one of the burgers on the floor, and there was a second one for him to eat! I had no idea how much my little dog was supposed to consume, but Hector was gobbling them up fast. Something else was on the ground near Hector's meal.

One of my Beanbag Babes!

I reached down to pick it up. Hector, sensing a new game was afoot, seized my doll and dashed away into the cafeteria. The young cook ran after him, with Reginald and I close behind. After running around the cafeteria, creating chaos with the diners, Hector finally hopped onto an empty couch in the recreation room. The young cook grabbed the Beanbag Babe, still in Hector's mouth.

"Nice doggie…give that back."

Hector growled, and a tug of war ensued.

"Hector! No!" I yelled.

My dog ignored me. He tightened his grip around my doll, and with an aggressive shake of his head, he dislodged it from the cook's grip and stared at us proudly with his prize in his mouth.

"I give up," said the cook. He left the room to resume his duties in the kitchen.

"Bad Hector," I said.

Hector responded to my stern voice this time, and sat, dropping my toy.

"My poor Beanbag Babe…" I picked up the damaged doll. The Beanbag Babe did not survive the ordeal. The dog's teeth had completely disfigured it. "You know how much you cost me Hector? This is worth a fortune!"

Reginald put his hand on my shoulder while Hector lay down on the couch.

"Larry, do you know this dog?"

I went on to tell Reginald about how I saved the dog from certain death, and how I helped a poor family in need. I might have exaggerated the details about how depressed the girl, Courtney, was, and that poverty drove the family to send the dog for adoption—just to add a bit of drama to the story. Despite that, Reginald seemed impressed by my good deed.

"There is much responsibility in owning a dog, Larry. You must feed it, walk it, wash it, take it to the vet, and given the state of this dog's fur, you might need to take it to a specialty groomer. Have you considered all of this and the costs?"

No…

"And we have never had a dog at the hospice before. It's known that pets are great for people's mental health, so I am not completely against the idea." He looked over towards Hector on the couch. The pup advanced over towards Reginald and stood up on his hind legs, pleading for Reginald to pet him.

"This cheeky blighter is adorable. Aww…we'll figure things out." Reginald scratched Hector's ears. "Larry, there will be many rules to abide by if we keep him. You will be expected to be responsible for his care."

I nodded. *He is my dog, after all!*

"He'll be with me all the time, Reginald. In fact, we have a big excursion planned to the Highland games in Coquitlam. Don't we boy?"

Instead of responding to me, Hector stood up on his hind legs again and placed his paws on Reginald. Reginald chuckled and raised the dog in his arms.

"Do you think that's a good idea?" He scratched Hector's ears. "That might be a huge outing for this little pup after so much change for him. I will care for him while you are gone…just this once. Then we'll establish the rules for having a dog here." He returned Hector to the couch, and the little dog sat, staring up at Reginald.

I thanked Reginald, and as I walked away, I heard him say, "Aww…look at that! You want your tummy rubbed…bloody hell!"

Reginald never swears! I turned around, and Reginald was looking in disgust at a wet sleeve of his blazer. *I was warned that Hector "piddled" when excited.*

I pretended not to notice and dashed back to my room. I secured the remaining Beanbag Babes in a drawer and decided to send them off to Mama tomorrow to "protect" my investment. She would treat them well, since she had a huge doll collection. Maybe she could even fix the damaged one.

The train pulled into the small city of Coquitlam, a little over an hour east of Vancouver. I had never been before but heard nice things about it. It reminded me of suburbs I'd seen on TV, but with a beautiful backdrop of mountains and rivers.

I found my way to the games. Greeted by the sound of the bagpipes, I ventured onto the grounds to check out the action. There were many activities, such as highland dancing, marching bands, and Scottish sports. I took in some caber tossing, which bored me, so I went to do some whiskey drinking at the cultural tent. I sloshed back samples while learning the fine nuances of the beverage. I didn't understand the fuss after sampling several. Taste one, you've tasted them all.

Near dinner time, I wandered to the food court and bought some haggis. I practically puked at the taste. *Do people really eat this? Yuck!*

I threw my plate in the trash and settled for some more palatable Scotch eggs with a pint of ale. When I polished off my beer, I opened my whiskey bottle and refilled my cup and staggered to the area of the park designated for concerts.

The *Piobaireachd* promised to be entertaining, being an open competition for pipers who played Scottish classical music. I sat myself down in an empty row sipping my drink. A skinny young man, maybe touching nineteen, sat next to me. He wore a kilt, but no shirt. I wish he had one. He smelled strong and his skinny hairless frame left little to the imagination. Poor boy shouldn't shave his head. It made him look much older.

He smiled. His two front upper teeth, and one lower, were missing.

"Hi, I'm Larry Johnstone." I extended my hand.

He shook it. "Hi Larry, nice to meet you. I'm Danny."

We chatted while sipping our drinks, sharing a common passion for Scottish tradition. He knew his tartans well, correcting me when I mistook his Campbell kilt for a Gordon—and like a true Scotsman, he enjoyed his ale. He waved his empty beer cup after downing it.

"Hey," I said, "would you like some of my special Scottish drink? You haven't lived until you tasted this stuff." I filled his cup, emptying my first bottle.

He took a sip. "Wow! This stuff is the bomb, man!" He gulped some more. "Hey, you look like the type of fella who can help me out."

"Sure." Always happy to offer my bottomless pit of knowledge to someone.

"You may have noticed; I'm not wearing a shirt."

Really?

Danny continued. "Yeah, I came up to these games from Saskatchewan. I bought my ticket early this morning, and the place was pretty empty. Some asshole pushed me over and kicked me in the gut a few times. I tried to get up, but he pounced down on me and knocked out my teeth."

"That's horrible! Did they catch the guy who did this to you?"

"No, he bolted off with my bag and wallet. It has everything I brought with me for this trip, including my return tickets. It'll cost me near four hundred bucks to buy another, and I gotta return home to Regina tomorrow for my mum's bypass surgery. Can you help me out?"

I inspected him closely. No sign of bleeding or swelling on his face. "Danny, I know the master of that con." *Peter.*

"This is no con, man. I'm telling it like it is. I got beat up and need cash to get home."

"Saskatchewan, eh?"

"You bet. Born and raised."

"Which grid are you on?" I knew how to speak Saskatchewan, thanks to a man I met at the hospice from Moose Jaw. He had a lot of fun with teaching us the dialect.

"Huh?"

"Never mind. Are you a grich or a groch? The answer will determine if I help you or not." The terms for male underwear can create quite a rift amongst native Saskatchewanians, so I've been told.

"A grich."

"Sorry, can't talk to you. I'm a groch. I've been in a groch family for generations. Can't associate with griches." I happened to be wearing a blue groch that day.

"What the hell?"

"Just messing with you," I said. "Here. Have another drink." I topped his cup. "Can't pull a fast one on Larry. I'm too smart for that old trick. I learned from the master—a guy named Peter Van Wagner."

Danny sipped back the drink. "No shit? You know Peter? I sell and smoke his dope!"

I had known Peter's business grew, and he'd hired helpers. I never met any of them, figuring there'd be plenty of time for introductions when I'd inherit his empire one day.

"Yeah, I know him. So, you're from Vancouver, eh?"

"Nah, born in New York, but I moved to Kelowna a few years back. I ran away from home. See this?" He pointed to his teeth. "My dear old dad pummeled them out of me. I couldn't take his shit anymore, so I split. Peter was the only man I knew around here, and he helped me make some coin in order to live."

"You're earning for Peter at the games?"

"You bet! This is the best place to sell pot!"

He had a point. Everyone around here looked like they were wealthy. We spent the evening sharing about our lives. Danny's was horrible, filled with abuse, and I empathized for him. It's a sad story we often hear at the hospice. My life story was bad, too, but at least I didn't get beat up in the process.

"You're right Larry, this whiskey is the nectar of the gods," Danny said finishing the latest cup. He was well on the way to inebriation.

"Told you."

"Can you buy me a ticket back into town?"

"Sure, no problem. Where are you staying?" Instinct told me he lived in the streets.

"A Vancouver hotel, on somewhere street."

"Tell you what, I work at the Hospice of Good Hope. We can take you in, and maybe even help get you a job and a real place to live, if you're up for it."

"Man, you're too kind."

The *Piobaireachd* ended. I took out my Polaroid and asked a stranger to take a photo of Danny and me, then we headed back to the hospice. He passed out on the first available bunk.

I might've not had the cake and candles, but my selfless heart helped someone in need. I'll never forget my fortieth birthday.

10 p.m.

I returned to the hospice. I couldn't find Hector anywhere, and given the dog's size, it would take an eternity to search every nook and cranny in the building. After walking around calling his name for a while with no success, I settled in the office. A note was glued to the computer monitor. It was from Reginald, saying that he brought Hector to his home, given that it was getting late. He also implied that Hector required a "lot" of training. I huffed in disbelief. *My pup is very well trained, thank you very much!* I logged in to the new computer.

The hospice had bought a scanner, and I went about digitizing all my photos of my son, Heather, Dana, the Browns, and the ones I took with Danny that day. I didn't have too many—there wasn't much to my life to capture on film. The task took a half hour, then I decided to see what was going on in the world of the internet.

The hospice now had a high-speed connection. We no longer had to listen to the hiss and whir of the horrible modem and wait for hours for a page to open. After reading some news highlights, I reviewed my email. I clicked through my messages, mostly the typical stuff—women all over the world wanting the 'ol Larry action. I no longer read them, since they all pretty much said the same thing, so I began the laborious process of deleting them, one at a time. I stopped when I saw an email from the Golden Oaks Hospital, embedded among all the other messages. It looked important.

The message was an official notice from the hospital saying now that I am forty, I'm no longer eligible to donate sperm.

Nuts to that!

Day one of being forty. Job one. Donate sperm. *Who cares what the hospital says?*

I bounced out of bed and before I could rush to Jumpin' Java's for my first cup of coffee, Reginald, sitting in the cafeteria, flagged me down. He held a lead while Hector ate some dog food.

"Ah, good morning, Larry. Just to let you know, I walked your dog this morning. That is something you should do each day at 6 a.m. Here, take him now."

How could I forget about my dog? "Thanks so much Reginald for taking care of him. You two seem to be bonding well. Do you mind looking after him? I have an important appointment at the hospital."

Reginald didn't seem to need to have his arm twisted. He was quite taken by

Hector. I left them alone for my daily coffee fix.

Fully caffeinated, I grabbed the bus to the hospital and waited for the clinic to open.

Margo greeted me warmly from behind her counter. "You here, again?"

Smiling had such a positive effect on her!

"Yes silly, I'm here like always—to donate." *Maybe she isn't aware I turned forty.*

Margo nodded. "Larry, there's a couple of new policies now in place." She turned and typed a few notes in a computer. "From now on, you'll have to book your time in advance. Also, you won't be allowed more than fifteen minutes in the room alone. Isn't that right Enrique?"

The janitor, mopping the floor, turned and nodded his head.

"He's a great conversationalist," Margo said while chuckling. She placed her hands on the keyboard. "Let's book your appointments now, and you can return to donate. Sound good?"

"That's all I want. Thanks, Margo, you're too kind. But why the new policy?"

"I don't make the rules Larry, just follow them. By the way, you won't need biannual exams anymore. The doctors reassessed your chart. They determined there is no sperm deterioration for you. Your sperm quality is off the map and will always be welcome here!"

Enrique burst out laughing—no idea why. Margo sounded more pleasant than usual, too.

"Great! I hated when they poked and prodded my nether regions. Let's schedule some times. Is there an opening first thing tomorrow morning?"

"You're in luck, there is."

"Thanks Margo. You're amazing!" I beamed happily.

"I know, but you helped me change my life. Who knew all I had to do was smile!" Her grin broadened.

"See?" I responded, "Told you so!"

"Oh, one more thing before you go."

"Yeah?"

"Doctor said your sperm was so special, we have to compartmentalize it separately from the others."

About time they recognize it's a cut above the rest.

"See this?" Margo pulled out a yellow bin from the side her desk which had a lid labelled, "Larry Johnstone's Donations." The bin was adorned with a symbol resembling ancient Klingon.

"Yes, cool! How'd you know I loved *Star Trek*?"

"If I'm not around and you're finished, simply deposit your sample in here." Margo's eyes watered, despite her radiant smile.

Enrique's face reddened and tears rolled down his cheek. I should be emotional, too. I'm being recognized as the donor hero that I am. But outputting the same quantities in fifteen minutes? Might be tricky.

"Thank you, thank you, and thank you. We'll see you tomorrow!"

"Yes, see you tomorrow, Larry," chuckled Margo. "Resist temptation and keep fresh."

Part Three: Sudden Fame Larry

2007 — 2015

Chapter Nineteen

Forty-Two

June 2007

Forty-two. According to the *Hitchhiker's Guide to the Galaxy*, it's the answer to the ultimate question of life, the universe, and everything. For me, life's mysteries were answered many years ago in church through prophecy. Since celebrating my forty-second birthday a few weeks ago, my stresses about my life's purpose kicked into a higher gear. Convinced my super sperm was fathering a nation through the clinic, I still needed to validate the "married to the voice of a generation" part. In a sense, I was still married to "the one," but I hadn't seen or heard from her in eons—apart from the odd call to pick up stationary for Little Larry. It was the least I could do to honour and respect her, as dictated by the prophecy. But, given my situation, not surprisingly, I struggled with the question—how can I make my marriage complete?

I rolled out of bed.

"Arf!" Hector, like most nights, cuddled into me while I slept. He was pretty much the same size as when I acquired him a couple of years ago, and he became a fixture at the hospice. Most days, he'd bring his toys to play with the homeless men who visited. Everyone loved him and pitched in with his care. Some residents had much experience with pets of their own, and they trained Hector to deal with some of his "problem" areas. Staff took him for walks and paid for his food. I still had to fork out cash for the vet, but I kept his grooming costs to a minimum. I found Hector's scruffiness gave him character—as did his morning routine of barking to get me out of bed. After a few woofs, my dog ran out of the room to the stairwell expecting me to follow him to the kitchen.

Instead, I hit the shower. I'd been up late over the last little while. My hometown hockey team had me glued to the TV while making a run for the Stanley Cup. The water dripped out of the nozzle on a day where I needed a "wake up call" more than ever. *Will they ever fix the water pressure?* Hector barking outside my stall interrupted my shower.

Half-dead to the world, I strolled in my bathrobe to the kitchen, fed Hector, and went to the office. I'd been so consumed by hockey that I neglected my email. Blasted with hundreds of messages, I didn't know where to begin. Most were the usual ones from all my girlfriends. Some newer ones, though, caught my eye asking me to "Friend" them on a website whose name didn't make much sense to me.

Curious, I clicked the link and a cheerful-looking page filled with blah-blah-blah welcomed me, promising to connect me with all my friends. I never learned to type, so I was glad the account creation process only required my email and a password. Took me a while to figure a good password out. I typed "password." *No one will think to use that!*

A screen prompted me to upload my contacts from my email account. I had thousands, thanks to my fan club accrued over the years. *Why the hell not?* Someone called me to the kitchen, so I pressed the button and left the computer to do its thing.

The hospice appeared more run down than normal. It might've been natural erosion over the past seventeen years: the furniture was worn out, the kitchen resembled the aftermath of the Battle of Britain, and the tables and chairs in the dining area were filled with etchings of rather crude sentiments. It's sad to see everything falling apart. I grabbed a plate of eggs and parked myself in front of the TV. Hector, having finished his breakfast, cuddled up beside me, begging for some greasy bacon. I gave him a piece while I flicked through the channels.

10 a.m. and they're running infomercials? Unless you had premium channels like HBO, the only thing broadcasting on TV was mind-rot—either commercials or reality shows.

Screw TV.

It'd been a while since I read a book. I only keep a few prized ones, like my Bible, biblical commentaries, and some classic Greek mythology in my small room at the hospice. I loved reading, and some of my fondest memories of being in Vancouver were those quiet moments watching Heather leaf through business papers in heavy binders—her choice literature—with glass of asparagus water in hand, while I studied my scriptures.

Maybe I'll venture out and buy myself a Harry Potter novel. Never had read any, and the latest lands in bookstores in July. I was several books behind, and I had heard fans were obsessed with the series—they'd line up for days in advance of any new release. I had a month to catch up, but being a busy man, I knew it wouldn't happen. But still, I wanted to understand what the fuss was all about.

Books were a huge part of my life growing up. Mama insisted Dad read to me when I was little. She felt it important to introduce me to literature. I didn't mind. I loved bonding with my father. He often read from old books that he still had from his childhood. Their age, combined with his aristocratic British accent, made the bedtime stories come alive and have an enchanting aura about them.

Curious George became the first story I memorized from stem-to-stern. Dad sometimes teased me by messing up the words, which I proudly corrected. I also enjoyed Dr. Seuss—but British author, Enid Blyton, became my go-to bedtime favourite. We both bonded over the *Secret Seven* series. He also read to me—and simplified because of my age—more child-friendly Shakespeare, like *As You Like It* and *A Midsummer Night's Dream*. His collection of all of Shakespeare's works was by far the largest book he owned. I laughed while Dad awkwardly balanced the tome on his lap, and as he read, I thought it odd how he had to keep tucking away something that threatened to fall out of the book.

Each night, shortly after supper, we'd eat a bowl of Frootie-ooties, then brushed our teeth. Both dressed in comfy pajamas, he'd read to me until I felt drowsy, and tucked me in. He'd then stay by my side in bed with his arm wrapped around my shoulder until I dozed off. On nights where I didn't feel too sleepy, we'd talk. Dad never said much—I had plenty to share about my life, even at such a young age.

He taught me to read during our bedtime routines. When I hit seven, we were taking turns reading passages from the stories. Most kids at school called me "sissy" for having this tradition at such an age. I didn't care. I had special time with my dad—they probably didn't.

Growing up in a trailer in Ottawa, my room didn't have much space. For my eighth birthday, Dad bought me a bookshelf that spanned the entire height of the wall. Two of the six shelves were immediately filled with our "bedtime" books.

Dad lost his job after my ninth birthday. It might've been 1974—the time during the recession in the States, which impacted Canada. Jobs were scarce, but my father did what he could to make ends meet. Must've been challenging for him. He sometimes came across shy, so interviews might've been difficult. Despite that, he took on commissions at weird hours of the day. When he had to work nights, Mama insisted on doing her part to keep his tradition alive by reading to me in his place.

Each night, she'd remind me of the sacrifice she made by missing her favour-ite TV shows like *The Waltons, Little House on the Prairie*, and *Barnaby Jones*.

It made me feel important. She did all that for my sake, recognizing the royalty I'd become—she did, after all, call me a prince.

Even though she complained, I enjoyed her spin on the routine at first. She read to me from a book she loved as a child called *Biblical Bedtime Stories*. Well-illustrated, it featured some classics such as "David and Goliath," "Noah's Ark," and "Daniel in the Lions Den." She had several volumes, and by the end of the summer, we completed most of them. It offered a nice change of pace from the Enid Blyton mysteries.

I endured a huge life change later that summer. My best and only friend, Greg, moved from our neighbourhood. With him gone, and Dad working irregular shifts, I was forced to spend more "alone time" with Mama.

Before then, my only real interactions with Mama occurred when we'd attend church each week. Dad never accompanied us, stating I needed quality time with my mother. I rather enjoyed the pompous Anglican ceremony, and I excelled at Sunday school—learning scriptures faster than the lesser brats in the class. Mama seemed pleased I took to her traditions, and she'd take me out for my favourite double burgers after the service. I looked forward to Sundays.

Mama rarely ventured from home. We never talked much, unless she needed me to do a chore. She'd yell at me from her perch in the living room ordering some task or other, and I'd ignore the request. She'd shout a command again, and I'd retort, "You do it!" It had little avail. She'd continue barking until I stopped what I was doing and fulfilled her bidding. The orders felt like an hourly occurrence until Dad came home. Then she'd pass on the squawking and chores to him. She ruled the roost in our household, spending hours in front of the TV.

After struggling to find employment, Dad found permanent work in Montreal that fall. He had a weird schedule and stayed in the city with a friend during the week, only returning to Ottawa when he had a few days off in a row. I thought it fortunate he had a "foreign" city to visit, and he always seemed enthusiastic to leave our house and return to his work.

He mentioned his friend to me a few times. She sounded nice, and I wanted to meet her. Dad denied my requests to visit and warned me to never tell Mama—citing that if she knew about his friend, it'd risk him losing his job. I kept his secret safe. It had taken him a long time to find employment, and I'd hate to be responsible for him getting fired.

I did miss my bedtime routine with him when he was away, which Mama continued. When we finished all her story books, she decided to read the whole Bible to me from the old King James. Starting from Genesis with language containing many thees, thous, and thus's, we ploughed through the scriptures one chapter a night. Often, I fell asleep dreaming of Shakespearian characters, wearing panty hose, while walking on water and slaughtering rams.

Dad found a home for us to move to in a rural part of Ontario near Alexandria the following spring. It promised to cut his travel time to work and would give us additional land and larger rooms to live and play in.

Ironically, Dad didn't spend more time with us, being closer to Montreal. In fact, he returned more often for "business trips," which sent my mother in a foul mood each time he left—and yeah, he was around sometimes, but he seldom spoke to Mama. They would spend their time sitting quietly in the living room, Mama watching her TV, and he, reading his newspapers.

I hated Alexandria.

Yes, there was enough space for two bookshelves in my room, and a large floor to play various games. I read more in my first few months there than I ever did in my life. Dad, seldom at home, bought me my own Bible along with many books on Greek mythology, science fiction, and fantasy. My creative mind thrived, and though some of the academic books were slow to plow through, I savoured them, reading and re-reading them.

The larger home permitted Dad to unpack from storage old newspapers and magazines he enjoyed from his youth—some dating back to the 1950s. He kept them piled close to his chair in the living room and read from them often. I understood their appeal—they always featured a gorgeous woman posing half-nude on the third page. For the first time in my life, I felt an attraction to women, and my curiosity was piqued by the photos. The majority were blonde, which I found most alluring.

In fact, thanks to those newspapers, I began noticing women's beauty. I remember falling hard for an actress in a movie I watched on TV and getting all choked up and teary when the film ended. I wanted to see more of her. Dad said her name was Goldie Hawn—a blonde. He, too, thought she was cute and had first seen her on a show called *Rowan and Martin's Laugh In* when I was a toddler. He spent hours re-enacting some of the funniest sketches from that program, and "sock it to me" became one of our inside jokes—one which Mama never understood.

And even though some were blonde, I never took interest in Mama's doll collection, which was displayed throughout the house. Like Dad's newspapers, they, too, were unpacked from storage when we moved to Alexandria. She had hundreds, and the dolls were of different skin tones, shapes, and types. Some talked, others had blank expressions on their faces. The collection lined stacked shelves nailed to the walls of our dining room and along the main hallway of our little bungalow. The ones near my parent's bedroom were the creepiest. They scared me, reminding me now of the *Children of the Corn*.

Mama maintained her routine, parking herself in the living room to watch

TV. She did dress every day, wearing her brown hair in a beehive hairdo and caking her face with make-up. She told me you always need to look your best for anyone who might drop in unexpectedly. It never happened. No one ever visited us.

Alone, I read and played games in my bedroom to kill time. There were more books in my room now, mostly Dad's. Many were cool histories of England. I remember excitedly leafing through these tomes. They were laced with pictures of knights and royalty decked in funny clothes. I often imagined myself sitting on a throne being served by subjects—wearing long velvety robes, feeling the silk against my skin.

I worked my way through most of the books on the lower shelves. The topmost ones were the largest and out of my reach. Curious, one day I went to retrieve a chair from the dining room. It was an awkward size, and I couldn't lift it.

"What are you doing?" hollered Mama from the adjacent living room. The chair scraping over the hardwood floor had broken her trance with the television.

I explained, and she volunteered to help me retrieve the books.

"I don't think I've seen this one," she said pulling down the largest. It was an older one with damaged binding. "This looks like a collection of Shakespeare. Your dad loved studying it in school." She leafed through it. "They have *Macbeth…Antony and Cleopatra…*oh, and look here" — she lowered the book to show me — "*Romeo and Juliet.* They are such great romances. I'm going to start reading these to you tonight!"

A pile of postcards fell out of the book, surprising us. I picked them up, and Mama and I inspected them—mostly pictures of Montreal. Sandwiched between them was a photo of my dashing dad arm in arm with a blonde woman! Mama shrieked, snatched it, and stormed out of the room. The sound of frantic back and forth pacing filled the house while I browsed through the postcards.

I loved the images of the picturesque city and wanted to visit it one day. They didn't have any writing on the back, though. As I rifled through the postcards, I found a second photo of the woman hidden in the stack. I studied her features and deemed her one of the most beautiful I'd ever seen. I flipped over the picture and struggled to read the bad penmanship. *Did that say "miss you," or "fun?"* The signature was clear: "All my love, Amélie xxx."

Amélie had a warm and youthful expression that immediately drew me in to a world of fantasy. I imagined we were best friends doing fun activities together, like going to a museum. I envisioned being able to share my deepest concerns with her and receiving warm cuddles of affection when needed. My feelings of attraction and security to this woman left me confused. *Is this love?* I hid her picture in the drawer next to my bed intending to pull it out whenever I felt lonely and needed comfort.

The familiar chatting on the television resumed. My stomach growled—must be lunchtime. *Funny. I don't hear any activity in the kitchen.*

I ventured out into the hallway to the living room.

"Mama, I'm hungry."

My mother turned from her seat. The make-up around her eyes was smudged and wet.

"I'm not making lunch today."

Not sure what to do, I served myself some Frootie-ooties and returned to my room.

Dad didn't return home for supper. Whenever his plans changed, he'd call home maybe an hour beforehand to tell Mama he'd be staying in Montreal longer. It never was an issue, though Mama would mutter about wasting the food she toiled to prepare.

The phone rang at its usual time…and rang. Mama didn't answer. The ringing irritated me, so I picked it up.

"Hello?" I said.

The line clicked on the other end, and I heard the dial tone.

"Was that your Dad?" barked Mama.

"It hung up. Hey…when's supper?" I had noticed Mama hadn't moved from the living room for a while.

She stood with a huff, retrieved a loaf of bread and jar of peanut butter from the pantry, and placed them dramatically down on the dining room table. From another cupboard, she grabbed a plate and a knife and put them in front of me. She filled a glass with milk, then returned to watch television.

I stared at the food not knowing what to do next. I had never made myself a meal, though I watched Mama make sandwiches in the past. It didn't take long to figure it out, and I prepared myself two. I didn't dare ask Mama for the jelly.

Finishing my dinner, I placed the plates in the sink along with the others. It was weird. Mama kept the kitchen spic and span. Peering into the living room, I noticed she hadn't budged from the sofa.

"Are you okay, Mama?"

"Fine," she replied with a sharp tone.

It was a quiet evening, me, alone in my room. Mama didn't visit for bedtime stories. I opened the drawer by my bed and pulled out the picture of the beautiful Amélie and spent my evening staring at it.

It must've been sunrise when my feet hit the floor to start the next day. I couldn't sleep a wink. A little unsure of myself, I grabbed my bathrobe.

Mama sat alone at the dining room table, holding the photo of Amélie she had found with both hands. On either side of her arms lay two of her favourite dolls. They were the exact same type. They weren't babies like her *Children of the Corn* collection—more like the skinny models you'd see on some TV shows. One was brown-haired like Mama, the other blonde. She named them Betty and Veronica.

She didn't notice me staring at her and placed the photo down. Without lifting her head, she reached for the brunette doll and began buttoning its vest.

Mama didn't play with her dolls too often, though she'd sometimes talk to them while cleaning the house. "Penelope, how'd you get so dusty?" she'd say, for example.

Peeking in at Mama from the hallway, I didn't want to interrupt her, but she caught me skulking in the shadows. She placed her doll down and lifted the photo so that I could see the image.

"Do you know who this is?"

I gulped as I stared at the photo of Amélie and my father. *Is this the woman Dad visited in Montreal? Better keep his secret.* "Uh, no."

"Hmm…He never said anything about her?" She waved the photo in front of me so I could have a better look.

I thought the photo I had of Amélie hidden in my drawer more flattering.

"No, never mentioned her."

She slowly placed the photograph on the table and glowered at it for what felt like an eternity. She grabbed the dark-haired doll, and with a miniature comb began grooming her hair. "Veronica, you are gorgeous," she said. Mama stared woefully at her toy, each stroke, painfully slow. She looked up at me. "Do you agree?"

Unsure what to say, an image of my cute Goldie flooded my mind. I studied Veronica, then my eyes lowered to the blonde doll, lying on its back on the table. I must've stared at it for a while.

"What?" Mama said with distain. "You prefer Betty?" She reached down and waved it from side to side.

"Yes, I like her better."

"You are such a shallow child." Exasperated, she stood and a braid from her brown hair fell. "Why does every man in this house fall for the blonde? Larry, you need to see beyond that. Brunettes are much better!"

"No way! Betty looks more like Goldie Hawn. I love Goldie, not this dark-haired Veronica."

A frustrating discussion ensued. Mama insisted never to judge a book by its cover and that brunettes were prettier than blondes. I didn't say a word. I clenched my fists and slammed them to my sides. She had no right dictating preference like that over me! Angry, she returned to bed, letting me tend to my breakfast.

Funny, the dishes hadn't been cleaned from the night before.

The next few days were beyond weird. Mama insisted on conversations about "opening my mind" to seeing the beauty in brunettes. The two dolls were left on the dining room table to remind me of her point. Sometimes Mama would change Veronica's clothes with the hope of bringing out her beauty more. My opinion never changed, prompting further chats about colour and what goes well together.

Apart from those painful lectures, the house remained somewhat silent. Mama's routine had changed, though. She no longer made my bed or cooked my dinners. She spent her time either watching TV or playing with the Betty and Veronica dolls.

I had learned how to make meals and mastered boiling soup and using the toaster.

I was quite pleased with myself when I prepared a TV dinner—which included a tasty apple treat dessert. I savoured my third Salisbury steak meal of the week when Dad opened the front door returning from his latest trip. He wrapped his arm around me and noticed the two dolls lying on either side of my plate.

"I've always been one to like Betty," he offered unsolicited. "You son?"

I didn't have a chance to answer before Mama demanded I return to my room and began ripping into my father. I heard her say words like "sin," "fornicate," and "the child," and I heard him plead, "but Snookie" several times. The argument de-escalated as fast as it erupted.

A few minutes later, Dad entered my room with a tumbler of whiskey and sat before me on the bed.

"Not a word about my friend in Montreal. Remember?" He pinched his lips with thumb and forefinger and twisted his wrist like he was locking his lips.

I understood. He must've planted a doozy of a lie on Mama about the woman's identity in the photo. Dad never shared with me how he spun that tale. Instead, he tucked me in and told me a story about Hercules. Funny, Hercules was born out of Zeus' unfaithfulness with a mortal and victimized by the jealousy of Zeus' wife, Hera.

The sound of my mother's soft moaning woke me from a deep slumber. It lasted for a while and stopped. I couldn't fall back to sleep, and a while later, I heard a sizzling sound from the kitchen. When I got out of bed, a huge stack of pancakes greeted me at the breakfast table—and no dolls that morning. Dad sat by his papers in a comfy chair in the living room drinking some coffee.

Mama finished cleaning the dishes, then poured me some orange juice, kissed my head, and went to my room to make my bed. Dad stood to leave for work, and Mama hugged him goodbye.

Business as usual…until the phone rang near dinner time.

Dad was summoned to stay in Montreal again.

Mama kept her cool over the next few days. Though, she brought out the Betty and Veronica dolls again, thankfully, there were no lectures.

Maybe it had something to do with my newfound obsession that week. Each night, I watched the women's gymnastics on TV during the Montreal Olympics. I earnestly watched the battle between Olga Korbut and Nadia Comăneci—both were brunettes, both amazing, and both super cute.

Mama first noticed me ogling them when she caught me attempting the "splits" in their honour. She approved, indicated that if they weren't from "communist" countries, they'd be the marrying kind. She seized the opportunity to spend many hours speaking to me about the merits of marriage, and how love extends beyond looks. Mama did paint a nice picture of the comforts of having a lifelong companion, white-picket fence, pets, and children. The images she conjured contributed to my reflecting that week of my potential future wife. *Could it be a Nadia, or an Olga?*

Mama and Dad sent me away to choir camp that August, where I met a great Counsellor-In-Training named Connor. We became close friends, and he contributed greatly to an experience that I loved—though my spare time was consumed with dreams of my gymnasts, Goldie Hawn, and Dad's friend (I had brought her photo to camp). I had a blast and returned to a relatively calm home.

My first night back, near Labour Day weekend, Mama was alone because Dad, again, had to stay in Montreal. She seemed a little unsettled, but after dinner, I turned on the TV. A rerun of the *Bionic Woman* aired, and I fell hard for the blonde actress, Lindsay Wagner. Any dreams of Olga and Nadia were replaced by this bombshell, running in slow motion to robotic sound effects.

Mama picked up how smitten I'd become with Lindsay. She scoffed while grabbing my suitcase and stormed down the hall to my room. I continued to enjoy the show when I heard her scream. She ran back to me with my photo of Dad's friend in hand.

"Why on earth do you have this?" She pointed to the back of the picture. "This is a love note!" She glared at me. "You knew about *her* and lied to your Mama! Wait until that man comes home."

She ragged on me. Needing to escape, I ran to my room, and she followed, carrying her Betty and Veronica dolls, talking non-stop about being honest, chivalrous, and every now and again asking why we men preferred blondes over brunettes.

Dad arrived in mid-barrage. He couldn't squirm his way out of being found out. He pleaded with her, but to no avail. I fell asleep that night to a horrible argument.

I had weird dreams of Mama's two dolls always moving side to side in front of my face, and a voice saying to me in the background "Who's prettier, Betty or Veronica?" repeated over and over.

I yelled back a thousand times "How many times do I have to tell you! Betty, Betty, Betty!"

I woke up in a cold sweat.

Fed up with the dolls, I snuck quietly to the kitchen in the middle of the night. Both Betty and Veronica were perched on the dining-room table. I wanted to wrench their heads off to remove any more comparisons between blondes and brunettes. Unfortunately, they were glued too strong onto their bodies, so I took a pair of scissors, and removed all the hair from the brunette, leaving the blonde unscathed. Satisfied, I left the dolls sitting in their original positions on the table. *There. No more arguments.* I returned to bed.

Mama woke me up with a scream.

Several minutes later, Dad entered my room. "Son, your mother and I have a lot to work out. We're going to have to send you to the city for a while."

Dad let it slip that Mama was concerned about my "psychological" problem. By the end of the weekend, my parents packed all my games and books and shipped me off to the foster care of Father George—a priest from our former church in Ottawa.

I lived there until I moved to Vancouver.

I gave my father credit. He found a way to stay married to Mama, despite his misgivings and her lack of trust. I never knew what became of my dad's friend, Amélie, but it was funny how she was a dead ringer for Heather.

Odd. Mama got along well and approved of my Schnookums—a blonde. I wonder what on earth changed Mama's mind?

I bought *Harry Potter and the Order of the Phoenix*, figuring I could read the latest two books in a month before the release of the newest one in July. The eight-hundred-page epic weighed heavy in my arm while I walked back to the hospice from the bookstore. The size and weight of the book reminded me of my father's Shakespeare collection, making me have thoughts of my parents and the state of their marriage.

As I reflected on their problems, I counted my blessings for the time my wife and I had together, and for the beautiful child we produced. Dad stayed married to Mama—and he worked hard at it. I often questioned why he did. She wasn't easy to get along with, and since the Amélie incident, he did everything in his power to satisfy Mama. It meant, for him, no more overnights in Montreal, or anywhere else, and he gave in to all of her demands. He cleaned the house, made the meals, and ran the errands while Mama watched her TV shows. To his credit, he did whatever he could to keep the marriage going.

I, too, have kept my marriage with Heather alive. But is there another woman, though, who could take her place and actually want to engage with me?

Then another thought hit me. My parents never divorced despite their difficulties. *Was that a good idea?*

I pondered on this.

Maybe I should put my Heather saga to rest.

Someone had left the computer on, and the monitor lit the dark office on my return. I found the link to the social media website I had logged into earlier and completed my "profile." I decided to use the photo Danny and I had taken at the Highland games on my fortieth birthday—a perfect profile picture to remind me of the good work I do for people. Danny had done well for himself since crashing here when he was down and out.

A page prompted me to type my "status." Not really understanding what "status" meant, I read through several on the web page, all posted by my women—likely my email contacts. They all were similar, like: Hi, I miss you! Why don't you click the link and see me?

I had no idea what to write, so I typed, "My sperm continues to augment the population! Four vials produced in fifteen minutes today!" That should impress everyone who's a part of Larry nation.

While continuing to read statuses, a red box with a number one in the top right corner of the screen seized my attention. I clicked it:

Tabitha Tatas likes your status.

Of course she does.

More notifications appeared "liking" my post, and many more of my contacts accepting my friend requests. This may be a nice way to keep in touch with all my followers. And less typing than email! I like *Larrynet!*

We had a staff meeting the next day. I couldn't pay attention—daydreaming of all my loyal subjects on *Larrynet. Could one of these women replace Heather?*

"…and next week we're going to have to put extra effort in cleaning the building because we'll be having our annual general meeting. We need to put our best foot forward for our donors." Reginald sighed. "Our poor building needs so many renovations."

"Tell me about it," a staffer replied. "The kitchen is becoming a cesspool to work in. Any idea how old the appliances are?"

"We just don't have the money," said Reginald.

"The showers have been brutal for years," another one added. "They barely produce enough water to soak your armpits, never mind your hair."

"Ever use *Larrynet*?" I asked, not realizing I said that aloud. "Trademark pending." I quickly added.

The conversation stopped, everyone giving me full attention. I commanded this respect when I spoke at our meetings.

"Sorry? What are you talking about?" Reginald asked after a brief silence.

"You know, this thing on the computer that makes contacting your friends so easy."

Our Director of Communications at the hospice answered. "Ah yes, I know what he's talking about. Yes, the hospice has an account, and we plan to use it for fundraising once we develop a *social media strategy* to inform all our stakeholders. Personally, I don't see the point of it. I believe it's geared mostly at young folk who aren't our target demographic."

You're such an old fart.

"Well, I created my account yesterday, and I now have all these friends. May I use the computer later today to develop my own 'social media strategy?'" I liked the expression. Sounded officious.

"Yes Larry, go ahead. Where were we…ah yes, the showers," Reginald resumed their discussion about the annual meeting.

Our director had said young people used social media. I might now be forty-two, but always young at heart. I made it a point to master the application and attempt to tap into the tool destined to increase my flock. I spent many hours posting statuses sharing my knowledge of women, the Bible, mythology, and my sperm for the edification of the world.

Initially, I never thought about tracking down old friends with it, but out of the blue, I received a notification from Dana. Odd receiving a friend request from her. Hadn't heard from her since she dumped coffee over my jeans.

She sent me a couple of photos of our time together, and I accepted Dana's request despite our past—bygones. Maybe she caught me in a good moment. I vaguely recall reading a Bible verse on forgiveness that morning.

True to Dana form, she invited me out on a date before I even had a chance to log off the computer. She messaged that she had a son and sent me his picture—handsome lad with dark hair and eyes. The photos of the two of them triggered memories of Little Larry and my Schnookums who were in Toronto. *Maybe I could find them on Larrynet?* A quick search proved fruitless.

Dana mentioned she graduated top in her class in med school and now delivered babies for a living. I hoped the burning desire to have her own children slowed with age. I recalled the advances she had made on me and shuddered—glad I rebuked her.

Curiosity, though, seized me, so I accepted her invitation to go out. We went to the swanky Duck's Path Restaurant. For what it's worth, we had a lovely time. She permitted me to talk for a bit, and like any excited parent, showed me millions of pictures of her son, Ethan. He could've been me at twelve. It saddened me Ethan had no father. The kid seemed bright, having a passion for music, and played many board games, mostly by himself. He struggled to make friends in school, so Dana tried to encourage him to play sports to meet people. Despite her efforts, Ethan preferred retreating in his own world, dreaming of his goals in life.

Funny, I did, too.

I showed her the pictures from our beach day, and we laughed at the memories. Dana asked our waiter to "capture our moment" by taking a picture of us using Dana's smartphone. Smartphones were just being introduced, and the technology fascinated me. She digitized my photos in the back of my Bible with her device, I permitted her to log into my *Larrynet* account, and she showed me how to upload and display them for the world's pleasure on the internet.

With Dana's help, I posted a comment under our photo at the restaurant, "Dana and I at Duck's Path Restaurant—and she paid for the meal in honour of my company. BA-HA-HA."

I hugged and kissed Dana goodnight. I didn't think I had anything to worry about with her. She was moving to Toronto in the coming weeks where she planned to start a new practice.

Returning to the computer in the hospice after our date, a burst of nostalgia hit me, and I wondered what my old gang was up to. I hadn't heard from my best friend Brad since leaving Ottawa. I clicked the friend search to look him up. Yup, there's a picture of an older Brad. *And who's that dark-haired woman in it? Is that Jen, the girl I set him up with? She's still with him? Wow, she's aged!*

I couldn't recall what on earth could've boiled Brad's bottom the day I left my hometown, but it would be nice to reconnect with him. I clicked the Add Friend button by his photo.

I spent a few hours searching and Friend Requesting many people from my life. For some reason, I could not find Jacquie Brown, but I was able to track down Troy. He had many photos of his kids and posted one of Angelica with a group of businessmen. I read the list of names under the photo and discovered that Angelica now went by Elizabeth. The comment under the picture read she was joining the board of directors of some East Coast art gallery. I was so happy for her success. After staring at Angelica's photo for a while, I elected not to send Troy a friend request.

Angelica's picture did make me think of how I initially thought she was Trisha in the dark strip club. The memory took me back to when I dated Trisha—she knew me as Ridiculous Rick's stage name, Dick Wank. I rubbed under my eye, remembering how he slugged me out cold at my stag.

I searched for Rick and found him. *He's gained weight! Sort of looks like a pear!* I clicked the Add Friend button. *What the hell...*

The rest of the evening was spent researching the web. The internet was a huge encyclopedia of knowledge, and I now had a *Larrynet* audience to share my findings and opinions. I posted many interesting tidbits of information to my virtual gang. No doubt, they'll all be duly impressed.

I continued to receive dozens of Friend Requests from women daily and hit over a thousand after my first week online. I accepted them all, even though I didn't recognize their names— except for Dana, who communicated with me directly.

They all loved my posts. Each time I logged in, I'd have hundreds of notifications awaiting! It became too time consuming to bother reviewing them all, but one stood out above the rest—a woman named Jaqueline Rousseau with a profile picture of a cat sticking out her tongue. She liked and commented on all the photos I posted of Hector.

A brunette stood with a colourful retro backdrop decorated in sixties psychedelia. Facing me, she screamed, "Sock it to me." Water doused her from above. She exited the scene.

An old woman marched on. "Sock it to me." A small elderly man snuck behind her and poured a bucket of water over her head. He exited stage left, she, right.

The camera panned to a cute blonde, but her face morphed. *Heather*? "Sock it to me," she said in a helium voice. She bent down, picked up a giant rubber hammer, and hit herself on the head knocking herself out.

"Ow!" I woke up startled as my giant Harry Potter book crashed my cranium. *Man, it's thick.* Hector sat on my nightstand, wagging his tail.

Did you knock it off?

I shook myself awake and rubbed my head. *Crap, I have a huge bump.*

"Bad dog!" I yelled.

"Arf!" Hector hopped onto my bed and sprung himself down onto the floor. He ran in circles, barking, expecting to be fed. I didn't move, frustrating the poor dog. He figured he make his intentions clearer and scratched on my closed door. I slowly rose out of bed, opened it, let him out, and shut it behind him.

Someone will tend to him.

I picked up my book and sat in my bed. *Where did I leave off? Page ten?* Thought I'd be deeper into it by now.

Determined to finish the book this week, I began reading. Halfway through page eleven, my mind wandered. I couldn't shake the image of my wife from my dream. It was too lifelike.

Oh, Heather, Heather, Heather. Where are you now?

I turned the page.

I need you Schnookums.

I flipped to the end of the book. Only 10,000 pages to go? I've been at this book for three days, and all I can think about is my Schnookums. *She's a virus I can't shake.*

Sighing, I placed the book back on my table and left the room. *Can't get into this Potter Hoof and Poof stuff, anyway.*

I meandered to the cafeteria. Hector was eating away at some kibble, served by someone in the kitchen. Apart from a few staff, not many people were around, and no wonder, it was near 10:30 a.m.

Nothing worse than sleeping in and waking up with the sensation of being run over by a truck. I chanced a glass of water and today the faucet poured clear liquid into my glass. *No brown stuff. Good.*

No one in the office, I turned on the computer. The familiar beeps and whirs filled the dimly lit room while the hard drive came to life. While I waited for the slow machine to boot up, Hector dashed into the office and jumped on my lap. I scratched his ears when I noticed a stickie note stuck to the monitor.

"Larry: your wife called. You are to arrange to send her the usual package."

Ten minutes later, the login screen prompted me to type my credentials. I reached around my dog and began typing. After an eternity, I connected to the internet. *I must find Schnookums. If not on Larrynet...*

Heather's weird stationary request went to her via PO box, not her home address, so I figured I could track her down via a web search. *I'm so clever!* I typed "Heather Mackenzie infomercial" and a wealth of data flooded my screen. I rather liked the hot pictures displayed of her but couldn't find Schnookums' home address. If not her, maybe...

I found Sven Lindgaard. A giant photo of him with a goofy grin filled the page for a company called Euro-Can Productions Inc. headquartered in Toronto. Hector was not impressed. He began growling at the Swede on the screen.

"Good boy!" I said. I reached into my pocket and tossed a dog biscuit on the ground for a reward.

"Arf!" Hector bounded off my lap and carried his treat out of the office to enjoy in the cafeteria.

I checked the Euro-Can Productions' website which featured the *Bärbar Ugn* and many advertising campaigns. I jotted my findings in my diary. Honey-Bunny must be working there. *I'm going to fly down for Canada Day weekend, deliver your package, sweep you off your feet, and bring you and Little Larry back home to Vancouver!*

I had a week. Plenty of time to get ready.

I looked up Air Western to price some tickets.

$650?

Where the hell am I going to find that kind of money?

Chapter Twenty
The Devil and Mrs. Jones
June 2007

Monday morning. I rushed out to grab my usual coffee at Jumpin' Java. My clothes were the same I had on yesterday, but I didn't care. I needed money fast—only had a few days until Canada Day weekend. I couldn't wait for my next paycheque, and I only had $120 cash from my work for Peter—no way near enough to cover a trip to Toronto.

I couldn't figure out why I felt the need to fly over for Canada Day, but I couldn't suppress my urge to visit my Schnookums. I travelled to The Happy Apothecary to place her usual order. It always frustrated me that a two-dollar item would cost fifty to ship.

"Ah, Larry," said the young lad behind the counter. "The usual?"

I nodded while he went in the back and dropped a pad of legal-sized paper on the counter.

"Fifty-two dollars. We'll send it out to her tomorrow."

"Today, I'll forgo the shipping costs."

The young man appeared shocked. "You don't understand. We *have* to ship it to her."

I shook my head. "Nah. I'm flying to Toronto soon. I'll bring it to her in person. It'll be a nice surprise." I removed my wallet and dropped a toonie on the counter.

"She might be a little more than surprised," the guy said staring at the coin while I left the shop.

Next stops: my appointment at the hospital, then Peter, hoping he'd have a "special" job for me to earn some cash.

I boarded the bus and before commencing my visualization exercises to prepare for my usual donations, I inspected the loose-leaf paper for Schnookums.

She can't buy this in Toronto?

"Hmmm…" said Margo examining my partially filled specimen cup—way less than my usual. "You spent your entire fifteen minutes for this?" She threw my output in the "Larry" bin, then smiled brightly while shuffling through some files.

Enrique returned from cleaning my office. "Maybe the 'fifteen-minute' rule is too stressful for you, Larry."

"I *am* stressed this morning. I need cash fast. I must visit Schnookums in Toronto. Can you lend me $650, guys? I'll pay you back next week."

Margo shook her head.

"Sure," Enrique said. He dug deep into his pocket and produced a few dimes and a nickel. "Here, hope this helps."

"Thank you, Enrique." I grabbed his coins. *Poor generous soul doesn't make much. Let's see…I had $120 to start. Less two dollars for Heather's paper. Add thirty-five cents from Enrique leaves me…I'm well on my way to buy that ticket!*

Outside the hospital's main entrance, cars drove by dropping off and picking up people. Peter taught me that success in making money depended on two key factors—emotion and product.

I stared at the vehicles stopping and going. I didn't have a product to sell. I didn't have several minutes to tell each passer-by my life story and why I wanted to raise funds to go to Toronto. I needed an idea fast.

An orderly pushed a man in a hospital-owned wheelchair to a car waiting by the curb. The orderly opened the door, and the man gingerly stood and took his place in the passenger seat. I rushed over to them.

"Hi, I'm Larry Johnstone."

The orderly was taken aback.

"I need the wheelchair," I said.

"What for?"

"I'm a patient. I just had surgery."

She glared at me. "Not likely, you wouldn't be left unattended."

She spun a one eighty and returned to the building. I followed her in, figuring there might be some other wheelchairs I could use, but struck out. A gentleman, sitting in a director's chair by a security stand in the lobby, left the room. I snatched it, returned outside, parked myself by the curb, and flagged down the first vehicle that pulled over.

The passenger door opened. A young woman walked out, and before she could close the door, I yelled, "Hi, I'm George Featherstone. Can you help me?"

The woman appeared a little startled. "Sorry, gotta rush. I'm late for my appointment." She slammed the door and turned on the jets to rush to the entrance.

A small hatchback arrived next. The driver exited the car and opened the door for his passenger.

"Excuse me," I said from my chair, "I need some urgent help."

The man stopped and looked down to me. "Oh, what's happening?"

"I just came out of day surgery, and the hospital insists someone take me home. My ride didn't show up, and I don't have any cash for a cab. I need to grab a taxi to go to Burnaby. Can you spot me fifty bucks to cover it?"

"Sorry, no cash on me." He helped an elderly lady out of the car and returned to drive it to the parking lot.

Peter makes this look so easy.

A minivan pulled up. The passenger seat was empty, and I beckoned the driver to lower the window. He obliged.

"Hi, I'm Peter Van Wagner," I said. "Can you help me out? I just came out of surgery and the hospital insists I have someone drive me home. My friend stood me up, and I didn't bring any cash. Could you spare fifty dollars? I need a ride to Burnaby, so need cash for a taxi."

The man, in his sixties, looked sinister with his Van Dyke beard and '50s-styled rimmed glasses. His fedora complemented the look.

"Hi Peter, beautiful day, *yes*?" The man raised his eyebrows and rubbed his beard with his right hand. "Sorry, didn't quite catch all that." He had a posh-sounding British accent, like Reginald's. "Did I hear you right? Needed a *taxi* you say?"

"Yes, a *taxi*," emphasizing the word like he did.

"We've been expecting you! I'm Dale Jones." The sprightly man hopped out of the car and dashed around the front. He grabbed my hand with both of his and shook. "Come in, come in." He opened the back door.

What the...have we met?

"Uh...I only need some mon—"

"This is going to be so exciting, Peter, *yes*?"

I shifted in my seat looking for the seatbelt.

"Let me get that for you. It's a bit tricky." He reached around my waist and helped me buckle up. "This is a happy coincidence, *yes*? We've heard so much about you."

He's heard of me?

"Of course," I said. Flattered, I didn't know what else to say.

"You did say Burnaby, *yes*?" asked Dale. "We live there, too. We can drive you there and talk shop."

Bloody good Samaritan. I shouldn't have told him where I'm going! Sigh. There was no way out of this. I made myself comfortable.

Odd. He winked at me before shutting the door. He nearly tripped over the deck chair I had brought to the curb.

I rolled down the window. "Would you mind bringing that back to the lobby?" I asked.

The man nodded. Within a flash, he returned, walking in front of the car while rubbing his beard. He took his place behind the steering wheel.

"I'm glad it's not raining," he said, grinning. He turned to face me. "I'm surprised the hospital left you unattended after a surgery—"

Why did he wink at me again? And does he have a skin rash under his beard? He keeps stroking the damn thing like a cat!

"—and Peter… Don't they use wheelchairs?" His smile grew wider.

Why is he smiling? Is he on to me? Think fast Larry. I scanned the area and noticed staff congregating around a designated smoking area. I recognized one.

"Yeah, you'd think they would. Look, the orderly who wheeled me out is taking a smoke break." I waved at Enrique through the open window. He tapped a friend's shoulder, pointed at me, and started cracking up. "Enrique is the one laughing."

"I see him," said Dale. "I would love to join them for a puff, but alas, I quit twenty years ago." He tapped the steering wheel in awkward silence. "It's a beautiful day to be outside, *yes?* We are waiting for my wife to be discharged, then we'll go." He raised his hand to pick at his beard again. "We're near the university campus. Work for you?"

"Yes, that's fine. I live near there."

Near, as in it's going to take me an hour and a half to return home.

I wiggled my bum on the nice cushiony chair. *Much better than the deck chair.*

My tummy growled. Embarrassed, I clutched it. "I guess you can tell I haven't eaten in a while. Do you have any snacks?"

"As a matter of fact," he reached into the glove compartment, "I do. Like kale chips? They're homemade and a favourite amongst our friends." He produced a sandwich bag with some schlocky green crap.

Who eats this?

"Is that all you have?"

"Yes, they're delicious." The man opened the bag and helped himself to one.

"I'll pass. Have anything else?"

He returned the bag and laughed. "Sorry." He chuckled, lifting another bag out. "Not everyone eats sugar cubes."

Must be die-hard tea drinkers.

We engaged in some basic get-to-know-you conversation, and Dale interrupted me in the middle of my fertility trials story.

"There she is!" He opened his door and stood and waved at a gorgeous woman being pushed in a wheelchair by an orderly. She looked too young to be married to him.

They reached the car, and she acknowledged Dale who had rushed out to open the passenger door. The tall beauty gracefully left her wheelchair and took her seat in the car. Her chestnut hair, wrapped in a neat ponytail, flung over the headrest while Dale helped her buckle a seatbelt.

"Winnie, looks like they barely touched you." The man smiled to his wife when he returned behind the wheel.

"Ooooooh!" The woman sang out the word "oh." She, too, had an accent from across the pond. "You know it was only a cyst removed on my leg, dear. I'll survive. Who's our friend?" She turned to me and smiled.

At close range, one could see the wrinkles in her face. Still, looked great for her age.

"Winnie, this is Peter. He needed a *taxi*." He emphasized the word again.

"Oooooh, a *taxi*?" she seemed confused and turned back to her husband. Her ponytail brushed my knee. "Dale, I thought you said we were going to meet him in a couple of days." She leaned forward and opened the glove compartment.

"Oh, did you offer Peter some kale chips?" she said, grabbing and opening the bag. "They're our favourite. Want some?"

Do I have to eat this?

I shook my head, and she quickly gobbled a couple and returned the bag. Winnie then helped herself to a sugar cube and fed one to her husband and patted the back of his head like a puppy-dog.

Dale spoke to her in hushed tone while chewing. "Our contact did say we would meet someone asking for a *taxi*…and needing a ride to Burnaby." He turned the key, and the car came to life.

Is "taxi" some sort of secret code?

"Oooooooh, Dale. How exciting. He's the one everyone's raving about." She flashed a dazzling smile at me. "It's the first time we've met someone outside of a hospital, you know."

Am I in a James Bond movie? I rather liked that idea. Dale screeched the van out away from the curb and headed to the main road.

"Winnie, darling, we'll get to business later. Did you know our boy came out of surgery, too?"

"Poor thing. Then it makes sense he's here. He picked a very nice day to have an operation. Not a cloud in the sky," she said, staring out the window. The streets were full of people carrying Earl of Latteigh coffee cups.

"Oooooh, Dale," said Winnie, after driving a couple of blocks, "you wouldn't believe the people in the hospital. All chatting and gossiping away. I was sitting next to this rather boorish fellow while waiting my turn. He was going on and on about having to wait for his surgery for months. He then went on to tell me about his slot car collection. Oh, it was horrible. Then they admitted me, and they kept asking me which leg my cyst was on. Isn't it obvious? And this man pushed me in a bed to the surgery and…"

She prattled on throwing in the odd "oh" and describing every microscopic detail of her adventures in the hospital. I learned about the unshaven intern, the smelly waiting area, and the hard-as-rock doughnut she was offered. Her "ohs" began irritating me, most being held for at least three seconds each.

We headed eastbound.

"What were you being operated on, Peter?"

I didn't respond.

"PETER?"

She's taking to me? Think quick Larry. "I had a vasectomy."

"Oh," said Winnie, mercifully shortening the annoying word. "You had one several years ago, didn't you Dale, dear?"

"Yes," answered Dale. "I didn't have much fun in my recovery. I had difficulty urinating and lots of pain down there—if you know what I mean."

"If what I'm feeling now is any indication of what's to come," I responded, "my next couple of weeks won't be fun. Man, this bandage is itchy." I rubbed my legs together for effect. "I needed to put my sperm to rest. I've impregnated many chicks with my seed, and there are too many little Larrys running around the world."

"Little Larrys?" asked Winnie. "I thought you said your name was Peter."

Crap. She's sharp. "Um, yes, I'm Peter. Larry Johnstone is my best friend who served in the Gulf War. I nickname the seed of my loins after him."

"Oooooh, that's so nice. Isn't it Dale?" said Winnie.

"Yes. It is!" said Dale rubbing his beard with his left hand while driving with his right. "How many children do you have, Peter?"

"More than I can count," I laughed. "But I've put an end to all that now."

"Must've been a difficult decision, *yes*?" Dale said continuing to stroke his chin.

"You bet." I sighed for effect. I shared my life woes with women, and how I ached to be married with someone who gave two flying effs about the institution. They seemed most interested about Heather and her quirks. I happily answered all the personal questions they had about my wife.

The scenery outside my window changed entering the suburbs. We drove through a well-to-do neighbourhood.

"Oooooooh, you poor man," said Winnie. "Where did you say you worked?"

"I'm a professor in philosophy. I actually have to present a lecture at the university in Burnaby this afternoon."

"Philosophy?" said Winnie. "How interesting! But shouldn't you rest after your surgery? Dale had such a miserable time after his."

"The doc told me I should take a couple of days off work, but I feel fine. I'm too busy to take time off."

"Look dears, we're home," Dale interrupted.

"Will Peter be coming in?" said his wife.

Dale turned down a side street. "Winnie, did I not mention that Peter told me he needed a *taxi*?"

"You did. Silly me. Must be the meds the hospital gave me. So, you're sure he's the one we were supposed to—"

What is she going on about?

"Yes. I'm sure he'll fit right in," said Dale. "Peter, you must join us for a late breakfast. It will be good for you to give your lecture on a full stomach."

Winnie turned to look me in the eye. "You'd like that, wouldn't you, Peter? We have so much to talk about!"

How could I say no to such a beautiful lady who wants to chat?

"Thanks," I answered, "love to. Do you have any Frootie-ooties?"

"Oh, no," said Winnie. "We're vegan and prepare everything fresh and organic…" she blabbed the rest of the way of every detail on how to prepare breakfast, including picking the fruit, squeezing the juice, and the steps Dale would take to whip up some pancakes. "I promise you, though, you'll never eat anyone else's pancakes again after having ours."

Dale pulled into a driveway, and we entered their beautiful Tudor-style home.

"Ooooh, Peter," Winnie sang to me we while walking in, "why don't you wait in the living room while we change into something more comfortable."

"Okay," I said. "When do we eat?"

"Shouldn't be too long." Winnie replied. "Maybe fifteen minutes?"

"Okay. I can't stay too long. I have a busy day ahead." *I need money!*

Larger than a barn, the Jones' living room was a far cry from the one in my condo in the Kits. The wall paneling reminded me of something one would see in a saloon of an old Western movie. Its colour blended with the wood floor. Each corner in the room had a large wooden play horse, fully loaded with saddles, stirrups, and bridals. The walls behind them were adorned with jockey whips—stacked linearly above the horses—along with a few sets of spurs, and riding chaps in various sizes. *I never seen this type of interior décor in Ottawa.*

A burgundy leather couch with studded arm panels sat prominently against the main wall. Above it featured several columns of large black collage picture frames—each one contained groupings of three photos.

I walked over and studied the first group of three. A label at the bottom read "East Vancouver Equestrian Club—1995." My eyes floated to the left-most image captioned "Dressage Riders." A group of a dozen men and women were neatly posed in tight fitting breeches, blouses, and protective riding caps. They all held jockey whips and wore boots with golden spurs. Even though they had "Batman-styled" masks, I recognized Dale in the group. Another man with a thin moustache also stood out. *Could be Reginald's twin!*

The middle photo had the word "The Stable," written beneath it. It featured a group of men and women dressed in black leather underwear supporting horse tails, and they all wore these weird horse-head shaped masks. They were all different shapes and sizes, some hairier than others. All in all, a well-groomed lot.

The final photograph in the series contained people wearing outfits that would've made Spider-Man proud, except they were black and wore masks with zippers shut over their mouths and mesh eye coverings. The sign under the image read "The Stable Hands."

Each photo grouping represented a club year on the packed wall.

Opposite the couch rested a large bureau with locked drawers. Above it hung a series of traditional whips, all with unique tips, surrounding a large painting of Winnie wearing a latex version of the Dressage Riders' costume. It dominated the room. I walked over and read the silver frame label: "Queen of the East Vancouver Equestrian Club." *Schnookums would look lovely in that getup!*

The elegant Winnie entered the room carrying some envelopes. I barely recognized her. She had donned a latex cat woman suit top, a Lone Ranger mask and a hair band with pointy ears. No longer in a ponytail, her long hair flowed around her shoulders. Her pants didn't match, being silk. *Is this essential suburban loungewear?*

I couldn't shake the image of the man who looked like Reginald in the photo. I went over to check again. *Sure looks like him.* I dismissed the possibility it could be. Reginald was conservative and pompous. The Joneses on the other hand, were quirky, energetic, and warm.

"I hate these trousers," Winnie said awkwardly sitting on the couch. "So uncomfortable, but my usuals are too tight to wear after surgery. Dale is getting the pancakes ready. I'm famished. You, Peter?"

"I can eat a horse."

"Oooooooh, you probably shouldn't say that here," she laughed. "Have you not noticed? We have a thing for horses."

I love horses, too! But in your living room?

"Of course, I noticed." Some people have the knack for stating the obvious. "I didn't realize horseback riding was so popular in East Vancouver."

"Oh, Peter, you'd be surprised what's popular here. We have to turn away many who want to join our exclusive club. They all come to us anonymously—like you—recommended by our members. We only accept the healthiest in our stable. You might've guessed," she said, pointing to the hobbyhorses, "we have to improvise because there aren't any stables or horses around here."

I used to play make-believe, too. It started with my playing board games by myself as a kid. It evolved into role-playing games, where I spent days creating fantasy kingdoms filled with castles, princesses, and monsters. I often imagined being a paladin, riding on the back of a beautiful white warhorse, rescuing the damsel in distress. This could be fun.

"So, your club has different roles," I said pointing to the framed photos. "You have riders and horses."

"Oh, yes," she said. "We ride the horses here."

"But what do the stable hands do?"

"Oh, let's just say they clean up after the horses, groom them, and tend to the needs of the riders. We'll talk more later, Peter… would you mind checking in on Dale? I'm famished and am craving his pancakes." She ripped open an envelope and began to read her mail.

The smell of food led me down the hall, and I almost stopped in my tracks at the entrance to the kitchen. A man stood with his back to me tending to some pancakes. His exposed bare bottom had a thread emerge from its hairy butt cheeks.

Hmmm...they must be from a different part of England. Reginald would never wear anything like that.

The thread was attached to a thick strap that connected to a belt leading to a choke collar around his neck. Sort of reminded me of what a wrestler wore on TV once. Dale faced me with spatula in hand.

"Ah, there you are, *yes*?" Dale smiled, rubbing his Van Dyke. He turned to the stove and flipped some pancakes in the air from a grill to a few plates. "Please be a good lad and place these on the table by the corner."

Glad his nether regions are covered with that small triangular patch of leather. I placed the plates on the table. It had already been set with maple syrup, utensils, and coffee cups.

"Please pour out the coffee, *yes*? Wiiiiiiiinie," Dale neighed, "breakfast is on!"

A few seconds later Winnie entered. "Oh, sorry honey, I couldn't put my spurs on for our meal."

"No worries, dear. You just had an operation."

The pancakes were as advertised—the best I ever ate.

The Joneses were a lovely couple, permitting me to continue where I left off in the car sharing all about my sperm donation history and the many children I spawned. They were impressed! We had a wonderful chemistry. *I could really get used to hanging with these horsey people.*

The fact that I didn't dress in leather or latex didn't seem to faze them in the least—though it did provoke my curiosity. *Should I buy some for lounging around at the hospice?*

We took our coffees back to the living room. I inwardly sulked because they didn't serve cream. I didn't care for black coffee, but they were so nice, I couldn't refuse their hospitality.

"Oooh, Peter," said Winnie stretching comfortably next to me on the couch, "are you ever concerned for your children's well-being? You have so many mouths to feed."

"You bet." I answered. "I'm the best caring father out there. I'd give my blood for my kids!"

"Peter, darling," said Dale, straddling a saddle on the horse in the corner facing us, "what we mean is… how will you provide for your children if you die. With so many, it must be expensive for you to ensure they are properly cared for—even with a university professor's salary."

"It's hard, it's true, but I never thought about it that way. I guess I have nothing to help them out with when I'm on the 'other side.'"

"Peter," continued Dale, "we can certainly help. Your capacity to breed might make you eligible to be part of our stable in the East Vancouver Equestrian Club. How'd you like that?"

I looked around the odd room, then the wonderful couple. They smiled and made me feel at home.

"Oooh, Peter," said Winnie. "There are so many perks to being in our stable. It'll be such fun."

"I would love to join your club! I have loved horses all my life. They are such majestic creatures. As a teen I often imagined myself being a paladin, riding a beautiful white warhorse named Blondie. I adored it. I spent hours drawing pictures of him."

Dale raised his eyebrows and rubbed his beard. "That's wonderful, Peter. We do use our imaginations a lot here."

I was confused. "But what do my children have to do with horses?"

"Let me explain how this all works, *yes*? As mentioned, we are exclusive, and you came to us on a recommendation from a member." I averted my eyes while Dale lifted his leg over the saddle and walked to unlock one of the drawers in the bureau.

"Member?"

Dale appeared puzzled. "You did use the codeword *taxi* to be picked up at the hospital."

"Of course." *What is he on about?*

"Yes, we have lots of fun here" — he waved his arms at various objects in the room — "but the East Vancouver Equestrian Club is, in fact, a private life insurance company, *yes*? Everyone in our club owns a policy through us. We care not only for our members, but also their loved ones."

Dale retrieved and opened a file folder filled with colourful images, graphs, and numbers. He explained them using expressions like term, group, perm, and complex processes like "variable rate annuity." I didn't pay attention. I stared at a horse in the corner and imagined riding it.

"There are winners and losers in this world," he blathered, "those that are prepared for unavoidable life changes and those who are not. Peter, you can have financial security for both you and your family—"

Neiiiiiggh.

"—we offer three levels of club membership, coinciding with insurance premium costs and benefits. Tier 1. The Stable Hands—offers compensation of $50,000 on death to your loved ones. Tier 2. The Stable—offers up to

$300,000 of coverage. Tier 3 is for the Dressage Riders—offering benefits of over $500,000."

"Oooohh, based on his stock, and recommendation, Dale, I think Peter is a stallion," said Winnie placing her hand on my thigh. "He should be a part of The Stable."

"Yeeeeeees!" I applauded. *I want to be a horsey!*

"Oh, Peter, I love your enthusiasm," purred Winnie. I failed to notice the jockey whip she held beside her. "Neigh!" she ordered, then playfully tapped my lap with it.

"Easy dear," said Dale. "The poor man just came out of surgery for his most delicate bits, and he might not be used to our ways."

Winnie glared at her husband.

"Whi-hi-hi ba-ha-ha!" I couldn't contain my laughter while doing a crappy imitation of a horse.

"Not good enough! You want to be a horse in our stable? Or a stable hand?" She lifted the whip again, but before she brought it down, I let out my best imitation of a horse. It was perfect.

"Oh, yes!" she said in partial moan. "I can feel you'll be an amazing breeder!"

"Of course," I said. "That's what I do."

Dale drew my attention back to his papers. "Would you like to become a member and sign up for a policy? It seems like you are interested in Tier 2. The Stable," said Dale.

"I'm not sure. It depends on the cost."

Winnie lifted her whip again. Before she brought it down, I added, "I can afford one hundred dollars."

"Oh...we can admit you into The Stable for a hundred dollars...*a month*," said Winnie. "In turn, you will receive a free horse costume after three months of payments. Until then, you can enjoy the many pleasures and learn more of our club as a stable hand. Sound good?"

I don't want to be a stable hand. I reflected on it a bit. *Ah hell, I won't be one too long; and the horse costumes are wild!*

Dale continued. "One hundred dollars a month enables you to receive a $300,000 death benefit, while enjoying our exclusive club. However, you need to make an initial deposit of $300 for your first month. Coverage will begin on payment."

I had $120, to start. I needed $650 to fly to Toronto. I spent two on Schnookums stationary. I earned thirty-five cents from Enrique. I needed $300 for membership. *How the hell will I know how much money I need?*

"Our equestrian meetings are held here monthly. We leave the garage door half open, and members can walk in, change into their costumes in complete anonymity, and proceed to the basement where the fun begins.

"With your membership, you'll be entitled to a 'plus one.' This means you can come to our meetings with a partner or good friend. The 'plus ones' can only participate as stable hands, though. You'll receive two of our special 'cowls' if you sign up today. One for you, one for another. Of course, this is a secret club where only a few know the identity of our members. For that reason, we encourage members to wear, at minimum, masks for all club activities."

Sounds like a fancy-dress party!

"On that note, Peter, all our members never use their real names. When you sign up, you will be the primary policy holder, and a nickname will be associated to you from this day forward. You cannot enter our home for club functions out of costume. Failure results in immediate expulsion from the East Vancouver Equestrian Club, and policy terminated. No refunds. Do you have any questions?"

"Hmmm...?" Shaking the pony daydreams from my mind, I said, "Yes, I mean no. All very clear. Where do I sign up to be a pony?"

"Oh, Peter," said Winnie seductively. "I can't wait to ride you."

"This is very exciting news, Peter," said Dale. "I simply need your information and signature on this document." Dale handed me a legal-sized piece of paper. "We will also walk you through a medical questionnaire."

I recalled the warning Schnookums had given me when I signed the "condo agreement" and started reading the contract.

"The following are definitions of some of the terms used, blah blah blah..." I completed the form.

Name: Peter Van Wagner.
Address: Hospice of Good Hope.
Beneficiary: Larry Johnstone.
Beneficiary address: Hospice of Good Hope.
Signed: Peter Van Wagner.

"Excellent!" said Dale clapping his hands. He asked me some questions about my medical history. I was surprised he had some medical equipment stored in the bureau, and he explained, while taking my blood pressure, that after a year, I could make money by bringing in new members.

"How will you be paying your first contribution?"

"Cash." I took out my wallet and gave him a hundred dollars. "I'll have to come back later. I'll need to go to a bank machine on campus for the remainder."

I started the day with $120 in my wallet. I paid two at the store for Heather's paper. Enrique gave me thirty-five cents which is not in my wallet. I paid a deposit of 100 dollars to Dale. *Oh, bloody hell, I can't keep track of all this!*

"Don't forget to give him the complementary zipper hoods," Winnie sang.

Zipper hoods?

"Yes," said Dale. He got up and opened another drawer in the bureau and retrieved two masks. "Sorry, one size fits all. We'll be home all day. For our membership records and admittance, what will be the name you will use."

I recalled my fantasy horse. "Simple. Blondie."

"Oooooh, what a pretty name," said Winnie. "Dale, could we get a Palomino horse costume for Peter?"

Dale grinned. "Splendid idea. Peter would look fetching in one. And the name of your plus one?"

"I don't know, yet. How about Binky?"

"Perfect." Peter completed writing some details down and handed me a carbon-copy receipt. "I'll give you a copy of your signed policy when you return with the 200-dollar balance you owe. The original stays here, safe and sound. We'll expect cash payments every second visit, or you can mail me a void cheque if you prefer.

"Here's a list of members nicknames, roles, and dates of our upcoming meetings." Dale presented me an envelope. "We don't use phones or email to communicate. We only print newsletters, available here on departure from our gatherings. Looking forward to seeing you and Binky at a future session! We have lots of mares and stallions who I'm sure would look forward to meeting a stud like you."

"No doubt! I love stallions. This is going to be a blast," I said.

"Oooooh, Dale," sang Winnie. "Didn't you promise to drive Peter to the university?"

"Right," said Dale. "Peter, the campus is only a few blocks down the road. I realize you just had surgery, but could you walk? It's a bit of a pain to change out of my comfy clothes."

"Oh, meow," said Winnie, waving to me as I left.

What a wonderful start to the day. I boogied over to the campus, doing a little jig. *I'm going to be doing some role-playing games! And we'll be dressing in costumes!* In my happy state, I had completely forgotten that I didn't visit Peter that morning to pick up some dope to sell to the rich brats. I would have to go back to the city to obtain some merchandise from him before returning out here.

The university was a ghost town, anyway. I doubted I'd be able to sell anything. Needing cash, I read a school newspaper, searching for a creative spark. Leafing through it gave me an idea. *Peter says you need a product. Maybe I can sell this paper to tourists?*

I took a large pile and skipped back to the train station for my ride home.

Tuesday morning, I grabbed a milk crate from the kitchen at the hospice and stuffed the school newspapers I brought home the day before in a duffle bag. The hospice's office had some fancy stationary which could be used for invoices. Now with product in hand to sell, my challenge would be to devise a pitch to play on people's emotions to earn the $650 needed to fly over to Toronto, and $200 to cover my club membership. Extra cash would be a bonus, too.

The Vancouver Aquarium drew many tourists who might be interested in buying a souvenir or two. I forwent my usual coffee and rode a bus out to Stanley Park. One of my favourite spots in Vancouver, the views of the city, the greenery, and the animals were amazing. It offered a peaceful place to sit and reflect.

I broke a sweat walking to the aquarium on the unusually hot day. Still too early for crowds, I placed my crate down by a shady spot and sat. I killed some time reading the Bible, but couldn't keep focused on the Word, so I leafed through my photos. I stared at the one of Little Larry and I at the beach.

I'll see you soon, son.

An hour passed, and crowds meandered by. *Time to get rolling.* I stood on my box waving a copy of the school newspaper.

"Want to experience Canada's finest school? Sign up for our campus tour. Check out the university that produced the most Canadian professional football players. Witness life at a school which offers athletic scholarships to all. Wanna see what a roof worth $100,000 looks like? Sign up now! For fifty dollars, take a copy of this souvenir school paper, and I'll take you to and from the campus, and give you a personal tour."

Many people stood around and listened to my pitch for near an hour. The folk seemed genuinely engaged, but I only sold a measly four tickets to a couple who didn't speak much English. They bought them when I mentioned the cast of *Baywatch* was part of an artists-in-residence program. I filled out some invoices and told them to meet me at the train station the next morning.

This is way too much work.

I ditched the remaining newspapers in a garbage bin.

Needing more money for the trip and running out of ideas of how to make more, I hunted Peter down at his usual corner after eating an unpalatable liver-based lunch at the hospice. Business had been slow for him, too, over the last several weeks. Knowing Peter being crafty at earning cash, I figured he might have some suggestions up his sleeve on how I can earn more.

Peter suffered in the heat, sweating while playing his guitar for passers-by that afternoon. He wore a sleeveless undershirt that left little to the imagination. His skunky odour was stronger than usual.

"Hey, brother, how ya doing man," Peter stopped strumming his guitar. He gestured a peace symbol with his hand.

"Hey, Peter," I said returning his hand greeting.

A youth wearing an aqua polo shirt, shorts, and sandals stopped in front of him. Peter read his coded look, and without missing a beat, took out a few baggies from his duffle bag. The youth gave him the correct amount of cash and dashed down the road.

"Been picking up a bit today, man," said Peter. "Hey, can you go to the local Earl of Latteigh and buy me a mango smoothie? They're awesome."

He gave me five dollars, and I walked to the store and returned with the beverage. He snatched it from me and downed the whole lot in one swig. He spilled some drink on his beard, wiped it with his hand, and belched.

"Ha-ha, sorry about that man. Guess I needed that," he said. "Do you want something?" Another young couple bought baggies from him, and I let him finish his business before answering.

"Yeah, sorry to bug you, but I need, like, a $1,000 to fly to Toronto. I need to see my wife…"

"I'm not falling for your long sob story, brother. You remember…I showed you that trick!" After seeing my shock at his severe look, he became pleasant. "I'm messin' with you. You need $1,000? I can loan it to you."

"Really? That'd be great! Will I have to pay you back?"

Peter's eyes narrowed. "What do I look like, man, the Bank of Fuckin' America? Of course you do. I expect you to pay me back $1,200 by Labour Day, or I'll cut your balls off." He stopped to think. "Oh, and there's also a catch, man. I need a favour."

"What could I possibly do for you?"

Peter took me aside and placed a heavy arm on my shoulder.

"I need to confess something. I'm missing the 'free love' I enjoyed living off the land in San Francisco. These yuppie shits don't get that. Can you, maybe, introduce me to a woman? Maybe someone who wants to live in the moment with no strings attached? I don't want someone who is bought. That ain't the same, brother. It's been way too long, man, and from what you tell me, shouldn't be a problem for you to hook me up." Peter lowered his arm, then offered me his hand. "You set me up, and maybe share a few of your secrets for meeting women, I'll lend you the money."

I thought about it for a moment. It's impossible to pass the old Larry charm to someone else, especially someone with social ineptitude, like a Peter. But this is easy money, and I can figure out how to make this happen.

"You got a deal." I shook his hand. "I'll come back tomorrow. You give me the money… I'll give you the keys to scoring a fun woman."

"Deal, man."

Dale greeted me at his home the next day in "normal" clothes.

"I thought you quit on us, Peter. You were supposed to pay us yesterday."

I waved the cash in front of his face.

"Excellent," he said, taking the money I had earned in Stanley Park. "Your timing is good. Our next meeting is this Friday. There'll be a bit of a Canada Day theme. The horses will be dressed in red and white. Hope you can make it. I'm sure you'll love it."

He left me at the door and gave me a copy of the contract, newsletter, and zipper masks.

I returned to town reading the newsletter on the way home. The equestrian club planned a break from meetings during the summer. *Odd, summer is the best time to ride horses.*

Too bad I'll miss the session. I'll be in Toronto with Schnookums!

Peter was still on his corner singing "Kumbaya" at 4 p.m.

"Peter, as promised, I'm going to give you my secret of how I score with women. Do you know I'm a super popular socialite in this city? I'm often invited to various galas and social events." I presented the equestrian club newsletter to him. "Check this out. I just received this invite for one on Friday to the East Vancouver Equestrian Club. It's ritzy. The details are all in here.

"It's a high-brow, fancy dress party where people do a 'role-play' type thing. Most of the members are horse lovers, and they meet monthly for tea and crumpets." *At least, that's what I imagine they'll eat.* "Plenty of women come out to their shindigs. I tell you, Peter, you just have to show up, and you'll score. They are always looking for a stud stallion."

Peter cocked his head. "That's your secret? You make it seem so easy, man."

"It is! And what makes it super simple is that this club runs on total anonymity! All guests must wear costumes." I pulled a zipper mask from my bag. "I reserved you a place, and you'll be attending under the pseudonym of Binky. No one uses or is allowed to use their real name. See how you like it. If you do, their newsletter has a schedule of future events at the club, which you can pick up when you leave."

Peter wiped sweat from his brow. "Binky? That's what my nephew called his pacifier."

"Well, yeah, can't change it now. Those are the rules," I said. "Anyhow, I can't go to the party, cause I'm off to Toronto, but you'll be my guest. C'mon"

— I presented the zipper-mask — "try this on. It'll be your disguise, and it's compulsory uniform for club functions."

Peter took it from my hand and tried to figure out how to put it on. "How the hell do you drink tea with that? That looks like some pretty kinky shit, man."

"Kinky? No, this is more like what Spider-Man wears. I figured that you'd be open to trying this out it, given your desire to meet people."

"You're right. I'm open to anything."

Peter pulled off his glasses and handed them to me. He struggled to pull the mask over his head, and with considerable effort he succeeded. His beard flowed around his jaw from underneath the latex.

"MMMmmph, mmph. MMMPH mmph?" Peter asked.

"Sorry, I can't quite make out what you're saying."

"MMMmmph, mmph. MMMPH mmph," he repeated flailing his arms.

"Let me try something." I reached over and pulled the zipper across his mouth. His tongue stuck out the moment his lips were freed.

"That. Is. Hot. And. Slimy." Peter puffed and panted. "I hope the women at this place are worth it."

"Oh, they will be. I've seen photos of their members. They're hot!" *Well, at least photos of past members.* "When you go, the house will be easy to spot. It'll be the one with the garage door half open. You can slip on your mask before going in. I guarantee you'll have a time like you've never had."

"Huh. Should be a blast, man," said Peter.

Peter struggled a few minutes to remove his mask and took his glasses from me. He dug deep in his bag for a money-purse and counted out ten one-hundred-dollar bills.

"Remember. You owe me $1,200 by Labour Day. Otherwise your sperm will cease to exist."

"No problem, and you have a blast, *Larry style*. See you soon, Binky!"

Chapter Twenty-One
The Big Smoke
June 2007

Air travel had changed since the last time I flew when I moved to Vancouver. One: no one gave me any money at the airport. Two: no handsome flight attendant. Three: they have this category of seats called Premium Economy, which cost double the regular base fare. Being stuck in regular economy class, the cheapest possible seats, sucked all the joy out of flying. No free vodka oranges flowing down my gullet at a torrential pace. No free food. Instead, I had to settle for a half a can of OJ and a five-dollar bag of chips.

Crammed in between two large travel buddies, sleep was near impossible. One played a hand-held video game and pointed his elbow in my gut. He continually jabbed my stomach while he twisted, turned, and jumped. The other yelled to her friend who sat across the aisle.

I tried watching an in-flight movie, something called *Material Girls*. The premise sounded interesting, about two sisters who were heiresses to a family's cosmetic fortune. I became frustrated at not being able to hear any word the fine actors, Hillary and Haylie Duff, uttered. Annoyed, I closed my eyes and attempted to sleep for the duration of the flight. The noise of my fellow passengers, screaming children, bad food, and overall discomfort in my seat made this flight a hellish experience.

The announcement of our pending arrival in Toronto woke me. The instructions were clear—stay seated with seatbelts buckled until the aircraft came to a complete halt. No one obeyed. People stood grabbing their bags and belongings, creating chaos while the airplane rolled to the gate.

The plane slowed to a stop and the captain thanked everyone for flying Air Western. I forgot about the time difference. Now Thursday afternoon, I'd have to try to visit Schnookums tomorrow.

My back hurt leaving my seat at the end of a long flight, and I hobbled out of the aircraft with my bag. Many signs advertising local businesses in "Mississauga" caught my attention in the concourse. *Am I in the right place?*

A long line snaked in front of an Air Western attendant. I had important questions, too, and cut ahead of the queue, interrupting her discussion with an elderly man.

"Excuse me, did I get on the wrong airplane? I booked a ticket from Vancouver to *Toronto*. It looks like I'm in *Mississauga*."

"Excuse me, sir. But can't you see I'm helping this other passenger? Wait in line," she answered.

I looked back at the queue. "They aren't that important. I need to know now!"

"Help this insolent cad out," the old man said with a poker face.

Insolent cad? The nerve!

"Very well," replied the attendant. "Sir, you have arrived at Lester B. Pearson International Airport. It serves *Toronto*. Most people understand that many international hubs like this one are not located in the city centre for reasons like congestion, noise pollution, and available land; therefore, they are built on the outskirts of the city. *Mississauga* happens to be about a half hour drive from downtown *Toronto*. You'll need to take a taxi or a bus to go into town. Now if you'll excuse me, I have to help this gentleman you interrupted and others in line with more pressing problems."

I didn't care for her patronizing tone, and I made a note to write a complaint to the airline later.

Before leaving Vancouver, I had left a message at my best friend Brad's house in Ottawa asking him to pick me up. There'd be little doubt he'd be excited to see me after all these years and make the trek down to Toronto.

He didn't show, and after waiting an hour, in hindsight, I hoped he'd understood "airport in Toronto" meant Mississauga. I waved down a taxi. The cab driver greeted me with a warm smile and bright eyes.

"Welcome to Toronto, sir, I'm Anil," he said with pep in his voice. "Where will I be taking you today?" He grabbed my suitcase and dumped it in the trunk, then opened the back door.

"Hi, I'm Larry Johnstone, but please, call me Larry," I answered, stepping into the back seat.

"Did you come off that Air Western flight, Larry?" he asked, assuming his seat behind the wheel.

"Yes, I did. Horrible experience. Damn it. I forgot to ask the attendant what hotel I'm supposed to go to. Would you know where Air Western typically books their passengers?"

"It so happens I've been instructed to take passengers from your flight to their hotel. I can't imagine how uncomfortable it must've been for you all to stay in a crammed aircraft for so long."

"You wouldn't believe it! My back will never be the same again after being jammed in that seat!"

"How long were you stuck in there?"

"Would you believe over five hours, Anil? I'm never flying economy again."

Anil laughed. "From what I heard, I don't think it would make any difference if you flew economy or not. Okay, Air Western has booked rooms for its passengers at the Executive-Traveler Inn downtown. It might take a while to get there. Rush hour traffic might be a bit intense."

Anil must've owned a crystal ball. We were tied up in bumper-to-bumper traffic for most of the ride to the downtown core. To pass the time, I shared my life story with Anil, as well as my desire to reconnect with my Schnookums. He cared for me, and on realizing my stresses, he attempted to calm me by raising the volume of his radio with soothing music. The sound of the sitars made me want to explore India one day.

I enjoyed the view of the lakeshore and Toronto's landmark tower in the distance as we approached the city centre. My mind drifted in a daydream of my pending visit with Schnookums while staring over the waters of Lake Ontario.

The driver dropped me off at the hotel and refused payment for the ride, saying Air Western covered the costs for my inconveniences! It was a difficult flight.

The Executive-Traveller Inn stood in the heart of the city near the train station. I never stayed in a hotel before, never mind something so swanky like this place. In fact, apart from that one brief trip to the Pentecostal camp when I was a kid, my family never travelled. Mama never had the urge to leave home.

I advanced through the lavish lobby. *Now this is what I'd expect from Air Western!* Soft chamber music piped through the crowded halls where people were congregating, mostly dressed in business suits. I stood in line to check in.

A handsome young man with dark hair and eyes greeted me at the front desk. *What a dapper uniform. Bet I'd look hot in that.*

"Good day sir, welcome to the Executive-Traveller Inn. Do you have a reservation?" He seemed pleasant, with a warm deep voice. His name tag read Leon.

"Hi Leon, I'm Larry Johnstone. I believe I have a reservation with Air Western?"

"Let's see, Mr. Johnstone. Such a horrible ordeal you must've endured on your plane today." He typed at his computer. "We hope at least you'll have a nice night to unwind from that terrible experience."

Everyone seems to know about my brutal flight in "economy."

Leon made eye contact with me. "Hmm, we don't seem to have a Larry Johnstone on file. We have a Johnathan Johnstone though."

I didn't feel like arguing with him about Larry versus Johnathan. Johnathan was my middle name, after all.

"Johnathan is my legal name. I go by Larry."

"Very good, Mr. Johnstone. May I see some identification?"

I presented some government-issued ID which contained my middle name.

"Thank you. Here are two sets of keys for your room."

Two keys? How posh is that? I'd love to bring Schnookums back here.

I dug into my pocket and pulled out twenty dollars from my wallet and presented it on the counter. "Leon, do you think I could ask you to find a suite? Let's say, I have a special family reunion I'm organizing, and it'd be nice to have some champagne, too.

Leon looked to his left and right, and quickly moved his hand across the desk to snatch the money. "I certainly can offer you an upgrade for your special occasion. Especially given the difficulties of your day. Let's see. Hmmm. Looks like our presidential suite is the only other room available. Let me get your keys for it. Not a word to anyone." He winked. "I still have your original room in the system, in case there are issues. Gotta cover my behind."

I nodded, understanding.

Leon passed the keys. "The beds will be turned down at 9 p.m. Enjoy your stay sir."

"Oh, wait," I said pulling out another twenty and placing it on the counter. "My flight home won't be until Saturday. Will the room be free until then?"

Leon surreptitiously took the money and looked at the monitor. "As a matter of fact, yes. I blocked it off." He leaned forward and whispered, "Don't bother with checkout. Just be out of the room by nine on Saturday morning."

Leon was the best. I thanked him and took my bag to the top floor of the hotel. The room stole my breath. The entrance featured a living room with a small office space, and a stairwell leading to a king-sized bed with huge bathroom. The bath had a hot tub jet with tons of shampoo, conditioners, and soaps, free for the taking. There was a knock at the door and a waiter delivered a bucket of champagne on ice.

"Complements of the house, sir."

I gave the man a loonie. He snapped a spin and left the room. *My generous tip must've left him speechless.*

I popped the cork and poured myself a glass. *Where were you on my nightmare flight?* The drink glided down my throat. I poured a second, then a third. Comfortably numb, I turned on the TV. The news blared the latest headline.

"Air Western Flight 573 took a turn for the worse today. The flight, destined for Halifax, had to make an unexpected stop in Toronto early this morning. Coming from Phoenix, the passengers were in the air for over four hours, but the aircraft started losing power forcing an emergency landing. Airport officials say the passengers and crew were all safe. All the power on the aircraft shut down shortly after landing, leaving it stranded a significant distance from the tarmac.

"Air flow and lavatory were not functioning, and it took airport officials a couple of hours to retrieve all the passengers. The problems on the aircraft were deeper than expected…"

Pffft, that's nothing. Bet they didn't have to endure the horrors of flying "economy."

Feeling a bit peckish and in my happy haze, I ventured to seek food in downtown Toronto. A busload of tired people was joining a long lineup at the hotel's front desk. One man, with a partial bald head, round face, and moustache, yelled at a poor clerk.

"What do you mean Johnathan Johnstone has already checked in? I'm Johnathan Johnstone! Do you know what type of day I've had stuck on that plane?"

"I'm sorry, sir. There must be some mistake, and we're completely booked. I'll try to call some hotels for you, but it's Canada Day weekend. We might still have some space at our location in Mississauga…"

How freaky is that? Not too many days where someone with the same name as you stays at the same hotel.

I walked out to grab some dinner.

The city pulsed the Friday before Canada Day weekend. I slept in my glorious room until I called room service and ordered the American Breakfast. The forty-dollar dollar price tag for the meal didn't concern me—Air Western's flipping the bill, and it came with a huge pot of fresh coffee!

I planned to visit the Euro-Can Productions offices in the afternoon and figured on killing some time meandering the streets of this magnificent city.

In the distance, a building with white windowpanes and awning over the entranceway caught my eye. It belonged to our national television broadcaster, and they allowed tourists to walk in and browse their free museum. The place triggered some wonderful pangs of nostalgia—being laced with many photos and props from great shows from my childhood.

I should've been on TV. I would've impressed the hell out of Mr. Do Bee on *Romper Room*. Mama recognized my potential for child stardom, but insisted I practice singing instead of acting. According to her, singers were the most diverse entertainers and could take their craft anywhere—TV, radio, or the stage. It motivated me to practice daily, and it was worth it. Mama'd reward me with a favourite treat—Toasted Frootie-ootie Tarts. I couldn't get enough of their sweetie goodness, and I ensured I earned two or three a day! In hindsight, I think the Toasted Frootie-ootie Tart's could've been the secret to my super sperm.

A pretty university-aged woman accosted me as I exited the museum into the hallway. About a head shorter, she had long, jet-black hair pulled back with a rich blue headband. She wore an earpiece, connected to a radio on her belt, and carried a clipboard. I liked her uniform, a well pressed pair of black pants and white dress shirt with a name tag pinned to it.

"Hi, how are you doing today?" Her bright eyes sparkled with her smile.

"Hi, I'm Larry Johnstone. I'm doing quite well." I read her name tag. "You know, Ronnie, I trained to be a TV star ever since I was a small child. I really should have pursued a career in acting or writing, oh well."

"Oh well, indeed." Ronnie glanced down at her clipboard, and she quickly wrote something. She looked back up and smiled. "Hey…I'm asking people this morning if they'd like to sit in as part of a live studio audience for a TV recording. It's great fun to watch a show before it hits the air. You might even be on TV!"

"Glad to see the network recognizes my potential and talent. I'll grant you permission to have my face shown on TV. What do I need to do?"

"Excellent. Please fill out this brief form."

She handed me the clipboard with a document full of blah, blah, blah. I signed it, and she ushered me to the studio. The cushioned seating reminded me of a small movie theatre.

Pretty much full, I found a place in the middle of the back row in the dimly lit room. I had no idea what I'd be watching. The stage had a backdrop of a beautiful foggy seascape, with a boat in the middle. To my eye, it looked realistic. A petite woman walked around testing microphones and verifying wiring around the stage. She might've been my age, and with straight brown hair, I could've sworn I had seen her before. Then it hit me.

"Sandy!" I screamed from my seat. She looked like the girl I had set Revolting Rick up with when we were teens. *What is she doing here? Poor Rickie pined for her like nothing else!* "Sandy! Over here! It's me!"

The woman stopped her work and turned to scan the audience, now silent. I guess she didn't recognize me in the crowd, even though everyone stopped their chatter, wondering where the voice was coming from. I waved my arms frantically, but she ignored me and resumed her work. *Why didn't she come up for a hug?*

Three young adults walked in front of the stage: one man flanked by two women. They wore bright yellow shirts making them stand out from the rest of the crew. The man announced we were part of television history, participating in the taping of a pilot entitled *Dildo's Head*—a sketch comedy show set in a small Newfoundland town.

I stood and cheered loudly. I loved shows like *Codco* growing up in the '80s.

The man at the front grinned. "We love your enthusiasm. But please sit down." I obeyed. "In the future, we ask you remain silent until you see the applause signs light up." The two women pointed, drawing our attention to the now lit signs. Automatically, people cheered.

The trio walked through a bunch of dos and don'ts during the taping while "pumping us up" for the show. They were entertaining and made us all excited. We were ready, they exited, and the show began.

It opened with a traditional Newfoundland song, followed by a few comedic sketches. The humour and accents always tickled my funny bone. They knew how to have a good laugh. *Newfoundland is another place I must visit one day.*

Time flew. At one point, the cast joined together on stage dressed in sou'westers and chimed an acapella version of "I'se the B'y," — a classic song.

Feeling the urge to make my mark on television, I stood and bellowed along with them in my richest bass. I knew my voice boomed as the people around me leaned away and covered their ears. As I'd hoped, the cast stopped singing and stared up into the crowd, probably wondering who delivered those angelic tones. *That'll propel me on TV!*

"Get that caterwauling creep out of here," one of the cast members bellowed.

I kept on singing. An usher walked over to my seat and tugged my arm. "You're going to have to leave now, sir."

"What?" I said. "Am I being asked to join the cast on stage?"

"Uh, yeah," he said. "Will you follow me?"

The man led me to the exit. Ronnie, the young lady who recruited me, was talking to the small woman who'd been setting up the microphones before the show. She sure looked like Sandy from a distance but wasn't.

Ronnie whispered in the usher's ear, then dismissed him.

"You see, Ronnie," I said, "I'm quite the talent, eh?"

"Yes, Mr. Johnstone," she said, "so much so the producers asked me to get you to sign this form." She handed me her clipboard.

"Another one?"

She nodded, while I looked at it quickly. More legal mumbo jumbo about terms and conditions or something.

"What's it for?"

"Just a consent form to permit us to use some material you provided us in the next half of the show."

Material? I didn't write anything for them.

"You mean, like my singing on TV?" I asked.

"Something like that."

"I knew it! Do you need me backstage to put on a costume?" I signed and handed the clipboard back to Ronnie.

"No, Mr. Johnstone. You already gave us an amazing performance, and we don't need any more footage."

"Great. When will *Dildo's Head* air?"

"We're thinking sometime later this summer. Have a good day Mr. Johnstone."

I left, stoked that I was going to be a TV star!

I meandered around the Entertainment District and walked westbound until I reached my destination.

Ping-ping. The doors inviting me into the office of Euro-Can Productions.

A young receptionist, maybe in her mid-twenties, filed her nails from behind her desk. She paused a moment and looked up. "We're closing soon for the weekend." She returned to work on her cuticles. Behind her, a huge, framed portrait of Sven overlooked the office. Painting aside, there was artistic charm to this place, with brick in the walls and hardwood floors.

Photos of Sven accepting awards for marketing greatness adorned the walls along with some charts promoting impressive sales figures. My eyes gravitated toward some trophies in a glass display case. A placard in the centre boasted the "Most successful advertising campaign—*Bärbar Ugn II, 2002.*"

Sven obviously had done well for himself, branching out into the world of advertising—which was more Heather's domain—and relying on the internet for his work. Might have accounted for why he's not on TV as much.

Funny, there are no photos with Schnookums.

The stylish woman stopped filing her nails and stood.

"May I help you?"

I didn't think what she wore was appropriate for the office. Most women wore tight fitting dresses to go clubbing, not stenography. However, she was stunning.

"Wow Marika," I said, reading the nameplate on her desk, "look at you getting all gussied up! Going on a hot date tonight?"

"Sorry?" Marika said, frowning. "Are you here for a reason?" Her voice had hint of California in it.

"As a matter of fact," I replied, "I'm Larry Johnstone, here to see Schnookums."

"Who?" Marika suppressed a laugh and pushed her long brown hair over her left shoulder.

"Schnookums. Heather Mackenzie. My wife."

"Heather's married?" Marika appeared surprised.

"Well, it's complicated."

"I heard she had divorced some loser."

What's being said in the office gossip circles?

"No, we're still married, though I haven't seen her in a while. I flew in from out of town to surprise her for the weekend…and I have an important delivery." I waved the stationary.

"I see," she said. "Then being her husband, you should know she doesn't work here."

"Of course I do…but she partnered with Sven on promoting that little oven. So you do see her every now and again, right?"

"Yes, we still do, and it so annoys my boss! She pesters Sven—often—always wanting in on his latest business ventures—especially his plans to create reality TV shows. We've already won some awards for our webisodes. They document six people's lives driving across Canada in a compact car." She walked over to a shelf along the far wall that contained photos of the recent accomplishment.

"What's this?" I said pointing at a photo of Sven standing in the middle of a punk band.

"That's pretty new. Sven's got a bug for music. He's sort of managing and promoting those guys. They're a hot act out of Sweden called *Rännrottorna*. Maybe you've heard of them?"

"No, should I? And what the hell is a *Rännrottorna*?"

"I don't know. I think I heard Sven mention it means gutter rats or something. Anyway, not a household name here."

Marika returned to the desk, picked up a large pile of files and began placing them one at a time in a cabinet. When she finished, she noticed I was still standing around, staring into space. "If you have no further business, I'll have to ask you to leave."

I parked myself in a chair in the lobby.

"If Heather is not here, I'll see Sven."

"You actually *know* Sven?"

"Of course. Like I said. I'm Heather's husband."

Her expression changed from officious to friendly.

"Silly me. Sure you know him! And if you *are* Heather's husband, I bet he'd *love* to see you." She chuckled, then shook her head. "Okay, sorry. It's been a long week. Well…since it's a Friday before a long weekend" — she returned to sit behind her computer — "Sven'd kill me for telling you, but he's scheduled to be back later this afternoon. He's at the ball game with his two boys."

"His two boys?" I felt insulted. "One of them is mine!"

"Huh?" She stopped her typing and looked up.

"Yes, Little Larry."

"You mean Lars?"

"Okay, Larry, Lars…Potayto, Potahto. I call him Little Larry."

"Oh…this is too good," Marika said under her breath. "No one calls him that, you know? And he's not that little."

"Of course I know!" I cried. "His full name is Rupert Lars Mackenzie. I prefer to call him after me, his father, Larry!" The mention of the lad's last name placed a shiver down my spine. "Heather likes to call him Rupie. I never liked either of those names."

"Oh, you do seem to know them quite well." Marika clicked on the keyboard. "Uh, oh. Heather's dropping by, too." She quickly drummed her nails on the desk's blotter. "Might be some fireworks," she said, smiling. "Any case, you're in luck. Heather will be here."

Marika flicked a rocker switch to turn off the computer and began walking down the hallway towards a kitchen. "It's been a boring day, anyway. You might as well stay. Can I get you a cup of a coffee?"

The receptionist returned with a couple of mugs filled with *kaffe*. Marika joined me for a chat. She was gossipy, and we got along like a house on fire. I shared my story of moving to Vancouver to marry Heather, the birth of our son, and her leaving me to pursue her career with Sven. Marika focused on her nails.

"I find it hard to believe you're Lars' Dad. He looks so much like Sven."

"No, he doesn't!" I pointed at myself. "Look closely at my face! You'll see the resemblances."

She absorbed my features. "Nope, don't see it." She sipped some coffee. "I'm surprised you came here to track down Heather."

"Oh, why?" *It's only natural I'd come.*

"Well, for one, she hasn't worked directly for the Euro-Can Productions in years."

"But her infomercials say you guys do all the filming."

"Yes, it's true. But Sven put a stop to that when he and Heather started having their 'issues.' He's been ranting of late about how Heather's company had been embezzling him for years—that's the latest scoop. It might explain why he started Euro-Can on his own, to do everything Heather's company did."

"Issues?" I sipped some coffee. I cringed at its bitter taste. "Let me tell you about issues." I went on to describe the "ancient Viking rites" that bound Heather and Sven for "all eternity."

Marika giggled. "That's a riot! Haven't heard that before! Can't wait to tell *that* to the gang here. You know, the older staff at the office have some amazing stories about them… Well, I guess *eternal* to Sven got quashed when he had a baby with another woman."

"What?" I said, trying not to spit out this bile they called coffee. Oddly, I felt a bit sympathetic to Schnookums.

Marika giggled and leaned forward like she was going to share some tasty gossip. "Well, Heather isn't exactly a saint, either…Rumour has it, Sven's second son, Elias, is the product of a fling with an infomercial dancer in Halifax," she whispered. "He didn't tell Heather about the kid until Elias' mother showed up and raised a fuss at some business function they attended. The woman wanted Sven to take full custody of the child."

Sven must've loved that!

Marika's eyes lit as she shared her juicy story. "Heather blew a gasket, refusing to raise the other woman's baby and Lars while travelling. I think Sven's fling with a younger woman must've hit her, too. I might be guessing, but Heather started dabbling in cosmetic surgery around that time. Anyway, there was a running gag in the office about Heather wanting a 'househusband,' whatever that means, to solve their childcare issues. Sven, though, hired a nanny to be his kid's guardian. I heard she was a beautiful young Russian woman, new to the country. That added fuel to the fire between he and Heather. Heather despised the nanny, and the new *au pair* moved into Sven's home here in Toronto.

"Anyway, childcare was a point of contention for them. If things didn't sour then, it really did when Heather got pregnant. Personally, I think it was a bit of revenge sex, but she insisted the child was Sven's. I think Sven was initially excited, but Heather didn't want the Russian to have anything to do with the upbringing of her kid. Created another sore spot for them."

"It makes sense," I said. "I was the best for Little Larry, and Sven never seemed interested in babies, anyway."

Marika tapped my forearm. "Well, soon after Heather's baby's birth, it became obvious it wasn't Sven's child." Marika lifted her left hand to her face and studied her nails. "In fact, Sven accused Heather of breaking her 'eternal vows' to him…Hey, is this the Viking rite you were telling me about?"

I nodded. I threw in additional details like how Sven sat in some poison ivy and had an itch in his nether regions for years after. *Maybe it didn't happen, but I found it amusing.*

"Can't wait to tell the gang that," Marika laughed. "You know, most people would want to flush those vows right down the toilet if their partner screws around on them. To me, it seemed obvious Sven wanted to move on—but Heather didn't. She's really quite tenacious." She stood. "Want a snack?"

"Yes, please." I answered. "I'm amazed you know all this."

She walked back to the kitchen and returned with a banana in one hand and an apple in the other. "Are you kidding? This place is a constant soap opera. Heather and Sven argue all the time when they are in the same room. Never a dull moment. It baffles me why Heather still wants to be part of Sven's enterprises."

"I love soap operas." I grabbed the banana and peeled it. "*General Hospital* is my favourite." I slowly took a nibble off the tip of my treat.

"You know they separated. Sven refused to raise Heather's child. Maybe you're right," Marika took a bite out of the apple. "Maybe he's not too crazy about babies, but for sure he wasn't caring for one that isn't his.

"I feel sorry for Elias. Poor child." Marika walked to the wall of photos and took another bite out of her apple. "Being raised by a nanny and part-time brother can't be fun. It's a pity. Heather and Sven used to make a beautiful couple. Anyway, Heather hasn't had any business dealings here for a long time."

Ping-ping. The front door interrupted our lovely chat.

Chapter Twenty-Two
Family Reunion
June 2007

"EEE HEE HEE HEE," a familiar voice filled the lobby. "Marika, dear, were you able to send out the monthly invoices this afternoon?"

Marika brushed her hair around her right ear and twirled it with her hand while standing. "Yes, all sent off." She giggled, smitten by the dashing Sven.

My back had been to the door, and I turned to face the man, standing beneath the huge portrait of himself.

Sven squinted at me, put on a pair of glasses, and reviewed some letters at the desk. A little overdressed for baseball in a dark business suit, Sven looked striking, still having the natural charisma from his paid commercials. Two boys, one a later teen and the other barely hitting puberty stared at me. They both had Sven's ice blue eyes.

Sven stopped shuffling through the mail and looked at me again. "Wait… Larry? Is that you? What the fuuh!" He stopped himself from swearing in front of his boys. "What a surprise! I'm so happy to see you! What brings you to town?"

To my shock. Sven rushed over and wrapped his arms around me in a warm hug. He caught me off guard with his "European greeting." I stood rigid.

The older boy spoke. "Hey, aren't you Uncle Larry? The guy that took me fishing?" The lad had Hollywood celebrity good looks, with long blond hair, and athletic build. "I still have the Pocket Fisher Pro you gave me."

"Little Larry? I mean, Lars?" I said. "Wow, you've grown so big!" I opened my arms and beckoned him for a hug. He didn't budge.

"Papa…" he said.

"Yes," I answered.

"Not you," he said and faced Sven. "I told Erica I'd meet her in fifteen minutes for dinner. You know how Mama gets about my dating. Mind if I split before she gets here?"

Sven stood stiff as a board.

"What? I told your mother you'd be spending time with her! She won't be pleased when she finds out," Sven glared at his son. After a moment, he looked over to me. He then smiled and messed up Lars' hair. "No problem, I understand. I don't really want to see her either—"

"Nor me!" yelled Elias defiantly.

"—but I really wish you told me sooner. We wouldn't have had to come back here."

Sven walked over, placed his hand on my shoulder, and grinned. "But now that Larry's back, maybe he can explain all this to her. Hey, maybe he can take that woman—his wife—away from us for good!"

I lowered my shoulder away from Sven's heavy hand. *I'd be happy to "take Heather away from you for good."*

"Who's Erica? Your big date?" I asked the lad. "Hey, why don't we meet up at my hotel later on. It'll be nice to catch up."

"Uh, okay," said Lars. Before I could give Lars the hotel address, he said, "Dad, can I have a hundred bucks?"

"Of course, son," Sven said, producing his wallet. "Have fun." He gave him the money and winked.

Ping-ping opened and closed the doors while Lars exited.

Sven turned abruptly and narrowed his eyes.

"Okay. You've been out of our lives for how many years, and you just show up out of the blue? What the hell brings you here? Did *she* put you up to this? I do hope you are here for her, and, well, make that witch happy!"

"Yeah! Witch!" echoed Elias.

"She'll be here in five minutes," said Marika, tapping her watch.

"Yes, yes. We'll be gone before she arrives," said Sven. "Well, Larry?"

Not quite sure what to answer. I waved the stationary. "I brought this for her."

Sven stared in disbelief.

"What? You flew across Canada to bring her *that*? She can buy that at any drugstore."

I turned over the package and inspected both sides. "Well…it's special stationary, from this naturalist store."

"Ohhhhh, *that* place." Sven lightened up. "Hee-hee, you might find she's a little disappointed with what you brought. You do realize the paper is a cover. They usually ship something else to her, too."

I scratched my head, confused. "What? She only asks for this."

"Nah! She buys some contraband beauty crap exclusive to that store. They mix this cream with some illegal drug. It's supposed to smooth wrinkles or something. Honestly, I don't think it works for her. It's why that store only takes cash—can't have that prohibited stuff on the books. Anyway, she can't purchase it anywhere else. She probably told them some 'mule' would come to their shop asking for paper, and they'd take care of the rest—shipping a parcel full of 'stationary.'"

Which explains why it costs fifty-two bucks.

He rushed into a back office and returned a minute later with a few files. "I'm so glad Lars has his date." He dropped off the folders into a briefcase on Marika's desk. "Means, Elias, we don't have to see Heather! Isn't that great?" He snapped it shut. "Saves me having to explain Erica to her, too! Larry can do that now, eh? Hey Elias, want to go out for some *lax*?"

"With fries?"

"You bet," said Sven. "Marika, will you lock up, dear?"

"Yes. You'd better hurry." Marika checked her watch. "Heather'll be here any second."

"Bloody woman's timing's like clockwork," said Sven shaking his head. He walked over and gave Marika a kiss on the lips. "Have a nice weekend, dear." He waved to me and left with Elias.

Ping-ping chimed the doors a few minutes later.

A tall woman entered the office wearing a red dress. She held a boy's hand who might've been about twelve. I liked the kid's look. He had dark hair and eyes like mine and wore preppy clothes, like I did at his age.

She glared at Marika and me from the entrance. Her blonde hair flowed in waves down her back.

"Where's Rupie-Bear?" she bellowed. Her voice sounded huskier from what I remembered. She had work done on her face, too. Her lips had ballooned, her eyes were narrow slits, and she must've had cheekbone implants, which made her look sterner. I wouldn't have recognized her in the street, but I admired her attempts to keep youthful in her later forties.

Marika picked up my coffee cup and banana peel, and she rushed to the kitchen.

"Where is he?" Heather demanded.

"Little L-l-l-arry?" I stuttered. "He left. He had a hot date with some chick named Erica."

The anger cloud over my Schnookums lifted when she recognized me. "Honey-Bear? Is that you?" she said sweetly.

"I flew all the way over from Vancouver, just for you Schnookums. I missed you so much!"

Heather advanced, opened her arms for a hug, and stopped. "Wait," she said, tone changing to anger, pulling out her phone. "Rupie's on a date?" She sighed. "I haven't seen him in weeks. Whenever it's my turn to take him for the weekend, he has some excuse not to be with me—like going out on dates or being away on hockey tournaments! I wonder who the trollop is this week." She texted a message. "He'll be home later."

The cloud lifted from her, and she hugged and kissed me.

"I got something for you!" I said, extending her the stationary.

"What? You brought the stationary I asked for all the way from Vancouver?" Her eyes narrowed shut. "Wait. Where's the rest of it? Didn't they give you a small jar?"

"No. They only charged me two bucks for the paper, and that's it."

Heather scoffed. "You'll have to go back to the store and have them send my usual over when you return. There's a reason why you shell out over fifty dollars every time you go. Shipping is not that expensive." She took a deep breath and softened her tone. "Anyway, you must be hungry. Come."

I grabbed her hand and followed her out of the office.

Ping-ping. The doors said their good-bye.

Heather drove us in her sporty SUV—a minor step up from a clichéd mini-van. The high-end sound system cranked a track called "Make them Suffer," a song by Cannibal Corpse, at least, that's what the title read on the car's dashboard. The singer was incomprehensible. Heather insisted I remain quiet and absorb the "deep lyrics" while she slammed her hand frantically to the song's 400 bpm tempo. Thankfully, it only took two minutes until the singer vomited out the final note, and the alarming noise was replaced by "It's My Life." Heather permitted talking during the No Doubt cover.

We grabbed the child a burger, drink, and fries through a drive-through.

"I love this food! Thanks Mama!" the boy cried out.

"No eating in the car!" yelled back Heather. "You'll eat that when you arrive at your little friend's house."

The young lad introduced himself. Oscar was far from a grouch. In fact, I've never met anyone so full of themselves in my life. He wouldn't stop talking!

"I'm the best at school. I get straight A's in everything! And I never study!" he bragged.

Hmmph. School's so overrated. I never needed an "A" to succeed in my life.

"Do you know how many bricks were needed for the Egyptian pyramids?" He waited for an answer which never came. "Two point three million. Ask me anything. I know everything."

Bloody brat.

"Okay know-it-all…how many books did Paul write in the Bible?"

"Pfft…easy. Thirteen of the twenty-seven in the New Testament. That's the stuff written about the early days of Christianity. Everyone knows *that*. Know how many books there are in the *entire* Bible?"

I should know…

"Sixty-six! I know, and we don't even go to church. Pity. Church looks like fun. Oh, and I love games. When I turn twelve next spring, I'm going to ask for a gold-plated dice set so I can get into role-playing games. I need a new challenge. Board games are so boring."

Heather didn't say much while heading north on Spadina. She turned off the stereo, giving our eardrums a break. When she drove down Eglinton, she announced we were taking Oscar to the "Forest Hill" district. I found the modest homes there appealing.

"I'm going to my friend Pierce's cottage this weekend. I'll be showing off my superior windsurfing and will dominate him in horseshoes! He has no chance. Oh, and there'll be Canada Day fireworks on Sunday, too!"

Heather drove into the driveway of a mansion.

Nice pad.

Oscar jumped out of the car. "Hey, if you are here on Monday, you should come to my school. I'm going to be retelling my version of 'The Highwayman' at the schools' poetry recital—by heart! Bet you can't do that!"

Bet you can't sing Gregorian chant.

Heather unloaded a large suitcase from the back, took Oscar by the hand, and led him up the long pathway to the house while I remained behind in the car. He goose-stepped quoting "a highwayman came riding—riding" in cadence with his march.

A woman opened the front door, while Heather was speaking sternly to Oscar, waving a finger at him. I couldn't hear a word, but it looked like the poor lad received a barrage of "thou shalt nots" in a span of two minutes.

Heather jumped back into the car, started it, and turned the stereo back on. It played a depressing song called "Love Will Tear Us Apart."

"Ready to eat?" asked Heather.

"Yeah, I'm starving. I only had a banana since breakfast."

"So am I. We're near one of my favourite restaurants." Heather grabbed her cell phone. "Hi. Yes, for two. You have VIP? Excellent. Mackenzie. Yes, the usual. Ten minutes please." She put the phone down and drove away from the house.

"Who's that child?" I asked.

Heather glared from the corner of her eye.

"Yours?" I said. I couldn't believe she had another kid.

She returned her focus on the road.

"Why didn't you tell me you had a child?"

"I did," she said.

I closed my lips tight and cocked my head. *She did?* "No, you didn't."

"Yes, I did!"

"No."

"Well, I might've mentioned it once, when he was born."

"That was what? Twelve years ago?"

"It might've slipped my mind. I've been busy."

How could I possibly have forgotten THAT? No way!

I wanted to blow a gasket but told myself to remain calm. I had travelled a long distance for my wife, and I figured we'd have a lot to catch up on. The last thing I wanted was to let my anger ruin any chance of reconciliation—and Heather, so far, had been consistently nice.

I figured, if we were going to be together, I'd better put the interests of her children first. I asked if she had life insurance for her kids. I don't know why—maybe because "legacy" had been on my mind of late, and I had just bought a policy from the Joneses.

"Yes, I do. From a small company called the East Vancouver Equestrian Club. Lovely couple who run the place. If you're interested, I can refer you to the owners. My company ran a nice advertising campaign for them…until Sven snatched them up."

"I like their horses," I said.

"You've heard about *that*? How?" Heather gave me a knowing look.

"Well, yes. I have a policy with them."

"Wait a sec," said Heather "*You* have a policy with them? Who do you know in the club?"

"No one. They thought I was someone else when they picked me up at the hospital. I didn't let on."

Heather seemed to understand. "Their membership is quite complex." She snickered. "In fact, the restaurant we're going to has quite a history with that equestrian club. I'm sure you're going to love your dinner—it's more a dining experience than a meal in of itself…No more talk about the club. It's secret. Even among members."

She cranked, "Godspeed to your Death Bed," another song I couldn't sing to, while we drove northward to a wooded area, void of homes. After a while, we passed a large property surrounded by a white wall with trees peeping over the top, providing additional privacy. I spotted the sign by the side of the street simply reading "The Chamber," at the entrance. We turned onto a long roadway that cut through an open field before finally pulling into a horseshoe driveway, leading towards the restaurant. A large courtyard appeared to our left, with a long rectangular pool in the middle with a statue of a large bronze stallion at one end spewing water from its open mouth. Riding on its back was a nude couple, posed in similar fashion to Rodin's *The Kiss*. The Greek god,

Poseidon, stood at the other end of the pool with arms open, holding a trident. Below him, statues of horses were splashing around in the water.

I found the main building a bit gauche. Its modern rectangular design with two-storeys looked like two boxes stacked on top of each other. The bottom floor had grey stonework, the top, white. Two windows spanned the front on both floors, but the sides had none, though they had a couple of small trees in planters for decoration. Heather stopped the car under an overhang that covered the main entranceway. A valet opened the car door for her.

"Nice to see you again, Ms. Mackenzie."

"Yes," Heather replied, dismissively.

Many people lined up outside. I felt a little underdressed, as most of the gentlemen wore ties and blazers. The doorman recognized Heather and ushered us in.

The Maître D stood in front of a large dining room. He snapped his fingers at someone, then pointed to me. A man rushed off and brought me a blazer—a perfect fit on first try.

We were led to the back of the dining hall to "Pomp and Circumstance" playing over a sound system above the loud chatter and clanging of cutlery. Awesome choice of song to announce my arrival with my Schnookums. We approached a door at the rear of the room.

My heart stopped because a "VIP" sign hung on the door. I remembered how costly my last VIP experience at the strip clubs turned out, so I whispered to Heather, "I can't afford this."

"Don't worry Honey-Bear," she said. "My treat. I've missed you!" She rubbed my back affectionately.

"Then why didn't you come back?"

Heather placed her index finger to her lips. "Shhh. You'll ruin the mood with your whiney talk."

The Maître D opened the door, and we went through. Another gentleman greeted us.

"Ah, Ms. Mackenzie, so nice to see you again," he said. His voice had a classy hint of Eastern European in it. "We have your usual booked. And who is your escort this time? I don't believe we've seen him before. He looks a bit older than your usual."

"Hi, I'm Larry Johnstone, and I'm only a few years younger than my Schnookums." I reached my hand forward to shake the man's hand.

"Please to meet you sir. Follow me."

"Pomp and Circumstance" gave way to *Eine Kleine Nachtmusik*. Another song I loved. It's so Mozart—all chirpy and uplifting.

The man led us down a hallway, and I offered my arm to Heather. We passed several doors on either side with signs: The Junk Yard, Prehistoric, Hells Angels, Scientific Experiments, and Fuzzy Bear Central. We stopped outside a door with "Medieval Dungeon" posted on it.

"Here we are, Ms. Mackenzie," the man said. "Will three hours and dinner suffice?"

"Yes."

He opened the door to the "Medieval Dungeon," and we entered the room, dimly lit by torches. The grey stone and walls added to the somber atmosphere. *How on earth did they make this place so cold and damp?*

The middle of the room featured a dining table designed like a medieval rack with a waxed man lying on it. His hands and feet were attached to automated wheels that stretched and relaxed him every few seconds. A recorded scream complemented the stretch, which cast an ironic counter to the happy Mozart piece that'd been playing. Other images of medieval torture devices adorned the walls, and sounds of screaming, whips, and creaking doors filled the audioscape. Four iron grated doors to prison cells faced us on the far wall.

"Perfect! So cozy!" said Heather clapping her hands.

Were those real hands holding the bars in one of the cells?

"Dinner will be arriving momentarily." Our escort turned and left.

The rack had a couple of dinner plates and chairs already set. Heather removed her overcoat and instructed me to sit next to her. Her red dress clung to her surgically altered figure.

"They have an amazing steak here," she said.

"I wish I can 'ave steak," a cockney accent said. *Where did the voice come from?*

Crack. "Aaaaaah!"

"Can't wait." I said, looking over towards the cells. I noticed silhouettes of prisoners in three of them.

The wheels turned on the table. Squeak, squeak. "Aaaaaah!"

"Give it to him!" another voice yelled. *Is he talking to me, or the wax figure on the table?*

"I missed you, Honey-Bunny," I said, "Little Larry's so big now."

Crack! "Aaaaaah!"

"Harder," bellowed another prisoner.

"Yeah! He looks like he's enjoying himself!" yelled another.

I couldn't believe my eyes. Amidst the cheerful classical music and screaming in agony, a tear welled up in Heather's eye. I held her gaze for a moment and lowered my head.

She's wearing the pendant I had bought her many years ago!

Heather noticed me staring at it. She opened it and showed me the photo I had inserted of Little Larry, still in place. "That Rupie-Bear is growing up too fast." She took a deep breath while she snapped it shut. "He'll soon be away from his Mama."

Squeak, squeak. "Aaaaaah!" The music changed to the familiar waltz, "The Blue Danube."

"Bloody hell! This song is torturous!" The original prisoner screamed.

Crack! "Aaaaaah."

"Little Larry must be quite the ladies' man!" I said. "He's got great looks, just like his old man." I couldn't be any prouder he's going on a date tonight.

"I never see him anymore. He prefers spending time with Sven or his hockey friends."

I've never seen Heather almost cry before—or express any emotion, apart from anger, for that matter.

"Every time I see Rupie dating like crazy, I'm reminded of his horrible father," she said.

"What? I'm not horrible." I replied.

Crack! "Aaaaaah!"

Heather looked at me with vulnerable eyes and placed her hand on my cheek. "I know. You came all this way just to see me. And bringing my paper was noble, even if you didn't have a clue what you were doing." She kissed my cheek.

Crack! "Aaaaaah!"

"Let him have it," yelled a prisoner.

I never saw my Schnookums in such a tizzy. She told me how Little Larry trained hard and became an accomplished hockey player. He'd wake up at the crack of dawn most days to hit the rink and practiced a few hours after school. It paid off. Professional scouts were now attending his league matches. He had many female admirers which particularly concerned Heather—they were mostly girls his age or a bit older. Then she confirmed Marika's story that Sven had an affair and child with another woman.

Crack! "Aaaaaah!"

A door squeaked open.

"Feeding time," croaked a prisoner.

All three put steel mugs between the bars of their cells.

A man dressed in an executioner's hood wielding an axe pushed a trolly into the room with our meals covered. He served us first, and from the bottom tier of his cart, he picked up a tray with six slices of bread and a jug of water. He served them to the prisoners.

"Bloody 'ell, why do they get steak and wine? And we 'ave to watch them eat?" yelled a prisoner.

Odd we were served rare steak on china with nice silverware in a dungeon.

I took a few bites of my meal. "This is the best steak I've ever had," I exclaimed.

"Aaaaaaah!" the recording from the wax man on the rack agreed.

"This is the best stale bread I had! No mould!" someone bellowed sarcastically.

Heather nodded.

We ate without speaking, and when Schnookums took her last bite, she asked, "Have you masturbated?"

"Crack!"

"All the time," a prisoner responded.

Heather glared at the cells. The silhouettes retreated from their doors. The power of the Honey-Bunny death stare!

I dropped the last bite of a dinner roll on the floor. The question took me back to our first date when she asked me that in front of Nauseating Rick and his friends. I explained how I now masturbate for science, and how my seminal emissions made world records after the clinic trials.

Heather didn't acknowledge and stood when I finished talking. She offered me her hand.

"Come."

"What about dessert?"

She didn't flinch.

The prisoners began catcalling and rolling their mugs against the bars of their jail cells. I took her hand, and she led me to the narrowest grated door along the far wall. It creaked as she opened it, and I jumped out of my skin when the door slammed shut behind us.

"I love this place," she said. "Makes me in the 'mood.' You?"

Do I have to answer honestly? I kept quiet.

I looked around the room. The only lighting came from the entrance, revealing a cold stone floor and a hard bench spanning the length of the wall. Apart from that, there was only enough space for the two of us to stand.

"You come here often?" I asked somewhat rhetorically.

"Lie down," Heather said, "and close your eyes."

I obeyed, and all the screaming, whips cracking, and classical music dissipated in the background as Heather became the sole focus of my world.

The executioner scraped the bars of our cell with his axe handle later. He threw a key in our jail. "Time's up." He walked out.

Heather stood from our hard love bench.

"Thanks, I needed that," she said. She straightened her skirt and fluffed her hair.

"What time is it?" I said rubbing my eyes. I had no idea how long I slept.

"Its 10:30 p.m. We need to leave. This room is popular, and I'm sure someone has booked a midnight feast."

"Will you take me back to my hotel?" I buckled my belt and put on my shirt.

"Yes. I need to hurry. My little Rupie-Bear will be home soon."

We marched out of the torture chamber to Bizet's Carmen's "Overture" amongst the screaming inmates. It always reminded of the movie, *Bad News Bears,* for some reason—not the screaming, the music.

It didn't take too long to return the hotel. Heather turned to me from the driver's seat and looked lovingly in my eyes. I could tell because her eyelids were slightly closed, like a content cat.

"You were useful, tonight," she said. She grasped the pendant and lifted it towards me. "I remember the special occasion you gave me this. Do you?"

"Of course I do," I said. "Then you left."

Heather stared at her necklace and opened the locket. She showed it to me again. The same pictures of us and Little Larry were still inside. It moved me for a second time that night.

"There isn't a day I don't look at these photos," she said. "I've missed you, even though you cheated on me." She clasped the locket shut.

"I never cheated on you."

"Don't lie. I *always* know when you're lying. Nevertheless, I forgive your infidelity."

"What are you saying? I'm a little confused."

"Don't be so simple. Isn't it obvious? Seeing you in the office took me back to when I first met you. I want you back in my life again, to be with our son!"

Are my ears deceiving me? The prophecy will be fulfilled after all? I have fathered many children with my super sperm, and Heather's TV career could be construed as the voice of a generation! My patience and faithfulness will pay off!

"I would love to be back in your life," I said.

I leaned forward and kissed my Schnookums. She parted her lips and moaned gently. *I can't believe how my life will turn out. Schnookums has the wealthy lifestyle I dreamed of. Flashy cars. Beautiful home. Gourmet food. I'll be out of the gutter for good and back with Little Larry!*

"Oh, Larry," she purred. "I've had such challenges raising the kids. Having you as househusband again will be wonderful. I need you." She drew me in for a tight embrace. "I need to convince Sven he needs me too. He might forgive me my transgressions if I have more time to focus on him, and you care for the children."

I went limp in her arms, my chin embedded in her shoulder. She gently pushed me back and looked me in the eye.

"Think about it. We could be a family again—like when we were first married. Wouldn't that be nice?"

Househusband? My life with Heather during our first several months of marriage flashed in front of my eyes: alone at home with my son; Sven waltzing in and out of my house, seducing my wife; Heather performing some sort of everlasting love ritual with him; and her accusing me of having an affair and ditching me to the streets to take my home at the hospice. I balled my hands in fists behind her back.

"No! No! No!" I yelled. "It's me or him. Not both!"

"Honey-Bear," Heather said, voice slightly more frustrated, "be reasonable. You're the only househusband for me. That's your function in my life. Besides, I must get on board with Sven's new business ventures. Infomercials are dying, and his new ideas are going to be stratospherically successful!"

I didn't want to waste my breath on this discussion. I opened the door, left the car, and slammed it shut. Heather put pedal to the metal, and her SUV screeched away from the hotel.

The doorman rushed out. "Are you okay? Quite the hot babe that you left behind."

"Piss off."

I walked to my room where the maids had left the lights on and had turned my bed down.

I stripped off my shirt and pants and crashed on the couch in front of the TV in my underwear. More news coverage flashed on the screen about the airplane that was stranded on the tarmac yesterday for hours. *Poor sods.* A bottle of champagne rested in its ice bucket. I reached for it and swigged a huge gulp down, then passed out.

Crappy trip. Crappy wife. Crappy cab.

The taxi driver claimed Air Western didn't pay for my return ride to the airport. He took all but five dollars of my remaining cash.

Crappy flight.

I swore I had booked my tickets for Saturday morning. Ended up being Friday instead. I could've knocked the block off the ticket agent. He refused to change my flight because I'd bought the cheapest seats with a no refund, no exchange rule. Blowing up at him, the guy learnt I couldn't be jerked around, and he sent for his manager to discuss the problem.

I figured I'd try Peter's con on him. He listened to my huge sob story about my best friend being unexpectedly on his death bed in a Toronto hospital yesterday—why I missed my flight. I admitted my mistake and pleaded his forgiveness. He did and offered me the last seat available on the next flight—fifteen hours later. Never was so bored waiting.

Given my crisis, I expected to be at the front of the plane, being served a late-night snack of Cornish hen and champagne with the other first classers. Instead, they threw me in the last row, in a far corner seat, where crowds of impatient people were lining up, walking in and out of the bathroom all flight long. The stink of lavatory chemicals made me feel like puking all night.

I couldn't even afford a bag of chips.

The seat didn't recline, either. I worried that my spine would be permanently fused by the time we landed. I had to beg for a few bucks in order to catch the first train from the airport to downtown.

I made my way to bed at the hospice at 6 a.m.

The crappiest few days of my life had ended, but the worst was yet to come.

Chapter Twenty-Three
The Narcissist
July 2007

Couldn't sleep on my return home, reliving and fuming over my experience of the past couple of days—running the memories through my mind over and over. Why on earth did Heather still cling to her unfathomable dream with Sven? Unbelievable!

I needed a new beginning. It's Canada Day, and I'm in one of the coolest cities in the world. I decided I'd check out what was going on. Maybe the national holiday will offer a gateway to my renewal.

I shook the cobwebs from my brain, grabbed a book, and strolled down to the empty recreation room. At 8:00 a.m. on a Sunday morning, the place was deserted. Crashing in the comfiest chair, cuddling with Hector, I started reading *Narcissus and Echo*, a story I enjoyed as a youth.

Echo was a nymph who was punished by the goddess Hera to only be able to repeat the last words spoken to her. She fell in love with Narcissus, a handsome young man who rejected her advances, hurting her so badly she ran away, retreating to a cave in the forest.

Soon thereafter, Narcissus saw a reflection of himself in a pool of water. Day after day, he stared at himself in the water, falling in love with his own likeness. Narcissus began to waste away from grief at not being able to share his love with himself—and felt himself dying. "Good-bye, my love," he said to his reflection with his last breath.

"Good-bye, my love." Echo cried to him from her cave.

After he died, the wood nymphs searched for his body. All they found was a beautiful white flower beside the hidden pool. The flower was called a Narcissus.

And for poor Echo? Depressed after Narcissus' death, she didn't sleep or eat, and faded away, becoming thin. All that was left was Echo's lonely voice, forever heard in the mountains, repeating all the last words anyone said…

Why the hell did I like that story?

My mind wandered to thoughts of Canada Day, so I grabbed the newspaper off the floor to search for events. Typical headlines: BC Lions lost, something about *Dancing with the Stars*, an ambulance called to a suburban swingers party Friday, and, finally, Canada Day in the city. I read through the page—lots happening on Granville Island, including a parade! No doubt, the place would be filled with families and kids. *Wonder how many are mine?* Seemed like a perfect distraction from my problems.

I resumed my reading and fell asleep.

"Where have you been?" snapped a sharp voice, jolting me from my slumber. Hector was running in circles around a young man, barking in attempt to gain his attention.

Danny, whom I rescued from the pits of Hades when I met him at the Highland games on my fortieth birthday two years ago, reached down to pick up my dog. He patted him and glared at me.

"Didn't you get my note?" asked Danny.

"I have no idea what you're talking about. I've been out of town."

"You? Bullshit," said Danny.

Danny placed Hector on the couch and stormed out of the room. I hadn't seen Danny often. He had responded amazingly to the hospice's program. In fact, he had mentioned to Reginald that he had worked his way to becoming a manager at a hardware store—Reginald couldn't have been more pleased, though I had my doubts it was true. Danny spent the bulk of his time with Peter, aiding him on his runs to the States. The two were close and had become inseparable.

Danny returned with a piece of paper. I read the chicken scratch, demanding I call a number and go straight to the hospital.

"Was there a problem with my sperm donation last week?" I asked.

"It's not always about you, Larry," Danny exploded. I'd never seen him so stressed. "It's Peter!"

"Peter? I never knew he donated sperm!"

"No! He was taken to intensive care late Friday night. He's on a ventilator!"

The little I knew about hospitals was from my visits to the fertility clinic and the soaps I had watched. Ventilators were serious business, and my experiences with Peter "spreading the love" flashed through my brain. I sat, speechless, and stunned. *He's a huge part of my life in Vancouver. What could've happened?*

"You really should pay him a visit," he said, scribbling Peter's room number at the hospital and handing me the note. "I have some business for Peter to deal with." He turned and walked away.

"He's in good hands," I called after him. "I'll go after my work!" I had no idea why I said something so inappropriate. It might've been a combination of stress and fatigue.

I reclined back in the chair. Since I missed church that morning, I did something I hadn't done in a long while—I prayed, specifically for Peter—but fell back asleep after the first few sentences.

I had vivid dreams of my Schnookums and Little Larry—and a lifelike nightmare about Peter being in intensive care at the hospital. The lunch staff clanging about in the kitchen woke me. It must've been near noon, and the hospice was unusually inactive. *Maybe everyone is enjoying Canada Day.*

I changed into some fresh clothes and ventured out with Hector to Granville Island. What a wonderful afternoon! Didn't think about Heather once, though Little Larry popped into my brain as I wondered how he was celebrating the national holiday. I also hoped that the poor child, Oscar, had fun with his friends, too. Cute kid. A bit of a pompous brat, but I liked his spunk and obvious intelligence.

Like at lunchtime, the hospice was empty near dinner. Meant less mouths for me to feed. *Maybe I can sneak out early for more festivities and the fireworks.*

A few men lined up for supper when Reginald burst into the cafeteria. He looked exhausted. It might've been the first day he hadn't shaved in years. In fact, it could've been a couple of days growth.

"Reginald," I said, "what are you doing here on your day off?" He didn't often come on Sunday evenings.

"Oh, I'm so glad you're back, Larry," he said. His pale face and bloodshot eyes hinted he might've not slept for a while. "I wasn't sure when you'd return from your trip, but I wanted to tell you your friend Peter was taken to hospital Friday night."

It wasn't a dream?

"You really should visit," said Reginald sternly. "He had a severe heart attack. The doctor explained he's lucky to be alive. They had to operate because he had a total blockage of the artery. Poor Peter was lucky. He might've been within minutes of death."

Peter did smoke and wasn't the healthiest person.

"That's horrible," I said. "Peter's tough. He'll be okay. I'll stop by later."

The flood of stresses cycled through my mind again, and it occurred to me—I didn't have the money to pay him back. Money should've been the last thing on my mind, but like everything else of late, it weighed me down.

Knowing that hospital food sucked big time, I prepared some meatballs in the old *Bärbar Ugn*. Peter loved them, and I hoped they'd lift his spirits. All the plates in the kitchen were left in the dishwasher, so I threw the meatballs in a freezer bag. *I'm sure Peter won't mind.*

Hector, either wanting some meatballs or thinking he was going on a walk, balanced on his hind legs. His eyes stared longingly at the bag.

"You are cute, but I must go see Peter and deliver his gift." I waved the bag in front of Hector, and he whimpered. Unable to resist my dog's begging, I threw him a meatball from the bag and left him to demolish it.

I stopped off for a coffee before grabbing the 7:00 p.m. bus. I cursed the Sunday schedule at the best of times, but given the national holiday, each bus was jam packed. I squeezed my way on and rode off to visit Peter at the hospital.

Walking down the empty hospital hallways creeped me out. They would have the makings of a terrifying horror movie setting. Reaching Peter's room, I opened the door. He lay asleep in bed with a tube coming from a mask over his mouth.

Beep-beep-pffft-beep-beep-pffft, the heart monitor and ventilator sounded, answering and calling each other in steady rhythm.

"It's dark in here," I said flipping on a light switch. The lights blinded me for a second, and when I regained my sight, I noticed Peter didn't move. I'd have thought for sure he'd wake for me, but the man didn't budge. He laid there, flat, on his back.

Beep-beep-beep-pffft.

"Peeeeeeter," I yelled waving the meatball bag in the air. "Oh Peeeeeeter! I brought your favourite treat."

Beep-beep-beep-beep-pffft.

I inched closer, opening the bag.

Beep-pffft-pffft-beep.

"Peeeeeter, look what I have." *Hmmm....is meat supposed to smell like manure?* I took one out to inspect.

Can he smell it with a ventilator on?

"Peeeeeter, do I have a treat for you!" I reached out to place the meatball over his mask and...

Pfft-pfft-beep-beep-beep-beep-beep. The monitors accelerated in cadence.

Peter's eyes opened and turned towards me with alacrity making me jump out of my skin. With a great surge his arms raised in attempt to hug me. He clumsily knocked my meatball bag out of my hand onto the floor.

He mumbled something. *Did he say "Larry. Legacy. Inheritance?"*

I couldn't quite make it out. I sat on the bed and leaned closer for a better listen.

"Can you repeat what you said?"

Pfft-pfft-beep-pfft-beep-pfft-beep-beep-beep, the two sounds now competed at an electrifying tempo. If Peter repeated anything, I wouldn't have heard it.

Peter's eyes closed slowly, and his arms rested limp.

"Beeeeeeeeeeeeeeeeeeeeeeeeep."

What's happening?

A rapid-fire high-pitched alarm filled the room. Startled, I instinctively covered my ears. Within seconds, a team of two male orderlies and a woman in a white lab coat rushed in with a crash cart. I stepped back.

One man stepped on the meatball bag, skidded, and fell over top of Peter.

"Quick, get up," the woman hissed. She had a sense of urgency while the team prepared a defibrillator.

I sank into the corner of the room, not knowing what to do.

"Clear," said the doctor. Peter's body jumped a foot in the air.

"Is there a chair I can sit in?" I asked.

"Get out, now!" the other orderly yelled.

"Clear," I heard the doctor yell as she applied more voltage through Peter.

Not sure what to do, I left Peter in the care of professionals.

I returned a little later to find out what happened. The hospital staff did not permit me to visit him but informed me Peter had stabilized. Feeling relieved, yet sad and exhausted, I skipped the fireworks and went straight back to the hospice, and to bed.

The next morning, I awoke feeling heavy. After a useless shower, I went downstairs to the recreation room before heading out for my morning coffee. Danny, with Hector cuddled beside him, and Reginald were huddled in a corner, heads bowed, whispering to one another. An acoustic guitar was leaning against the arm of the couch.

"Is that Peter's?" I asked.

"Larry, please," said Reginald, "we're having a private conversation."

"Oh, okay." I stared at the nylon-stringed instrument, picked it up, and did a single strum.

"Larry!" Reginald's tone had a hint of anger in it.

"It's okay, Reginald," said Danny. "You play?"

"I do!"

"Good! Take it," said Danny. "Peter wanted you to have it."

"He did? Out of the blue like that?" Peter giving me his guitar was odd. I still owed him a lot of money for my trip to Toronto. I hoped he wouldn't add the instrument to my "tab."

I put my foot on the corner of the couch and placed the guitar on top of my thigh. "Look, I'm a rockstar." I windmilled my arm like a guitarist I saw on TV once and hit all the open strings. I needed practice, but I only wanted to bring some levity to what seemed like a heavy chat.

"Larry, please," said Reginald, "leave us alone. Danny lost his uncle last night."

"I didn't know you had an uncle!" I said, putting the guitar down.

"Well, technically, more like a godfather," replied Danny. "He was close friends with my Ma's older brother. Poor guy died in Vietnam. Here's a picture of him." Danny dug a wallet out of his pocket and showed me a photo. "His name was Artie Greenburg."

Name sounded familiar but couldn't put my finger on it.

"I'm sorry to hear that," I said. Figuring that Danny needed some cheering up, I put on my Scottish accent. "Ach, but ye'er a strong lad. Chin up." I punched him gently on his shoulder, trying my best to solicit a smile. Like my guitaring, it failed.

"Larry, please," said Reginald, "Danny's been through a lot. I'm going to insist you leave us alone. When Danny's Uncle Peter died last night—"

Something clicked. The ventilators. How still Peter was in his bed. The sounds of erratic breathing…the doctors rushing in to treat him. *Peter, you were fine when I left you. No!*

Stunned, my relationship with Peter flashed in front of my eyes—how he oriented me to West Coast living by introducing me to marijuana, how he got me my first job spreading the love, how he wanted to take me under his wing so one day I could own his company, and how I helped him score with a woman by inviting him to the Joneses' party—*could that have been one of his last memories?* A tear welled in my eye.

"I can't believe it!" I said. "He was stable when I visited last night. He was surrounded in the care of some awesome hospital staff!"

"Well, he died shortly after 11 p.m.," said Reginald. "He did prepare a will, entrusted to his godson. We were just discussing it before you interrupted. Danny inherited all his assets."

Danny wiped his eyes with his sleeves.

"He often mentioned to me your love for music," said Danny after a long silence. "He wanted you to have his guitar, Larry. He thought it could help your singing."

"Danny," I said, "you know my singing doesn't need any help, but I'd love to master the guitar. I will cherish this." I picked up the instrument and hugged it.

"Oh, almost forgot, he also wanted you to have this, too," said Danny. He stood and reached into his back pocket and removed a necklace—Peter's peace symbol he always wore.

Does this mean Peter wants me to continue his mission, spreading the love?

Moved, I put on the necklace and plucked a couple of strings on the guitar. The sorrowful tones encouraged a couple more tears to roll down the side of my face. I recalled my one and only trip to Seattle with Peter. He talked a lot about legacy. He implied he was planning to leave me his business! *Why didn't I do a return trip with him or learn all the other aspects of it?* My thoughts shifted to Schnookums. I wasted years waiting for her. In a single moment, my life of laziness and lies pummeled me, filling me with regret. More tears flowed.

"You got the business, Danny?" I asked, wiping my wet cheek. "He often said he wanted to pass it to me to continue his vision of spreading the love."

"Larry, how can you think of that right now?" said Danny. "The only person besides my mother I ever cared about died last night. Besides, you never showed any interest in the business beyond sales."

"Of course," I replied, patting his shoulder, "you're right. We'll talk more about this another time."

I couldn't shake a dominant selfish thought, though: *He gets the business? I get the guitar and this peace symbol necklace?*

"Now…leave us alone!" I didn't like how Reginald raised his voice.

I obeyed, returning to my room, and even though I've never played a the guitar in my life, I vowed to produce glorious music in Peter's memory. I strummed the strings once and broke down, crying with the force of Niagara Falls.

It didn't take me long to master the two-note intro to "Jaws" on Peter's guitar. The music helped me quell my sadness. Proud of my progress, I worked on a more challenging piece, "Mary Had a Little Lamb." The gentlemen at the hospice were courteous, often leaving me alone to practice in the recreation room.

"Larry, office, now!" Reginald bellowed the Thursday after Canada Day. He must've had crabs in his shorts all week, being so bad tempered since Peter's death. A sure-fire sign of grieving.

Given Reginald's current condition, I thought it best to leave him alone and continue practicing.

A few minutes later, the sound of footsteps interrupted my play.

"Stop it! I can't take it anymore." Reginald snatched the guitar out of my hand and returned to the office.

You've gone too far, mister. I followed behind.

I closed the office door. Reginald sat in a chair behind his desk. In his hand, he held a yellow envelope, tapping its edge on the table.

"Sit," he barked.

Despite being mad at him, I obeyed.

"Do you know what this is?" He waved the envelope in front of my face.

"The only thing I know is that you rudely interrupted my guitar practice." I scanned the office and found my guitar on the far desk.

"Stop looking at that noise maker. I mean this." He shoved the envelope in my hand.

The return address looked familiar—The East Vancouver Equestrian Club.

"Hey, I joined them!"

"What? You're not supposed to talk about the club to anyone, remember?" Reginald stopped himself. "Ahem. Why on Earth would they be sending you something?" His eyes narrowed.

Something clicked. The photos hanging in the living room at that nice couple's home—the Joneses. Reginald might've been in one of them.

"How do *you* know about it?" I said sarcastically. I ripped open the envelope and unfolded the letter. A piece of paper fell to the floor. I bent over to retrieve it, and Reginald snatched the letter from my hand and began to read it.

"Peter Van Wagner was a member? And he left you what?" Reginald's face flushed.

I picked up the paper from the floor. "A certified cheque for three hundred thousand dollars? To me?"

Reginald stood, walked around to the front of the desk, and sat on its corner. He crossed his legs and folded his hands over his knee. "I know, for fact, that Peter, or should I say, Binky, was at the last club meeting last Friday. Hard to miss him with his size and beard poking through his mask. I mean, who else would yell, 'Wanna doobie, man,' selling dope all night long at a horse-riding event in my friends' basement? Most people say 'giddy up' or 'woah.'"

I remained speechless, trying to picture Peter at a club function.

"He was unmasked for the ambulance. Of course, I recognized him. I later asked the Joneses in confidence how long 'Binky'—of course we never address each other by our real names—had been a member, which they confirmed, was a recent addition…Seems his poor heart couldn't handle the stress from the demands of being a stable hand in our horseback riding club—"

He did smoke like a chimney.

"—Not a pleasant job having to cleaning up after us and setting down new straw. When Peter died, and thinking he'd been a member of the club, I submitted a death certificate on behalf of his beneficiary, Danny."

Reginald shook his head, stood, and pointed at me. "But Peter never joined the club, did he? I mean, after all, you admitted to joining two seconds ago. And this" — he waved the letter — "is his life insurance policy naming *you* his beneficiary? No, something isn't adding up, my old friend. He gave everything else to his godson, Danny."

"Really? You actually believe that Danny is his godson?" I remembered Danny trying to con me at the Highland games. "Besides, why wouldn't Peter leave me money? I worked for him for years!"

"Actually, I do believe Danny. He ran away from home and his horrid father, and he landed here a few years back. Peter took Danny under his wing—even helped his mother move out of that man's house, I think." Reginald looked down at the letter, then back to me. "I mean, Larry, why would Peter leave you anything? If you were so close, why didn't you attend the funeral? You just stayed here playing 'Jaws' all day!"

A rare surge of guilt hit me. *I missed my friend's funeral? Did anyone tell me about it?* Someone probably did, and I forgot.

Reginald flipped to the stapled second page of the letter. "Good, the policy is included." He glanced over it, grunted, and returned to his chair behind his desk and produced a pen and paper.

"Larry, even though Peter attended a club function, I don't believe this is his policy. You see, even on the off chance you both decided to join, Peter was a stable hand the night he died. This policy is at the tier-two level, meaning he should've been one of the horses last Friday."

"Maybe he wanted a change of role for the night." I then remembered something the Joneses said. "Or maybe he was new and waiting for his costume to arrive."

"Not likely. The benefits are much nicer for a horse. However, you're right. My proof is a bit circumstantial. Let's try something else, hmm?" He pushed the pen and paper in front of me. "Sign Peter's name, then yours."

"No way, man."

"Okay, we'll have a drive to Burnaby and find out if the Joneses call you by your real name, Larry, or Peter."

"Fine!" I placed the check on the desk and signed Peter's and my name.

Reginald grabbed the paper with my signature and compared it with the one in the policy. "Just what I thought," he said. "You're quite the con man."

I was taken aback by the accusation from a "Christian" man participating in these equestrian events.

"I don't care! I never dreamed Peter would die." I felt a tear on my cheek. "I just wanted to be a horsey in the club!" I stood and reached for the cheque.

"Sit back down. We're not done yet." He snatched the cheque away.

For the second time, I obeyed.

Reginald remained silent for a few seconds. He reflected, then smiled.

"You know, Larry, you've been living here for some time."

"Yes, yes, hard to believe how long it's been. What does that have to do with the money?"

"Everything. You see, our poor building is falling apart. The plumbing is old and decrepit. The kitchen is a fallout from the 1940s. The furniture and décor are severely outdated. I'm going to suggest you donate your cheque to the revitalization of this hospice. Need to make something good come from this, let's say, error in your judgement." He placed the cheque in front of me, along with a pen. "Endorse it to us."

I lived this life of squalor because of Heather.

"No way! The money is mine."

"Larry, you don't have any leverage. Besides, you've never given a dime to this place."

"You're wrong! I do have leverage. If you take my money, I'm going to tell everyone, including our church, that you belong to this secret equestrian club."

That got him. Reginald stared intently at me. "Can you honestly tell me you've never done something you want no one to know about?"

I couldn't think of anything.

After a moment, Reginald scoffed. "I haven't met anyone who doesn't have a single vice. This is mine.

"Shortly after my parents died, I was concerned for my legacy. I love my work here...sort of married to it, and I never had children of my own. My sister's husband had abandoned her with near nothing and two beautiful toddlers. I helped her financially for many years, and I wanted to be sure they'd be protected in the event I pass.

"A friend approached me in church one day—not the one we attend, Larry, it was Anglican. We had much in common including a love for the monarchy, and admired Princess Anne for her amazing horseback riding. I stopped attending that church, wanting a more expressive form of worship; however, I met my friend often for coffee who told me of a great deal for life insurance.

"One day, I received an anonymous letter saying I had been nominated to join an equestrian club with instructions and passcodes of how to meet the owner. It was so *Secret Agent*, and I loved horses. Though I thought it odd their group was in a suburb, and not a farm, I joined their bash and had a blast...and signed up for the most expensive life insurance policy they had.

"I don't think anyone in our church besides you, Larry, knows of my, let's say, interests. I want to keep it that way."

I didn't know how to respond to this man I'd known all my Vancouver life. "I want my money," I said, though my desire for it weakened.

"I can't let you, Larry. If you do, the police will take this insurance fraud seriously. I think you'd prefer to stay in a newly renovated hospice than a cold dank jail cell for the next twenty years."

He's bluffing.

"If you turn me in, I'll have you arrested as an accomplice who didn't return the fraud money." *Hah! Got him again!*

Reginald grimaced. "I'm going to let you think about what you have done for a while." He rose from his desk with my insurance letter and cheque in hand and flashed them in front of my face. "Forgive me, but you understand I will not let you have hold of this until this is resolved." He walked out of the office and closed the door.

Beyond frustrated with Reginald taking my money, I turned on the computer. *I'm going to post my dilemma on Larrynet for the world to see! I am sure most will agree that I should keep the cash!* Before I could update my status, the computer beeped, indicating I received an incoming *Larrynet* message from Jacqueline Rousseau.

Hey Larry, it's me! Jacquie Brown...well used to be Brown...not anymore. I guess you've been too busy to drop me a line since we reconnected online. That's okay. You probably didn't recognize me from my cat profile picture, or my name! Loved all your dog pics! He's very cute!

It's been a long, long, time since we last spoke, and I'm not sure if you're still thinking about me. To be honest, you really hurt me when you brought Peter over and he boiled pot around my baby! I've struggled to come to terms with it. However, the more I think of all those fun memories we shared, like talking about trashy romance novels and that scrumptious dinner you made, the more they reminded me what you mean to me. You're a special person, Larry, who has so much love to share.

I don't think I've ever laughed so much in my life as I did with you. I certainly didn't laugh as much since leaving for the States, following Vaughn's dreams— and he never was able to latch on to a pro football team like he hoped. He kept getting cut. Larry, he became impossible to live with, not wanting anything to do with our first child...and he kept blaming me for not producing "his" children! I'll leave it at that.

My family moved out East to Montreal, and they introduced me to an incredible guy. I married him and we have two wonderful boys. Things are great for us, Larry, and I hope they are for you, too.

I hope one day we can put that bad stuff from our past behind us and reconnect. I've been thinking about you a lot. You have a kind heart, able to see the good in people, even your wife (who I still think is horrible for what she did to you), and your friend Peter. I shouldn't have judged him so harshly. I do have a fiery temper, and I should have realized that if you saw something in him, I should have trusted that. I'm sorry. I know you wouldn't hang out with con artists or criminals. I was just angry about him calling me your girlfriend to my ex-husband! Now I get how it was an innocent misunderstanding.

The internet is making for a smaller world, isn't it? Maybe you can find time to write?

Speak to you soon,

Love,

Jacquie.

It had been a very long time since I heard from Jacquie, and I could hear her sweet voice through her words. I reread her note.

"I know you wouldn't hang out with con artists or criminals…"

I am a con artist, and I lied to Peter, telling him stories about my Jacquie and I being an item. Yet, Jacquie still loves me. I placed my head down on the desk and broke down crying—just as Reginald entered the office.

"Larry, what's the matter?"

His compassion surprised me, since we had just come out of a heated argument. I simply pointed to the monitor, and he read Jacquie's message over my shoulder.

"She's an incredible woman, Larry, and you know what? I too, have seen too much good in you—"

It hit me like a ton of bricks. *No one in my life has ever said I am good. I've always been so egocentric!*

"—and I trust that you would not blab my secret to the world. Do you remember who took you in when you had no home?" He put his hand on my shoulder. "Who gave you purpose to your life, helping others in need?"

"You?"

"Not me. Think again." He pointed to the ceiling.

God?

"Someone has been looking after you—and me. We are both human, and weak. Think deep my friend. What are your skeletons in your closet? You know mine."

It didn't take me long. "I attended strip clubs," I confessed. "I lie—chronically, mostly because of…" I choked on the next word—insecurity. Thoughts of my self-centredness and hypocrisies flowed through my brain. I spilled them all to Reginald. His hand on my shoulder gave a gentle squeeze.

A wave of grief hit me. Biblical verses I had read on attitudes towards money, forgiveness, self-sacrifice, and serving others flooded my mind. *I did resolve to put others before myself.* My inner voice haunted me—I could do more with my life. I took it as a spiritual prompting. The emotions weren't over. The grief of my friend's passing hit me again. I broke down in tears.

"You're right Reginald. I'm sorry. I am horrible. I haven't represented our faith as I should."

Reginald crouched down, gave me a hug, and me held tight. "No, Larry. We are *both* horrible. I, too, need to do better."

I wiped my eyes with my sleeve. "Okay, I'll donate the money to the hospice."

"And since we have shared each other's deepest secrets" — he released me from his grasp — "may I suggest we hold ourselves into account for them. If either of us feel the urge of sin creeping up, we share with each other immediately."

I nodded.

"Okay. May I ask a favour, though?"

"Sure," he said.

"May I keep ten thousand dollars, just to have a little something in the bank to show for all the years I've been here?"

Reginald thought about it. "Agreed, on one condition—you take twenty-thousand and promise to do good work." He grinned and stood.

"Deal." We shook hands.

For once in my life, I had some cash. I bought myself my first cell phone, but without a data plan. It permitted me to keep connected to all my loyal subjects on *Larrynet* when I didn't have access to a computer and Wi-Fi was available.

Reginald announced to the board of directors that a generous and anonymous benefactor donated $280,000 to the hospice for the explicit purpose of renovating the entire building. They agreed to the project, and contractors were hired to take on the task.

A few days after the cheque was cashed, a team began to work on the recreation room. Within a fortnight, two large screen TVs were mounted on the walls, and new flooring and furniture replaced the old. Even Hector had a special "couch" of his own, where he could keep all his favourite toys. The room felt cozy and modern.

When the work was completed, Reginald hung a brass sign in the middle of its main wall.

It read simply, "The Peter Van Wagner Lounge."

Chapter Twenty-Four

The Social Media Phenomena

July - August 2007

I struggled to snap the ingrained habits of being "me" for the last forty years. Even on the first day after "the talk," I bragged to a young man about how easy it was to score with California girls—like I did. I directed him to a website to find some. Of course, I didn't tell Reginald of my transgressions, even though I had promised I would.

Larrynet didn't help. My flock grew, and my old self wanted to post messages of my "great accomplishments" to inspire them. If Reginald had seen my online account, he would've banned me from using the office computer.

I woke up one morning in late July feeling ill and bad tempered. The narcissus I purchased shortly after Peter's death greeted me from its vase on my bureau. Peter's peace symbol necklace lay by its side. They were daily reminders of my late friend.

I selected a narcissus for a reason. Apart from being a cheery plant, it reminded me of the Narcissus and Echo story I was reading the day of Peter's death. Its presence represented my departure from the "old" Larry, which Reginald encouraged me to move away from during our "talk." The poor flower was wilting.

Forcing myself out of bed, I crawled to the office and logged into *Larrynet*. Notifications from my loyal followers always lifted my spirits. *Odd, there aren't any today.* Equally annoying, I had reached out to Rick again trying to reconnect. *Jerk hasn't accepted my friend request!*

Pissed, I updated my status, "Reign as Hospice of Good Hope's ping-pong champ continues! Unbeaten in over fifteen years! Bring it on losers at our next tournament Friday and enjoy our new table!"

Ha! My old snark made me feel good despite my groggy headedness. Having fulfilled my philanthropic duty for the day, promoting the hospice, I dressed and meandered out under the drizzly sky to grab my morning coffee.

I'd been grieving Peter's loss of late, and my headache that morning compounded my bad mood. My daily Bible study on hope offered a small respite from my ill temper, but not much. A man joined me uninvited at my table.

"Are you Larry Johnstone?" he said cheerfully.

Most days, my energy would have spiked if a stranger recognized me. Today, I sneered at the man.

"Yes…you are?"

The man pulled up a chair opposite me. "I'm Mark St. James, a reporter for CHLN, Canada's national news network. Would you mind answering some questions for a story I'm working on?"

A reporter?

"Fire!" His enthusiasm and the fact he was from TV got my adrenaline running and lifted me out of my dark mood.

He peppered me with questions about my life and Little Larry, though weird he referred to my son by Heather's preferred name, Rupert. Despite finding that odd, I happily shared my lifelong mission, and how I've yet to see it come to fruition. I was so into telling him about myself, I didn't get a chance to ask why he's asking and when would the story air on TV.

The discussion had contributed to a better start to the day than I expected—large output at the clinic; met my new friend, Mark, at the coffee shop; ate a fantastic egg sandwich on a sesame bagel—on him; and now off to help prepare and serve lunch at the hospice. The only thing missing was my daily joint—a habit I had stopped since Peter's death—and missed.

I strolled to Peter's old corner under the dark skies, wondering if someone else was peddling weed. Some tattooed hoods were aggressively selling hard drugs, not pot. They looked more interested in pushing the sale than a loving connection. I missed Peter's laidback friendly groove at his "corner shop." I decided to forgo the joint.

A sudden downpour soaked me, and it slowed to a drizzle by the time I arrived back at the hospice. My head uncharacteristically was beading with sweat, and my cheeks were burning. *Do I have a fever?*

A panel van labelled CHLN was parked outside the building. It was the first time a news crew had come to the neighbourhood since an unfortunate stabbing a few years ago. A woman with long black hair had her back to me in the distance. She stood near the entrance holding an umbrella, talking to a cameraman filming her. He lowered the camera as I entered the shelter.

Needing to brush a sesame seed caught in-between my teeth, I went to the bathroom in the kitchen, removed and washed my dentures—a constant reminder of Vaughn knocking me out. I placed them on the counter, grabbed a hand towel, and dried my hair with it.

"Larry, do you have a second to help finish chopping some lettuce?" someone bellowed.

"No problem, coming out." I dropped the towel and joined the cook.

Demonstrating my mastery of swinging a "samurai sword," my knife diced vegetables faster than anyone on staff. I placed the chopped lettuce in a deep tray and dropped it in the cold bar in the cafeteria to be served for lunch. I returned to the kitchen to grab the hot plates.

The line of hungry men advanced to receive their bowls of chicken gumbo surprise—mostly surprise. From behind them, the dark-haired woman approached.

My word, she's gorgeous!

Tensing, my tongue circulated the interior of my mouth. *My teeth! Where are they?*

Dropping the ladle in the soup cauldron, I bolted through the door leading to the kitchen.

The reporter yelled after me, "Mr. Johnstone, a word please." She trotted behind me with camera guy close behind.

I ran to the bathroom, splashed cold water on my face, did my best to groom my hair, and quickly slipped in my false teeth. *Phew.*

The reporter and cameraman were standing right behind me! *Time to turn on the old Larry charm!*

"Mr. Johnstone," said the woman.

"Please, call me Larry." I smiled.

"Larry, I'm Kendra Kwok from CHLN. We'd like to ask you about your son."

Something weird was happening. A reporter this morning was asking about my son—now her? And I'm being broadcasted on TV?

Her questions about my wife, Heather, annoyed me, especially after recent events. I went on an angry tirade, exposing to the world all the horrible things she and Sven did to me while living in the Kits. It irritated me that Kendra, like Mark had earlier, referred to my son as "Rupert" all the time.

When I finished, Kendra threw me for a loop.

"I can see this is all very upsetting for you, Mr. Johnstone. We saw a picture of you with the Red Angel just recently. You both looked happy. Would you care to comment?"

I had zero understanding of what she meant. *What is a Red Angel? Is it some ridiculous nickname the media gave my wife because red is Heather's favourite colour?* Anyway, for the life of me I couldn't remember the last photo we took together looking "happy." Heather always looked depressed in most shots with me, and I didn't recall posting any online.

I lost control and yelled at the camera, calling Heather a "Red Demon." I might've done a few rude gestures, too. Reginald, hearing the noise I was making, emerged from the recreation room and crossed his arms, shook his head, and left. His disapproving look and immediate departure made me regret putting down Heather.

I reflected on a few nice moments with my wife. I snatched the microphone from the journalist. "Aw, listen, my Schnookums. I didn't mean that. And I forgive you. I'll come back to you, if that's what you want. I do want to be a family again with Little Larry, or Rupie, or whatever you choose to call our child. Just say the word, and Daddy's coming home."

Kendra grabbed back the microphone and pivoted to face the camera. "For those of you just tuning in, Canada's sweetheart known as the Red Angel married Larry Johnstone, gave birth to his child, cheated on him, then left him to rot in a homeless shelter. Rest assured we'll keep you apprised of any developments as we get them. This is Kendra Kwok. Back to our main newsroom in Toronto."

She left me scratching my head. I couldn't figure out for the life of me why they called Schnookums the Red Angel.

Reginald approached me in the recreation room before lunch. "How could you? We just talked about sin and holding each other into account. Not only did you slip up...but on live TV?"

I cocked my head. "What do you mean?"

"You were spinning up all those stories to Kendra about your wife, her lover, Sven, your women on social media, and all those other unmentionable things you said."

"No, no, no." I waved my finger at Reginald. "They were all true."

Reginald scoffed. "Surely that's rubbish."

"Larry, you're a celebrity!" a young man interrupted, pointing at the TV.

CHLN displayed a red banner on the bottom reading: "Breaking News—Father of Red Angel's son found."

Red Angel? Like from my interview?

"Hey, they're showing a photo of the hospice!" I said.

Reginald stepped in behind me.

A broadcaster announced, "Pop singing sensation, Red Angel—"

My Schnookums is a pop singer? No! Really? She sings? I'll need to listen to the radio more often.

"—kept secret the identity of her son's father. News broke this morning on social media that she's with a man in Vancouver who claims to be the father of her son."

A photo displayed on the screen of me and a tall, stunning, red-haired woman. We were standing arm and arm on the beach.

That's not Schnookums!

Is this redhead the Red Angel? Surely I wouldn't forget someone so beautiful. *Did I go on a bender again? Freak, those blackouts are quite unsettling!*

"Larry, do you know *her*?" asked Reginald, voice lilting in excitement.

I think so... She's a celebrity? Just can't place the name to the face.

Reginald jolted my memory. "That's Cheryl Smith! The Red Angel! Why didn't you tell us about this? We're going to have a chat." He rubbed his hands together. "I had so many dreams for this shelter. With you and the Red Angel heading up our fundraising…"

The men in the recreation room cackled watching the news story. They were having a great time learning of my fathering a child with this vixen.

Why didn't she call me about it? When did we consummate? Did the news just say the Red Angel's child was five? What was I doing five years ago? There was that one time I blacked out at a strip club when I indulged in that new "blue baller" cocktail—and woke up at the hospice with no memory. Did I meet her there? Did we have a one-night stand? I probed deep in my memory and concluded my strip club days predated this kid.

Wait...Cheryl Smith? I flashed back to my youth. *Is she the little girl my one-time friend Rick babysat Friday nights? The one I sang songs with so many years ago? She's famous?*

I watched the news stories flash across the screen.

Why can't I remember posting this on social media? How is this all over various networks on the web? I only have a Larrynet account!

A picture of the Red Angel's kid on my shoulders displayed. *His name is Rupert, too? I already have a child named Rupert! Why the hell would I have two sons with the same horrid name? When was this photo taken?*

I took another glance before the station cut back to the news anchors. *The child does have many of my features…*

Flashing images of the Red Angel circulated non-stop on the TV. I wish I could've remembered her. *She's famous! Even more so than Heather.*

Why can't I recall making that beautiful baby? It must've happened. The news wouldn't lie...would it?

I couldn't answer the question. What I did know was this sudden fame and attention was going straight to my head. Like a drug, I needed more.

Later, *Larrynet* raged with notifications about the Red Angel, including these:

"Hold up, Larry...the Red Angel?" (From Jacquie.)

"What's going on?" (From Dana.)

After reviewing more comments, I spent the rest of the evening researching this celebrity. Embarrassed I didn't recall my encounter with such a star, I invented a beautiful romance story to share with the world.

The Red Angel's history was easy to find. Born Cheryl Smith in Ottawa in May 1978, the Red Angel rose to fame when offered a chance to perform at the *Make Grunge, Not Babies* festival in Ottawa, in August 1996. An unknown local band named Scottish Rot, led by Talentless Rick (aka Dick Wank), invited her to join them for their encore set. She stole the hearts of the crowds, along with a few music executives present.

Cheryl captivated the audiences with her original song, "Father," co-written by her long-time friend, Bastard Rick. "Father" became the first single on her debut album, and a smash hit.

Wait a sec. She wrote music with Reptilian Rick and performed in his band, Scottish Rot? This proves this is the Cheryl that Slovenly Rick babysat when she was knee high.

The Red Angel went on to produce five albums. Before touring the fifth, Cheryl inexplicably pulled away from the limelight. Rumour had it she needed a break from the industry and bore a child.

There were many stories surfacing on the web that day. Some mentioned she'd been in Ottawa with new boyfriend, "Rick Duncan," but others claimed she'd been in Vancouver with the father of her child, "Larry Johnstone." All stories cited social media as sources. *Hmm. Why on earth would such a beauty want to go out with an amphibian, like Rotter Rick?*

I found an online article, displaying the two pictures I saw on TV earlier. The one of me and Red Angel on the beach looked familiar, but I couldn't place where or when we took it. Another had me and our "son" on my shoulders.

The Rupert in the photo wore the same shorts with suspenders my Little Larry did on our beach day. They were identical except for their faces. *Cheryl's Rupert looks like a mini-me! The story must be true! He must be my child!*

I logged into *Larrynet* and browsed through my photo library and found the photo of Dana and me arm in arm on the beach. They were almost identical to the photos with me and the Red Angel, except the women's and the boys' faces were different! Comparing the two closely led me to one conclusion:

I must've taken many dates to the same beach.

I bookmarked the page containing the images.

I'll get back to that later.

Reporters swarmed me the next morning outside the hospice. They bombed me with questions about the Red Angel while strolling to Jumpin' Java for my morning coffee. I was still confused how this story came about.

"Larry, how long have you been seeing the mother of your child?"

"Why did you abandon your son?"

"Did you know the child even existed?"

"Why did the Red Angel choose *you* for a father?"

"Are you relieved the truth is finally out there?"

Truth? I wish I knew it.

Jumpin' Java had a longer queue than usual. People in line recognized me—some even wanted my autograph.

"Come in. Come in." Caleb, the owner, ushered me through the door. *Place is packed solid!*

"I have your usual table reserved for you and am preparing a special lox and bagel breakfast. Did you watch the documentary, *Sins of an Angel* last night? All about that pop star—"

"Yes, yes, the Red Angel."

The episode covered Cheryl Smith's early life before she turned ten. They didn't have much footage, and I found it amazing that they patched the show together in less than a day.

A few reporters grabbed chairs around my table. Over coffee, I regaled them with stories of how I taught Cheryl to sing, how I babysat her when I was a teen, how we watched films like *Robin Hood* and the *Fox and the Hound,* and how she loved Gregorian chants and choral arrangements—which had deep influence in her music. That garnered a chuckle.

"Do you keep in touch with the Red Angel?" someone asked.

"Not really. I do send letters to her management with the hope she'd receive them. On rare occasion, she'd write back. Often, she'd say how she misses me. Hey, you want a great scoop about the Red Angel? She never shaves in winter! She's such a hairy little gnome!"

I downed the remainder of my drink before continuing. I described her as promiscuous, dating around a lot and how I disapproved of her "bed fun" outside the bounds of marriage; and how she sent me some backstage passes to visit her after a show in Vancouver.

"We went out for drinks later. The evening wore on and we got a little, let's say, affectionate." I stared at my empty mug. "Caleb!" I yelled, waving it in the air. "More!" The owner retrieved my cup while I returned to my story.

"Cheryl emailed me telling me she was pregnant a few months later," I continued. "She wanted to take a step back from the limelight to raise her baby, especially away from the prying eyes of the media." I pouted a bit. "I wanted to connect with my child-to-be, but she insisted on keeping me distant, wanting to keep the identity of her father a secret. It was particularly difficult for me. I'm a professional sperm donor, and I don't connect with children I father."

I concluded my fibs by mentioning the Red Angel took pity on me living in the run-down hospice and invited me to crash in her pad in Vancouver, though it didn't last too long before she booted me out.

Did I go too far with fabricating my Cheryl story? Reginald had wanted me to change my ways. *Maybe I can do some good with my fame?* The hospice had always struggled to raise money—one of the reasons why the place fell to shambles. The renovations would deplete most the windfall I "inherited," leaving them in the same financial mess they were in before. *They will need more funds to keep them afloat, and maybe even could do more...*

"The shelter desperately needs renovations and will need more funds to keep operations going. They help so many people on the street get back on their feet again," I told the reporters. *Reginald will be happy to have more money. Maybe with more funds, his dreams for the place will be realized.* "If you can find it in your hearts to donate, please visit the Hospice of Good Hope's web page. We need your help."

Caleb brought me a huge plate of bagels, cream cheese, and salmon. I asked him to dismiss the reporters to leave me in peace to read my Bible. I stared at the blue seeds attached to my bagel.

"Caleb," I said. "Take this back. I want sesame seed bagels. Not poppy! Oh, and don't forget my refill."

I parked myself in front of the TV in the hospice's recreation room waiting for more Larry interviews to air. They never did...*My celebrity status can't be declining already?* I went to the office to solicit some encouragement from my online family. The office phone rang non-stop, but I ignored all the calls and continued my important reading.

Reginald bolted into the office from the hallway. "Why aren't you answering?"

"Not my job," I replied. I typed some posts promoting my desire to connect with my children.

Ring-ring.

Someone please pick up that accursed phone!

"Hello, Hospice of Good Hope, Reginald speaking." After a pause, "Oh, I see. Yes, he's here. Just one moment please."

"For you...again," said Reginald handing me the phone. "Answer your own calls next time."

Have to appease the plebs. "Hello?"

"Is this Larry Johnstone?" a stern and officious voice responded.

"Hi, yes, I'm Larry Johnstone! You might recognize me from all those news stories about Cheryl Smith and fathering her fine young son. If you'd like an interview, I'm pretty much booked all week."

"Mr. Johnstone, I'm Gerald Fraser of Farber, Fraser, and Hooper. I am calling you from Toronto, and I'm the attorney representing Cheryl Smith."

"Hi Gerry! I'm so glad to hear from you! Are you calling for me to sell you the rights for my life story? It'd make a great made-for-TV movie and will have a huge appeal for the twenty- to thirty-year-old demographic, which you undoubtedly know is prime amongst broadcasters. I have some A-list actors in mind who could play me."

"Mr. Johnstone, I don't think you understand. We've tried several attempts to contact you, and I'm now officially forewarning you that we will be launching a defamation lawsuit if you continue to promote your false allegations about your relationship with Ms. Smith after our conversation today. Our client insists she never had any personal communication with you in over fifteen years, and we can prove it. You'd better take us seriously. The major news outlets terminated the story shortly after erroneously airing it. We expect you to comply with this directive."

His warning irked me. I was having too much fun riding this popularity wave.

"No way! I have the right to say what I want, when I want. Sue me, see what I care."

"Mr. Johnstone, I'd advise strongly against—"

I hung up.

How dare they try to shut me up!

Later, I visited the office to chat with the hospice's new summer student, Amber. She was a cute and bubbly university student who worked hard and fit in well with our staff. She was giggling mischievously while working on the computer.

"What gives?" I asked.

"This is too funny." She waved me over. "Have a look."

Amber pointed to an image of Danny sleeping on the couch in the recreation room. Typical Danny, had no shirt on, and his head tilted towards the camera with his mouth gaping wide open. Surrounding him were several body-builder-type men, all wearing banana-hammocks, showing off their giant muscles. *I don't remember these guys. I would've loved to "pose down" with them.*

"Aww, I missed their visit. When did they come over?" I asked.

"They never did," said Amber.

"Huh?"

"Yeah, you see, Reginald asked me to create some promotional flyers for our annual Thanksgiving fundraiser using this cool image editing software." She clicked a few times, and she superimposed a photo of a skunk she found on the web into the corner of her creation with Danny and the bodybuilders and laughed. "*Voila!* Easy peasy!" She giggled again. "When I saw Danny sleeping on the couch earlier, I had to nab a picture of him to muck around with. Couldn't resist."

Danny did come around to visit every now and again—

"—But where did the muscle men come from?"

"Oh, just like the skunk, they're from the internet."

"BA-HA-HA, that's too funny," I said. "Danny will be so impressed when he sees it!"

"Nah, I won't show it to him, I'm just messing around." She exited the photo software. "Shouldn't you be preparing dinner now?"

"Oh, right."

My brain clicked with ideas.

Couldn't shake the call from Cheryl's lawyers from my mind.

How dare they interfere with Larry-fame? Can't they see I'm doing good for the hospice?

I needed to build more momentum and find more photos of Cheryl and I together. *There must be hundreds on the web.* I scanned the internet but couldn't find any, including the image I had bookmarked.

Amber's creativity with the photo editing software gave me an idea. *If I can't find pictures, maybe I can create some.* I reviewed some digitized photos of myself and set aside several I liked.

One had me standing in front of an altar of a traditional church. Must've been in a cathedral I visited a couple of years ago. I found a great image of Cheryl in full costume during a show. The Red Angel lived up to her name, with red shorts, high-heel pumps, giant angel wings, and halo. Perfect for my church backdrop.

I superimposed a copy of her photo into mine to give the illusion we were posing together. *We look great!*

One click and... *Boo-yah! Online!* Almost immediately, my browser screamed with notifications.

I downloaded more images of Cheryl and created a nice collection of pictures with the two of us.

Hmm. Why stop with just Cheryl?

I searched randomly on the web for other popular celebrities, and after a few hours of downloading and manipulating photos, I now had a small following of the most popular and beautiful people in Hollywood. Someone called me to the kitchen.

If Cheryl brought me fame, these people might, too. Maybe I'll post these later.

The lawyer, Gerry, was right. The news stories dropped off the face of the earth, at least on TV. Some media outlets on the internet, though, still published how I fathered Cheryl Smith's child. *Pfft, lawyers. No way they're going to shut me down. I'm still getting calls for interviews.*

Smokingbanditmedia.com became the first in a string of cancellations in early August. It might've been a coincidence, but something was different on my *Larrynet* homepage that day.

"What?" I screamed to myself. *My church photo with Cheryl was no longer online!*

Angered, I accessed the folder on my computer with all the doctored images I created of Cheryl and myself. I logged into *Larrynet* and created a Red Angel album, and when prompted, I selected all my images.

Before I clicked to upload them, a thought struck me. *What good are you hoping to accomplish, Larry? The Red Angel doesn't deserve this.*

Defiant, I stared at my collection for a moment.

Reginald suddenly burst into my office, breaking my trance. "Larry, do you know a lawyer named Gerald Fraser from Toronto?" He looked over my shoulder. "What on earth are you doing with all those images of Cheryl Smith? Get rid of them, now!"

Reginald attempted to grab the mouse from my hand, but I brushed him off.

"Larry, he is ordering you to cease your interviews about his client the Red Angel."

"Yes, he's such an asshole!"

"Don't use that filthy language!"

Reginald's stern voice grounded me. "Sorry, Reginald. What can I do to help?"

"Larry, I'm going to beg you. Please stop talking about Cheryl Smith. The lawyer reviewed your financial situation and determined you're not worth the effort to sue. But since you're continuing to do interviews from our offices, raising funds for us using her name, and uploading photographs of her, he's claiming the hospice is liable for supporting your false claims." He nervously rubbed his moustache. "Is that true? Is all of this a lie?"

I sat silent. The guilt surged through me again. "Forgive me?"

"Do you realize he's threatening to sue us?" Reginald placed his hand on my shoulder. "Can you please promise to stop any discussion about this Cheryl person, now, and delete all those photos."

Reginald appeared desperate. He was right. I should give this up.

"Okay, Reginald," I said. "I was sincerely trying to help the hospice." *Sort of...*

I turned back to the computer and deleted all my images. Reginald patted my back and left.

No phone calls from reporters, no emails from enquiring minds, but more friend requests on *Larrynet* from total strangers. It didn't matter. I no longer cared my name didn't appear first when I searched the web. In my heart, I was still a star, thanks to all this nonsense.

Chapter Twenty-Five
The Psychedelic Glee Club
September 2007 – May 2015

Kitchen renovations were well under way at the hospice the first week of September, forcing me to eat out often. I discovered a neat place called Hungry Herman's Breakfast Shop by the wharf. They'd piled on a huge plate of blueberry pancakes for me to bring back home.

Danny sat across from me in the cafeteria, salivating at my meal. Like Peter, when he visited, Danny spent time soliciting the regulars.

"Your celebrity charm sure is doing this place some good, dude," said Danny.

Good? The hospice looks like it's been hit by a bomb!

"Business has been a bit slow since Uncle Peter died," he continued. "I'd expect the kids heading back to school would be buying up more stash this week, but I'm thinking I need something catchy to reel them in."

Maybe Danny needed me selling for him. I never had an issue moving product to students in the past, though I hadn't been too inspired to do my old job since Peter's death and Danny inheriting the business.

"You can't exactly take out an advertisement in the school newspaper," I said.

"No, of course not… but dude, I have tons of weed I got to unload."

I was still bitter Peter's godson inherited everything, and I didn't care for his personality much, either. A reason why I didn't bother going back to work for him, though I missed it.

"I'm with you on the cash flow problems," I said. I had burned a chunk of the money from Peter's life insurance on new preppy clothing, phone, fine dining, and many hours in a tanning salon. "I'm seriously missing my commission I earned from Peter. Maybe I can help." I looked pensively in the distance. "We need something to draw people's attention back our way. My fame can help.

Everyone will flock to me." I stuffed a whole pancake in my mouth, and slowly masticated it.

"Dude, you don't get it. It's been completely dead. I hung out on campus earlier this week. It should've been the busiest day of the year." He leaned back in his chair and raised his arms behind his head. "Would you believe I stood by myself for nearly an hour? Not a single dude approached me. Being alone, though, got me thinking. Next week's gonna be 'Freshman Week.' There will be tons of events, and kids will be registering for school clubs and shit. We might be able to offer something different than, let's say, chess."

"What's wrong with chess?" I haven't played a good game in decades, maybe because most of the pinheads who challenged me never met my intellectual prowess.

"Nothing, dude, but I thought maybe we can create a school club, and offer a discount for joining," Danny said. "This weed stuff Peter sold doesn't really turn much profit—it's too labour intensive. Maybe we commit these students to paying for the pot in advance, and we deliver to them each month. Saves our asses hauling the shit up to campus every second day and make way more money up front!"

I reflected on what he said. I, too, had hated carrying around the duffle bag for Peter on that long train ride. "I like that! Great idea!" I cut up my last pancake. "We can give them bulk discounts for buying in advance. It would stabilize our financial foundations, and we could invest the extra funds for greater return. I see one problem with the plan. How on earth do we pretend to be a school club?" Of course, I knew, but I felt it important for Danny to figure it out.

"I read in the school paper they have clubs for everything—chess, games, orienteering," said Danny with a hint of excitement. "I thought of this idea for something I call a 'Psychedelic Glee Club.' I mean, universities already have acapella societies—"

They do?

"—but our offering will be different. We can name it after Peter."

"You mean," I said, "like the Peter Van Wagner Psychedelic Glee Club?" *Sounds pompous. I love it!*

"Yeah! I'd just have to get a friend to register it for us with the school. We can set up a table with a big sign with the club's name and an image of a cannabis plant! No one will take it seriously. It's the perfect cover! And Larry, with your fame, and my amazing tenor voice—"

"Ahem," I interrupted, "I have an even better bass voice. And I play guitar. I'll have you know I just mastered 'A Horse With No Name.'"

"Yeah, uh, okay…with our voices, we can write songs to draw the students in, sign them up to our service, and *voila*, instant moolah. We'll make sure the tune is simple and catchy."

I had to admit, I was intrigued. The "glee" we sold wouldn't come from singing, though, but songs and weed fit well with Peter's credo. I'd be open to help "share the love" this way.

We gathered our lyric and song ideas on paper and mapped out the melodies and vocals for our road trip the following week.

9:45 a.m.

Monday morning, we joined the other clubs in the largest hall on campus. Danny created an amazing blue tie-dye banner, laced with peace symbols and cannabis leaves. The letters Peter Van Wagner Psychedelic Glee Club stood out boldly in its centre. We taped it up under our table and placed many of Peter's remaining beaded jewelry on top. It made for a colourful display! Despite what our poster implied, we didn't showcase any smokables.

Danny went to buy us some coffees while I tuned the guitar. By the time he returned, the hall was packed with students who were browsing club tables.

My partner pushed his way through the crowd, placed our coffees down, and went back outside to smoke up. He returned relaxed, ready for showtime.

I strummed the chords of our tune. People stopped their chattering while we sang our song in two-part harmony.

If you think
School's a joke
Come on by
And take a toke
Buy just one
Or grab a bunch
You'll get over
The scholastic crunch

[chorus]
Marijuana, Marijuana
Brought in fresh from
Califor-nah
Smoke all night - ah
Or all day - yah
School's more fun with
Marijuana

No more stress

Once you start
Smoking up
Will make you smart
Healthy treat
You'll not sneeze
Not unless
You got allergies

[chorus]
Marijuana, Marijuana
Brought in fresh from
Califor-nah
Smoke all night - ah
Or all day - yah
School's more fun with
Marijuana

The day flew buy. Students recognized me, and I personally autographed "club" cards in the "authorized by" space for any student purchasing our six-month subscription package.

With one hour left in the day, Danny announced we sold so much pot, we wouldn't have to peddle the streets for the rest of the year. We broke out into another rousing chorus of our marijuana song, when a familiar looking man caught my eye. He stood, videoing us singing with a digital camera, and when we stopped, he approached our table.

"Hi Larry, do you remember me?" he asked.

"You do look familiar. Would you like to join our club?" I held out a card listing various membership options.

"Ha-ha, no thanks. We met a couple months back. I'm Mark St. James, the reporter from CHLN? I interviewed you at Jumpin' Java and broke the story about you and the Red Angel."

"Oh yes, I remember now. Did you buy me coffee?"

"I did…" He looked over the sign and the table. "I can only guess what you're selling here."

"Hey dude," chimed in Danny to Mark, "we're running low on stock of our good stuff, but I see you eyeing this cool beaded jewellery. I personally guarantee you'll never need Viagra if you wear this bracelet." He held out two samples for Mark.

Mark laughed. "I'll take them. I've been hard up these days." He paid Danny and shoved them in his pocket. "Larry, there's been a lot of confusion about the story between you and the Red Angel. I understand you have a son through your wife, who is also named Rupert. You call him Little Larry, right?"

"Yeah, what's it to you?" I asked angrily. Questions like these annoyed me. They reminded me of my diminishing fame because of Cheryl's lawyers.

"I've been doing my homework on you, and even though we can't prove or disprove you had a relationship with Cheryl Smith, you have an interesting life story. I think it should be shared with the world."

"I do, too! I'm a bit sad. I'm doubting my capacity to achieve my lifelong mission."

"Mission?"

"Yeah. Long story."

"I'd love to hear about it. Can we grab a coffee sometime to chat?

"Yeah, okay. I'll spill my life to you when we meet. Will we be on TV?"

"Well, CHLN suspended me for not checking up on all my facts about your relationship with the Red Angel. But I still write a blog and have a huge internet following. Your story has a drama which I believe will fascinate people, and my colleagues who read my posts might share them with their outlets." We finalized our "date."

"Looking forward to our chat." Mark left the building.

Larry, your star will rise again!

Mark scribbled notes at a torrential pace during our interview at Jumpin' Java. It'd been well over a month since the story broke that I'd fathered Cheryl Smith's child, but it died a fast death. Any evidence on the web of my paternal ties to her Rupert disappeared, extinguishing my only foray into fame. Part of me still believed the Red Angel's child was mine, but convincing Mark of that was fruitless.

"Did you see those photos of the three of us on the beach?"

Mark nodded.

"I mean, I have no idea where they came from, and they all mysteriously disappeared. My question is, why? I think Cheryl must be hiding something." The waiter returned with my coffee, and I nodded in acknowledgment. "Have you looked closely at the photo of her child? I swear it could very well be my kid."

Mark acknowledged in agreement and continued to record my every word. We gabbed for a couple of hours, discussing my mission and the prophecy, and how I've been changing my focus to put my fame to philanthropic use. I vented a bit about missing "spreading the love" for Peter, and how my friend had wanted to pass the torch to me. Mark seemed interested that Danny inherited Peter's business.

Mark scribbled down a note. "Do you work for Danny?"

"Not really. I've too many fond memories of working with my late friend Peter, and…well…the way Danny seems to be running things—it's not the same." I felt myself choking up on my words. "I volunteered to help Danny with the Psychedelic Glee Club. It was sort of my idea." *In my mind, it was.* "I wanted to find a new way that would appease Danny and somehow maintain the loving spirit Peter intended."

"You might want to consider what doing an illegal activity does to your profile, Larry," said Mark, putting away his notebook. "You have so much capacity to do good now."

Mark had a point. He asked me for my email address and told me he'd contact me when he published the story. He reiterated he had a huge following of journalists, and my pathetic life would draw lots of interest.

I couldn't wait.

My star meter sky-rocketed again through the month of September thanks to Mark's "blog." Blogs were intriguing. I figured out how to create one but didn't bother writing anything. Didn't have to. Mark did all the work, and besides, all my thoughts were documented on *Larrynet*.

Mark wrote my life story and painted me out to be a regular "Cassanova" who struggled to find dates. He even interviewed my best friend, Brad. It saddened me to have lost touch with him since moving here. We were close. Funny how I haven't heard boo from him since my ill-fated bachelor party—the day before I left for Vancouver.

He concluded his blog by talking about how I'd been living in the hospice for over fifteen years and resorted to selling pot to forge a living. He included a link to a site I never heard of containing videos, where he had uploaded one of Danny and me singing our marijuana song to the students. The movie-clip had been played over thirty thousand times in only a week!

I hadn't heard anything from Danny since our Psychedelic Glee Club success. You'd think he'd piggyback on my new internet-video fame, but he never invited me for an encore performance at another university. It pissed me off. I missed singing to my adoring public and spreading the love—both at the universities and in the streets.

Apart from spending on myself, Reginald had encouraged me to invest most of the twenty thousand I inherited in mutual funds—something I knew little about but was quick study. I enjoyed following their progress online, buying and selling stock became a bit of a fun game which, of course, I excelled at.

The last of my available money had evaporated watching the movie, *300*, a dozen times. Determined to transform my belly into Spartan warrior abs like the men in the film, I discovered the "Spartacus" workout online. I completed half of it and rewarded myself with an ice cream.

With no "liquid cash," I wanted to return to my old job peddling pot. I figured restoring Peter's old street corner mission would've been something my friend would've wanted. I thought it in poor taste that Danny never followed in his godfather's footsteps, singing and selling weed.

I grabbed my guitar and walked to Danny's condo, just a half-click away from the hospice. My plan—to demand enough weed to sell on the streets to resurrect Peter's work. I walked by Peter's corner *en route*, and the toughies were out hustling drugs to those interested. I ignored them and continued to walk towards Danny's home.

Danny's building overlooked Coal Harbour. He had moved in soon after Peter's death and extended me one of those "you are welcome to visit me any time" invites, but not really meaning it. I had asked on several occasions if he wanted to get together, but he always was "busy." It annoyed me—almost as much as his disappearance from my life since we performed at the university.

My anger increased while I strolled down the road. *Maybe a joint will help take the edge off.* I'd been going cold turkey pretty much since Peter died, and thinking about the number of hours I toiled for my friend only to be pushed aside by Danny frustrated me more. I arrived at his building, and he buzzed me in.

He greeted me at his penthouse condo, wearing flip-flops, inverted baseball cap, basketball shorts, and no shirt. "Dude! Welcome to my humble *château*!" he yelled over the rap blaring through his stereo.

Humble?

"Danny, can you turn this noise off?" I yelled back.

"Aw c'mon, dude." He turned down the volume. "Eminem's 'Lose Yourself' is the bomb!"

They name artists—if you can call this art—after candy?

"It's all noise to me. Vivaldi would sound much better with that sound system." I stepped into his "pad" and was overwhelmed by the mountain view from his wall-to-wall living room window. The pine wood flooring and white furniture screamed affluence. "This must've cost a fortune. Are you holding anything back on me?"

"What? Me? Nah! I gave you the 250 bucks I promised for our day at the university."

I walked around the living room and studied a Rodin-esque statue near the far wall.

"You realize, dude," said Danny, "that I inherited all this from my Uncle Peter, right?"

"Peter? Owned *this*? And he only gave me this guitar?" I lifted it in front of Danny's face. "I thought he said he lived 'off the land.'"

"Him? Only when the weather was decent. He had several investment properties along the West Coast. He was quite real estate savvy and needed a place to store his money. He didn't trust institutions, like banks."

Is this, like, money laundering? Who was this Peter?

"I wish I'd known he lived here," I said. "Hell, I would've house sat for him if he wanted to keep to his hippy roots and live in the streets."

A high-pitch giggle emanated from a room at the end of the hallway.

"Dude, I hate to be rude, but I have some, ahem, business to attend to. Happy for you to come and visit anytime, but you need to leave."

I had no intention of leaving until I got what I came for.

"Listen," I said firmly. "I want Peter's street business. That old street corner he worked on misses that grass roots spirit. Need I remind you that your Uncle Peter wanted me to have all this?"

Danny crossed his arms angrily.

"Not what he said, nor was it in the will. This is mine. I'm like his family. Got it? You? You're just a street seller, dude. You should be thankful I even let you up here."

Just a street seller? How dare he!

"Hey, I paid my dues on the street. I never see you hauling bags of product to the universities. In fact, I don't think I've ever seen you sell dope on the streets like your Uncle Peter. You don't know how he wanted to run things! He was about building a utopian love society."

Danny stood there, expressionless.

"I can bring that spirit back if you cut me in. Besides, I need to earn!" *I need to smoke, too.* "Now that I'm famous, I can probably bring in triple what I used to."

Danny took a deep breath.

"Listen, dude. I don't need to hit the streets selling weed anymore," he said calmly. "Nor do you need to." Danny walked over to his stereo and changed the CD. More ambient soul played through the speakers. He closed his eyes and swayed to the smooth rhythms.

A thought occurred to me. "Those hoods on Peter's corner. They work for you?"

Danny stopped dancing.

"Haven't you ever noticed Peter never had a problem with rival gangs? He had respect out there, dude. I don't. Besides, the harder stuff is where the money is at. Why I have that tough crew out on the streets." He faced his window with the gorgeous view. "No, I'm happy here. Can't go back to the old ways. Too risky being so close to the action." He turned back to me. "Sorry, dude. I'll call on you to help sell more subscriptions for the winter term. So, I won't need your services 'til then."

"But I need cash now!" And I didn't want to pay for joints by subscribing to Danny's package.

"Danny," the voice sang from the bedroom. "Are you going to play 'Puff the Magic Dragon' with me?"

Danny's face turned red. He dashed over to a stack of CDs on top of a speaker. He rifled through them, some falling on the floor. "Ah-ha!" he said pulling out one. He showed me the cover with a large green dragon on it. He inserted the CD and the familiar Peter, Paul, and Mary children's song lulled out its melancholy melody.

"Tell you what. You owed my uncle $1,200. He wouldn't want the debt unpaid, even if he's dead. You sell this bag by the end of the week, and return all the earnings, I'll give you $500 and erase your debts." He threw me a large duffle bag—much heavier than usual. "It's the last time I'll let you work the streets." His voice turned sterner. "There's about three thousand dollars of the stuff there…so be careful. The cops have been sniffing up our trail more these days. Now go and come back when you're done."

I shouldered the bag and left Danny to play his dragon game. Sounded like fun, and I resented he didn't invite me to join them. Even more so, I was pissed I was pushed out of the business.

Hitting the street, I opened the bag to check the contents. Joint paradise. I grabbed one and lit up.

Aaaaaaah.

People turned their heads to admire my celebrity as I walked among them in the streets, toking away. Peter had chosen his location wisely, being one of the busiest intersections in the neighbourhood. I didn't care if this was "Danny's turf." I'm here to reclaim Peter's former glory! *Funny, Danny's "thugs" weren't around.* I broke out my guitar, just like Peter, and brought back his magic.

I strummed our Psychedelic Glee Club song, chanting away the marijuana-based lyrics. No doubt, people would recognize the internet video sensation in front of them. A few said "hello" when they passed by, and I replied "peace" to them. Two well-built gentlemen, both dressed in trench coats with a stern posture, stopped and applauded—at which, I took a deep bow.

"Hi, I'm Larry Johnstone, man. You fellas look like you need to relax. Want to buy some reefers?" I smiled and opened the bag. "I have tons! I can sell them to you at a discount if you buy by the pound."

"Mr. Johnstone," the taller man said flashing a badge, "we're going to have to arrest you for peddling without a license, and possession of drugs."

"What? But I've been doing this for years!"

"Even worse. Turn around."

I heard the clip of the handcuffs slapping around my wrists.

What?

The door clanged shut behind me to my prison cell. It was dark and smelled like my high school washroom that hadn't been cleaned in months. A man at least twice my size sat still on the floor in the corner by a bunk bed, and he was staring at me intently. He could've been from an outlaw biker gang, and a long scar stretched from his left cheekbone just below his eye down to the side of his lip. Its edges were rough, and the scar stretched and retracted with the movement of his mouth as he chewed away on a toothpick. I was a little intimidated, so figured on making nice.

"Hi, I'm Larry Johnstone, your cellmate. Which bunk is yours?"

"You look flammable." His voice growled in a dull monotone.

I know I'm hot, but no one's ever called me that, before.

My roommate's bare arms fashioned tattoos of demons entrenched in fire. He never averted his intense gaze.

"I like your muscles." I responded attempting conversation. "Did you see the movie *300*?"

"You're lucky I don't have a match."

"Don't worry, maybe the guard has one. We can ask him next time he swings by. Hey, if you want to pass the time faster, we can sing. I'm awesome."

"Huh?" His mouth opened wide, dropping his toothpick.

"I know just the appropriate song. Listen and join in. I'm sure you might've heard it. It'll turn your frown upside down." I cleared my throat and belted with my deepest bass the old spiritual "Nobody Knows, the Trouble I've Seen." I thought it *apropos*. I've heard it sung in many movies by prisoners.

I finished the verse. "Your turn."

"No," he said, picking up his toothpick and placing it back in his mouth. "I'm gonna commit arson on your ass."

"I understand," I said ignoring his ramblings. "You want to hear me sing some more." I began the second verse, except I couldn't remember the words, so I made some up. My cellmate enjoyed it. He sat in the corner, raised his knees, and placed his forehead on them. That old song brings everyone to prayer and tears.

An officer rudely interrupted my sixth time singing the same verse. "Mr. Johnstone, a word." He opened the jail door and let me out.

"Thank you, officer," said my cellmate.

The policeman led me down a dark hallway to a room with a table in the middle. He handcuffed me to the chair. "Detective Khalid will be here soon."

I fixed my hair with my free hand, using the reflection on the mirrored wall while I waited.

A man wearing a nice tie and white dress shirt walked in carrying a file folder. He slammed it on the table after introducing himself.

"Do you know what that is?" Khalid pointed to the table.

"Yes. That's easy. That's a file folder. Pfffft. You're going to have to ask me a harder question to stump me!"

Had him! It took the gentleman a few moments to gather his thoughts.

"Mr. Johnstone—" he sat down, opened the folder, and leafed though some of the pages "—peddling drugs on the streets of Vancouver is a serious offence."

"It can't be that serious," I said. "Peter Van Wagner, rest in peace, and I have been selling pot for *years*. You don't know how many lives we've touched with our service! But you're right. Peddling *real* drugs is serious. May I have a glass of water?"

The detective motioned to an officer at the door who left the room.

"Look," I said, "there's a gang of hoods who hang around the corner where you picked me up. They've been operating there since the summer and are selling the *real* hard stuff. It's a bad scene detective." *Did Danny mention the name of the drug they are selling? Can't remember. I'll make one up.* "They're pushing *heroin*. So, yeah, it makes pot a tough sell downtown now. But do you know where the best spot is?"

"No," said the detective, eyebrows rising. Like most people, he's riveted by every word I said. He took a seat opposite me with hands clasped together on top of his file folder.

"The university!" I answered. "Those rich brats buy the stuff by the gallons. In fact, I'm a bit miffed that they buy so much."

"Why's that?"

"Because they no longer buy marijuana direct from me anymore. They buy via subscription. It's pretty much home delivery in bulk, and it's put me out of a job."

The detective rifled through some papers. "We had noticed a huge uptake in drug use on various campuses around the city the last couple of weeks," said Khalid. "No idea how the kids got so much." He tapped his index finger on the table a few times. "Mr. Johnstone, is that your bag we caught you with? Were you going to the universities to drop off the monthly 'subscriptions.'"

"Nah. It's been made clear to me I don't belong to the business. Like I said, I miss working the streets with my friend, Peter Van Wagner. Blessed memory."

"Who owns the bag?"

"Well, when my dear friend Peter died unexpectedly on Canada Day, his nephew, Danny, took charge. He's working to convert Peter's 'corner business' into this huge enterprise. He had the brainchild of selling copious amounts of drugs to the kids via a monthly subscription. It was so easy for him. He asked me to write a jingle to help promote his idea." I threw in a further exaggeration of the truth. "I had thought his idea of the Peter Van Wagner Psychedelic Glee Club a clever joke. Ended up being a front for a large drug operation. Hey, want to hear my little song? It's been played millions of times on the internet."

"No, I don't think that's necessary…"

I began singing. The officer remained stoic. *Hard audience.*

I finished to no applause. "Like I said, I've been pushed out. I live at the Hospice of Good Hope and have no easy means to make money. Danny is the one selling weed in bulk to children, and he's also behind the *heroin* traffic downtown. I have no more income! In fact, he used me for my musical talent, then dumped me!"

"Well, that wasn't very nice." I couldn't tell if Khalid was being sarcastic. "So, you're saying you weren't going to sell the contents of the bag on the street when we nabbed you?"

Save your bacon, Larry.

"No, just returning my unused 'street stock' to Danny. He ordered me to. But to be honest, I saw my usual corner free of Danny's hoods that I wanted to relive old times. Sorry. I didn't mean no harm."

"Where'd you say he lived?"

I gave Danny's address. "He should be able to answer all your questions. Oh, but wait. He mentioned not wanting to be disturbed. Something about playing a 'Puff the Magic Dragon' game with some chick."

The detective smiled. "Thanks, Larry. I think we can let you go once we finish things up at our end. You've been very helpful." He stood, faced the mirror, and nodded. I did the same, smiled, and waved at Khalid's reflection.

He left, and a minute later the police officer returned with my water and escorted me to the front of the station. The room was filled with desks and bustled with activity. He pointed me to sit in an empty chair and walked me through some paperwork—a lengthy process.

A couple of hours flew by. I entertained the officer at our desk with stories of my life woes. He seemed impressed, typing nonstop on his computer the whole time.

Two policemen burst in, leading Danny down an adjacent corridor away from us. He didn't see me as they ushered him to a back room. That's good. Danny should be able to answer all their questions. He might also be able to visit my cellmate, too.

Detective Khalid approached my desk. "Thanks again, Mr. Johnstone. You've been a big help. With your information, we're in the process of busting a huge drug operation. You're free to go."

"That's great." I grinned. "Hey, do you want my autograph?"

The officer passed me a clipboard. "Please. Just sign the release form on the line on the bottom."

"Gladly." I signed it "With love, Larry Johnstone xx."

I turned and left for home content that not only did I bring joy to a poor man in jail, but also performed an important civic duty by assisting the police in their work.

"How ya gettin' on, by?" a woman with a Newfoundland accent said from the hospice's new large screen TV. A horrible low-pitched growling noise filled the background, like a recording being played in super slow motion.

"I'm rotted! That farting sound is driving me to tears!" a man replied.

The post dinner crowd relaxed, taking in a TV show. Hector, sitting in his special couch was watching, too. *Can't believe the crap on the boob tube.*

"What'cha watching?" I asked, taking a seat.

One of the men replied, "Shh, it's a pilot called *Dildo's Head*. It's set in New-foundland and hysterical!"

"That's not a fart," a woman replied to the man on TV over the caterwauling. "Luh!" she pointed in the distance. "That racket must be a poor ol' confused puffin!"

The men in the room laughed.

"It must be really shitbaked," the man said, "having found its way here at Toronto. Have to admit, so am I!" The man placed his hands on his stomach. "The food here is the pits and I'm gutfounded. Fire up a scoff!"

"But we don't have anything to eat," replied the woman.

An off-screen singer hit a piercing high note. Hector sat upright, cocked his head, and growled. The screeching continued, and Hector ran out of the room to avoid the irritating sound. We all laughed at the actors covering their ears in agony.

"I su'pose something choked the life out of that poor bird," said the woman. "I'll set to making it up."

The low growling started up again.

"Arrgh! The damn things been back to life again!"

The hospice gang roared as the horrid singing trailed to a commercial. Reginald beckoned me from the back of the room.

"Larry, a couple of gentlemen came looking for you earlier. They claimed to be officers of the court."

"It makes sense. I had to work with the police today. Something about busting a drug ring in one of the universities."

"Hmmm, well they insisted on looking through your room. They had documentation permitting them to do so."

"No worries, I have nothing to hide."

Hector returned, carrying something in his mouth…something square, made of plastic, and about five centimeters wide. I didn't want him to chew and choke on it by accident.

"Hector!" I scolded. "Drop that!"

The little dog obeyed, placing the square object at Reginald's feet.

"Hello?" said Reginald, "What do we have here?" He bent forward to pick up Hector's gift. "Cock Sock condoms?" Reginald waved them to everyone in the room. "All right people. Who do these belong to?"

I might've flushed a bit. I had no idea where Hector dug up one of the condoms Heather gave me many years ago.

"Where the hell did you get that?" I said to Hector. My dog ran away guiltily.

Not surprisingly, no one took ownership of the condom. Nevertheless, I returned to my room to see if anything else was missing. Everything seemed to be in order, except I couldn't find my hairbrush. *Did Hector steal it, or did the officers of the court take it?* Happens all the time to celebrities with fanatical fans wanting a piece of their action. *Perverts.*

"Drug Scam Busted," screamed the Thursday headlines in the newspaper. It'd been a couple of days since my visit to the police station. I read the article while sipping my free coffee at Jumpin' Java.

Blah blah blah, million-dollar ring, blah blah blah, led by kingpin, Danny, blah blah blah and ran by blah blah blah. City reveals debt of gratitude to an INFORMANT whose revealing evidence led to the arrest and seizures of blah blah blah.

INFORMANT? Why didn't they say my name? I was pissed. I could've used a bit of a fame boost—attention to the stories about me posted by Mark St. James on his blog were beginning to subside. Caleb walked by with a coffee decanter.

"You in the news again?" He raised his eyebrows as I showed him the article.

I asked Caleb why my name didn't appear in the headline.

"Who knows?" he said, "maybe it's for security…to protect you from repercussions for their arrest."

Pfft. I'm sure the cops busted them all!

Annoyed, I finished off my coffee and returned back home.

Reporters and cameramen swarmed the hospice's entranceway when I arrived. *Are they here for me to discuss my heroism in stopping a huge drug cartel?*

They were talking to Reginald who was holding a big parcel.

"Oh, look, there he is!" said Reginald.

The crowd turned and cheered. I gathered word leaked out that I was the "informant" that led the cops to their major coup. I prepared to share tales of my detective genius, and looked forward, for once, to talk freely to the press about myself, and not the Red Angel and her son. I faced a cameraman and brushed my hair around my ears.

"I guess you are all here to talk to me about the drug bust in the city the other day?" I asked.

Reginald interrupted. "I have no idea what you are blathering about, but this came in for you, in a special truck, followed by the media." He offered me the package. It weighed a ton.

The return address read from Ottawa. I removed the wrapping. *A box containing a huge twenty-pound ham? Odd.*

I waved my meat for all to see and read the attached note to myself.

Please accept this gorgeous ham with love. Hope you
appreciate it!
From Cheryl, Rick, and Rupert.

Red filled my face, and I scratched my head. *Why is the Red Angel sending this to me? Is she sorry for siccing her lawyers on me? Or does she pity me for where I live? And why the media?*

"What does the card say?" asked a reporter.

"It's from Cheryl, the Red Angel, and from her wonderful child Rupert. She's sending me her love." *And Rick?* "I'm quite moved. I have such amazing friends. Thanks to Cheryl, and darling son Rupert for this wonderful gift. They see how I live; now we shall feast on this delicious meat. I wish I could share this with my family this Thanksgiving. I miss my Little Larry."

A silence filled the air.

"But I do have family." I faced Reginald. "The gang here at the hospice. We will enjoy this wonderful ham this holiday weekend, and if any of you out there would like to help the homeless of our city, please visit Hospice of Good Hope's web site to donate."

The reporters joined in a chorus of questions. One voice stood out in the din. "When will you see your child next?"

Not wanting to discuss my children, I pivoted the discussion.

"I'd rather not talk about all that. The conversations on social media and some articles about me and my life are still on the web. Read them, if you like—but that's all in the past. Let's focus on the now and continue chatting about what a hero I am for busting up that drug operation."

Why the hell are they laughing?

It might've been my fame, or the Red Angel sending a ham, but the hospice's donations increased dramatically over the coming years. It presented a quandary for the charitable organization—the hospice couldn't make a profit and had to strategically spend its windfall of funds. The Board of Directors debated what to do with the money, and they elected to hire more staff to extend their work in the streets. Reginald was never so excited. The hospice's outreach was growing, and there was even discussion of obtaining a second building, or maybe a bus that'd deliver meals directly to the homeless.

The place hustled with new employees joining the team. It meant I had less to do. No one played ping-pong anymore, I no longer sold pot, and I only served meals. With a lot more time on my hands, I continued to study how to invest money online. Reginald had already given me a few tips to get started, and I loved following the trends of the market. I started making enough cash to live on.

Jacquie was proud of me for my financial success. We communicated often online, resuming our heart to hearts like we used to in person years ago. She always encouraged and validated me, and when needed, kept me on the straight and narrow. Jacquie might have been the only one who could read through my lies. She wasn't the only person from my past I chatted with on the internet.

My father, too, became a huge web user. We'd been messaging online daily and had grown close. I never spoke to my mama, though she was always a popular point of discussion with Dad. I admired Dad's dedication to her, warts and all. It made me feel a little guilty about not pursuing Heather.

Speaking of pursuit…Dana tracked down Rabid Rick on social media. When she told me, her message hit me like a bomb. I couldn't understand why, but I felt a pang of jealousy. By the way she sounded, you'd think they'd gotten engaged. She had obviously lost all her taste in men! The timing felt a bit odd, coming right on the heels of Rick's wedding fiasco with the Red Angel—that's a whole other story. The Red Angel and Rick never married, and when I heard that news for the first time, I felt an unexpected twinge of sympathy for the poor sod.

Early in 2015, Reginald announced his retirement after forty years of service at the Hospice of Good Hope. Satisfied that his work was done, and pleased to see the hospice's mission expanding, he figured it was the right time to say goodbye. He longed to travel and catch up with old friends. We organized a farewell bash for him, and many members of our original small group from church, including Jacquie and her husband, joined the celebration. Despite Vaughn not being present, it felt like the first days when I arrived in Vancouver.

On Reginald's last day, he introduced me to the new operations manager of the hospice, who agreed to keep me on staff as supervisor in the kitchen. The cold jerk of a manager insisted I pay a rent to continue living in the building. He also wanted me to get rid of Hector, fearing that some residents could be allergic. The man refused to believe my dog was hypoallergenic, and we argued often, not only about my Hector, but also about how things should be run.

With all my long-time friends gone, the vibe at the hospice was changing.

Part Four: Superstar Larry

2017

Chapter Twenty-Six
The Waiting Game
February – May 2017

Dad sat in the living room of our home near Alexandria, Ontario, slumped over with hands on his knees. Father Barry, the priest from my youth, placed his hand on Dad's shoulder and talked to my father in hushed whispers.

Mama had died.

I plugged a kettle needing something warm to drink. Standing outside for the funeral had reminded me how nut-shrivelling cold the winters were in this rural town.

Dad had messaged me earlier that week when he had called an ambulance to take Mama to the hospital. Even though I had arrived the following day, it was too late. I hadn't spoken to her in over twenty-five years! Consumed with bitterness and regret, I had broken down in tears.

The home hadn't changed much. The halls were still enshrined with dolls, and my bedroom remained the same. Many of my childhood books were still on the shelves. I browsed through the *Biblical Bedtime Stories* my mother read me, reliving some positive memories. I retrieved the old Shakespeare text from the top shelf, and the postcards from Montreal were still there, though no picture of my father's "friend" Amélie.

Father Barry shook my hand when I joined him in the living room. "It's so nice to see you again, Larry. Been way too long, praise God. I will never forget the last time I was here. You remember? When we had that New Year's Eve engagement party. Hey, where's your lovely wife?"

I walked over to the kitchen to make a cup of tea. Barry didn't read the signal I didn't want to talk about her.

"Larry?" he asked with concern.

Father Barry and I had many heart-to-hearts in my adolescence. Seeing the compassion in my former pastor's eyes made my heart melt, but for the first time in my life, I closed right up.

"Are you still married?" persisted the priest. After an awkward silence, he placed his hand on my shoulder. "Larry, you've been such a huge help to me and the church when you were a teen. There is little doubt that your life accomplishments would've made your mother proud."

I recalled the last words my mother had said to me when I phoned her the night I arrived in Vancouver—something along the lines of my decision to move out West to "fornicate" with Heather. She had gone on a tirade about my living in sin, and her final words to me were: "You can come home only when you are ready to repent. I don't expect to hear from you again until you do." I hadn't spoken to her since.

I looked up to Father Barry. "I need to do a confession." My father gave us some privacy, and I unloaded everything to my former priest—my life; my difficult relationship with my mother; my marriage; my failures to be accountable for my ego and lying; and failing to fulfill God's mission, laid by the prophecy when I first landed in Vancouver. Father Barry took in every word and provided comforting advice.

A weight lifted off my shoulders.

"Mama left me her dolls," laughed my father in a moment of levity the next day. "Would you believe it? They were all she had. All she loved..." He sipped some coffee.

I chuckled. "What are you going to do with them all? There must be hundreds."

"Maybe not that many," said Dad. "Want them?"

I couldn't imagine the gang at the hospice playing with them, not that I had space for their storage, anyway.

"We can sell them!" I said.

"Those Beanbag Babes you sent are still here. Do you think they might be valuable like you said?"

I shrugged my shoulders. I couldn't imagine anyone buying any one of Mama's dolls. I mean, who'd want them? Some of them are outright terrifying!
Like those "Children of the Corn" dolls.

"There's always a buyer," I said. Peter would've sold them in a snap.

"Want some irony?" Dad asked. He left the room and returned with two dolls.
Betty and Veronica?

"Mama wanted you to have these."

What? The dolls that ultimately led to my eviction from this place?

"Veronica has a full set of hair?" I recalled shaving her head.

"Yeah, Mama was very good at mending things," said Dad. "What did she call fixing Veronica's hair? Re-rooting? Anyway, she was very upset at what you did to her favourite doll." He stared up for a while at a now empty shelf where some of Mama's prized collection lived. "Your mama wasn't all that bad. In fact, I re-discovered her kind heart soon after you left."

I couldn't see it. Dad had become her lap dog since the Amélie incident, but I nodded for my grieving father's sake.

"Have you been singing much, son?"

I had to admit, not as much as I liked. Mama did invest a lot of time in my singing, so I nodded.

"Your Mama always thought you had a beautiful voice." Dad left the table and came back with a huge stack of choral music scores. "I think she would've wanted you to have these, too."

He left me leafing through the pages remembering how I learned to read sheet music at choir camp. There were some with my old vocal solfège exercises. I sang a few bars quietly—*I still got it!*—while my Dad rummaged in the back of the house. Dad returned with a box and smirked as he placed it on the kitchen table. "By the way, she also knew how much you loved these, too."

I gasped when I opened it—the *Children of the Corn*! The dolls freaked me out so much, I couldn't finish breakfast.

I put all of Mama's dolls up for auction online before returning home to Vancouver. I felt bad leaving my dad behind in Ontario, but I needed to go back to work. My new boss at the hospice was too demanding, and he only granted me a few days of bereavement leave. He ragged on me the moment I stepped through the front door, because—according to him— Hector had snuck into his room, and systematically stole and hid most of his socks. I doubted my dog could have been that smart. I guessed my boss simply lost his socks in the dryer and blamed my pet for it. Given my boss's bad mood, I scooped up Hector, made my way to the office, and logged into the computer to catch up with my email.

Reginald had messaged me. He was pursuing his passion for travel, and we made a point of getting together whenever he was in town. I always enjoyed his tales of the countries he had visited, but often his stories would conclude with him speaking of his struggles with his vices. After all these years, he still wanted to be accountable for his actions. I scheduled a get-together with him at an Earl of Latteigh.

After reading the rest of my email, I checked the bids online for Mama's dolls and almost had a heart attack! The latest cruised around $50,000 for the *Children of the Corn*, and there were still five days left of bidding.

When the auction closed, the winner had bid 80,000 bucks! *Did Mama know their value?* I had no understanding of why those hideous zombies were "priceless," but I gladly accepted the cash. All the other dolls didn't earn much—maybe enough to cover shipping costs to their new homes. At least they would be enjoyed by a new family.

Dad missed Mama, and he had dreamed of travel since arriving in Canada. I booked him an airline ticket to fly over in May, and he fell in love with Vancouver—so much so, he wanted to move from Alexandria.

While he visited, we thought it'd be fun to tour some condos, and there was one in the West end he wanted to buy—then we saw the price tag. *How on earth can people in this city afford to live here?*

My dad and I had a long chat. The market value of his home in Alexandria might've covered a third of the cost of the condo. I offered him the earnings from the dolls and promised to cash in my stocks—which were doing well—to bring him over. It would've left me skint, but it didn't matter. My father was near eighty and alone, and I wanted him closer.

He said he would think about it and went back to Alexandria—the day before my birthday.

I hoped he'd move. With so many transitory people I've met since landing here in Vancouver, it would've been nice to have had family.

The next day, I had an appointment for my bi-weekly fertility donation. The overcrowded bus drove me back from the hospital to Jumpin' Java. Like most mornings, the line extended out into the street, and I strolled into the coffee shop waving to the chorus of "Hello Larrys." The place always buzzed with noise, and today a "grunge" song sung by a woman cut through the din:

And here comes douchebag, scum of men
The cock dumped by his latest hen
How fast can this guy's black heart mend?
Cause now he's back at it again.
I'm still of little worth to him
My chances looking pretty grim
Looks like I'll never get away
From all that crap he's gotta to say

Talk at me
You make me puke

Whine at me
I'll wine from you
Shout at me
I'll shout to you:
You're such a dickhead!

"Good morning, Larry, and happy birthday!" said owner Caleb Schwarz.

I grabbed my usual chair by the window seat, removing the "Reserved for Larry" sign from the table.

"Thanks, Caleb. Fifty-two sucks a little less than fifty-one," I said, winking at him. "Does that mean I get a free coffee?"

Caleb scratched his dark hair above his ear. "I don't know. You've been coming here for years, and come to think of it, I don't think you ever paid for a coffee, or anything, for that matter. Usual bagel and cream cheese?" He beamed a smile.

Talk at me
I'm in the loo
Whine at me
You've got no clue
Shout at me
I'll scream at you:
You're such a dick…heeeeeaaaaaad

"Yes, please. By the way, what's this horrible song you keep playing?"

"I don't know much, Larry, about any of this new music the kids like. Maybe my daughter, Sarah, can tell you?" He left to serve other customers while I picked up today's paper on my table.

The May 8, 2017, headline on my paper read, "Auditions Today for Canada's Next Superstar." They were looking for all types of talented people—singers, dancers, and comedians. A slender forearm, tattooed with two butterflies, placed a plate with a bagel and a large cup of coffee in front of me.

"You going to that?" said Sarah, a smiley eighteen-year-old. I couldn't help but notice the black roots in her bleach-blonde hair, and her dark eyes sparkling mischievously in the florescent lighting. She spoke with an endearing German-Yiddish accent like her father, Caleb.

"Know what? I think I will." The article reminded me of how my mother had believed my vocal talent would earn me fame. I hadn't even looked at the sheet music I'd inherited since returning from her funeral—and she always encouraged me to sing. *That's it! I'm dedicating this contest to you, Mama.*

My star meter had all but faded out. Maybe the talent show could propel me back to the limelight. "You might not be aware," I said to Sarah, "but I'm a trained singer. I do mostly choral music, but with my skills, I can sing any style. Winning this thing should be a snap."

"That's sooo awesome. I wish I could sing. I would've joined you. Do you really think you have a shot at winning? With no disrespect, most pop singers are my age."

"I'm not old!" The horrible noise they called music blared in the background. "Well, I can certainly sing better than that crap. By the way, meant to ask you. Who wrote this nonsense? I feel bad for the poor sod she's singing about."

"C'mon, you of all people should recognize the Red Angel's music."

That's the Red Angel? Yuck.

My face must've given my feelings away.

"You don't like this? C'mon! This song's amazing!" Sarah, always the music geek, explained: "It never made the cut on any of her CDs, but apparently they put it on as an extra on her remastered twentieth-anniversary release of her first album. It just came out a few weeks ago. It's been a hit ever since and is a bit of a throwback to the grunge era." She sighed. "Wish I grew up in the '90s listening to Sarah McLachlan and the Indigo Girls. They had the best music!"

Never heard of them, and how could anyone survive on this garbage every day?

"Yeah, of course I recognize the Red Angel's music. Poor thing really needs some vocal lessons. Maybe I could teach her a thing or two."

"Yeah, right…Hey, when are you heading down to the Canada's Next Superstar audition?"

"Dunno. Maybe later this afternoon. I don't want to be there too early. The other contestants might be insecure if they know a star like me is in the competition. Hey, do you think your dad could pack me a few sandwiches to tide me over? I love his smoked meat."

"If there's a chance you'll be on TV again, you better believe he will. His business had exploded because of you, and I drive a *De Renzio Sports Coupe* because of it! Well, okay. Gotta run. Need to help the baristas."

She drives a sports car, and I only get free coffee?

I saw a young woman pass the shop's window walking down the street, holding twin dark-haired boys in tow. *They're mini versions of me!*

I leaned my head against the window to get a better look at them. I noticed they were walking towards a crowd of people in the distance. They appeared to be chasing after a tall blonde woman in a trench coat. I could only see her back, but the blonde hair, clothing style, and gait reminded me of—*Heather? Schnookums? She's here drawing a crowd?*

I left my bag and Bible on the table, bolted out of the shop, and ran after them. I gasped for air when I reached the crowd who were surrounding the woman—escape for her was impossible. I still couldn't see her face as she bent over towards a little girl. The child handed the woman a magazine and a pen.

"Schnookums!" I screamed between breaths. "It's Honey-Bear!"

She ignored me. I tried again to gain her attention.

"Honey-Bunny, it's me!" I said, hunched over catching my breath. "It's been way too long. I miss you so much!" I stretched my arms wide to offer a hug.

The woman's head turned.

Wait a sec, that's not Schnookums! This woman's way younger!

She lowered her sunglasses to the tip of her nose. Her striking green eyes glared at me.

"Dickhead?" she said. "What the hell?" The crowd laughed.

Dickhead? There was something familiar with her voice and how she said that horrid word. Couldn't place my finger on it.

"No," I said. "Sorry. I thought you were someone else." I flashed my best Larry grin and trotted back to my table at Jumpin' Java thinking about my wife, surprised I mistook someone for her. *And when did I last see Little Larry? He must be in his late twenties.*

The twins and mother walked by the coffee shop again in opposite direction.

Sarah refilled my cup, and I grabbed the newspaper.

Between my brain spinning about my wife and child, and what song I'd sing for my audition, I couldn't read another word.

By the time I arrived, the lineup for the Canada's Next Superstar auditions stretched around the block near the hockey arena. Most folk wore jeans and jackets on the cool spring afternoon. Tents were erected near the front where some people huddled around butane stoves sipping warm drinks.

Wanting to cut in front, I offered to trade my sandwiches to a couple of blond, stoned "emos" for their place in line. They snubbed me harshly, even though they complained they were starving. Pity. Caleb's smoked meat would've been a life changing experience for them.

Frustrated, I strolled towards the back. Several beachballs bounced in the air over the sea of people, soliciting approving roars from the crowd with each successive pwoomp.

I found it odd no one stopped to say hello or ask for my autograph, given my history with the Red Angel. I guessed these kids were too young to remember.

Fwop.

"Ow!"

Something bounced off my head back to the crowd.

Finally, some cheers!

"Larry?" sang a low voice with familiar lilt in the distance.

About time someone recognized me!

A hand emerged from the horde near the back. Moving closer, an older bald man with goatee waved emphatically at me. I couldn't place the face.

"Larry, it's me!" the man said pointing at his chest with both hands. "You haven't changed a bit!"

The man looked familiar. My brain cycled back connecting some old memories to this guy. *Wait! He's from Camp Kinchora, my beloved choir camp where I mastered choral singing as a kid!*

"Connor? Is that really you?" A jolt of adrenaline filled me seeing my old friend. I slapped my thighs in disbelief that he was here.

"The one and only, darling." Smiling, he opened his arms wide beckoning me with his hands.

I rushed through the crowd and embraced him in a huge bear hug. "Oh my gosh!" I said wide-eyed, releasing my grip and patting his back for several seconds. "I haven't seen you in nearly forty years!"

"I know, I know! It's amazing to see you here of all places. Guess what! I live in Victoria now. You'd love it out there." He tapped my forearm. "You know what they call it? Home of the newly wed or nearly dead!" He laughed. "I'm both!"

"Newlywed? Wow! Congratulations! I bet you landed a hottie! What's her name?"

"Honey, I'd never call my prince a lady. He wouldn't be too happy. It's Kyle."

"What? You're gay?"

Connor chuckled. "Don't worry, Kyle knows."

Connor donned a biker's hat made with black leather. He resembled a heavy metal singer I once saw on TV.

He broke our brief silence. "What a coincidence to see you out here. How long you've been out on the West Coast?"

"About thirty years. Can never go back to Ottawa." I pointed what I thought was an easterly direction.

"Hear ya, babe!" Connor patted my back. "I made my way out west in the early '90s. Couldn't make it into the music biz in the Big Smoke, so tried my luck out in Alberta. I struck oil performing in Broadway shows at the Queen Anne Boleyn Theatre in Edmonton. Did some small theatre bits, too. In between, I taught vocals. Hey! What's your story? We got a lot of time to kill. The auditions for this thing don't start until tomorrow."

"What? I thought they were today. It said so in the papers."

Connor shook his head. "Sorry hon. They permitted people to start *lining up* here today. But you can see there were a few rule breakers based on the tents up front. So, spill."

I did…and in less than an hour!

The line still didn't budge. Connor reflected on my sad tale and went into his story…

"I, too, had much heartache. It began shortly after I stopped counselling at

Camp Kinchora. I left Ottawa and fell in love with…."

My mind drifted back to the days at my Anglican choir camp.

Connor, a counsellor-in-training (CIT for short), greeted me with a warm embrace when I, as a child, first stepped off the bus at Camp Kinchora. He directed me to join a group of kids huddled around the far end of the field, then continued hugging others disembarking.

I felt a rush of freedom from my home problems, walking towards my new mates. The gang invited me to join them in a singalong, and a few minutes later, Connor led us single file down a path through the woods. The trees surrounding us swayed in a light breeze, enhancing my "spiritual connection" to the place. When we arrived at our log cabin, we dropped off our bags on assigned beds and settled into camp life.

The routine was amazing. Each morning, I dashed to be first in line for our skinny dip in the lake. The chill of the mist-covered water not only ensured I was fresh and clean—it also woke me up!

We engaged in a variety of music lessons after breakfast, and there were many sessions on church liturgy and history. I adored anything having the ol' pomp and circumstance.

Campers were organized into teams based on vocal range for afternoon hymn sing. I was thrown in with the sopranos, given I hadn't hit puberty. Connor, ever encouraging, suggested if I worked hard, I might be able to do a solo during the first Sunday morning mass. I loved that idea of performing in front of my peers in the rustic chapel in the woods.

One practice, during the first week at camp, the organist suddenly ceased his playing in the middle of "All Creatures of Our God and King." He gave a signal to the choirmaster, who stopped conducting us and advanced to the middle of the traditional choir stalls of the old sanctuary.

"What's that voice I hear squawking like a howler monkey in heat?" yelled the choirmaster, English accent flailing. A couple of lads giggled. He slammed his palm atop the wooden crest that separated him from the front row of choristers. "Someone here does not want to sing with the rest of us! Who is it?"

The choirmaster faced the first boy in the pew. "You!" He pointed. "You! Sing me the first verse."

The lad obliged.

"Beautiful. You!" He pointed to the next soprano.

Poor boy couldn't hit the high "Alleluia."

"No worries, lad. You will be singing like an angel within a fortnight."

The choirmaster continued down the row until it was my turn. He ordered me to sing the chorus.

Thinking this was my chance to audition for that solo, I closed my eyes, tightened every muscle from shoulder to buttocks, and belted out every ounce of air in my body.

Perfection!

"I've heard emus chirp better with their heads buried in the ground!"

Cackles erupted from the stalls. The choirmaster raised his hand silencing the group.

"What's your name, son?" he asked.

"I'm Larry Johnstone. Hi."

"Larry, I don't want you to belt that Alleluia as if it were your dying breath! You must hit the harmony note higher, and more controlled. You must use your breath properly… and e-nun-ci-ate all your words! Do it again!"

I tried a second time. The choirmaster still wasn't satisfied. He stared intently in my eyes.

"Need more breath from the diaphragm to hit that note! Follow me."

I concentrated on the man who encouraged me to mimic his lip motion for articulation. He also exaggerated inhaling to cue me where to breathe.

"You're getting it," the choirmaster encouraged. "One more time."

He closed his eyes, counted me in, and…

"Allelu…" Rip. "Yaaaaaaaaah." I screeched.

Two older boys behind me released the torn waistband of my underwear letting it flop over my belt. The remainder of what were my briefs were deeply entrenched between my butt cheeks. Let's say, it was a little uncomfortable.

I winced in pain while looking over my shoulder. The brats sat in their places, acting all innocent. They're faces reddened and tears rolled down their cheeks while they attempted to suppress laughter.

"Perfect!" said the choirmaster. He turned his head, and the organist also nodded his approval. "Best top C I heard you do, yet. Keep it up."

I revelled in the compliment despite my discomfort. *That solo will have my name written all over it!*

The choirmaster's kind words encouraged me to focus more on technique. I noticed a few days later my voice soared above the others. Unfortunately, those two beasts kept performing their choir stall antics. "Wedgies" became a near daily occurrence. It amazed me how they timed it without our choirmaster noticing. They ruined many pairs of my undies, including my favourite Aquaman briefs. Despite those jerks, I still received an opportunity to solo—they didn't.

Connor mentored me on being a soloist after hearing the good news. He introduced me to contemporary music, which I didn't care for. That said, there were some useful techniques I picked up from some of those tunes he liked. It helped set me apart from the rest of the gang—including some cool harmony tricks, which we practiced each morning walking to chapel.

It was a nice stroll down the dirt road with long grass and trees along its sides. The quiet, which was interrupted by Connor's and my singing, made me feel at peace, something which I never experienced at home.

"If you can choose to do anything in the world Larry, what would it be?" Connor asked once while we meandered one morning.

"I love this camp. I'd stay here forever! I can bring my wife, raise my kids, and have pets! I'd spend many days out here playing in the woods, all while singing Gregorian chants."

"What's stopping you?"

I smiled thinking about the prospect of living there—but my pleasant dreams were suddenly interrupted. The two wedgie-holics were walking towards us in the distance.

"Hey, let's do something different to soprano boy today," the bigger of the two said as the closed in. "Ever hear of a Melvin?"

"A what?" said the other.

A what?

"Melvin. It's a front wedgie. It will guarantee soprano boy will sing those high notes for a long time to come."

"Cool! Yes!" said the other.

"No!" I said retreating.

"Aw, c'mon," said the smaller boy. "Choirmaster will love your top C even more."

They surrounded me, but Connor stepped in.

"You heard him, he said no." Connor's usual soft voice carried a tone of authority.

"What are you going to do about it, *CIT*?" sneered the bigger one. He stood face to face with Connor. The lad must've been close to Conner's age, and they were the same size.

Connor's head snapped over his left shoulder, and he assumed a karate stance. Doing two quick side steps to the edge of the road followed by a round-house kick, he knocked a low hanging branch off a nearby tree. Knees bent and arms raised ready for action, he snapped his head back, glaring at the boys for what felt like an eternity.

"As I was saying…" Connor continued walking down the road with me, leaving the two bullies speechless.

"Seniors are always terrible to first year campers," said Connor once we arrived at the chapel. "It's an unfortunate tradition we are trying to correct. This will be their last year here, so I hope they didn't ruin camp for you. Sounds like you have some wonderful dreams about this place. Hate for them to be tarnished by those Neanderthals."

After lunch, during break time, Connor wanted to distract me from the altercation with the lads. He took me down to the lakeshore and taught me to fish. He brought along his Pocket Fisher Pro, a cool portable rod and wheel I coveted. It was something I had wanted ever since watching the TV ads the previous Christmas.

Seeing how much I loved trying to catch fish, Connor lent me his Pocket Fisher Pro. Every afternoon thereafter, I'd returned to the lake to enjoy the tranquility of the waters for many an hour. It made little difference that I never caught anything—the experience was all I needed.

The day before leaving camp, I secretly packed the Pocket Fisher Pro in my bag. The next morning, I ran to Connor.

"Connor, I wanted to do one last round of fishing before I left," I lied, "but I can't find your Pocket Fisher Pro anywhere! I looked all over the place for it. Someone must've stolen it!"

"Don't worry," he said, "I think I know who did it. Probably that bully. No sweat. I never really used it much, anyway."

I never saw Connor outside of camp, but we became closer friends with each passing summer. He stopped attending when he completed university. He, too, had his dreams—to become a successful rock musician.

"...I've lived in Victoria since February," continued Connor. "We love it out there."

We killed a couple more hours, reminiscing a bit about our camp days. Tiring, we sat on the ground. Connor pulled out a deck of cards, and several more folk joined us in a circle to play. Towards 9:00 p.m., the sun began to set. A chill filled the air, so one of the young ones volunteered to do a coffee run. Connor "spiked" our drinks with lovely Irish Cream. That, combined with the game by flashlight, provided much levity and fun.

A couple of them were still playing cards early the next morning. The rest of our gang were dozing, trying to make themselves as comfortable as possible on the sidewalk. Connor, returning from a morning coffee run, woke them by singing a cool medley of rock songs. *He has an amazing voice.*

Sudden screams from the front jolted us to attention.

The line finally moved a few feet.

After a couple of hours, the entrance was in sight. They registered people in groups, and they stopped me after they let Connor in. After a few minutes, I followed.

My over eighteen-hour wait was over, and it wouldn't be long until the world fell in love with me again.

Chapter Twenty-Seven
The Audition
May 2017

A man with a megaphone paced around the middle of the hockey rink. The arena had filled to two-thirds capacity, with a few more stragglers taking their places. We were all wearing large stickers with handwritten numbers on them, assigned to us by volunteers.

Our seats were near ice level. Connor grinned from ear-to-ear pulling his shirt from his chest showing off his number sixteen to the crowd. Several cameras flashed while he bounced up and down like a hyperactive child. Even though I followed Connor in line, I received the number twenty-four—they weren't sequential.

"Thank you for participating in the largest talent search ever in Canada," megaphone man addressed the crowd in sharp staccato voice over the thunderous cheers. He went through some administrative information before explaining the procedures.

"You all have numbers. Do not remove these labels, otherwise you will not be admitted to the audition. Listen for when we call your number. When called, come down to the rink and join your group. Your group will be split into four and led to the pre-audition room. We'll be calling out the number ones soon."

He did a bunch of blah-blahs for several minutes about some rules, legal nonsense, etc. Only one in five of us would have a chance to advance to audition in front of the show's producers. From there, an even smaller subset would be selected to go on the show. That's where the real fun would start. We'd be doing a second audition in front of a group of celebrity judges on TV. They're the ones who would ultimately decide who'd enter the competition. I felt badly for those poor sods who waited for days only to be told they had to go home.

"The process will take a while," the megaphone man concluded. "If you are feeling hungry, help yourself to the sandwiches, donuts, and all the coffee you can drink in the pre-audition room—courtesy of our sponsor, Earl of Latteigh."

It looked like I'd be spending the better part of the day here, so I napped.

Megaphone man woke me. "Group sixteen, you're next!"

"Wish me luck." Connor waved while he departed.

I didn't have to wait too much longer—the leader called my number an hour later.

Split into four groups and assigned a team lead from the show, we were herded like cattle to a large room in the arena. It was packed with wall-to-wall people hustling about in excited commotion. Curtains sectioned off four enclosed areas. My group lined up outside one.

"You'll be ushered in one at a time where we'll film a brief video clip of you," said our lead. "We'll signal you to start. Simply state your name, where you're from, your age, and something interesting about yourself. Be yourselves in front of the camera. Be fun. Be unique.

"Most importantly…be brief. You only have two minutes, and the time will fly by faster than you'd expect. We'll signal you when you have fifteen seconds left—so finish up quick. We cut the cameras sharp at two minutes. Any questions?"

I raised my hand. "Hi, I'm Larry Johnstone. I'm a national celebrity, and I'm thinking I'm entitled to a two-*hour* interview and a ticket straight to the competition."

"Thanks for your comment," the lead said. "Next question?"

There weren't any so the lead opened the curtain. The first in line entered.

The waiting was annoying. *Doesn't anyone recognize me?*

A man finally invited me in to take a seat in front of a camera mounted on a tripod. Three people—wearing headphones—worked the lights and equipment. A middle-aged woman, wearing a business suit, walked in and stood behind the crew. The tiny space was crammed by our five bodies.

A crew man cued me in.

"Hi, I'm Larry Johnstone!" I spoke clear and slow to ensure nothing would be misunderstood. "I'm thirty-five" — *did someone cough?* — "and am originally from Ottawa, where I dated many women who all dumped me. I donate sperm for the betterment of humanity." *Unique enough?* I placed my face directly in the camera lens and waved.

The woman tapped the shoulder of the camera man, drew the curtain, and exited.

How dare she leave during my shoot?

Recovered from my brief distraction, I continued. "Uh, uh, oh, what I meant to say is that I have fathered many…"

"CUT!"

Filming stopped.

"Where was my fifteen second cue?"

"If you didn't shove your face so close to the lens, you would've seen me waving. Please wait a sec."

A couple of moments later, the woman returned. "Larry Johnstone?" She smiled ear to ear.

"Yes."

"To confirm, you're *the* Larry Johnstone? Weren't you the guy in the news about ten years ago?"

"Yeah. What gives?"

"I knew it! I'm Jeri Wildman. I'm one of the producers." Jeri smiled, shook my hand, and handed me a blue ticket. "Keep this, Larry. Congratulations! We're going to bypass all the steps of our process and place you on TV to audition in front of our celebrity judges! How does that sound?"

Someone who recognizes my talent and charisma. But…

"What about the song I prepared?"

"Save it for later. We'll need you to fill out some forms for the TV auditions."

She summoned her assistant, a lad in his late teens, to escort me on a long walk around the perimeter of the building to an isolated section of the arena. A group of young people were lining up outside a door marked "Registration." They all excitedly waved their blue tickets to a camera. My escort whispered to a security guard who nodded, and I joined the back of the line. It advanced slowly into the room.

When my turn came around, a woman in her thirties welcomed me from behind her desk. She requested my ticket, and I completed many forms filled with boring lawyer jargon. The woman explained they were confidentiality agreements, meaning that from this point forward, I couldn't legally talk about the show without the permission of the producers, and all film and interviews could be used by the show any way they saw fit.

Everything needed to be a secret, including the contents of the manilla envelope she passed to me.

I opened it.

The official invitation to audition in front of celebrity judges on TV.

The secret location for the audition ended up being in a downtown hotel's conference room. The past week had flown by in nervous anticipation for the event, and I arrived early for the official show taping. Sitting alone, I read some *Oedipus* to kill time.

I had this weird feeling my every move was being watched. Several TV cameras, perched around the room, were pointing straight at me. Ignoring them, I put my book away and reflected on a Bible verse from Timothy I had read in Jumpin' Java that morning. It talked about how an athlete isn't declared a victor unless they compete by the rules. *Pfft. Rules here are simple. I sing, I win.*

Contestants filed in. A familiar face came through the door.

"Connor!" I stood. "You made it through!"

"Never a doubt!" Connor said, giving me a deep hug. He explained how long he had to wait to meet the producers after the initial video interview. It was a long time, so I was glad to miss all that nonsense!

"I'm so happy," I said. "I need some competition for this thing. BA-HA-HA!"

The producer who helped me during the auditions stepped to the front of the group and interrupted our banter.

"Good day. I'm Jeri Wildman, a producer on Canada's Next Superstar. Congratulations! You've all made it to the next level of our show." She clapped her hands, and we all applauded.

"Would you believe nearly 10,000 people auditioned in Vancouver, and you're among the few who have the privilege to perform in front of our celebrity judges. In a few minutes, we'll be distributing personalized badges, and coupons from our sponsor, Bruce's Burger Emporium. It's a small thank you for coming out and making it this far."

They handed out the envelopes containing coupons. "I'm going to be famished after this," I said. "Wanna celebrate by eating some of Bruce's beef? They have amazing shakes, too."

"A most brilliant idea!" Connor glanced at the vouchers. "Uh, wait a sec. Did you read this?"

Get 30% off any purchase of $100 or more, or free beverage with order of $15. Offer valid until May 23, 2017.

"What's the date today?" I asked.

"May 22," said Connor.

"How much food do you think you can eat?"

"Well, given that the cost of Bruce's overpriced burgers is about fifteen bucks, maybe I can at least get a free drink."

"No, worries, I'll buy you a meal," I said. "I can take advantage of the coupon and buy some extras for some friends at the hospice."

We chatted a bit. Even though I arrived first, they called us in a random order. Connor only waited fifteen minutes but promised to meet me at the restaurant for dinner.

After 1:00 p.m., a security guard led me from the room and down the hall to a private elevator. He unlocked it, and we ascended to the top floor.

"Welcome, Mr. Johnstone," a woman greeted. "Please wait here. We're all settling back in after lunch hour."

Staff were busy positioning cameras, wiping tables, and adjusting the lighting. After a few minutes, my greeter showed me where to stand for my audition, about twenty feet in front of a desk. Two familiar men sat behind it facing me. A third chair remained vacant. The windowed backdrop contained a beautiful scenic view of the city.

"You!" I yelled out to the handsome one in the centre.

"Eee HEE-HEE hee hee," the middle-aged man cackled. "Househusband! What on earth are you doing here?"

The other judge was a guy from that *Dildo* show. He spoke with a strong Newfoundlander accent. "I remember you. You sang that lovely tune for us." He looked down at the paper. "Larry Johnstone, eh? Hee hee, this is certainly a surprise."

"Sure is," said Sven beaming a sarcastic smile. "I haven't seen this guy in years. I miss you, Larry."

Swine.

The Newfoundlander spoke. "Hey, you said we're on a busy schedule. No time for chit-chat." He glared at the empty chair. "Where the hell's she at? She in the bathroom again? She's spent more time in it than out this morning!"

"Be patient, man. She needs to go often in her condition, you know—and besides, we just got back from lunch," replied Sven.

I knew all about women's "conditions," because they used them as excuses to get out of dating me.

The Newfoundlander lifted the clipboard. "Says here you like to wallop the cod and read Greek mythology."

"Eee HEE-HEE hee hee, cod you say? That can't be what's written." Sven nudged him while peering over his shoulder. "According to Larry's wife, he's more like a minnow." He glanced at his watch. "What's taking my dear so long this time?"

He has his "dear" here? It couldn't possibly be Heather, could it?

"I wouldn't make fun of my sperm donation, Sven," I said, "or make any cracks about my manliness." I placed my hands on my hips. "Remember? I impregnated your *dear* with Lars!"

Sven's eyes narrowed. "Are you on crack? Lars is my child."

He pissed me off with his lie.

After an awkward silence, an idea hit me.

"No way. I'm going to prove it."

"What in blazes are you babbling about, Larry?" Sven replied.

"Tomorrow," I pointed to him, then to me. "Fertility clinic at Golden Oaks hospital. I have to make a donation and will permit you to take my DNA sample. That'll prove I'm *Little Larry's* father."

Sven's eyebrows raised. "Are you fucking with me? That's absurd. I'm not going to put my son through this."

Dildo man interjected. "Larry, you don't need to go to a fertility clinic for a DNA sam—"

"Tut tut," interrupted Sven placing his hand on the Newfoundlander's arm. He looked over at the camera, beamed a charismatic smile. "You know what?" he said. "Why the hell not?" He stood and pointed at me. "Larry? You're on. We'll play your silly little game. Have the hospital put aside a sample for us to test, and let's end this nonsense." He looked back to the camera. "You're getting all this on film, right?"

The man behind the lens nodded.

A tall blonde woman entered wearing an oversized red dress.

The woman who I mistook for Schnookums...she's pregnant...and she's Sven's "dear?"

Sven attempted to give her his "European" greeting by kissing her full on the mouth. The woman placed her hand on his lips and stepped back.

"Whoa, whoa, whoa," she said turning her head and feigned gagging. "What on earth did you eat for lunch?"

The woman completely ignored me and sat in her chair, removed her blonde wig, and placed it on the desk. Her crimson red hair was braided and pinned.

"You know the rules." She patted the chair next to hers. "No kissy, more 'sit'-ty. We have work to do."

Sven obliged.

She looked past the Swede and did an aggressive swiping motion at the cameraman. "You'd better not be filming this." He didn't really react.

A hairstylist and make-up artist rushed in, stood in front of her, and worked with alacrity to prepare the third judge for filming. They partially blocked the woman from my view while they did their work.

"Don't have time for a full treatment," said the stylist. "Maybe a ponytail— and a hat? Is that nice Fedora around here somewhere?"

The red-headed woman dove into some documents in front of her while her two helpers performed their magic. They didn't have to do much—just a few floofs for the hair, and some dibs and dabs of foundation. A stagehand brought the hat and placed it on the woman's head. She barely budged from her reading.

"Hey," she said the moment the stylist finished. "I'm dying for an ice cream sandwich and some of those funky garlic-cheese chips. You know...the one's we had at the Winnipeg auditions? I hope they sell them here. Can you get some?" She smiled innocently and blinked at her helper to her left.

The man blushed, nodded, and rushed off to a back room.

"But you just had lunch, dear," said Sven.

She waved Sven off, dismissed her team, and returned to her papers.

"Wait a sec," she said. "NO!" She emphatically pointing to her document. "What's this?"

Mr. Dildo and Sven smirked from their seats.

The woman stared up at me. Her glaring green eyes had laser-like aim.

That's the Red Angel!

"No!" she said in disbelief, doing a doubletake. "What the hell is Dickhead doing here?" she demanded. *There's that name she's been calling me since her childhood!* She forced a laugh to her co-judges. "This is a joke, right?"

The two men tried to contain their laughter.

She turned to me. "Not…funny!" She re-read the paper in front of her. "Shit! This is not a joke? I thought it was him I saw yesterday…" She turned to her colleagues. "You really want him to sing? Have you not heard him? He sounds like the wrong end of an elephant."

Nice…

"Eee HEE-HEE hee hee. Angel, dear, Larry has just been telling us that he's the *father* of your child." Sven said with a devious glint in his eye.

Liar!

"Wait, what?" I retorted. "No! I never…"

The Red Angel flushed in a millisecond and exploded from behind the desk, making a beeline for me. She raised her hand and wound it back as she drew near.

I held out my palms in front of me. *What's making her so hostile?*

"No, wait," I said.

Sven, with the speed of a rabbit, intervened from behind, and the production crew created a human barrier separating us. I couldn't figure out what was going on.

"You deluded douche-canoe-faced dickhead!" she said.

Such a foul mouth!

The woman raised a fist, but Sven whispered something to her. She pirouetted around and rushed off stage in a huff.

Things calmed. "What the hell just happened?" I asked. No one responded. "Do I sing now?" I broke out into my rendition of "All Shook Up" by Elvis. I was doing a fabulous job when I heard a woman grrr in exasperation from backstage.

What's going on back there? Maybe the Red Angel can't hear me.

I sang louder, and the Newfoundlander gestured to a security guard who walked over and escorted me to the elevator.

Jerks. I'll show them!

I yelled over my shoulder, "Sven…Tomorrow! Be ready for the bad news!"

The show's producer pressed the down button.

"That was great, Larry, but we need to move on."

"When will the live competitions begin?"

"Sorry, Larry, it's the end of the road for you, bud. But thanks. That'll make great television!"

The elevator doors opened, and I walked in with the security guard.

He didn't make sense. *Why would the best thing for his show not be invited to continue?*

I stormed out to the street.

"Goody," exclaimed Connor at Bruce's later. "Look what I've got!"

He produced an envelope and extracted a coveted "Rainbow Ticket." Connor was advancing to the live competition.

He let me read it while we waited for our meal.

"I'm finally going to realize my dream of being a rock star," said Conner. "If I can get down to the final ten, I'll have a record cut for sure! How'd you do?"

How the hell did he get the ticket, and I didn't?

I tossed it back to him. I didn't feel like telling him I didn't even audition. "Congratulations. But aren't we sworn to secrecy? I shouldn't really know about this. Nor you should know about what happens to me." I hoped my tone sounded positive.

"Aw, c'mon. We're both in the show," he said, "A little shop talk won't hurt. Hey, did you see the Red Angel? Did you know she is—"

The image of the Red Angel's green eyes and calling me that horrid nickname flashed through my mind.

"—fooled me with her blonde hair?" I said, finishing his sentence.

"Not what I was going to say, but no, her hair is red," said Connor.

"Yes, yes. I know. And yes, I saw the Red Angel. That nasty woman practically attacked me…totally unprovoked! I don't know what I ever did to her. Did I not mention to you while we waited in line for the auditions that I saw that crass woman, wearing her blonde wig, walking about in public outside Jumpin' Java the other day?"

Connor shook his head. I was a little surprised I hadn't, given how annoyed she made me at that encounter.

"Well, I ran after her in the street, thinking she was Heather, then she called me dickhead for no apparent reason." I shuddered at the sound of that name.

"What? You of all people didn't recognize her? Even with the blonde hair? Honestly, given her career the past decade, maybe not the best disguise for her in public."

"What do you mean, 'not the best disguise in public?'" I said, frustrated. "It sure as hell fooled me."

"Have you been living in a box, my friend? The Red Angel changed her image years ago. Don't you follow music at all? She fronted that Scandinavian metal band, *Isängel.*"

"*Isängel?*"

"Yes…means Ice Angel. They were amazing! I followed them closely. One of their founding members was in a punk band called *Rännrottorna*. Ever hear of them?"

The name rang a bell…but couldn't remember from where. I shook my head.

"Anyway, the Red Angel joined *Isängel* as their lead singer. The platinum blonde hair worked well with her stage gimmick. She's back to red, now that she's doing her Red Angel act again. I guess you're right. With all the hype she's getting about her upcoming twentieth anniversary tour, many people might've already forgotten her metal phase. It was years ago, anyway."

A waiter dropped off our food.

Connor talked about his successful audition in front of the judges while I daydreamed about my Schnookums.

"The Red Angel is such a sweetie!" said Connor. "She's so kind. Said nothing but nice things about my singing. She said my voice reminded her of someone from the New Kids on the Block. Who knew a metal queen would like boy bands?" chuckled Connor.

He took a bite of his burger.

"And she's so radiant in her condition," he said.

There's that "condition" word again.

"Must've been nice to meet up with the 'mother of your child' again, eh? Is her second one yours, too?" Connor winked.

His snide comment irritated me, and he continued to bore me for the next half hour talking about his admiration for the Red Angel.

"Thanks for treating me out," said Connor, wiping his mouth. "I must go to the loo. Can you order me a milkshake for dessert?"

I summoned the waiter and ordered.

"Oh," I said, "can you place those extra burgers I ordered in a doggie bag? And please use this coupon and bring me the bill."

The waiter looked it over. "I'm sorry, but this only applies to the new Bruce's that just opened in the east-end. It's not valid here."

He dropped the vouchers on the table and went back to prepare the milkshakes.

Connor's rainbow ticket stared at me from the table.

I had dedicated the show to Mama. I can't be booted out now.

The Bible verse from this morning returned to me. *I can only win if I play by the rules.*

Screw rules, I'm winning this competition.

I snatched the ticket, left the coupons behind, and ran out the restaurant.

Dine and dash, baby. Dine and dash.

"Morning, Margo," I said, entering the clinic late the next morning. "I have a special delivery to make," I said. "Super urgent. My room's clean?"

"But Larry," Margo spoke with a slow and deliberate timber, "your next appointment isn't for another two days." Margo turned her head to the wall away from me and smiled.

"Don't jerk my chain. You know I rescheduled yesterday afternoon."

Margo nodded at the wall.

"Can't talk, now," I said. "Was there a tall Swedish fellow who came earlier, looking like a buffoon?"

"You mean Sven?" Margo sighed. "He's so dishy." She turned her head to the wall and smiled again. "Yes, he came by earlier to make an appointment for himself. I think he's coordinating a DNA test for his son, too. He's really determined to prove you wrong, Larry."

He won't.

"We have some paperwork to complete," Margo giggled like a little girl and blushed.

"What's up with you today? My word. Is the room free or not? This is an emergency."

"Yes, yes. I know. Sven told me all about it."

She raised my usual yellow bin labelled "Larry Johnstone's Donations" high above the counter, pointed at it, and faced the wall again. "To receive your sample we'll test." She turned and put the box down.

"Good," I said. "How long to get the results?"

"Shouldn't be too long," Margo sang out in an uncharacteristic lilt. "Here. Sign the consent form to permit you to release your sample to Sven. He mentioned something about there'll be some 'impartial judges' assessing the DNA." Margo turned her head to the wall and smiled again.

"What's with that wall?" I asked. Nothing had changed on it—just the same old posters explaining invitro fertilization. "Oh, just give me a pen."

Why can't forms be in plain English?

I signed it without reading. "Is the room ready?"

"Yes, of course, Larry. Remember, fifteen minutes. Hospital policy."

"Yeah, yeah."

I slammed the door shut and began my usual warmups including ten deep knee bends, and thirty seconds of arm and wrist rotations. Nice and loose, I dropped my drawers and plumped myself on the recliner and began "the drill."

Five minutes later. Nothing happened. *What's wrong with me?*

For the first time in my life, I panicked over my chore. I had to prove I'm

Lars' father. *Sven took my Heather. Sven was unfaithful to her. Sven is a lousy dad to my son.*

At that moment, I remembered Sven's cold blue eyes glaring at me in the audition room. *They sure looked like Lars'…*

Deflated at the possibility I'd been duped all these years, I sank back in my chair.

No! I need proof!

Bold and new measures were needed to complete the task at hand and prove him wrong.

I reflected on tempos of songs I loved. Closing my eyes, I began to hum the "Blue Danube."

"Dum-dum-dum-dum-dum.
Fap-fap, fap-fap.
Dum-dum-dum-dum-dum.
Fap-fap, fap-fap."

I continued my rhythmic beating until the climatic chorus a few minutes later, but alas, no special delivery. *What the hell?*

I tried another. Ravel's "Bolero." I sang and accompanied it with a one-two-three-one rhythm. After couple of minutes, I collapsed, my wrist sore and strained. *This never happens to me!*

Knock-knock-knock. "Five minutes Larry," said Margo.

"Damn it!" I yelled back. "Okay."

Gotta perform under pressure.

The "Flight of the Bumblebee" popped into my head. I sang it hyper-tempoed, and again, matched the rhythm of the song with my beat. Sure enough:

"OOOOOAAAAAAAH! Damn, that was AMAZING!" I yelled.

The sample size proved small but enough for the task.

"That'll do," I said aloud shaking the bottle around.

I cleaned up and left the room. Enrique was mopping the floor outside the door.

"You sounded like you were having a good time!" he said, laughing.

I ignored the janitor and handed the jar to Margo.

"I think that's a record low for you." *There she goes smiling at the wall again!*

"Doesn't matter. Should do the trick."

"Can I ask a favour?" She stood and wrapped her arm around my shoulder. "Face the wall and smile."

I humoured her. She held the bottle between us, then returned it to my special sperm storage bin.

Weird.

Chapter Twenty-Eight
Canada's Next Superstar
July - September 2017

I reread the instructions on the Rainbow Ticket for the millionth time. It'd been a couple months since the audition, and I had pestered Margo each subsequent visit to confirm if the DNA testing had been completed. Every time, she said it hadn't, saying something about the lab awaiting Sven's sample.

My anxiety mounted knowing the filming for the competition would take place in Vancouver in a couple of weeks. Only twelve people earned the right to compete in the regional final—most of the contestants were singers.

Reading the instructions one last time, I flipped the ticket to the front. It simply read "Congratulations Connor O'Connor."

Hmmm. There might be a problem. I stood in front of my mirror and removed my glasses. I don't look like Connor. *Need to change that.* I reached down for my handy dandy electric razor, grabbed a lock of my mullet, and stared at my reflection. *Can I really remove something that has been part of me forever?*

My life flashed in front of my eyes. At fifty-two, I accomplished much more than the average Joe, so why was I changing?

I must win the competition—for Mama. To do that, I need to look like Connor. I closed my eyes while I shaved my head bald.

Not bad! Should've done this years ago! Now, I have just enough time to grow a goatee and pierce my right ear.

Funny, no one asked me for any identification when I entered the theatre. I just presented my Rainbow Ticket to the security guard, and poof, was in. A producer approached me backstage.

"You've lost quite a bit of weight, and shrunk a few inches, Connor."

"I followed a grapefruit-based diet. Must look my best for TV, darling." I pointed to my glasses. "Also need my specs."

After running through a pre-show routine, including more paperwork, make-up, and general instructions, I joined the other contestants in a soundproof waiting area. They were mostly young adults—and highly immature—spending most of their time staring brainlessly into their phones and cackling like hyenas. They all stopped what they were doing when one of the show's producers entered and escorted the first contestant out—a young girl who had taps on her shoes. We all cheered for her, but I started to feel a little nervous. *This is actually happening!*

Time dragged while I awaited my turn, and I had no clue what was happening on stage. All I could do was watch one contestant after another, leaving the room.

A stagehand and a second man with a camera mounted on his shoulder entered. "Connor, you're next. When we cut to commercial, we'll be filming in this room. Wave and smile brightly for the camera."

I did, and they guided me to stand alone in the dark, offstage, in the back. My nerves intensified, and I felt my body begin to tremor. I breathed in and out a few times in attempt to relax. It didn't help, and my anxiety mounted.

No one has asked me what I'm going to sing! Panic set in. *What if they play a song Connor chose? I don't listen to his music!*

An image of Reginald staring disapprovingly at me and a surge of guilt suddenly replaced my nerves and excitement.

Will everyone think I'm Connor? Surely, they'll see I'm not him...and this was Connor's dream, not mine. I wouldn't be able to live with myself. I'm going to fess up in front of everyone.

Before I could make my announcement to the world, my voice boomed over the loudspeaker.

"Hi, I'm Larry Johnstone!"

What the...?

A giant screen above me filled the audience with coloured light.

"I'm thirty-five and am originally from Ottawa, where I dated many women who all dumped me. I donate sperm for the betterment of humanity."

Previous contestant's had video clips introducing them before they performed—that wasn't Connor's!

I ached to step out from behind to watch the video, but a producer lifted a palm forcing me to stay.

Laughter poured in from the crowd.

I heard some rhythmic grunts over the loudspeakers—like the sound one makes while lifting weights. Snickers smattered from among the horde.

It bothered me that I couldn't see what was going on. An orchestra kicked in playing the Blue Danube. I closed my eyes savouring each beautiful note.

"Dum-dum-dum-dum-dum." The instruments played.

Silence.

"Fap-fap, fap-fap," my voice sang.

What the...

The orchestra conveniently dropped out to for each fap line but doubled me for the other bits. Curiosity killed me. I bullied my way past the producer, rushed to the edge of the darkened stage, and turned my head to face the giant screen above.

Videos cycled filling the screen, synced to my singing and timed to the famous waltz: a time-lapsed sunrise; a beaver yawning; a wolf sniffing a tree stump; a chimpanzee sitting up from a lying position; a silent movie clip of a man's head with handlebar moustache slowly opening his eyes...

Then "Bolero" kick in. The montage continued: handlebar man slowly smiling—eyes looking left, then right; chimpanzee standing erect; plants straightening to face the sun; a male gymnast slowly dipping up and down on the parallel bars; bunnies hopping around; handlebar moustache man boarding a train; the locomotives pistons start their motion...

My "Flight of the Bumblebee" rendition flooded the theatre. The locomotive's pistons moved faster and faster; wildebeest in high-speed galloped down a grassy plain; a group of Russian men squat danced and split jumped; the chimpanzee, joined by some of his friends, bounced up and down at torrential tempos; another close up of handlebar moustache man—eyes closed, face straining; pistons moving faster and faster; llama braying; moustache man sweating, now expressing enormous struggle; bear scratching it's back; train; Russians; pistons...

My singing cut to the sounds and images of a volcano erupting.

Silence.

"Damn, that was AMAZING!" my voice cut through the sound system.

A tree fell in the woods; plants shrivelled; a donkey collapsed to the ground; moustache man climbed into bed and blew a candle out.

Black. Still. Quiet.

The video resumed with me leaving my room in the clinic and froze on a still image of Margo and me smiling, holding my sample bottle between us. A recording of my voice suddenly boomed through the theatre's speakers. "That'll do," it said, breaking the silence and concluding the film clip.

The house lights flicked on to a laughing crowd. Mr. Dildo and Sven were facing me. The third judge's chair was empty.

"I've never seen such talent," said the Newfoundlander judge. "Your vocals were...inspired. The audience loves you, Larry."

They do? Why?

"Eee HEE-HEE hee hee," cackled Sven. "That was the most creative act I've ever seen. Such fresh rendition of some classics. Brilliant Larry."

I stood, stunned. *The audience isn't loving you; they're mocking you. Wait. Where's the Red Angel?*

Sven noticed me staring at the empty judge's chair. "You looking for her? Sorry, but she stayed at home."

Sven faced the audience. "You probably are all wondering why the Red Angel isn't here with us tonight…but to find out why, you'll all have to tune in to our national finale in Toronto for the biggest and wildest ending ever seen on Canadian television. But I do have a small surprise tonight, of sorts, that will rock the nation."

Sven turned to me. "Larry, I give you your props. You had me a tad worried during the audition." He turned back to the audience. "You see, my ex-partner, Heather Mackenzie, would do anything to be with me—an international celebrity and multi-millionaire. I wouldn't put anything past her, including telling Larry here, that my Lars is his son—I mean, who wants to change diapers when you're in your twenties? I didn't." He produced an envelope and threw it like a Frisbee across the stage. "There it is, Larry. The proof that Lars is *my* child—and DNA tests, for your information, can simply be done by a cotton swab in your cheek."

The envelope lay still on the stage. For the first time in a long time, I had sympathy for my wife for pursuing a false dream with this jerk. She never actually said Lars was my son. I only assumed—and she did say Sven had little interest in caring for a baby.

"But I'm sorry to say, my dear Larry," Sven continued, "that we cannot advance you to the national finals." He turned to face the camera and yelled with excitement. "Because Larry stole the Rainbow Ticket from our real finalist—Connor O'Connor."

I hadn't seen Connor backstage with the other contestants. *Maybe he was in another soundproof room?*

Heavy metal blared through the sound system and the audience erupted as Connor took the stage with a blood curdling scream. Dressed in long leather trench coat and new earrings, he looked the part, rocking out on some horrible piece of music.

And I had dedicated my "singing" to Mama—not this humiliating display of my donating sperm.

Sven! You ruined my wife! And you ruined my life.

Angry beyond words, I flew towards the Swede, but two security guards intercepted me and escorted me off the stage while Connor continued singing. They grabbed me by my arms and forced me to follow them out of the studio and down a hallway. One guard opened the door to a small room with white walls and florescent lighting. The second dragged me in and directed me to sit in a chair in the corner.

"What am I doing here?" I asked.

"You're gonna wait and see if they'll press charges."

"Charges? For what?"

"Really? Think about it," said the guard before he left.

I leaned back in the chair and waited, not knowing what on earth I could've done that warranted an arrest. *This is all Sven's fault. He humiliated me!* It didn't take long for the door to open again, and Connor, still sweating from his performance, entered the room.

He glared, and the silence made me uncomfortable. I tried to break the ice.

"I'm so glad to see you, Connor. Did you see what the swine, Sven, did? I'm going to be the laughingstock of Canada!"

Connor placed his hands on his hips. "I don't believe this...that's the first thing that comes out of your mouth? You really disgust me." His tone was cold and direct, and his response took me aback.

"Larry, when we met at camp all those years ago, I felt badly for you because of those bullies. Do you remember how it felt to be picked on by them all the time?"

I didn't like it.

He continued. "And you know how you repaid me? You stole my Pocket Fisher Pro."

I was about to protest, but Connor wagged his finger at me.

"Don't deny it. I know you did. But given what you went through that first week at camp, I pretended to believe your story that the bullies took it. And after all these years, Larry, and through all your experiences living in a shelter, I thought you might've grown up a bit. But you stole from me again!

"I'm going to ask you, Larry, to instead of pretending to be me, imagine what it's like to *be* me at this very moment."

I didn't know how to put myself in his shoes.

"Imagine a close friend taking you out to dinner and deserting you to pay a huge bill. How would you feel? Imagine winning a ticket to this talent show for a dream opportunity of a lifetime, only for it to be snatched away by a thief who says you're his pal. And finally, Larry, imagine what it's like to see someone attempt to steal one's identity. I'd be surprised if I wasn't the first."

You were the third...I stole Peter's for the insurance, and Rick's stage personae, Dick Wank, just to score some dates.

The guard entered the room. "You have to go back on stage, Connor, they're going to announce the winner."

Connor acknowledged, and before he turned to leave, he said, "Larry, I have a forgiving heart, so I won't press charges, but I will tell you this. I'm completely done. I had a high opinion of you—once—and I cherished our friendship. That's gone up in flames. I never want to speak to you again."

He stormed out of the room.

I sat alone in the room, doing my best to imagine myself in Connor's shoes after what I put him through. It took a moment, but I finally understood what I had done—and deeply regretted it.

The men at the hospice crowded around the TV in the recreation room watching the Canada's Next Superstar West Coast regional final, airing after Labour Day. Word circulated around the internet of a mystery performer, arousing everyone's curiosity. I was still in a funk about what I did to Connor, and in turn, what Sven did to me, but I, too, was interested in what the fuss was all about. *Maybe the Red Angel will sing something?*

It didn't take too long to discover to my dismay that I was the one behind the show's hype. The room erupted in laughter and applause when Sven concluded my "performance" by complementing me for the "fresh new sounds." I didn't stick around to be mocked and went up to my room with Hector. I cuddled him while I reflected on my situation.

Jerks. The hospice hadn't been the same since Reginald retired. The new staff were cold, the residents were unfriendly, and the place had become impersonal and lost its charm. My stocks were paying high dividends, though—*maybe I should move into my own place? But Vancouver is so expensive...Maybe I can sue the Canada's Next Superstar?*

Beyond angry, I hunted for the contract I had signed with the show but couldn't find it anywhere. Never in my wildest dreams I'd have thought they'd air my humiliating "performance." After an hour of frustration, I couldn't find it.

The show had a contact number on their website. The best I could do was phone and leave a message. *Who knows if they'll return my call?*

After a sleepless night, I meandered down the rain-soaked streets to Jumpin' Java late the next morning. The regulars lined up outside the small shop— umbrellas open. Pissed that my usual chorus of "Hello Larrys" was replaced with jeers and laughing, I assumed my usual place in a wicked mood and snatched up the morning paper.

Not much on the main page... the usual coverage about President Trump and our friends down south. There was an article about Canada's Next Superstar. Connor won! My heart filled with excitement that my friend fulfilled his dream, but I saddened immediately. *My former friend.*

A thin forearm with two small butterfly tattoos placed a bagel and cream cheese in front of me.

"I almost missed you coming in," said the shop owner's daughter. Sarah had dyed her hair to match her dark eyebrows. "I didn't hear the good morning 'Hello Larrys...' and why do you look so sad?"

"You didn't watch me on TV last night?"

"Noooo," the waitress exclaimed in surprised. "It was on? How could I've missed it—especially since Sven Lindgaard was promoting a 'special' performance all over the place."

I cringed when Sarah mentioned the Swede's name. Yes, Sven had been advertising Canada's Next Superstar on TV, the radio, the newspapers, and the internet. It was everywhere. I sighed, munched my bagel, and resumed reading the article about the show...

"The Blue Danube Fap's a hit and can be watched with the rest of the show online."

What the...?

The article contained some usual nonsense about my history and lifelong sperm donations, the show, and interviews with network executives. My episode was creating a storm on social media ranging from offended people, claiming there should be more appropriate content on a family show, to those thinking my audition the funniest thing since the restaurant scene in *When Harry Met Sally.*

The execs separated themselves from the controversy, citing that Sven had full responsibility for the show's content. Of course, the Swedish interloper wasn't available for comment, but his staff mentioned my signing non-disclosure agreements had permitted them to use all footage they had collected, and the censors agreed the material was suitable for prime-time TV. *Why don't I read documents I sign?* The hospital hadn't made comment yet to their role in the show.

*The hospital...*I ditched my paper and dashed out the door to catch a westbound bus.

"Where's Margo?" I asked the young receptionist sitting behind the desk of the fertility clinic. Her bunny-filled scrubs reflected her youthfulness. Nonplussed, she broke her trance from her phone.

"Huh?" she asked, grey eyes half closed.

"Margo. You know, the old bat who is usually sitting in your spot."

"Who?"

"Oh for Pete's sake." *Must be new. Never seen her before.* "How about Enrique?"

"Enrique?"

"Will you stop it? I've had better conversations with doorstops."

The wall Margo stared at during my last visit still displayed the invitro posters. I made a beeline towards it. *Must've been a camera hidden there.* I placed my face against the photo and rubbed my hands along its surface. All I saw were some fallopian tubes and blurred text.

"Sir," said the woman, "I must ask you to stop…"

"There must have been a wiretap in my room."

I bolted down the hall. A shut door didn't deter me from going into the room where I donated sperm for so many years. A balding man, maybe in his thirties, sat at attention covering his privates with a largish cell phone. He clumsily reached over the chair and grabbed his pants. He placed them over his lap while I left him alone. *Oops, should've knocked.*

Returning to the reception, a familiar sound filled the hallway.

"Dum-dum-dum-dum-dum…Fap-fap, fap-fap."

The young receptionist chuckled staring at her phone. On seeing me, she quickly hid it under the counter out of sight.

"It's been a while," I said.

"For what?"

There she goes again.

"Since I last donated."

"*You're* a sperm donor?" She covered her mouth supressing a giggle.

I pointed to my face "Don't you know who I am?"

She stared with tight frown for several second. "No. Should I?"

"I can't believe this. Don't you watch TV or follow the news?"

"No."

"I've had enough of this."

"Are you done?" She lifted a clipboard. "I'm really quite busy."

Determined to search the room, I requested an appointment to provide a donation. The young woman broke down in laughter!

"You must be near sixty!"

"What?" My frustration meter peeked.

"Okay, okay, what's your name?"

"Johnstone. Larry Johnstone."

The receptionist typed something in the computer. She made a clicking sound and nodded her head while waiting for a response on screen.

"Nope," she said.

"Nope?"

"Yeah, nope. No such person as Larry Johnstone."

I couldn't take it anymore. "I've been coming here for over twenty years."

"Well, maybe you can make an appointment to see a doctor."

"I haven't seen a doctor since turning forty." It occurred to me, there might've been a reason for that.

"Oh," said the woman, "that might explain why you're not in the system. Your records would've been archived long ago."

What about all my donations over the years?

"That's impossible." I ran around the desk and began poking around for my special yellow bin.

The woman yelped, picked up the phone, and within a minute a burly security guard appeared.

"I think it's time for you to leave."

I begrudgingly followed him out the door, yelling back at the young woman to find my bin.

A week later, my "performance" was still trending on the web. The popularity of my marijuana song on the internet paled in comparison to the "Blue Danube Fap." The video yielded hundreds of thousands of viewings in such a short period of time. It completely overshadowed Connor's winning the regional final and led to a new trend, which I discovered when I logged into *Larrynet* one morning.

People were finding pictures of me online and manipulated them to make me have all sorts of distorted sex faces. They were posted everywhere, filling my news feed. Some of the images were also used for millions of memes, and "that'll do" turned into a huge catch phrase.

You'd think I would've loved all this attention. Quite the opposite. It made me want to permanently disconnect. Before I logged off, a message popped in from Jacquie. I hadn't heard from her since before the show, and she usually said the magic words that could lift me out of any funk. It only had one sentence.

> *Larry, I didn't have the words to write sooner. I watched the show. I'm so disappointed in you.*

Her message broke my heart.

Reginald was in town, so we grabbed a lunch at a posh fish and chips place. Reginald loved it. They presented the meal on newspaper, reminding him of his childhood in England.

He had returned from visiting friends in Montreal. It seemed his "equestrian" lifestyle extended beyond Vancouver and was curated by our insurance agents, Dale and Winnie Jones. Their events were supposed to be secret, but members always found a way to connect with their own kind. Reginald went into detail of how he, again, fell from grace.

"I'm so sorry for what happened on the show," concluded Reginald, changing the subject. "It must've been quite upsetting."

I went into detail of recent events. Sven had totally played me. The world was making fun of me via the internet. The hospice was no longer a place of refuge. I lost Connor who now hated me, and Jacquie hadn't messaged me in ages. My "friends," Margo and Enrique, at the hospital were just jerks—like all the bullies I had encountered in my life. I teared as my frustration was hitting apocalyptic proportions.

Reginald placed his hand on my arm. "Were you always bullied? I never knew." He resumed eating.

I reflected for a moment. "My mum always called me a prince when I was a kid. But you know what I never understood? Why other kids always picked on me. Me! Royalty! I mean, how dare they oppress me? But they did anyway. Called me names because my dad read to me. Insulted me because I loved mythology and church. Wedgied me at summer camp. Mocked me for my singing. Excluded me from fun stuff."

Fifty-two years old, and this is the first time I'm saying this aloud?

"I guess that's when I started stretching the truth," I continued. "I *needed* to be bigger than the bullies. If anything, in my mind. It helped me cope. It sometimes made me feel 'accepted' by building me up to something I'm not.

"Yes, lying did protect me—but now I realize I've been lying to myself all these years. Truth is, I'm not great. I'm pathetic. I was prepared to sing something amazing on TV, pretending to be someone who I'm not. That's how I lost Connor—and it ended up that Sven, like all the bullies in my life, had something else in mind, and took advantage of me. Now the whole world sees me as a loser...and in the process, I hurt others, too." I choked on my words. "I can't believe I did that to Connor."

Reginald finished chewing on some fish. "Larry, you are not a loser. Yes, you struggle with lying—and yes, your head at times is so swelled you have a hard time fitting through doorways." He cut some food. "But you've done so much since joining the hospice, lifting people's spirits through song and game. You brought Danny back and into the program. Too bad he fell in with the wrong crowd. Whatever became of him?"

"Who knows? He should be out of jail by now."

"Well, even if we came across some insurance money by dishonest means, it helped rejuvenate the hospice—and our little hospice has grown so much thanks to your fame. You know what else? The homeless in the city have more hope thanks to your fine work."

Reginald's words did encourage me; however, my speaking about lying reminded me of some other doozies I had spread—especially the one where I pretended to be Rick using his stage name Dick Wank. And what for? To score dates with girls? All these years I've been angry at Rick because he punched me out at my stag, ruining my original wedding plans with Schnookums. I had blamed him—but it wasn't his fault.

It was *me* who blabbed about getting his cousin, Heather, pregnant at the bachelor party. It was *me* who bragged about having sex with her. *I* stole Rick's identity which caused him traumatic humiliation—possibly even worse than I had endured on TV. Hell, I set him up with a girl he crushed on in high school, only to spread gossip about him which led to them breaking up—only because I was jealous of him. And for sure, my soaking in the limelight for fathering the Red Angel's child didn't help. *I* was the cause of all his grief.

My lying and manipulating him were no better than the bullies in my life. I'm the reason why Rick and I aren't friends. No wonder he knocked my block off at my bachelor party so many years ago. Rick never did anything wrong.

I shared my thoughts with Reginald.

He ate his last chip. "It's funny how life works. You arrived here shortly after that incident. Your life suddenly took hold of some purpose through that church prophecy. You've changed Larry, letting go of the old you, being transformed into something new. Transformation can be instantaneous, like the Apostle Paul, but it can also take a lifetime. The Bible mentions often about letting go of bitterness, malice, slander, and anger, and seeking forgiveness. Maybe that's the last thing you need to do to move on and complete your journey."

"You're right. I need to seek Rick's forgiveness."

I logged into *Larrynet* that night, and before I could send Rick another friend request, a message for me popped in from Dana.

Larry! I'm engaged! Can you believe it? Rick asked me to marry him! I'm beyond excited! We're going to Ottawa with Cheryl (you know, Rick's half-sister, the "Red Angel") and Cheryl's sister Sandy next Saturday to surprise him for his fiftieth birthday! Should be fun, but busy. Rick's mum is moving out of her house that day. BTW: Cheryl's newborn baby, Aubrey, is so adorable! Anyway, super excited.

Dana had attached a photo of her embracing Rick, with hand sticking out to the camera showing off a diamond ring.

Red Angel had her baby? Is that why she missed the show? Who is the father?

Cheryl had stopped Sven from kissing her at the auditions. *Were they having a spat?* If she was Sven's "dear," did that bastard impregnate her? It would've been the second time—that I know of—he would've gotten someone else pregnant. *Poor Schnookums.*

I shook my head in dismay and sent another friend request to Rick before logging off.

I spent the next morning in the office on the computer with Hector on my lap, trying in frustration to search for Connor online. Apart from some news articles about his win on Canada's Next Superstar, I couldn't find him on any social media platform. I gave up and checked in on *Larrynet,* read my notifications, and composed a long message to Jacquie, explaining how I was trying to mend things with Connor and change my ways. I didn't expect her to write back; I just felt I needed to share these things. My cell phone rang the moment I sent it.

Hector's ears perked up, and he stood upright. "Arf arf arf." He wouldn't stop barking.

I thought I heard a man say "Househusband!" over my dog.

"ARF ARF ARF." Hector barked even louder. He leapt and tried to snatch the phone out of my hand.

"Wait a second, I can't hear you."

I lifted my dog under my arm, threw him out of the office, and closed the door behind him. He started to howl in the hallway as I raised the phone to my ear.

"Househusband?"

"What the hell? Sven? How dare you call me?"

There was a brief pause on the line. "Larry…I'm sure you've seen how big a sensation you've become because of my little prank. Notice your view count on the internet? We're making a killing in advertising! So, Larry, I've got an amazing proposition for you! We can capitalize on this. Imagine—"

I hung up on the douche and blocked his number.

A memory of Peter telling me about my legacy hit me. What will I leave my children after I die? I wouldn't have minded them knowing I fathered a nation through sperm donation, but this national TV fiasco? And how would people remember me?

I need to turn things around.

Logging into *Larrynet,* I noted Rick still hadn't accepted my friend request. Maybe he doesn't use his computer much. Wait a sec. *Isn't he having a surprise party in a few days?*

Looky here. The Air Western website is promoting a flash sale. Flights to Ottawa for only $499! I booked first class tickets for $1,300 and logged off the computer for the evening.

Rick, I'm going to ask your forgiveness in person for your fiftieth birthday.

Chapter Twenty-Nine
The Party
September 2017

I had overslept, waking up at 8:30—Vancouver time—and had walked around my hotel room in a fog before remembering I was in Ottawa. The time was, in fact, 11:30. Knowing I'd likely be late for the "surprise" at Rick's place, I slipped on a new pair of khakis and polo shirt, bought especially for the occasion, and I called for a taxi.

The cabbie drove me to Rick's neighbourhood in the west end of Ottawa. The overcast skies threatened rain, despite the weather forecast promising sunshine. I asked the driver to drop me off a few blocks away from my destination, so I could explore my old stomping grounds.

It hadn't changed much—jammed with row homes, and lawns pristinely maintained. Parked cars lined both sides of the narrow streets. Like when I was a teen, the area made me feel claustrophobic.

The wind picked up when I turned down Rick's road. One of those giant windsocks towered above the homes in the distance—like the inflatable ones that are often displayed outside car dealerships. Yup, giant condom man was parked in front of Rick's house. It bounced around to the beat of blaring rock music.

A man was preparing a hot buffet under a pop-up canopy tent in front of "Windy Willy." The formally set table under the tent might've been the only decent looking thing outside the home. The edge of the yard was littered with boxes, garbage bags, and furniture. Inflated penguins crowded the remainder of the front lawn. They flanked a huge banner reading "Honk for Rick's 50th!" A few cars driving by obliged. A lot of love for Rick went into this. Pity they are moving his mother out of the house today, too.

Two uniformed men were loading a bureau in their "Three Men Will Do

Anything for a Buck" truck. They returned to the house, passing a co-worker carrying a large lamp.

I strolled past the tent inhaling the wonderful aromas that would be my future lunch and snuck a peek inside the truck.

"Hey, you! Get away from there!" a voice called from behind.

A tall pot-bellied man approached the truck's ramp carrying a bulky box. *Rick?*

"Hi brother," I yelled back.

The box fell to the ground accompanied by a shattering sound.

"What the hell?" said Rick bending over to open the box. "He pulled out two pieces of a blue plate and glared up at me.

"Pffft…looks cheap," I said.

Before Rick could reply, a tall thin brunette exited the townhome.

"Oh my gosh, you actually came?" said Dana. She put down a garbage bag, rushed forward, and embraced me.

"My grandmother's Wedgwood," Rick cried out and slammed a broken piece back in the box.

Dana and I, still hugging, turned our heads towards the birthday boy. A mover with a box passed between us and climbed the ramp.

"Wait," said Rick, squinting. "Who are you?"

"You mean, you don't recognize me?" I had kept my beard, and some peach fuzz had grown back on my bald head. "I'm your best friend from high school!"

"You don't look like Greg," said Rick.

His tone irked me. *Forgiveness takes time, Larry. Be patient.*

"Awww, c'mon Richie," said Dana, letting go of me. "Don't you recognize Larry? He told me he knew you. Looks like he came in all the way from Vancouver to wish you a Happy Birthday!"

A blue sports car vroomed past the house. Its brakes screeched, caroming the vehicle off the curb and on to the lawn, bowling over several penguins and the birthday banner. A prolonged honk blared. The driver reversed the car and parked it properly on the street.

"Rick," I said, "this is the best fiftieth birthday party I've ever seen in my life!" I extended my hand for a shake. "I'm sorry for—"

"Birthday? Sorry?" replied Rick, confused.

A tall thin woman—maybe late fifties—exited the car, distracting the birthday boy. Her face, caked with make-up, looked like it had been applied by a steam roller. She brushed her long blonde hair around her left shoulder and straightened her tight red skirt. "Good," she said bending into the car. "Looks like we made it on time, Oscar."

"Heather?" Rick yelled out to his cousin.

"Schnookums?" I said.

"By the way," Heather said to Rick with touch of sarcasm, "my mother, your aunt, insisted I be here. She sends her warm regards."

A handsome young man in his twenties exited the vehicle. I recognized Oscar immediately. Hard to believe it's been over ten years since I last saw him. His dark hair and eyes reminded me of myself at his age—including his clothes and John Lennon glasses. "I wish you let me drive, Mom." He joined his mother, who was popping open the trunk of their car.

"Heather's here?" Rick moaned. Looking back at me, something clicked. "Larry? We all saw you on TV. I mean…shit." I expected him to be surprised to see me, for better or worse, but his voice lacked any emotion. He looked over his shoulder where Heather and her son, Oscar, were carrying a large, wrapped gift to the canopy. "Huh, surprised she came."

"Of course she would," I said. "She's your cousin!"

Rick shook his head again. "Wait a sec," he said to Dana. "You know this guy?"

Calm Larry.

"And how'd he find out about my surprise birthday?" he asked.

"Rick," I said, "I came all this way from Vancouver to apologize for being such an ass to you and seek your forgiveness." I extended my hand again.

"Apologize? What? You want to say sorry after all these years?" Rick's face reddened. "Dana, you remember the guy I told you about who caused me so much trouble when I was younger?"

"Mom," Oscar yelled to Heather while advancing to the canopy. "They're serving wine." The caterer poured a glass which the lad sloshed back and beckoned the man for a refill.

"I remember you saying something like that," said Dana.

"And you hug him?" asked Rick pointing at me.

Dana flushed. "What? You mean, *he's* the one? Oh, my gosh, honey. I'm so sorry, but how was I supposed to know? You never bothered mentioning his name. Yes, I've known Larry for years. We chat all the time online."

Rick's temper erupted. "You talk to…" — he shook his head — "This douche better leave in thirty seconds."

"No," I said. "I'm happy to stay—"

A pair of hands cupped my cheeks from the side, interrupting me. Plasticized lips interlocked with mine, and a tongue navigated its way into my mouth. It tasted like a cross between a gallon of rubber meeting a strip of leather.

"Honeeeeeey-Bear…" Heather said. She flung her arms around me.

I stood motionless in her grasp.

Rick and Dana resumed their heated exchange while some perky song called "Happy" played in the background.

"Honey-Bear?" The handsome Oscar joined us by the truck. "Mom, you told me that you called my dad Honey-Bear." The young man stared at me. "Wait a second. I remember you. You're the guy who visited us in Toronto that Canada

Day week! I was going to my friend's cottage, and I dominated him at horse-shoes that weekend!"

Kid's memory is sharp!

"Yes, Oscar, I call Larry my Honey-Bear," Heather faced her son, sounding happy. "And Larry is your dad, you clever boy."

"My son?" I said.

"Uh, okay." Oscar emptied his wine glass.

Okay? I'd expect fountains of tears at the prospect of reconnecting with his father.

Oscar looked around. "Mom, I thought you said the Red Angel would be here."

Now I know where his priorities are—the hot rock star. Apple doesn't fall far from the tree.

Still hugging Heather, I spoke over her shoulder to Rick. "Hey, Rick! Is the Red Angel here?"

"Yes," said Heather breaking our embrace, expression turning from joy to anger. "I have few words for her, too."

"Do you have butt wad for a brain, Larry? You caused her enough stress to last a lifetime," said Rick, breaking from his conversation with Dana. "She just had a baby and doesn't need your nonsense now."

Oscar went back to the canopy, refilled his wine, and began dancing with the Windy Willy, mirroring his motions.

Kid has great moves!

Heather stroked my beard. "By the way, I think it's hot!" She whispered in my ear in her sweetest voice, "It's been too long, Larry..." Heather leaned away, and I had to admit, I was stunned. Her turn of character surprised me. Maybe she finally understood Sven never really wanted her. "Isn't your son handsome?" she asked.

What's she up to?

Before being able to question Heather's sudden surge of passion, another young man, about the same age as Oscar yelled from the doorway of the house. He, too, had dark hair and eyes like mine. "Mom, can you help me?" he asked Dana.

Rick stared out to the lad, then turned his head to me, and finally over towards Oscar dancing. "No! This can't be true!" he yelled.

Dana's son, Ethan, looks like Oscar?

Dana, frustrated with Rick's anger, shrugged her shoulders in attempt to regain her composure.

"Sure, Ethan," said Dana to her son, and left to enter the house.

Dana and Ethan returned carrying a huge box up the truck ramp. Rick dashed into the house without saying a word, slamming the door behind him. Heather, eyeing the wine bottles at the dinner table, walked to the canopy and demanded a glass from the caterer.

On exiting the truck, Ethan noticed Oscar dancing with the windsock and the caterer filling Heather a glass. "Oooh, wine!"

He bolted from the truck, served himself, and joined Oscar in his little dance party.

Let the festivities begin! Bring on the boogie! Getting in the spirit of the party, I grabbed a glass for myself and joined the two lads.

Rick stormed out of the house and into the tent. He exchanged a few words with Heather, who had taken a seat. She pointed to the large gift she and Oscar had deposited at the foot of the table. Rick wanted to return to the house.

"Open it," Heather barked before he could leave. We all turned our heads to check out what was going on.

"Later," said Rick.

"Open it," Heather insisted. "Now!"

Rick threw up his hands in frustration.

Dana, still looking miffed, joined Rick under the tent and begrudgingly placed her hand on his shoulder in mock support while he unwrapped his present—a giant military-grade footlocker! The perfect useless gift!

Dana covered her mouth. Rick was speechless.

"A place to store your old junk that your mother doesn't want to keep," said Heather.

"BA-HA-HA," I laughed.

Rick glared at me, exchanged some words with Heather, downed a glass, and refilled it. He returned his gaze at me and the two lads.

"Wait a sec," said Oscar to Ethan, "you look just like me."

They stopped dancing and faced each other. I couldn't help but notice how identical they appeared, except Ethan had Dana's largish nose. Their stare down lasted a long while before they both turned their heads to study me.

"You look like him, too!" Oscar said to Ethan pointing to me.

"Ethan, you are quite a handsome lad," I said to Dana's son.

Ethan pointed to Oscar. "You could be my twin." He looked back at me then to Oscar. "Who are these guys?" he asked his mother, Dana.

"Yeah, Dana," I said. "Your lad does look a lot like me." Dana had shown me photos of her son when we last went out a date many years ago. He resembled me more now than he did then.

Dana reddened. "I didn't want this to come out this way, Ethan dear, but Larry's your father. Sort of."

Rick stood aghast and downed his wine.

"Best party ever!" I said holding up my glass, swinging my hips to some song with too much awful reverb.

"When I was a kid," she explained, "I always wanted babies, and Larry's sperm was readily available to me at the lab where I worked when I attended med school. I was young, and, well, there you have it.

"I didn't know your father would come out today," said Dana to Ethan. "I thought by moving out here, I'd be able to keep it all a secret until the right time." After an awkward pause, Dana looked over my way and said sheepishly, "I guess this is it."

"No More Mister Nice Guy" cranked through the yard stereo.

"What the hell?" said Rick. "I thought you said Ethan's father was a boyfriend who abandoned you!"

"In a sense, Larry did abandon me..." Dana replied.

"You dated him? And you told him about my party?" Rick said.

"Yes, but he's changed. Richie, honey. I must've let the party slip when I told Larry of our engagement...I was so excited when you proposed to me that I wanted to tell the world!"

"I can't believe this," said Rick.

Everyone stared at Rick, while Alice Cooper continued to blare.

"Hey, is lunch ready?" The tall charismatic presence of the Red Angel holding her baby in the doorway of the house diverted everyone's attention.

Rick looked over to me. He aggressively wobble-marched over to her. "Cheryl, don't come owwwwwwwwwwt!" He tripped over the footlocker and stumbled forward several steps. He grasped hold of Windy Willy in an attempt to regain his balance and tackled the thing over to the ground, landing hard on his head.

"Awww... There goes my dance partner," I said.

Rick rolled off Windy Willy. He grabbed his head moaning, while the windsock jumped back to life. Dana rushed over to his side and cradled him in her arms.

"Dickhead?" the Red Angel's voice interrupted from the house.

I hate it when she says that!

A boy in his teens, about the Red Angel's height, swerved around her. His thick hair was dark like mine.

"Uncle Rick?" said the lad, concerned. He rushed over and knelt on one knee by his side, ignoring everyone else.

"Rupe?" moaned Rick lifting his head up. "Stay in the house..." and he rested his head back in Dana's arms.

This is the Red Angel's son?

After a moment, the Red Angel's Rupert, too, noticed the other two dark-haired men and me standing around. Though the lad was younger, he had striking features that resembled all three of us.

"Ha! I had a feeling it was all true!" I yelled out to the Red Angel. "I did father your son! Though for the life of me, can't remember when we did it!"

"What? You deluded, brainless, poombah!" said the redhead.

At least she cleaned up her potty mouth around the "kids."

The Red Angel, Cheryl, advanced towards us and studied the three young dark-haired men—maybe realizing she couldn't escape the truth. She cleared her throat and stated the obvious in a hushed tone. "You're right. Rupert is your son." Her baby began to cry, and Cheryl rocked him gently to try to calm him.

Though Oscar seemed nonplused, Ethan and Rupert reeked of consternation.

"I knew it!" I said. "The news stories were true!"

Rick moaned in Dana's arms. "My relatives, Oscar and Rupert, are *his* offspring? My stepson-to-be, Ethan, is his, too? How come I never noticed?"

Rick had never been observant. Maybe, given Dana and his short courtship, this might've been the first time the boys were meeting.

"Wait," said Rupert to Ethan, "you're my brother?"

"Just to keep your head out of your *derrière*, Dickhead" — the Red Angel adjusted her baby in her arms and faced me — "had I known the sperm from the clinic was from you, I would've burned the place to the ground to ensure it wouldn't infect anyone!" She stared me right in the eye. Her being a head taller intimidated me.

"Rupert…Ethan…" Rick grunted.

Cheryl sighed at Rupert, Ethan, and Oscar discussing their daddy issues amongst themselves. "They've figured it out," continued Cheryl, "Hell of a way to discover new relatives in this ballsed up family reunion." She stood and pointed to the three lads. "Yeah, they've got it all sorted out." She groaned. "It's gonna be a long trip back to Toronto."

"The three brothers look so handsome," said Heather sincerely, as she approached us from the tent.

"Where's Lars?" I asked looking around.

"He's busy with his hockey," said Cheryl.

Something sparked inside Heather. She folded her arms and glared at the Red Angel. "How would you know where *my* son is?"

Before Cheryl could answer, Heather threw in, "—and where's your baby's father…hmmm?"

Does Schnookums think the baby's father is Sven, too? Sven did call the Red Angel his "dear" at the auditions.

Cheryl bit her lower lip. "I didn't ask him to come. It would've upset Rick— they don't get along. Besides the move is stressful enough for Rick's mum."

"Yeah. Who is the father of your little baby?" I asked.

Silence, except for the flapping of Windy Willy's arms over Meat Loaf's "I'd Do Anything for Love."

Heather and I stared at the child's ice-blue eyes.

My Schnookums began to tremble, then tears poured down her cheeks. I never saw such an outpouring of emotion, nor understood what might've caused it. *Must've been "the menopause."*

"Bastard!" exclaimed Heather. "I knew it! It's Sven's."

"So did I," I yelled.

"No bloody way!" Infuriated, Cheryl returned to the house and slammed the door.

"Yes," I said. "I agree, Schnookums, the child has to be his." Though if it wasn't really Sven's, at the rate this day was going, I'd half expect it would be mine.

We stepped towards the entranceway.

"I saw how the two of you were galivanting on TV," Heather wailed.

The Red Angel poked her head out. "You must've watched a different show!" She slammed the door again.

"That fornicating prick!" said Heather, choking back her tears. "I'm going to get that asshole!" Heather leaned into me. "Want to help me?"

I didn't know how to respond. *Sven did cause me a lot of grief...* I placed my arm around my Schnookums shoulder and simply nodded.

Heather regrouped herself as fast as she broke down and brushed off my arm. "No, not here." She rubbed her nose then put her hands through her hair. "I'm gonna sue the blond off that Swede's head! We'll bankrupt that swine. He'll rue the day for leading me on all my life!" She looked over to me.

"Honey-Bear," she said gently, while stroking my head. "I'll make sure he pays for humiliating you, too." She clapped her hands together. "We're going to make a lot of money!" That brightened her up.

Dana continued to hold Rick on the ground and stroked his hair.

"Come," said Heather to me. She grabbed my hand. "Oscar!" she barked. Our son had resumed the Windy Willy dance while his newfound siblings continued their discussion. "Catch!" She flung him the car keys. "You're right. You should drive. Safe trip home."

We walked down the street leaving the chaos behind. By the time we hit a major roadway, a spit of rain fell from the sky, leading to a steady drizzle. Heather remained silent, occasionally weeping, and rubbing her eyes. I'd never seen her so upset.

After walking a few blocks, the precipitation soaked us to the bone. She permitted me to hold her tight under my arm, and I kissed her wet head gently. Heather turned into me in full embrace, and while we hugged, I reiterated the promise that we'd bring down the interloper's mighty Swedish empire. We kissed for a while in the downpour.

"You know," I said, "Sven promised you eternal love. He never meant it." We snogged a few more minutes. "I've kept true to you. Even after all these years. I promise to give you everything Sven didn't."

Heather loosened her grip and pulled back so we could look each other in the eye and nodded without saying a word.

Mascara ran down her cheeks, she reached up and stroked my beard again, and her mood shifted. She began giggling.

"You know," she said sultrily, "I like that beard...I can have fun with it!"

She flagged down a passing taxi. "You are famous now and your star will always be on the rise. Sven will fall...and hard." A cab pulled over, and Heather opened the door for me. "Come, let's go back to your hotel and have our honeymoon."

Though technically we already had shacked up, later that afternoon in my hotel, our union had a deep and almost spiritual connection.

Heather was the voice of the generation.

I had birthed a nation.

The prophecy was fulfilled.

Epilogue

December 2019

A gaslit fireplace heated the living room in my new condo back in the Kits. Hector, wearing a Santa hat, slept next the hearth, warming his old bones. Christmas carols provided a relaxing backdrop while I sipped a wonderful glass of holiday whiskey. I was back in the lap of luxury, thirty years after landing in the West Coast. The stillness and peace of my "den" filled my soul—a far departure from the noisy hospice where I had spent the better part of my adult life.

Heather had bought me a "smoking jacket" as a housewarming gift when we moved in last year. Basically, it's a dressing gown with an ascot. It made me feel suave and sexy, and I took up pipe smoking to replace my pot habit to complete the look. Heather approved, preferring the smell of tobacco to marijuana. She also loved my "playboy" image, too. I'd taken to wearing my smoking jacket in the evenings while I parked myself in front of the fireplace for my after-dinner smoke.

My mother's Betty and Veronica dolls stared at me from the mantle. Beside them, a narcissus stood proud in its vase. I always ensured a healthy one was there to remind not to regress back to the man I had once been. A necklace hung around the vase, dangling a peace symbol pendant. My friend, Peter, always remained in my thoughts.

It'd been a hectic time.

Heather invited me to live in her home in Toronto after Rick's "party." With vengeance as our common motivator, we became partners and strategized several ways to destroy Sven. We acted within a week of my moving in, suing the jerk for the embarrassing Canada's Next Superstar television show.

After presenting our intent to sue the network, they cancelled Sven's program immediately. I had felt badly for Connor, who had advanced from the West Coast regionals to the nationals. He was on track to winning the competition to that point.

Our investigations revealed that Sven had paid Margo and Enrique to wear secret microphones for a better part of that summer, looking for juicy sound bites to use on the show. Sven had compiled reams of material. Who knew if he had planned to use them in later episodes?

It was moot. We threatened the network with further litigation if they wouldn't obtain and destroy all the recordings, as well as forced them to never permit Sven to broadcast another show again. They agreed with little argument, and it spelled the end of Sven's broadcasting career.

We received a windfall of cash from the out-of-court settlement. I'd never seen Heather so excited when the money landed in our bank accounts—and knowing Sven wouldn't return to TV for a while pleased her immensely.

Admittedly, I was disappointed when I heard the hospital had discovered the "Larry Johnstone donation bin." They reported that Margo had gathered my samples illegally—all to satisfy her little joke. Who knew what she did with them? Anyhow, she and Enrique were both canned the morning after the show. It was no wonder they weren't around at my last hospital visit.

I had thought being fired was getting off too easy for them. Annoyed they wasted my time for so many years, I had wanted to sue their asses and go after the hospital at the same time. Heather, though, suggested I didn't. She had a plan...

Rick and Dana moved in together in Toronto. He refused my friend request on *Larrynet*, which upset me. I still wanted to make amends and peppered Dana with messages hoping she could help. She sympathized and thought it might be nice for the four of us to get together to hash things out.

A few weeks later, Schnookums suggested to Dana that she and Rick join us at that swanky restaurant Heather had taken me to years before—The Chamber. Instead of booking her preferred "medieval torture room," she chose a "Glam Rock" themed one. Dana accepted and was thrilled at the prospect of cosplaying as KISS. She knew Rick would love the idea of dressing up, too, and felt optimistic he might let the "past be the past."

Heather and I arrived at the restaurant that night. I was dressed as the "Spaceman," and Heather the "Demon." We waited a half hour when Dana entered alone dressed as the "Catman." Poor thing was so embarrassed. Rick refused to join us. We tried to make the most of the evening, but it felt oddly empty without her partner. My guilt for the harm I had inflicted on him mounted, and the regret still haunted me to this day. At least Dana and Heather got along, and even had a few laughs.

A couple of weeks later, Dana confided something to Heather and me over coffee.

Rick's half-sister, the Red Angel, Cheryl, through her professional associations with Sven, questioned a few of his business ventures. She suspected some could be criminal and mentioned some questionable partners she had met. That really got Heather's juices flowing, and we dropped the "seeds" of Sven's corruption to law enforcement authorities. They began investigating the allegations. Schnookums also launched several business-related lawsuits against Sven, ranging from defamation to breach of contract. The most potentially damning was one related to royalties on the still popular *Bärbar Ugn*.

Though I loved Toronto—a city filled with an exciting pulse—I pined for the West Coast. I missed the mountains and its laidback spirit.

Heather, like me, wanted to return, wanting to be closer to her aging mother and to distance herself from Sven. It didn't take long to find a condo near where we used to live, and we moved across Canada in time to celebrate my birthday. We even had a bit of extra cash to move my father over. He couldn't have been more thrilled about his new home—an assisted living residence with a view of a mountain.

"Honey-Bear," a seductive voice beckoned from down the hall. "Funsies?"

I admitted, my current married life exceeded all my childhood expectations, and we loved our new condo in the Kits. Over a year had passed since we moved here, and we were still awaiting final settlement on all those lawsuits against Sven.

Our son, Oscar, initially planned to move in with us, but he opted to stay in the Big Smoke to pursue an advanced degree, combining philosophy and classical studies. He and Dana's son, Ethan, became close friends, and, with our help, the stepbrothers found a place they could share while in school. The Red Angel's family still lived in Toronto, and Cheryl's sister, Sandy, invited the brothers to join her clan at their weekly Friday night gatherings—a tradition that began with Rick and his family when they were children.

"Are you guys going to do it again?" a woman's voice moaned from her bedroom—*our new roomie!* And no, there was no hanky-panky going down in our home.

Did I mention Dana was an obstetrician?

Dana, who once was jealous of Heather, became besties with her.

My wife became disillusioned with the sales and advertising game and wanted to use her talents to better humanity. It could've been all those years with Sven, but I've no idea what brought that on. But befriending a doctor, being married to a sperm donation dynamo, and having hold of a fertility clinic by the short and curlies (in a legal sense), all fed her master plan.

Fearing a lawsuit from me, and under immense pressure from Heather and her legal team, the Golden Oak Hospital in the west end agreed to repurpose their fertility clinic. Thanks to Heather, they now extended their services to support couples who struggled having children on their own, and who might not be able to afford the fertility procedures to have them.

See, people had to pay for any insemination services to that point, and it was a costly decision to make with no guarantee of success. So, Heather registered a not-for-profit organization. We struggled with a name—my suggestion of "No Vas Deferens" was totally shot down. We landed on Heather's—the advertising exec's—choice of "Sex Cells Fertility Clinic." It had a catchy ring to it.

We nominated Dana to be the head of the board of directors. She had been visiting us monthly ever since to attend meetings, monitor activities, and advise us—but never with Rick. Even Reginald pitched in. He had vast experience in not-for-profit organizations and helped with many of the administrative tasks.

When the first "Sex Cells Fertility Clinic" officially opened last month, Dana moved in temporarily to help set in motion the final steps of our plan—we wanted to go national, to extend aid to any couple wanting to have a family.

Yes, we were developing infomercials to promote the idea, and had raised some initial capital for the venture—but you know what Heather really loved most about our idea? It wasn't the philanthropic nature of it. It was that we planned to use Sven's money for our not-for-profit venture. She cackled at the notion, knowing Sven hated having his own kids, and now his money was being used to facilitate the birth of millions.

It had been a great year, and the day was ending on a high note. Mark St. James, the man who wrote so many blogs about my history during my rise to fame, called me. He wanted to write a book documenting my amazing journey to share with the world. Of course, I said yes.

Could this year get any better? You bet it can!

"Schnookums, ready for Honey-Bear?" I said, entering the bedroom.

My wife turned on the stereo in our room, and the speakers played "Endless Love." It didn't take me long.

"OOOOOAAAAAAH!"

Acknowledgements

Larry Johnstone was a character I loved to write in *Dissatisfied Me: A Love Story*. Since he saved me from several writer's blocks, I just had to write a spinoff book—and the many British comedies I watched since childhood, with all their absurd characters, helped me shaped Larry into the person he is today. I'd sit back with a cup of Cream of Earl Gray tea (which became my go to drink during the drafting of this novel), and write away. In a way, it was easy.

Or maybe…a little too easy.

I needed grounding. In my earlier drafts, I took absurdity way beyond the plausible.

To that, I am grateful to my wifey, author Cait Gordon, who showed patience listening to me ramble about Larry for hours on end, and identifying where I pushed the boundary of absurdity too far. If you have read her books, she has an incredible way with words, and her humour is contagious. Elements of it made its way to my story. She also wrote the lyrics sung by the Red Angel— including the song Dickhead (yes, it's about Larry). If it wasn't for Wifey's encouragement, I would never have attempted to walk down the path of author-dom.

And, I am thankful to my mother, Marilyn Gordon, who spent an enormous amount of time reviewing my work, editing, and positive feedback to improve the overall story. She also introduced some concepts which I will be bringing to my future writings. Her patience in reading and re-reading various chapters are hugely appreciated, and I've learned plenty from her experience.

For Nathan Frechette…his cover art is amazing; they're great conversation starters; and is a constant reminder of his passion for books and desire to bring out the best in author's works. Thanks to him and Renaissance Press for giving me the opportunity to publish my stories.

To authors John Haas and Jamieson Wolf, whose reading through my first draft gave me positive food for thought, and I took their comments to heart as

I continue to develop my craft. And thanks to my beta-readers who provided invaluable feedback. The idea for Rick Duncan, the narrator of Dissatisifed Me: A Love Story, writing a forward to the story came from one of them!

Some may ask why I chose Sweden as the home country for my antagonist. I really don't know why I did, except maybe my acknowledgment of a Swedish friend in my first book. That said, the more I researched about Sweden, the more I came to love the country and would relish the opportunity to visit one day. Special shoutout to my Swedish consultant with a special message: Min svävare är full av ål. Tack och rocka på. It might not make sense without knowing some Swedish, and watching a lot of Monty Python, but he'll get it…

Last, but not least, I want to thank all of you who continue to support this author's journey, laugh at his jokes, and who took the time out to read this book. You've all made my life somewhat satisfying.

About the Author

Bruce Gordon is originally from Montreal, Quebec, and lives in the suburbs of Ottawa with his wifey, Cait Gordon, who is also a published author. Bruce's love for writing was sparked by the challenge of NANOWRIMO 2017, which spawned this first book of a trilogy. When he is not working as a public servant or writing, Bruce enjoys playing his guitar, watching superhero movies, and listening to Iron Maiden.

Dissatisfied Me: A Love Story

Rick "Dickie" Duncan is turning fifty. Meh.

On the eve of this mid-century milestone, he finds himself alone in his mother's Ottawa basement, surrounded by gaudy decor and a carpet that hasn't been raked in years. Grabbing some brews and frozen hotdogs, Rick rummages through the clutter that's made up his dissatisfied life.

From the death of Santa to the last days of Scottish Rot, Rick meanders through the decades, mapping his existence amid the pop culture of the '70s to the present day.

Marking key moments of his unsated misadventures and real-life dating disasters, Rick reminds himself that his journey is a love story. Sort of.

The Reluctant Barbarian

Arthur Jenkins would have been happy to live his life the way it was until he finally died, but the angel in his office has different ideas. He's there to grant a wish Arthur made as a kid, and it's a doozy. It's also a wish he doesn't want in the slightest. After all, what grown man would want to be a barbarian hero? Seriously! Whether he wants it or not, Arthur is getting that wish granted. Angels have quotas too, you know. Join Arthur, Dead Mike and Valeria the Paladin on a quest across the land, having unwanted adventures while looking for a comfy place to sit.

Season One
Iris and the Crew Tear Through Space

In a galactic network known as the Keangal, where space is accessible…

Lieutenant Eileen Iris and the command crew of the S.S. SpoonZ haven't a clue what it means to be disabled. An unexpected conversation with an intergalactic janitor brings up the question but offers no answers before he's 'ported away.

Unfazed, duties resume as Iris manages an overprotective guidebot; Security Chief Lartha and her sentient prostheses offer kick-ass protection; Mr. Herbert's inventiveness is a godsend (although he's not quite grasped how to flirt); Commander Davan's affable personality comes through whether trumpeted, texted, or signed; and Captain Warq's gracious but firm leadership keeps everyone at their best.

Until on one mission, where the crew tears through space.

Just a little bit.

About Renaissance

Renaissance was founded in May 2013 by a group of authors and designers who wanted to publish and market those stories which don't always fit neatly in a genre, or a niche, or a demographic. Like the happy panbibliophiles we are, we opened our submissions, with no other guideline than finding a Canadian book we would fall in love with.

Today, this is still very true; however, we've also noticed an interesting trend in what we like to publish. It turns out that we are naturally drawn to the voices of those who are members of a marginalized group, and these are the voices we want to continue to uplift.

At Renaissance, we do things differently. We are passionate about books, and we care as much about our authors enjoying the publishing process as we do about our readers enjoying a great Canadian read on the platform they prefer.

pressesrenaissancepress.ca
pressesrenaissancepress@gmail.com